THE HUNDRED GIFTS

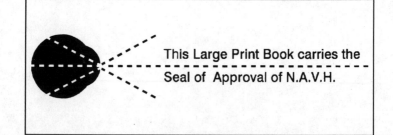

This Large Print Book carries the
Seal of Approval of N.A.V.H.

THE HUNDRED GIFTS

JENNIFER SCOTT

THORNDIKE PRESS
A part of Gale, Cengage Learning

GALE
CENGAGE Learning®

Farmington Hills, Mich • San Francisco • New York • Waterville, Maine
Meriden, Conn • Mason, Ohio • Chicago

GALE
CENGAGE Learning®

LIBRARY OF CONGRESS CATALOGING-IN-PUBLICATION DATA

Names: Scott, Jennifer, 1972–
Title: The hundred gifts / Jennifer Scott.
Description: Large print edition. | Waterville, Maine : Thorndike Press, 2016. | ©2015 | Series: Thorndike Press large print women's fiction
Identifiers: LCCN 2015038947 | ISBN 9781410486158 (hardback) | ISBN 141048615X (hardcover)
Subjects: LCSH: Middle-aged women—Fiction. | Interpersonal relations—Fiction. | Kindness—Fiction. | Large type books. | Domestic fiction. | BISAC: FICTION / Contemporary Women.
Classification: LCC PS3619.C66555 H86 2016 | DDC 813/.6—dc23
LC record available at http://lccn.loc.gov/2015038947

Published in 2016 by arrangement with New American Library, an imprint of Penguin Publishing Group, a division of Penguin Random House LLC

Printed in Mexico
1 2 3 4 5 6 7 20 19 18 17 16

For Scott, my gift

ACKNOWLEDGMENTS

Seeing my stories come to life in published books is always a gift, and just as Bren and her cooking class come together to make gifts happen for Virginia Mash, so do many people come together to make this gift happen for me. I'd like to thank some of them now.

Thank you to Cori Deyoe for coming to every single "cooking class," even the bad ones, when I burned the toast and the pudding was gloppy. Thank you to everyone at 3 Seas Literary Agency for your support and help along the way.

A huge thank-you to Sandy Harding for helping me refine all of my "dishes" without once making me want to cry or upend the entire pot into the garbage. Thank you to my NAL family for continuing to support and champion my books.

Thank you to my Jazzer-friends who inspired this story by showing me that

7

sometimes when random women come together, a whole lot of fun and sharing and kindness can happen. I want to give a special thanks to my 9:30 GB Thursday girls — Becca, Kelly, and Jen Squared — for scene inspiration (you will know which one). And, of course, to Roberta, who was my "Paula," and convinced me that I wasn't joining a workout; I was joining a friendship. So true.

Finally, as always, I want to thank my family, who has to, quite literally, endure my cooking, while also enduring my long hours of writing and revising. Paige, Weston, Rand, and Preston, you are homemade chicken and noodles with warm brownie sundaes for dessert, and I love you all.

Scott, you are my crème brûlée. Of course.

CHAPTER ONE

It was the fifth day of November, and Christmas commercials had been in full swing for weeks — sweatered, singing suburbanites holding power drills and cans of soda and Big Macs and mops as microphones and dance partners. All the stores had their decorations up, and the bell ringers were out in force, their cheerful *Good mornings* and *You have a nice day, now*s making Bren Epperson duck with guilt. Who carried cash anymore? She could hardly drop her debit card into the little red bucket.

Ordinarily, by the fifth day of November, Bren would be rushing from store to store, clutching a list of errands so long it could garland her tree. But this year, for the first time ever, she didn't know where she should go. Planning for the holidays was always such a pain, but not actually having holidays to plan for was maybe the loneliest prospect in the world.

She drove around, an open box of peanut butter cookies sitting in the passenger seat next to her, the radio set to a talk station, not that Bren was actually listening to it — back-and-forthing between two local hosts, one Democrat, one Republican, tedious and typical. She could have scripted their arguments for them. But the conversation in the background gave the illusion that she was not alone in the car. They were like friends, the kind who will let a third wheel tag along, but not really ever acknowledge her. At each stoplight, she tipped up a latte that was more flavored syrup than actual coffee. So sweet it made her jaw ache.

Stopped at a traffic light, she glanced to her left. A frazzled-looking mother and daughter sat in a minivan, the mom's hands clutched tightly around the wheel, her eyes fixed on the red light. Her mouth was moving, her head bobbing in such a way as to suggest an argument. Every so often, the daughter, in the passenger seat, would roll her eyes, say something, gesture wildly.

"Oh. Don't do that," Bren said softly, her breath fogging the driver's-side window. "Don't waste your time on that." How many nights had she wished she could take back arguments she'd had with Kelsey? How many regrets did she have, even if they did get along incredibly well compared to many of Kelsey's friends and their mothers? "Talk about good things instead. Cookies and coffee." She held up her cup, accidentally getting the attention of the mother, who glanced across at her. Bren smiled and waved, feeling embarrassed, but also kind of good that she'd interrupted their disagreement.

The woman gave a curious, halfhearted wave, and, to Bren's surprise, rolled down her window.

Bren pushed the button to lower hers, a bluster of cool air pushing right in on her.

"Do you need something?" the woman asked.

"Eight thousand," Bren shouted over the noise of the traffic, the first thing to come to her mind.

The woman's confused look deepened. "Excuse me?"

"Well, eight thousand six hundred and twenty, to be exact." Bren sipped her coffee. "From Missouri to Thailand. It's eight thousand six hundred and twenty miles."

"Okay?" the woman said. A car behind them honked, and both Bren and the woman checked the rearview mirrors, startled.

"That's where my daughter lives," Bren said. "In Thailand. Eight thousand six hundred and twenty miles. Not door-to-door, of course. That would be even farther."

The woman pointed through the windshield. "The light is green," she said.

"Oh!" Bren sipped her coffee again as the guy behind her held down his horn. "Sure thing. You have a great day! These, by the way" — she held up her cup — "are fantastic!"

The woman's eyes narrowed, as if she wasn't sure what she was supposed to be feeling or how she was supposed to react. Finally, on the third honk, she roared away, her window shooting up to close out Bren.

Bren laughed aloud, wishing she were feeling mirth rather than . . . whatever this was that she was actually feeling, and set her cup in its holder. She pulled forward just as the light turned yellow, leaving the window open so she could shout, "Merry Christmas," to everyone she passed, just because.

The cookies were gone, and she was still hungry. Hungrier, maybe, now that she'd pointed out three times — loudly — how very far away Kelsey was. She headed for the square.

Vargo Square was a place that for decades

had been desperately trying to be relevant in a world of strip malls and big-box stores. As county seat of Vargo County, the square was dominated not only by a massive centrally positioned courthouse, but also by the county jail, the juvenile detention center, and the sheriff's office, and every time someone important went to trial, also by a parking lot full of news vans. Yet at the same time, the square tried fiercely to appeal to small-town sensibilities, trotting out a rolling troop of kitschy shops, breakfast joints, antiquarians, booksellers, clothiers, and shoe repairers, all of which sprouted and failed at alarming rates around the sturdy and permanent Vargo County Historical Museum, inside of which Bren had never set foot, nor had she ever known of anyone who had.

The Hole Shebang, on the north side of the square, had been a favorite of Bren's since the day it opened. Not just donuts — although just donuts would have been enough, because weren't donuts always enough? — but the kind of donuts you put an "ough" into. *Doughnuts.* Food of the gods — that was what they were. The Hole Shebang's specialty seemed to be putting the most absurd things in and onto their doughnuts and somehow making them sound delicious — crispy bacon brittle doughnut, buttered cracker crunch dough-nut holes, candied anchovy Bismarck, long john with creamy black truffle icing. *Froofy food* was what Gary called it, but Bren couldn't help feeling just a little bit worldly while noshing on a sprout fritter.

The bell tinkled as she walked through the door, and even though she'd downed the last of her coffee before getting out of the car, and her body was positively slosh-ing with insulin, she couldn't help but feel a twist of hunger at the scent of sugar in the air. It was intoxicating, and in a way over-powering. But who minded being slapped upside the head with a cloud of sweetness?

"Good morning, Brenda," the young man behind the counter said when she walked in. She was torn between feeling thrilled at the familiarity of being a regular — made her feel like a townie, like someone who belonged — and ashamed that she'd fre-quented the Hole Shebang often enough for the staff to know her by name.

Tomorrow. Tomorrow I will eat right, she told herself. *No, today. I will eat salads for the rest of the day. Or fast. Yes, fasting is a great idea.*

"Merry Christmas, Tod," Bren said cheer-fully, wondering if she was feeling mirth yet.

He laughed, pushing his adorable baker's

cap back on his head. "It's not even Thanks-giving yet."

"Never too early to get into the Christmas spirit," she said.

"Well, I suppose you have a valid point there. What sounds good today?"

Bren tapped her bottom lip with her forefinger, contemplating what was left in the case. Not much, actually. She was a little later than usual, and the morning rush must have been heavy. "Any recommendations?"

He leaned over the counter, peering inside, as if he alone hadn't made all of the doughnuts and had no idea what was in there. "I've been playing around with a sage, potato, and pumpkin cream cheese filling." He stubbed a finger straight down. "If you're in the holiday spirit, it's supposed to evoke memories of Thanksgiving dinner."

"Like the Gobstopper in *Willy Wonka*," Bren said.

"Huh?" He was young. Far too young to appreciate a good Gene Wilder movie refer-ence.

"Never mind. I'll take one."

Tod pulled the doughnut out of the case and handed it to her, wrapped in a sheet of wax paper. It was still warm — their signa-ture, and her favorite thing about the Hole Shebang doughnuts. "Enjoy!"

15

She wasn't actually sure that she would. She was not the biggest fan of sage, and for all of her bluster about *Merry Christmas* and *Never too soon to get into the holiday spirit* and so forth, she was not fooling herself. The number 8,620 flashed in her mind over and over again as she paid for the doughnut, a numerical reminder of how far away her perhaps closest child would be on Thanksgiving Day. Did she really want to evoke that image with this doughnut?

Even though she knew Tod was watching, waiting for her to take a bite and give him feedback on his new creation, she suddenly just couldn't do it. The caffeine and sugar had all rushed to her brain, made her nervous and forlorn. She smiled — a shaky smile that felt as though it couldn't hold up her cheeks for longer than a few seconds — and backed through the door, thinking she would take a walk and discreetly dump the doughnut in the trash barrel in front of the vintage jewelry store around the corner. Do the right dietary thing.

But she was only a few feet away from the Hole Shebang when she noticed a piece of paper taped to the inside of the vacant shop's window next door. It caught her eye immediately.

LOVE THE HOLIDAYS? LOVE TO COOK? LOVE SHARING YOUR RECIPES WITH FRIENDS AND FAMILY? THE KITCHEN CLASSROOM NEEDS A TEACHER FOR A HOLIDAY COOKING SERIES. EXPERIENCE HELPFUL BUT NOT REQUIRED. CALL PAULA 555-1454 ASAP.

Bren read and reread the paper, her lips moving over the words. She did love all of those things. In fact, that had been her problem of late, right? It was almost too perfect that she should run across this paper on this day at this moment. She cupped her free hand and placed it against the glass, peering through the window. The shop was no longer vacant. A round, red-haired woman bustled about inside, a hammer in one hand, some nails pressed tightly between her lips.

There were several island counters, each with a small sink and work area on top, an oven beneath. One of the islands was elevated and facing the rest of the room. Behind it was a wall of wire shelves, empty baskets and bottles lining some of them, an accumulation of jarred spices at attention on one end. Bren's heart raced at the very sight of them.

The Kitchen Classroom. Cooking and teaching. Sharing recipes.

Maybe this was providence. A sign. Maybe this was exactly what she needed right now. Maybe she'd been led to the Hole Shebang and this awful doughnut — the smell of which was starting to turn her stomach a little now — so that she would discover what she was supposed to do with herself this holiday season.

Her hand plunged into her purse, searching out a pen. Without thinking, she stuffed the wretched doughnut into her mouth to hold it while she smoothed out the wax paper and wrote the phone number on it. She would give the job some thought. Sleep on it. Talk to Gary about it and give this Paula person a call in the mo—

"Hello?"

Bren blinked, looked up. The redhead was leaning out the door, the hammer dangling at her side, the nails between two fingers now.

"Can I help you?" the woman asked.

Bren shook her head, forgetting that the doughnut was in her mouth until it cracked, split, and broke, landing with an orange potatoey-cream-cheesy splat on her foot, a ragged chunk still clenched between her teeth. She had no choice but to chew and swallow, glad for her strong stomach. It definitely tasted like Thanksgiving. But not in a good way. More like if you'd perhaps licked the dirty dinner plates clean instead of putting them in the dishwasher.

The redhead ventured out onto the sidewalk, pretending as if she hadn't seen the doughnut fall. "I'm Paula. Are you interested in the position?"

Bren swallowed. "Yes. Well, maybe," she said, swallowing again. "I was writing down the number. I'm Brenda, by the way. Bren." She held out her hand and the redhead took it.

"You're hired," Paula said quickly. She laughed, self-conscious, breathless. "I'm sorry, but I'm desperate. I'm new here and I want to get up and running and I had a teacher all lined up for this class, but now she's going to Buffalo for Christmas and . . ." She shook her head. "Buffalo. Can you believe it? Anyway, the class was supposed to start this week."

"But I haven't filled out an application," Bren said.

Paula waved her off. "It doesn't matter. Can you cook?"

"Yes, I think so," Bren said. Nobody had ever told her she was the best cook in the world, but then again, nobody had ever complained, either. Not really, other than the one time she got experimental with the quinoa. In any case, nobody ever died from eating her food.

"Then you're hired," Paula said.

"I haven't talked to my husband. . . ."

"He can have the leftovers."

"I was going to sleep on it, and . . ."

"I'll pay you double what I was going to pay the other lady."

"I haven't really had any sort of job in over twenty years," Bren said uneasily, and it was this, she realized, that frightened her the most.

"This isn't a job. It's a friendship. I promise. You will love it. Please?"

A friendship. Bren liked that. Bren *needed* that.

And, without thinking about it, without really pondering what this would mean for her holidays, without even considering whether she could actually come up with a single recipe worth sharing, Bren found her shaky hand extending toward Paula's chapped one.

"Okay," she said. "I'll take it."

CHAPTER TWO

Virginia Mash hated her apartment. It was small and dark, always dark, and the windows were painted shut, thanks to her incompetent boob of a landlord. Plus, it was smack-dab in the middle of the square, perched atop a doughnut shop like a dusty old hat.

Square shopping had become trendy over the past couple of years or so, she had noticed. Virginia Mash hated trendy. And she hated square shopping. All those stores, thinking they were so original with their sheep's-milk soaps and their antique chests and their hand-sewn children's clothes and their crêpes. What on earth, Virginia thought, made a crêpe trendy? Hadn't they been around for centuries? It would be like calling gladiator sandals trendy, which, she supposed, some of the girls were doing these days, too. *Trendy* seemed to be defined as *I have it and you don't.*

And because the square had been revamped, the old, sleepy shops replaced by these new, trendy stores, that meant the square, and the space around her apartment, was always filled with noise and cars and exhaust and slamming doors and children throwing loud fits, and all the things that Virginia Mash hated most in this world.

It had been especially bad for the past year or so, once the doughnut shop had moved in directly below her apartment. The Hole Shebang, they called it. Virginia could not believe such a ridiculous name. Whatever happened to family names on businesses? Proud, anchored names with history. Ferguson's Rugs or Elliott's Pharmacy or Samuel's Furniture. Well, that one — Samuel — was so anchored it was downright biblical, wasn't it? Unlike the Hole Shebang. Virginia knew where she would like to punch a hole. And it wasn't in someone's shebang, that was for sure. Depending, of course, on what a shebang was, and where on a body it might be located.

Her apartment now smelled like sugar. And not in the good kind of way, either. Not outdoor festival sugar. Not Christmas cookie sugar. Cloying. Sickening. Overpowering, overbearing, overdone. Good Lord, did the irresponsible people of the Hole

Shebang think nothing of their arteries? Probably diabetic, every last one of them, or heading there. Dead before they were fifty, and when the medical examiner cut open their lardy fannies, what would she find? Doughnuts. The Hole Shebang doughnuts. Of that, Virginia Mash was certain.

But to make things worse, when she took her fourteen-year-old dachshund, Chuy, out for his walk today, there was a truck out front. A moving truck, parked right in the middle of the sidewalk in front of the Hole Shebang, making it darn near impossible for Chuy to do his business at all. Did these insensitive people think dachshunds could just hop up and down curbs all willy-nilly to avoid ill-placed ramps and boxes and dollies? Did they not realize that those short, stubby legs tired easily? Did they not notice that Chuy himself was nearly an octogenarian, half blind, arthritic? You would think these trendy people would have more respect for their elders, even the furry kind. *Especially* the furry kind. Animal rights were also trendy these days, after all.

The front door of the previously vacant storefront next door to the Hole Shebang was propped open wide, a flurry of movement going on inside, with several men lifting, grunting, sweating, sliding enormous boxes, and a red-haired woman, who looked to be in her mid-forties, wearing flannel and denim and boots directing them while simultaneously rooting through boxes and pulling quilts off countertops and . . . were those ovens? All of them? And with even more of them inside the truck?

"No," Virginia said aloud, hoisting herself up a few steps of the ramp that lolled out of the back of the truck like a tongue. As if the very truck were mocking her. She peered inside. Everything was covered, boxed, wrapped in cellophane. But, yes, she definitely saw at least one oven in there. "Cripes. Just what we need, Chuy. Another damn smelly restaurant at our feet. Don't people ever eat at home anymore? Why can't a good old PB&J be trendy?"

Chuy peered up at her through bleary old dog eyes that seemed to say, *Frankly, Virginia, I just don't give a shit.* Virginia harrumphed at him.

"Can I help you?" She whipped around and, seeing the flanneled woman coming toward her, Virginia quickly — or as quickly as she could, at her age — scuffled back down the ramp. Startled, the woman held out her hands. "Oh! Careful!"

"I'm fine, I'm fine," Virginia groused, swatting at the air between herself and the

24

woman's hands. There were few things she hated more than someone treating her as if she were incapable just because she was old. She'd driven a tow truck in her lifetime, for golly's sake. She'd fired no fewer than a dozen incompetents. She'd once installed a dishwasher with nothing but grit and determination and a single Phillips head screwdriver. "I can walk down a blasted ramp."

The woman's hands dropped to her sides. "Can I help you?" she asked again.

"Haven't you seen a woman walk her dog before?" Virginia answered, thumping down the ramp with her cane, because for some reason this seemed like an important point to make at that precise moment.

The woman bent down and scratched Chuy on top of his head. He wagged his tail gratefully. Traitor. Turncoat. Attention whore. "He's adorable. What's his name?"

"Speaking of, I suppose you're going to name this place something as stupid as the Hole Shebang," Virginia said, gesturing at the storefront. "I hope it isn't sweets."

The woman looked confused, turning to follow Virginia's gesture, but then she seemed to get it. "Oh," she said, her hand flying to her chest. "No. No, actually I'm calling it the Kitchen Classroom, because that's what it is, a kitchen where people can come to learn how to cook. Pretty straight-forward. I suppose I probably should have come up with something more creative, huh?" She'd turned and was studying the doughnut shop. "The Hole Shebang. Cute." She turned back to Virginia and extended her hand. "I'm Paula, by the way. Owner, manager, and only employee so far. But that will change soon. In fact, I think I may have just hired someone. I hope, anyway."

Virginia gazed at Paula's hand with such disgust, Paula retracted it, pinning it up against her stomach with her other hand. "A kitchen classroom? You mean a bunch of people who don't know what they're doing in a kitchen are going to be firing up ovens right below my apartment?"

Again, Paula glanced backward, this time tilting her head up to take in the painted-shut windows above the Hole Shebang. "I'm sure they'll know how to do that much," she said, but her voice was soft and uncer-tain. She turned back to Virginia, but her freckles had been clouded over with a flush. "We're more of a recipe instruction kind of place."

Virginia squinted one eye. "People need instruction on how to follow a recipe? I knew how to follow a recipe before I was ten. Can't they read?"

"We'll also be renting it out to culinary students and chefs who might want to try out new menu items and so forth."

"So there will be strangers streaming in and out at all hours of the night," Virginia said. "And I suppose it would be too much bother to have their backgrounds checked for criminal behavior."

The flush turned beet-colored. "So, are the — are the doughnuts good?" Paula asked, flicking a finger over her shoulder. "They smell delicious from here."

Chuy began to tug lightly at his leash, letting out a garbly whine. Virginia had no time for this Paula person and her recipe instruction. Plus, the weather was getting ready to turn. She could feel it in her arthritis. Her knuckles hurt when Chuy's leash grew taut around them. She glanced up at the sky, which was the flat gray of incoming winter. The tops of trees blew and swished. It wouldn't be long before a skiff of cold air swooped down onto the square and whipped her hair and clothing like those leaves. Chuy didn't like the cold. Virginia didn't like the holidays that the cold heralded in.

"Just make sure you have this sidewalk clear before I get back," Virginia said, ignoring the doughnut question. Did she honestly look like someone who would eat those nasty lard balls? She gestured toward Chuy with her cane. "My dog can't do curbs."

"Okay," she heard at her back, but she didn't bother to so much as take another look at redheaded Paula with the flannel and the boots and the ridiculous business idea.

With any luck, the Kitchen Classroom wouldn't be around for very long anyway.

CHAPTER THREE

It was what should have been dinnertime when the phone rang. Of course, it wasn't actually dinnertime. Not officially. It hadn't been officially dinnertime in the Epperson house since Kevin, leaving a trail of balled socks and loose change and mementos of a lost age — football cards stuck upright in the cracks of the baseboards, a Sanibel sand dollar plucked from the ocean an impossible decade ago, figurines from the imaginative days of childhood — had left the house with a passport and only half a harebrained plan. And quite a bit of cannabis, from the smell of him. Oh, he could deny it, but a mother knew when the eyes of her child weren't right.

Her youngest. Her baby. A once-treasured bedroom now home to only forgotten Super Balls and soccer pads and slippers, rock band posters and a rat's nest of old phone chargers, and the college textbooks he'd

29

foolishly purchased before he'd decided to admit that he wasn't planning to go, all abandoned.

Kevin had sprung the news on Bren that he'd never actually enrolled in college at a pancake house, of all places.

"Now, Mom," he'd said, holding his hand out to shush her, not even looking up from his plate of sunny-side-up eggs and congealed bacon grease, so condescending, so combatant, so very Kevin. "I know what you're going to say."

And she'd turned her face back down toward her plate, her Belgian waffles, her sausage links, her hash browns, and commenced eating, not even pausing the slightest while he went on about the confines of the American education system and his needs as an inquiring, and still growing, late adolescent mind — *no, make that young adult mind* — for the freedom to explore.

"If I see a flower that is beautiful, I need to be able to spend a day contemplating the folds of every petal on that flower — don't you understand?" he'd said, and Bren had nodded, made a muffled affirmative noise, and stuffed another forkful of strawberry topping into her mouth to keep herself from asking him when exactly was the last time he'd even noticed a flower. If, in fact, he

30

could name one single flower in existence.

He'd launched into his plans to travel abroad.

"And I don't mean just Europe," he'd said, stretching back, his hands folded behind his head, as if he were the god-damned king of England. "Europe, yes, but it's so cliché, don't you think? Finding oneself in Europe? As if we all exist only there. I mean, what if the true me exists in the Himayalas, you know? What if the essence of Kevin is in . . . in Kazakhstan or . . . or Beirut?"

He'd been so good at debate in high school. Well-spoken, extremely intelligent. Bren and Gary had been so proud, so very, very proud of his ability to think for himself, to put his thoughts together and present them convincingly. *He could sell ice cubes to an Eskimo,* Gary was known to say, a quip that made Bren feel uneasy — was it offensive to Alaskans? She could never quite tell.

Turned out Kevin hadn't needed to sell anything to anyone but her. By the end of the breakfast, she was so full she felt sick, stuffed to the gills with carbs and fat and sugar, but she was smiling, assuring Kevin that, yes, yes, she would talk to his father about these new plans of his. It sounded like an adventure, she told him between muffled belches. Something she wished she'd done while she was young and had a chance to explore the world.

He'd left with a jacket, a pocketful of snacks, and a sleeping bag harnessed along the underside of a backpack, for Christ's sake. *Isn't he taking this backpacking-across-the-world business a little far? How can he possibly have packed enough to live off of in that thing?* Bren had asked Gary, who'd sat on his parked motorcycle looking one-tenth worried for Kevin and nine-tenths envious out of his gourd. *Oh, he'll be fine, Brenda. Let him explore. This is important. You don't want him to turn around in thirty years and regret that he never went.* Bren had rolled her eyes. Of course Gary would make this about himself. Ever since the man turned the corner into the back side of his forties, he'd managed to make everything about himself. God love the old oafish bastard.

And so Kevin had hugged her and made promises about phone calls and postcards and a future that she knew would never come true and had hopped into his friend Tony's idling 2000 Toyota, checked his pocket for his passport one last time, and set off for the airport, a flick of his wrist through the passenger window for a wave,

Epperson family dinners whisked away on a fog of alternative music and car exhaust.

At last check-in — must have been at least three weeks ago — Kevin was just pulling into Český Krumlov, which Bren had made him spell so she could look it up on the Internet later. Somewhere in the Czech Republic, he'd said. He'd dropped his iPod in the Vltava River, but he didn't care, he'd said. He'd met a girl, he'd said. Her name was Pavlina, and she was an artist — *like, a real artist, not one of those weird girls who use creative stirrings as their excuse not to shave their pits, Mom.* Pavlina didn't believe in shoes, and she was the most beautiful thing he'd seen yet, and that included all of the Roman sculptures and paintings combined. He was smitten, but was telling Bren this as if dictating a travelogue, as he always did. Sounding removed, dutiful. Bren forever fretted that there would be a test at the end of his phone calls. She never talked to him without a pad of paper — what she thought of as her telephone pad — and a pencil so she could write down all the confusing foreign-sounding things he said. When they hung up, she felt like a completed chore he could check off his list. A *confused* completed chore.

But this time, the ringing phone had a

+66 country code at the front of it. Bren was eating cheese on toast — her fourth piece — and idly filling out a magazine quiz while the news blatted through the tiny kitchen TV, a persistent buzzing of negativity and fearmongering that both frightened her and made her feel superior. She jumped at the receiver.

"Hello?" and then, covering the mouthpiece with her palm, "Gary! It's Kelsey! Kelsey is calling!" Then back into the phone, "Hello?"

A strange click, some faraway hissing. "Mommy?"

Bren's breath caught. She loved that her daughter had never gotten too old to call her Mommy, but had to admit that hearing the word *Mommy* coming from her daughter, even at twenty-four years old, even married and a whole continent away, brought to mind skinned knees and Barbie dolls, an eight-year-old Kelsey who would never grow any older.

"Kelsey!" she exclaimed. "How's Thailand?"

"Oh, Mommy, it's beautiful. The rain has stopped, and it's so warm. Perfect, really. We're getting ready for Loi Krathong here. Do you know what that is? Have you ever seen it?"

Bren scrambled for her telephone pad and pencil, flipped to the *Kelsey* page, and scribbled down *Loy Rithong*. "I've never even heard of . . . Did you say *Rithong* with an *R*?"

Kelsey giggled. "A *K*, Mommy. A *K*. Krathong. We make these little boats and fill them with flowers and candles and coins — we're making ours out of bread to feed the fish, our boat. That was Dean's idea. Isn't that a great idea, Mommy, to make it out of bread?" Bren nodded, but there wasn't time to speak between Kelsey's breathless sentences. She always got that way, especially when she talked about her new husband. "He's so smart about things, even though we're still learning. It's like he's lived here his whole life. Anyway, so you float these little boats down the river during the full moon. It's like an offering, Mommy, but it's also symbolic. It symbolizes letting go of your hatred and anger and bitterness, and there are lanterns, so many lanterns, and, gosh, it just sounds so beautiful. Doesn't it sound beautiful?"

"Yes, beautiful," Bren said, but she'd gotten behind on her notes. "Wait, you have hatred and anger?"

"It's symbolic, Mommy."

"Symbolic hatred," Bren said, writing

35

down the words as she spoke them.

"So what are you and Daddy doing this evening? It must be about dinnertime there. I just woke up. I'm waiting for Dean to get out of the shower. We're playing hooky and going to the beach today. I'm telling you, Mommy, someday you and Daddy simply must come visit us. We have space. Dean said he would make space, isn't that the sweetest? He's so thoughtful that way, you know. Always worrying about everyone else. He would probably give you our bed and would sleep outside on the ground if that was what you wanted. You must come and let him be thoughtful to you, Mommy. It would mean the world to him. And you would be amazed by these beaches. The water, it's so clear. You've never seen water like that in Missouri, I can tell you that much."

Ah. There it was. The requisite Missouri-bashing that both of her kids had to do on a regular basis, now that they'd moved on to such exotic locales. As if nothing good could have possibly come out of a place so bland as the Midwest. As if they both had not come out of the Midwest themselves.

Bren wrote the word *beeche* — misspelled, after overthinking that it might have some foreign iteration like all the other things she'd been writing down — then scratched it out and wrote *hooky* instead, then scratched that out, too, and put down her pen.

"So?" Kelsey asked.

"So what?"

Impatient grunt, followed by a giggle. Kelsey's signature. The girl moved like a hummingbird, always zooming on to the next thing, the next conversation, the next song, the next location. "So what are you and Daddy doing tonight?" she repeated.

"Oh, that," Bren said. Her head felt swimmy, stuffed too full of information. She placed her hand over the phone receiver again. "Gary!" Nothing. She went to the garage door and pounded on it with the flat of her hand three times, marital code for *get your ass in here.* "Gary!"

"Daddy in the garage again?" Kelsey asked. "Still working on that motorcycle?"

"Yes and no," Bren said. "He's onto dune buggies now — it's a long story. I suppose we're not doing anything tonight. Although I'd hoped to catch up on some of my recorded shows."

"Well, that's boring. Honestly, Mommy, you should get out sometimes."

Bren's hand went to the back of her head. "I get out. I'm going to the hairdresser tomorrow."

"The hairdresser? What, are you ninety? I mean *get out,* get out. Do something fun. Go dancing. You're empty nesters now. You have freedom!"

Don't remind me, Bren thought, thinking for the thousandth time what an awful term *empty nester* was. So lonely, evoking images of things dried and barren. It was bad enough to feel that way without putting a name to it, too.

Bren found herself stuttering, nothing intelligible coming out, as her daughter continued to talk over her with suggestions of things to do — fancy dinners, romantic river cruises, day trips, double dates, clubs — followed by condemnation for sitting around and rotting at home, doomsday predictions of what happened to old couples who didn't thrive, old people who didn't leave the house.

"They die younger, Mommy, did you know that? Retired people who get out and do things live longer."

"We're not retired," Bren found herself saying, bewilderedly. "I'm only forty-five. Your father's not yet fifty."

"It's here before you know it," Kelsey said, in a very sage voice, as if a twenty-four-year-old knew the first thing about the advancement of time.

Bren considered telling her about the Kitchen Classroom job. Or was it the Classroom Kitchen job? And was it even a job? What kind of job could a person have if she couldn't even remember exactly the name of the company? She hadn't said a word to Gary about it yet. She hadn't even really convinced herself that she was going to go through with it, anyway. The further she'd gotten away from that strange encounter with Paula, the more hours that elapsed, the less likely it seemed that Bren could be a teacher of anything. Surely the woman didn't actually expect her to begin a job that was offered on the sidewalk with no background checks or résumé exchange or anything. What if Bren was a murderer? A kitchen knife–wielding murderer. It could happen.

There was a thundering of footsteps, and Gary came into the room, reeking of grease, wiping his hands on a filthy towel. Grateful for the interruption, Bren sat the phone on the table and hit the speaker button.

"Hey, there, princess!" Gary said, without waiting for an opening. Exactly where Kelsey got the chatty gene, right there.

"Daddy!" Kelsey squealed. If they'd been visiting in person, she would have wrapped her entire self around him, the way she always had. Such a daddy's girl. Although he'd taken her marriage and moving much more easily than Bren had thought he would.

She'd always had a vague fear that one of her children would move away. *Away* away, not college away or different town away, or even different state away. *Away* away, where she couldn't get to them within a few hours. But she'd never have guessed that one of them would actually go and do it. Not to mention both of them. Where had she gone wrong that both of them suddenly wanted to be *away* away?

Kelsey was married for exactly forty-six minutes before making her way to the middle of the reception dance floor, grabbing the mic, and announcing that Dean was accepting a new job (pause for polite applause) and that it was a really great opportunity (pause for excited grin) and that they would be moving (pause for hopping on toes) to exotic and beautiful Thailand (pause for confetti and balloons and a goddamned unicorn shitting puppies shaped like hearts and four-leaf clovers). Bren had smiled and clapped with the others, all the while trying to remember if Thailand was a place with big, scary insects or a place with big, scary diseases or a place with big, scary kidnappers. Or maybe all of the above. She was quite possibly the first mother of the bride in all of history to wonder aloud, at the reception, whether her daughter was up-to-date on all of her immunizations.

Oh, Gary had taken it hard at first. But he'd gotten over it so fast. How did he do that? Kelsey had now been gone for six months, and it already felt like six years, but to listen to Gary, to watch him as he putzed around on his dune buggy without a care in the world and as he casually chatted with his daughter on the phone — no pad and pencil required — you would never know the girl had been gone at all.

"How are things down under?" he asked.

This got the usual giggle from Kelsey. "We're not that close to Australia, Daddy."

"Oh, does that mean you don't have a pet kangaroo yet? Well, then I'm never coming to visit."

More laughter. They were so cute together, those two. It made the bridge of Bren's nose ache. She pinched it, wondering if she should write down *kangaroo.* Out of nowhere, her shoulder itched. She shrugged a few times, the friction from the bra strap scratching it.

"How's Dean-o?" Gary asked, his voice

booming, making Bren flinch.

"Oh, he's just great. His project is going well and it looks like he may get a contract extension, which we're so excited about. We haven't seen nearly enough of Thailand yet. We'd like to stay a few more years."

"Years?" Bren barked, and then slapped her mouth shut. She'd vowed to never make either of the children feel guilty about their decision to live lives separate from hers — even if they were so carelessly breaking her heart — but she couldn't help it. Years was a long time. Years was long enough for her to miss the birth of a grandchild. Years was long enough to put down roots, real roots, the kind of roots that you don't want to dig up.

"Well, you tell him we said hello and to keep up the good work," Gary boomed, as if Bren had never said anything at all. Thank God.

"So I can't talk for much longer," Kelsey said, her voice going down at the edges. "Trying to save money where I can."

"That's my girl," Gary said. "Level-headed."

Bren shot him a look. As if saving pennies by shortchanging her own parents on phone calls while lollygagging on a beach all day instead of working were a fiscally responsible decision.

"I just wanted to say hi. And to tell you I miss you both bunches."

"Bunches?" Bren repeated. Her pen scrawled it out of its own accord, but she was drowned out once again by Gary.

"We miss you, too, pumpkin. You take care of yourself down there. Don't forget to put another shrimp on the barbie."

Kelsey's laughter tinkled through the phone speaker again. Bren had more than once wished she could bottle up that laughter, keep it safe, keep it handy. It was a sound of such pure joy. But now it only sounded faraway, dulled by distance. A joy that she could only admire, but never fully experience again.

"Oh, just a reminder, by the by, that Dean and I won't be coming home for the holidays."

"Yes, yes, you've told us," Bren said tiredly. Did her daughter have to keep reminding her of that? Did she really think that having her first-ever Christmas apart from her children would be something Bren would absentmindedly forget?

"Got big Christmas plans?" Gary asked.

"Not really. It's mostly Buddhist here, so not a lot of Christmas celebrating goes on, I don't think. Plus, the place will just be flooded with tourists, from what I hear. We'll probably have a quiet dinner. Maybe some noodles, some fish. Just the two of us."

"Same here," Bren said. "Just the two of us. Only without the noodles."

"No Grandma?" Kelsey asked.

"She and Aunt Cathy have plans," Bren said.

"They're going to Vegas, those dirty dogs," Gary added. "Christmas with Elvis and all-you-can-eat steak." The way he said it made it sound fun, and not like the abandonment it was. Even Bren's own mother couldn't be bothered with Christmas this year. Imagine.

"Well, tell them I said to enjoy that! I hope they roll sevens. Or elevens. Or whatever it is that's good," Kelsey cried out, right back to her sunny self. "And you two should make the most of your alone time. A romantic Christmas dinner for two, for the first time in, what . . ."

"Twenty-four years," Bren supplied.

"Wow, twenty-four," Kelsey said. "You are long overdue."

"I suppose we must be," Bren said. She didn't have the heart to tell Kelsey that their grand Christmas Eve dinner plans involved a cafeteria, nor did she mention the cheese on toast or the pad and pencil with all the foreign words or even her incessant nightly scouring of the Internet for cheap flights halfway around the world.

"That we are," Gary said, snaking an arm around Bren's shoulders. She resisted the urge to pull away, though she knew she was going to smell like that damned buggy now even if she did.

Their good-byes were, as always, over so quickly it left Bren's head spinning. She clutched the pad and pencil, gazing at the words as if trying to memorize the conversation, file it away so she would have it to pull out on her next lonely evening filling out magazine quizzes and listening to the nightly death report.

Gary drifted away, taking the rag and a glass of iced tea with him. Terse, typical conversation, the amiable guy with the big smile and the cute turns of phrase snuffed out like a candle on a birthday cake.

"You eat?"

"Just some cheese toast."

"Huh."

"You want me to make you something?"

"Naw, I'll grab a bite later. Working on the buggy."

A shuffling of footsteps toward the garage again. "You gonna be long?"

Garage door opening, an echoey answer

45

that drifted into inaudible murmurings, and then a shut door: "Got to get to bed. Meetings tomorrow . . ."

Bren stared at the pad of paper. *Bunches* was the last word she'd written.

But off in the margin was the sad face that she'd drawn when Kelsey had told them she didn't plan to come home for the holidays.

Suddenly the cheese toast looked congealed and disgusting, postsurgery fleshy. She could feel the bread perching at the base of her esophagus, coiled, ready to launch as soon as she lay down for bed. She could practically see little orange pustules of grease popping into the pores around her mouth, on her cheeks, her forehead, suffocating them, making her skin dull and cheeselike itself. The very thought made her tongue curl back in a gag.

She got up and carried the plate to the sink, snatching up the remote control and turning off the TV as she went. The room hummed with silence. The sun had fallen.

She padded back to the bedroom, where her black long-haired cat, George, lay waiting for her, curled at the bottom of the bed. He made a *brrr* noise as she slid headfirst into the bed, and moved so his hind end pressed warmly into her side.

It was barely seven o'clock, but Bren Epperson went to bed anyway, thanking God, as she drifted off, for the short days of autumn.

CHAPTER FOUR

Bren closed her eyes, concentrating on the
shush of the water and the warmth that
spread itself over the crown of her head, the
feel of Nan's fingers snaking over her scalp.
She always kept her eyes shut during the
washing, the better to ignore how irregularly
long the sinks made her neck feel, and how
scrutinized she felt in that position —
stretched backward, throat bared, skin tags
laid out for anyone to assess or attack. Plus,
hairdressers could see right up your nose
when you were under the faucet. Nan probably knew more about Bren's nasal cavity
than Bren did. Mortifying.

Of course, she'd been going to Nan long
enough to go through the washing in silence.
Nan recognized a good, quality neurosis
when she saw one and understood when to
go ahead and humor it. Before Bren had
found Nan, though, she'd endured in-
numerable washing sessions filled with yam-

mering, the stylists raising their voices to be heard over the water — *Can you believe this weather? I didn't even need a jacket today! Do you have kids? Yeah? How old? What are their names? Blah, blah, blah.* From what Bren could tell, nobody particularly enjoyed this routine; they simply put up with it. Anything to keep everyone in the room from acknowledging the truth, that you were a grown-ass woman who'd just washed your own hair an hour before, because you were perfectly capable of washing your own hair, and because you were too vain to go any-where with greasy comb marks in your limp tresses, even to the hairdresser.

Or maybe these were just the things Bren thought about when lying back, giraffe-necking the sink, earlobes squished against the washbasin, expensive shampoo scent fog around her head, until Nan let the nozzle snap back into place and cradled her head with a towel, urging with her hands for Bren to sit up.

Then and only then would she allow herself to open her eyes. But she was never quite pleased with what she saw in the mir-ror. Especially these days. Her neck looked squat and squeezed under the collar of the brown cape. She looked, to herself, like someone who'd been buried chin-deep in mud. Or maybe at this point it was more chins-deep. Plural. The snap of her jeans jabbed into her gut as confirmation.

"So," Nan said briskly, combing Bren's hair into straight chunks around her shoulders, "Turkey Day's in nineteen days, huh?"

"Oh, is it?" Bren asked. "I had no idea." Out of the corner of the mirror, Bren caught Lucy, the impossibly young desk clerk, so skinny Bren would have worried if she'd been the girl's mother, stepping up onto a stool to pull down the orange and black Halloween garland that had been strung across the shop's front window.

Nan nodded. "And you know what that means."

Bren frowned, then, seeing her hideous frown lines in the mirror, quickly released it before pasting on a pleasant little grin. It was totally fake, but much nicer to look at. "No," she said.

Nan stopped brushing, met Bren's eyes in the mirror. Really, Bren thought, Nan had terrible hair. Frizzy, overworked, bleached within an inch of its life. And Nan was forever fiddling with it. Bren imagined she could hear Nan's follicles cry out in terror every time the woman picked up a teasing comb. "It means" — dramatic pause for effect — "only forty-eight days until Christmas." Nan laughed as Bren groaned. "Have you started your shopping yet?"

"No," Bren said, though she didn't elaborate, that there wouldn't be any shopping this year. Not really. Everything these days was so impersonal. Gift cards and money, money and gift cards. Even her nephews couldn't think of anything they wanted; her sister-in-law had told her, *Just get them gift cards or money.* And then she'd done that thing that wannabe-rich people so often did when conversations turned to money — the knowing-laugh thing — and added, *Money's always one size fits all, amIright?*

Bren had knowing-laughed along with her, but secretly, inwardly, she wondered what five-year-old boy or seven-year-old boy or twelve-year-old boy couldn't think of one gift to ask for. What were they going to do, line up their dollar bills on their beds and count them? Roll around on their cash a little bit? Was that what passed for recreation these days? Knowing her snooty nephews, that was probably exactly what they did.

So shopping was going to look a lot more like running to the ATM — *one size fits all, amIright?* — and maybe not even scraping together enough energy to buy fancy cards to put the cash in. Instead of heavy card stock laden with iridescent glittery snowscapes, she would probably end up tucking twenties into dollar-store flimsy getups, glossy and thin with some ridiculous animal, entirely unrelated to the holidays, smiling on the cover. *What the heck does a raccoon in a necktie have to do with Christmas?*

"I haven't even started to think about shopping," Nan said, shifting around Bren's chair to pick up a pair of scissors. "Nico's already got a list as long as his arm. And you know he'll get all of it. Just can't say no to him."

Bren smiled. "He is so cute. What is he, four now?"

Nan nodded. "Four going on fourteen. Spoiled seven ways from Sunday. Tilt your chin down."

"Not spoiled," Bren said to her breasts. *My word, but they had also gotten so big.* Was it her imagination, or was she unable to tilt her chin all the way down, for the breast barricade? "Just loved. You two went through the wringer to get that baby."

Nan stopped cutting and Bren tipped her eyes up just in time to see Nan pointing to the mirror with her scissors. "Boy, have you got that right," Nan said. She went back to Bren's hair, tickling the base of her neck with the scissor point. "Thought we'd be two old farts, all alone together forever. So depressing."

Bren felt a prickle inside her stomach. *Two old farts, all alone.* Just like she and Gary were now. And Nan had never been more right — it was depressing as hell. The top of her shoulder itched. She snaked her hand up through the cape and scratched it. Nan stopped clipping again.

"You ever tell Gary about that?" she asked.

Bren shook her head, glad to be in the chin-tilt position so Nan couldn't see her face. Nan made a noise.

"Girl, you better tell him. Sooner rather than later, you know."

"I will," Bren said. "It's just . . . there's nothing to tell yet."

"I suppose," Nan said. She combed a swath of Bren's hair down and ducked to clip it. "But you told me."

"Oh, Nan, you know that's different," Cara, the middle-aged stylist at the next chair, said. She switched on her hair dryer and picked up a large roller brush. The woman in her chair looked sleepy and serene, her lips pale and eyelids heavy. "We're like therapists here," she shouted over the noise of the dryer. "People are supposed to tell us everything."

"Vegas," Tomie, the only male stylist, said. "We're like Vegas. What happens at the salon . . ."

"Stays at the salon," Cara finished, and they burst into laughter.

"Still," Nan said, turning Bren's chair so she faced the mirror, Skinny Lucy popping into the background again. She had finished pulling down the garland and was now taping little cardboard turkeys and cornucopias to the window. "When you gonna say something, honey?"

Bren shrugged. "When I know something," she said, "I guess." And when Nan only raised her eyebrows questioningly, Bren added, "Gary's so busy right now, anyway."

Recognizing when she was defeated, Nan sighed, raised her scissors, and changed the subject. "Oh yeah? What's he into now? Still golfing?"

"Oh no, he was no good at that."

"What? He golfed every day."

"And he finally recognized that he stunk." Bren currently had twelve pairs of golf shoes in her bedroom closet. Twelve pairs! She wondered if even that adorable pro golfer — what was his name? Foaler? Fowler? Yes, that was it, Rickie Fowler — had twelve pairs of golf shoes. Gary couldn't sink a hole in one if the hole was the Grand Canyon, but he had shoes, by God. Shoes, and a god-awful pair of pink pants. "Now he's into dune buggies."

Nan stepped back. "Dune buggies? What does it mean to be 'into dune buggies'? We don't even have any dunes around here, do we? Where would we have dunes in Missouri?"

Bren sighed, having already been through this argument more times than she cared to count. Things like available dunes were details to Gary. He wasn't interested in hearing any sort of rational response. He was just interested in having something to do. "None that I know of. But that didn't stop him from buying an old beat-up thing. It's sitting in our garage — makes the whole house smell like a lawn mower — and every night he's out there tinkering around on it, dreaming of the day he can go God knows where in it. I suppose to the grocery store. That's the only place we ever go."

Nan raised one eyebrow, giggling. Bren couldn't help joining in — even though this was more than a sore subject in her house, Nan's giggle was contagious.

"Will I have to start styling around helmet head?" Nan asked.

"Oh, goodness, no. He won't get me in that thing."

"Where do you put groceries in a dune

buggy, anyway?"

"Bet if he bends over, I'll find a spot," Bren said sourly, meaning it, but again the giggles started, which threatened to rip her out of her snit prematurely.

The truth was, she was sick of Gary's midlife crises. First it was the motorcycle. Expensive as hell, but it took only one week for Gary to decide he was much too vain to show up at work with sweaty clothes and wind-whipped hair. Then there'd been a short stint of very dedicated boys' nights out, Gary coming home bloated from greasy bar food and beer farts so smelly she had, on more than one night, considered sleeping in Kelsey's bed just to get some relief. Fortunately, none of the guys in Gary's circle had the stomach, literally, for boys' nights out anymore, and they were quickly kiboshed. So Gary had dived headlong onto the golf course in his fabulous shoes and pink pants — a hobby he quickly realized he was no good at — and now here Bren was with a house that stunk like the inside of a gasoline can.

But at least he wasn't lusting after some blond intern, she thought. At least he wasn't blowing their retirement money on a red Lamborghini. Let him have his crisis. Soon (sooner than she wanted to admit, actually), fifty would get here and he would begin to settle into old age with her.

God. What a miserable thought.

"Well, dune buggy or no dune buggy," Nan said, breaking into her thoughts as she combed out the last threads of hair and bent to clip them even, "you really should let him know about this." She tapped Bren's shoulder twice lightly with her comb. The sensation made Bren's shoulder itch, but she resisted the urge to scratch. Leave it to Nan to always be able to bring a conversation back around to itself.

"I got a job," Bren blurted, shocking herself, but glad for the diversion.

Nan stopped clipping. "A job? Doing what?"

"Cooking," Bren said. "Well, teaching a cooking class, actually. So sort of teaching, I guess. I'm not exactly sure. It's a part-time thing. Seasonal. You know." She shrugged, suddenly embarrassed and anxious and wishing she'd said nothing. She still hadn't told Gary. She was still changing her mind on an hourly basis whether this job thing was going to happen.

"Well, congratulations," Nan said. "That's really great. I can't wait to hear all about it."

"And feel free to bring in leftovers," Tomie

shouted from his chair. "We will happily be your guinea pigs."

"If you insist," Nan agreed, and they all laughed, even Bren, even though her laughter was having to elbow its way around an enormous lump in her throat to get out.

CHAPTER FIVE

Lamb chops with mint gremolata. Turkey stuffed with wild rice, sausage, and apples. Crown rib pork roast and oyster stuffing moist with sage brown butter. Bren had made them all, sweating, littering every spare centimeter of her already-cramped counter space with spice bottles and measuring cups, spending a fortune on food she would soon throw out because Gary was too busy with his dune buggy to eat it and she was too full and too lazy and too sick of soggy bread cubes to so much as take another nibble. Her kitchen, outdated but usually clean and bright, was sopping with melted butter and thick with meat fumes and sticky with spilled broth. She had flakes of sage and red pepper and parsley permanently stuck to the bottoms of her feet. The hardwood floor felt as worn and gritty as a barn floor, and didn't look much better.

Yet none of it was right.

They didn't eat this shit on Christmas.

They ate smoked beef brisket, coated with so much salt it seemed obscene, and doused with sticky sweet barbecue sauce and tender enough to spoon off hunks and balance on expensive onion buns and those King's Hawaiian sweet rolls the kids loved so much. The house smelled like a tailgate party; the sides were beans and coleslaw and corn casserole with jalapeños and cheese dip with tortilla chips. Not a flake of sage to be found. Not a sprig of parsley. Not an artfully arranged circle of pork or a well-balanced stuffing.

Jell-O salad. Wheat Thins and Triscuits and a thousand pounds of cream cheese in varying forms to dip them into. Pinwheels. Brownies. The occasional fried chicken tender or pot of Kraft macaroni and cheese. Ordinarily, you could barely see the faded blue Formica of Bren's kitchen counter, much less the spot where Gary had dropped a highball glass and taken a hunk out of it or the spot where Kevin had gotten over-zealous with Easter egg dye or the little mound of dried Krazy Glue that had fallen off of one of Kelsey's never-ending art projects, for all the pots and bowls and handwoven hot pads.

On Thanksgiving, they did the traditional.

Of course they did. The same pumpkin pie that everyone else made. But Christmas, never. Picnic food was their Christmas. It was perfect for them. Bren loved it. She cherished it, actually. Wouldn't have wanted to trade her brisket dinner for all the turkey dinners in the world. Wouldn't have given a drop of her barbecue sauce for a gallon of browned butter. What the hell was browned butter, anyway? Why couldn't anyone call it what it really was — burned?

Bren had never considered before how un-traditional her family's Christmas dinner really was until she considered teaching others how to make it.

Holiday Eats Class #1: The Fine Art of Dipping Your Shit in Ketchup.

That was definitely not going to fly.

She remembered the first Christmas that she brought Gary home to meet the family. How his eyes had gone big and surprised when her mother had brought out the barbecued meatballs, and then followed those with two whole briskets. Nearly thirty pounds of cow. They were blackened — caramelized — on the ends and juicy in the middle, and tendrils of steam wafted up, sending out puffs of delicious smoke scent that brought to mind Amish fall festivals and touchdowns at Arrowhead.

"My family does turkey," Gary had whispered to Bren as they filled up their paper plates. "And ham."

"It's my grandmother's recipe," she'd said, blanching. "I'm sorry."

He'd hefted a spoonful of baked beans onto his plate and let the spoon thunk back down into the Crock-Pot, and then turned to her. "Are you kidding me? I'm so sick of turkey I could puke. This is the best."

It was then that Bren knew Gary was the man she would someday marry. And, she'd vowed to herself, when she did marry him, she would serve him smoked brisket and baked beans on Christmas Day for the rest of their lives together. And she did. And he would have it no other way now, either. Or at least he wouldn't have until the kids moved out. A cafeteria? Really? They were going to give up Grandma's brisket for limp green beans and bowls of tapioca?

But Bren was certain she could never convince a class full of people to accept brisket as holiday fare. They'd be coming expecting traditional recipes. They'd want to baste birds and simmer the piss flavor out of cranberries and bake loaves of bread. They'd want to eat some goddamned figgy pudding, for all she knew.

She made a quick mental note to suggest

a figgy pudding doughnut to Tod. He would love that.

Desperate, she dragged a chair across the kitchen and stepped up on it, patting the top of the refrigerator, what used to be home to junk food she didn't want the kids devouring, now only a hiding place for the occasional plastic alphabet magnet, a whole lot of dust, and a little metal box that held all of her grandmother's old recipes. Maybe she'd find something there.

But as she sat on the chair, flipping through what she'd found, nothing seemed just right. Coconut cake. Her grandmother might have made that a couple of times. Creamed spinach. Oh yes, Bren vividly recalled that failed experiment, otherwise known as "The Unholy Christmas Incident" between Bren's father and his aging mother-in-law. Nobody had known at the time that neither of them had more than five Christmases left in their lives. Of course, had he known, her father just might have blamed his mother-in-law's creamed spinach for his untimely, and quite deadly, heart attack. Scalloped potatoes, the homemade kind. Oh, how Bren loved those. But nobody could quite make them like her grandma — even using her recipe, which they'd all suspected had been partial, nobody else's as tasty as hers by design — and so they'd dropped them from their spread. Were they Christmassy enough for her to teach them to a class?

Ugh, she didn't know!

She slammed the box shut. Held it in her lap. Then stood and tucked it away on top of the fridge again. Quit. She had to quit; that was all there was to it. She could cook. But she couldn't do this.

Before she could talk herself out of it, Bren crossed the kitchen and grabbed the phone, dialing the number she now knew by heart. She'd started to quit at least a dozen times already that day, only to hang up the instant Paula answered. But this time she wouldn't disconnect. This time she would quit and be done with it.

"Hello?"

"Paula? Hello, yes, this is Bren Epperson."

"Oh, hey, Bren, I was just talking about you."

Bren blinked, thrown off. "You were?"

"Yeah, there was a lady here asking about the holiday cooking class. Said she's tired of the usual turkey and stuffing and was looking for a way to spice up her holiday menu. I told her you would have lots of unique recipes up your sleeve."

"You told . . . unique?" Bren flopped back

into the chair that she'd still never moved from next to the refrigerator. The fridge — old friend, bought before the time of fancy things like digital temperature readouts and built-in ice dispensers — kicked on with a whoosh and a hum. She leaned her head against it, feeling the vibration in her temple.

Paula laughed. "Don't sound so surprised. You look like just the kind of lady who would have out-of-the-box recipes, pardon the pun." She laughed again. "Maybe something literally spicy. Jalapeño stuffing, maybe? Chipotle gravy? Buffalo turkey wings?"

Bren gazed at the counter, where her recipe book was still spread out. "Or South-western corn casserole," she said numbly, hardly believing her ears.

"Exactly! Now, there's a holiday recipe nobody is expecting. Who eats Southwestern corn casserole for Christmas? It's brilliant!"

Bren forced out a chuckle. "Yeah," she said. "I don't know who."

"I'm going to start to bill your class that way, I think. Unique flavors for a Christmas they never saw coming. Oh! That's it! New class title: The Never-Saw-It-Coming Christmas! What do you think?"

"I never saw it coming," Bren said, only half joking, though her mouth turned up in a smile with Paula's laugh.

"So tell me why you called," Paula said.

"Oh." Bren was lost for words, no longer sure what to say at all. Why was she calling? What was it she'd been wanting to say? That she was going to quit? Well, she could hardly quit now that she was on the hook for Southwestern corn casserole. Not to mention, she would hate to have to explain to Nan that it was a brisket that took her down. "I was just wondering if you'd had anyone sign up," she lied.

"Yes," Paula said. Bren could hear papers shuffling in the background. "Just the one, actually. But she seemed really eager, and maybe she'll tell her friends. And I am going to go out and really plug the class today, especially now that we have a new title for it. Do you have any friends or family that might be interested? Because, you know, feel free to recruit some of your own people."

"Recruit. Yes. Of course," Bren said. "I'll do that."

"Okay, sounds like a plan. Well, then I guess I'll see you next Thursday. Send me your ingredients list by Friday, okay? Remember, two classes a week."

"Yes, sure," Bren said, on autopilot. She was still stunned that she would now be able to send an ingredients list that included KC Masterpiece and canned pork and beans without feeling like a total failure.

Bren hung up the phone and considered who this strange woman might be. The one sick of turkey — just like Gary had been — and looking for food with a little kick. The one responsible, really, for the new class title. Never saw it coming. Boy, wasn't that the truth!

Bren wondered idly if she would like this woman. If maybe they'd end up being friends. It had been a long time since Bren had any real friends.

Sure, there were neighbors. Even good neighbors, who would come outside for a drink on a cool fall evening. There were Gary's work friends, who became her friends, too — most notably John and Cindy, with whom they'd shared a great many rowdy evenings, but whom they hadn't really heard much from since Gary's last promotion. And there were school friends. Tight-knit mommies who tested out all their fears and insecurities on one another. But those friendships dissolved as the kids moved up to middle school, junior high, high school, beyond. She'd been invited to only one wedding. Just one — the wedding of a boy Bren had babysat for a short stint in early elementary school. And she had invited none of those mommy friends to Kelsey's wedding. It was as if that period of her life had never existed, as if those people had never existed.

Now her friendship circle was Nan, whose friendship was somewhat bought, if Bren allowed herself to really think about it, one rinse at a time; Tod at the doughnut shop, who probably wouldn't notice if she disappeared, except that would mean he would have to press his cockamamie concoctions onto someone else; and the enthusiastic-wave-from-the-flower-bed neighbor two doors down, who wasn't close enough for Bren to actually know her name. That was no circle of friends.

She knew people. People who knew people. Women who went on trips with other families. Women who lived for their GNOs. Women who bought one another birthday gifts and who probably celebrated Christmas at one another's houses. Bren had always been jealous of those women. Soul-crushingly, mortifyingly, profoundly jealous. She wanted Sunday-dinner friends.

The envy pressed in on her, as it had done so many times before, making her shoulder itch. She scratched at it absently, a stab of guilt working its way through her. Nan was right — she really needed to talk to Gary about that. Before it was too late.

She got up and leaned over the counter, picking up her pen and righting it over the paper where she'd been making her lesson plans earlier. Or more like the paper where she should have been making lesson plans, but had gotten nowhere. She wrote down *Southwestern Corn Casserole* and *Zippy Taco Dip.*

There. That ought to please her student.

Her one student.

God, how humiliating that would be! Just one student?

She set the pen down and reached for her purse. She didn't have friends, this was true. Nobody she could call in a favor on, beg for reciprocation, or help or anything much more than that flower-bed wave.

But, by God, she had family.

And family always owed one another.

CHAPTER SIX

Winter was not wasting any time showing up this year. It seemed to have swooped in on them all at once, Bren thought. Wasn't it only two weeks ago that she'd been happily tooling around in her flannel jacket, still sporting sandals with her jeans? Wasn't the neighborhood pool swarmed with kids the week before that?

Now the sky was more gray than blue, and the trees seemed to have dumped all of their leaves at once, their branches clicking and creaking against one another as the wind gusted through them.

Her mother's street was decked out for fall, as it was always decked out for every seasonal occasion. While Bren's neighborhood had definitely been a victim of post-middle-age fuck-its, her mother's neighborhood was as progressive as a bunch of twentysomething parents of preschoolers. Never mind that the vast majority of them had lived in their houses for upward of forty years, and not a one of them even had a preschool-aged grandchild left. They were decorating fools. Really old, really dedicated decorating fools.

Her mother's yard was tastefully done with three well-placed hay bales (which she must have had Bren's brother, Mark, bring over) topped with a cute stack of pumpkins. She had anchored a wooden sign, painted in orange, yellow, and red, with the stenciled word THANK-FALL! near the front walk. Her yard had been raked (that was Bren's nephew's doing, for a pretty penny at that, Bren was sure — *Money's always one size fits all, amIright?*), and she'd even hung a plastic turkey on the front door. It was cute.

Bren turned and glanced at the house across the street, which appeared to be not yet ready to let go of Halloween. The décor in that yard consisted of a garish-looking scarecrow, face drawn on in a terrifying grimace across a stuffed burlap sack, the arms covered with fake spiderwebs, one hand clutching a plastic amputated foot. A crow hung upside down from the general area of the scarecrow's mouth, its head ripped mostly off and dangling. Also, curiously, there was a half-eaten Milky Way dangling from the scarecrow's other hand.

As she was looking, suddenly the front door banged open, and out popped a familiar mass of tangled gray hair and rainbow clothing.

"Bren! Yoo-hoo!" the hair and clothing called.

Bren sighed. Of all the places her crazy aunt Cathy could have chosen to live, she'd chosen the house directly across from Bren's perfectly, or at least mostly, sane mother's house. Why her mother hadn't moved out the very day Aunt Cathy moved in was beyond Bren. But then again, her mother seemed to have more patience with Aunt Cathy than did the rest of civilized society. She even seemed to sort of enjoy Aunt Cathy's company, an anomaly Bren could only really guess had something to do with the post-WWII suffering that they had both endured as children.

"Hey, Aunt Cathy," she said. "I'm not staying. Just a quick visit."

Bren hated that she started every conversation with Aunt Cathy this way, specifically because starting conversations that way was nothing more than her hoping it would deter Aunt Cathy from making the slow, arduous trek down the long flight of steps that led from her front porch to her driveway.

But the old woman was too stubborn to save her arthritic knees from the torment of a stair climb. And, in turn, Bren's torment of having to listen to her half-insane rants. What would it be this time? Puppy mills? Obamacare? The French? Those were Aunt Cathy's top three.

"Can you believe that idiotic weatherman?" Oh yes. The idiotic weatherman. Top four. "He said it would be clear today. Clear! Ha! A lie if I've ever heard one. Clear is a snow globe. Clear is a window. Clear is not this . . ." Aunt Cathy paused midstep, gesturing wildly with both arms toward the sky. "This gray stuff!" Slowly she continued down the steps, which seemed to be growing, regenerating as she walked. It was like watching someone try to walk down the up escalator. "Soon there will be wind and snow, and what will the weatherman have to say for himself then?"

She had made it to the bottom of the steps at last, which meant Bren had to wait for the long pause for her aunt to readjust her knee-highs before the million-mile shuffle that would take her across the street.

"Well?" Aunt Cathy hollered, taking Bren off guard. She wasn't used to being asked for input during one of Cathy's rants. She wasn't exactly prepared.

"Huh? Oh. I suppose he'll be sorry then," Bren said, but only because she thought it was the right thing to say. Surely Aunt Cathy would have heard nothing else.

"Damn straight," Aunt Cathy said. "Someone ought to firebomb his car."

"Well, that might be taking it a bit far," Bren said, although she supposed that would make an interesting evening broadcast to watch during one of her solo cheese toast dinners.

At last Aunt Cathy was climbing up the curb to Bren's mother's house, grunting with the effort. God, Bren never wanted to get old. She wanted to stay this age forever. Actually, scratch that. She wanted to go back to twenty-five and stay that age forever. Back when her boobs were still something to look at and Gary was a man who still cared to look. Back when her kids begged her to put up the Christmas tree weeks too early. Back when she mattered.

But she especially didn't want to get old enough to be adjusting her knee-highs while ranting about the weatherman and getting out of breath walking across the street.

Not that Aunt Cathy even paused when she reached Bren. She just kept going, kept ranting as she made her way right through the front door of Bren's mom's house.

Bren really needed to talk to her mom about leaving her front door unlocked. It was unsafe. Plus, how did she keep Cathy out?

It was one of the scariest things about losing her dad — the knowledge that now her mother, fragile and timid, would be alone. And the knowledge that Mr. and Mrs. Moneybags — *amIright?* — wouldn't bother to so much as check to see if the woman was alive every now and then. If something horrible happened, Bren knew she would never forgive them or herself, so she'd been on high alert since the day they buried her father. It was sort of like being a new mother again, only worse, because it somehow felt easier to accidentally kill an old woman than a new baby. Or maybe that was just her fear talking.

She went in behind Aunt Cathy, noting immediately how hot it was in the house. She'd talked to her mother about the heat a billion times, but the woman never listened. She liked it warm, she insisted. But there was warm and there was condensation-dripping-down-the-windows warm. There was sunscreen-and-calypso-music warm. There was run-around-the-house-nude warm. Bren made a pit stop at the thermostat. Her mother had it set at eighty-four.

Who did that? Bren slid it down to seventy, wondering whether she could somehow open it up and bend the needle to point at eighty-four when it was actually at seventy. She bet she could. She felt deliciously deceitful, kind of like getting her back for all those Santa lies. She made a mental note to read up about it online.

She found her mother and aunt Cathy in the kitchen by the scent of the coffee, which was always fresh in her mother's house, and the sound of Aunt Cathy's ranting voice once again.

". . . firebomb the whole news station . . . ," Aunt Cathy was saying.

"Hi, Mom," Bren announced, cutting Aunt Cathy off before she started counting casualties.

Her mother, Joan, sat, small and white, at the kitchen table, wrapped up in a sweater, her hands pressed against a full, steaming coffee mug, as if she were hayriding through the Antarctic. How was she not a melted grease slick by now?

"Hello, Brenda!" Joan said. "Come have some coffee with us. We were talking about the weather."

"No, I can't stay," Bren said, waving off both the coffee and the conversation. Or at least she hoped. "I just wanted to come by to . . . invite you to something." Maybe if she made it sound like something fun and exclusive, they would be excited about it.

"Oh, are you having a party?" Aunt Cathy asked, and when Bren didn't answer immediately, she turned to Joan. "Is she having a party? I am so there. I want gin. Been craving gin for a week. I'll bring the gin. Lots of it. Gin for everyone. Especially me."

Actually, Bren could think of few things her aunt needed less than lots of gin, but she ignored and plowed on.

"It's a class," she said.

Her mother laughed. "I'm too old for school. I was never very good at it when I was young."

"I hated school," Aunt Cathy said. "Bunch of communists teaching in those schools anyway."

"No, no," Bren said, holding her palms out to stop the school rant before it started. "It's not a class in a school. It's a cooking class. In a kitchen. And I'm teaching it. And I'm not a communist," she added.

The two older ladies glanced at each other and then burst out laughing.

"What?" Bren asked. "What's so funny?"

"Nothing," Joan said. "Nothing, honey. It's just . . . you? Teaching a cooking class?"

Bren was stung. She'd had her mother

over for dinner countless times. Hundreds, probably. Maybe thousands. Millions? Was it possible to make millions of dinners in a lifetime? She thought maybe it was, and maybe she had. It sure felt like she had. She crossed her arms over her chest.

"What's so hilarious about that? I'm a great cook."

"You are." Her mother nodded. "But you're not the most patient person in the world. What if someone in your class can't cook?" She thumbed toward Aunt Cathy. A brilliant example of someone who couldn't cook, in Bren's estimation. Epically so. Aunt Cathy could do a lot of things — bitch, vent, rant, snark, snarl . . . dance — but she couldn't so much as toast a Pop-Tart without nearly setting the house ablaze. In fact, when she'd moved into her new home, there had been some surreptitious discussions about having her oven secretly disabled so she wouldn't accidentally burn down the whole neighborhood while trying to hard-boil an egg.

Once, Aunt Cathy burned a salad. It was Fryer family lore with long roots, and although Aunt Cathy swore on a stack of Bibles it never happened, there were a dozen Fryers who would swear on two stacks that it had.

But Bren thought about it. Thought about how she blurted out that bit about how far away Kelsey was to that woman at the stoplight the day she got the job at the Kitchen Classroom. Her mother had a point. She wasn't the most patient person in the world. And she only seemed to get worse as she got older. And if there was a time of year that her already-thin patience wore down to nothing, it was the holiday season. All those crowds and the noise and the shopping and the pressure. She wondered why on earth she felt blue about missing it. Shouldn't she be rejoicing that she didn't have to be part of that nonsense this year?

Bren schlepped over to the coffeepot and poured herself a cup, then slunk to the kitchen table, where the sugar and cream were. Her mother pushed them toward her without a word. Like the rest of her mother's kitchen, the table could be described as "retro diner." White Formica top, red vinyl chairs, full sugar bowl as a centerpiece. But the truth was, it was just plain retro. Bren's mother could make just about anything last forever.

"Well, of course we're kidding," her mother said, patting Bren's hand. "You will do great, and if you want us to be there, we will be there, Brenda."

"With gin," Aunt Cathy added.

"I don't know, Mom," Bren said. She stirred her coffee, laid the spoon on a napkin just the way her mother always did, but instead of taking a sip, leaned forward on her elbows, resting her forehead in the palms of her hands. "I swear I don't know what I'm doing half the time. Did you know I was getting ready to look up a recipe for figgy pudding? Figgy pudding, for Christ's sake. What, is it 1852? Who the hell eats figgy pudding anymore?"

"I would eat figgy pudding," Aunt Cathy said. "Is it made out of figs, or is it one of those things that sounds like a reasonable food and then when you eat it you find out it's made out of intestines and eyeballs and rotted stuff?"

"I don't know," Bren moaned into the cavern of her arms. "I never looked up the recipe because I got sidetracked thinking about goose."

"We used to eat goose on Uncle Wyatt's farm," Joan said. "Remember that, Catherine? It was supposed to be a treat, but it always tasted so dark and greasy to me. Our brothers got most of it."

Aunt Cathy leveled her gaze at Joan, silently and for so long, Bren peeked up over her arm at her.

"I've never had goose," Aunt Cathy said.

"Yes, you have. You don't remember all those weekends at Uncle Wyatt's house? The goose, the cauliflower with cheese sauce, the angel food cakes?"

Aunt Cathy shook her head adamantly. "Who is Uncle Wyatt?"

"Are you kidding me? He was Daddy's brother. Lived out in the country. How can you not remember him, Cathy?"

"I swear, you get more demented every day, Joan," Aunt Cathy said, and then they were off, talking over each other, arguing over the uncle who may or may not have ever existed. In Cathy's favor, Bren had never heard of an Uncle Wyatt, either. In Joan's favor, Cathy didn't remember most of her childhood, and seemed to have re-created one based mostly on old movies and the occasional Hallmark commercial. In Bren's best guess, Cathy lost her childhood memories right around the time Woodstock was ringing out with warnings not to take the brown acid. Coincidence? Probably not.

On and on they went, Bren following them as if following a particularly muddled and slightly schizophrenic tennis match while sipping her coffee. Finally, when she'd reached the bottom of the cup, and the two women had taken a long and winding road to the subject of unremembered childhood pets, she cleared her throat.

"You guys are coming to Thanksgiving, right?"

Joan blinked at her. "Well, why wouldn't we?"

"I don't know," Bren said, using her finger to pick up a few random sugar crystals. "Maybe because you're abandoning me on Christmas. Your only daughter. Your newly empty-nested only daughter."

"For the get-over-it files," Aunt Cathy said, and then elbowed Joan. "You hear that? Pretty good, huh? I heard some kid say it on Nickelodeon."

But Joan ignored her. "Brenda, don't take it so personally. We've wanted to take this trip forever, and neither of us is getting any younger. If we don't do it now, it might be too late."

"And mama needs to have cheap crab legs with one of them Vegas strippers," Aunt Cathy said. "You can't deprive an old lady of the essentials. Seafood." She held out one cupped hand, and then held out the other. "And buns."

"Gary is taking me to a cafeteria for Christmas Eve dinner," Bren said. "A cafeteria. So it feels pretty personal, wouldn't you agree?"

"Those places have good rolls," Aunt Cathy said.

"It's just this once," Joan said. "Next year we'll all be together. Look at it like a long-awaited break. Let someone else do everything for you for a change."

"Like a stripper!" Aunt Cathy said.

"You're not getting a stripper," Joan said.

"Bet me."

And they were off again.

No matter what Bren could or couldn't do in the classroom, it couldn't be any worse than enduring an entire holiday season of this.

"So I'll see you both on Thursday?" she asked, standing up and taking her cup to the sink.

"Where?" Aunt Cathy asked.

"What's Thursday?" Joan said at the same time.

Bren resisted the urge to scream. "My cooking class."

"You're still going on about that?" Aunt Cathy asked.

"Yes. Well, no. I never got the chance to go on about it in the first place, not with Uncle Wyatt and the strippers in the kitchen with us."

"There was never an Uncle Wyatt," Aunt

Cathy responded.

"Oh, Brenda, we're sorry. Of course we will be there. What time?"

"Class starts at seven, so you might want to get there a little before. But not a ton before. Don't get there, like, an hour before. I'll be setting up, and having you two there will make me nervous. Just come at around six fifty, okay?"

"Okay," her mother said.

"And I mean the real six fifty. Not the six fifty where you show up at four forty-five, okay?"

"Okay," her mother said again.

"And sit in the front. No, actually, the back. I don't want you distracting me with your talks about nonexistent uncles and weathermen and firebombing things. Wait. But if you're not up front, what if nobody takes the stations up front? That will be really awkward, me cooking up front and having to scream everything to the back. I don't want awkward. I can't deal with awkward. Ah, God, what kind of teacher can't deal with awkward? This is going to be a disaster. I'm quitting. I've got to quit. There's no other way. You know what? You should sit in the middle."

"What's wrong with her?" Aunt Cathy asked Bren's mom, thumbing toward Bren, who was half bent over the kitchen counter, trying hard not to hyperventilate.

"I don't know," Joan said, "but I think we should leave for the class around five, don't you?"

"Yes, definitely. You can't trust those traffic reports. God knows how long it will take us to actually get there."

"And Brenda won't mind if we get there a few minutes early," Joan added.

"We can help her get set up."

"Yes, yes. Maybe we should leave at four forty-five. What do you think, Brenda?"

Bren took several deep breaths, trying to collect herself. This was going to be a disaster, she had no doubt. But it was apparently going to be *her* disaster, because there was no way she would get her mother and Aunt Cathy to understand that they shouldn't come after all at this point.

"Sure," she said to her boots, which had come back into focus. "Four forty-five sounds perfect," she said. "I'll see you then."

CHAPTER SEVEN

The piecrust was sticky. Too sticky. So far she'd made crust that was heavier than lead plates, crust that was bland as drywall, and crust that crumbled into oblivion. And now it was too sticky.

Why the hell was crust such a pain in the ass?

"Was the butter too warm?" Rosa asked, fiddling with the stem of her wineglass. Bren resisted the urge to snap, *Do you honestly think I haven't thought of that yet, you twit?* But, even though Bren had seemed to be losing more and more of her etiquette the closer she careened toward menopause, she knew that in general circles, it would be considered impolite to call your friend names as she taste-tested your cooking disasters. Also bad etiquette to spit in her wine, as tempting as it might be every time she opened her mouth and a stupid question like *was the butter too warm?* vomited out.

To be fair, Rosa wasn't so much Bren's friend as her charge while Gary *crisis du jour*ed with Rosa's husband, Gilbert. Bren had met Rosa a few times before — always at awkward and uncomfortable office parties and employee-spouse gatherings, where any smiling face was a friendly face. But one-on-one, Rosa was a little too rhinestones-and-yoga-pants for Bren. Not that rhinestones and yoga pants were bad things, only that being friends with someone who looked good in rhinestones and yoga pants was. Rosa was a svelte and pretty mid-thirties with the style of a college coed and the personality of a best friend.

A loud twang vibrated the floor, followed by three loud thumps and the crash of cymbals. Bren jumped, as she always did. Rosa laughed, throwing her adorable head full of thick black curls over her shoulders like she was in a shampoo commercial. Bren gritted her teeth.

"They are getting better, no?" Rosa asked, sipping her wine.

"No," Bren said under her breath. She dumped the dough into the trash and ran water into the bowl to clean it and start over. She had to jostle dishes to make enough room in the sink to fit the bowl under the faucet. Effort number five. "I don't know what possessed Gary to think he could play the guitar," she said over her shoulder. "He flunked out of marching band. Teacher told him his ear was so dead she wouldn't be surprised if it fell off." It was one of the many stories Gary had told Bren about his childhood — injustices and triumphs, all the vibrant lives led before they met. He'd supposedly gone on to try out for the football team and become one of Summit Glen's star players. He owed his glory days to that marching band teacher.

The marching band teacher had been right, though.

For a week, Gary and Gil had been an official garage band — well, okay, basement band because the garage was too cold. Snow on the Roof, they called themselves — which they thought was hilarious because it was meant to be a hint about their virility, but Bren thought it made them sound like a Christmas cover band. Perfect for this time of year, if only they could play a single note.

So far all it had been was twanging and banging and a whole lot of hanging around the kitchen with their sweaty selves, wondering what there was to drink / snack on / watch on television, and, *Hey, is that pie?*

Cluttering her counters with guitar picks and drumsticks and beer cans.

"I'm just glad Gilly found something to keep him busy," Rosa said, stretching backward, her perky breasts straining against the front of her shirt. "He's been an animal in bed ever since he picked up those drumsticks." She laughed again and drained her wine.

Bren tried not to think about how Gary continually claimed that playing the guitar made him new shades of exhausted. He was asleep before his head hit the pillow.

The timer sounded and Bren pulled another pie out of the oven. Cranberry cherry pear walnut, which she planned to top with ice cream and a balsamic drizzle. If only she could get the crust right.

"Taste-test time," she announced, placing the pie right in front of Rosa.

"Oh, I couldn't have another one," Rosa said, rubbing her belly. "That last one did me in."

"This is my first lesson," Bren said. "If I don't get that crust right, I'm going to be done in. Now taste."

She sliced the pie, knowing good and well it was way too hot to stay together when she pulled it out, but too anxious at this point to wait on it. This was no longer pie;

it was a pie death march, and there would be no survivors. She slopped a steaming piece onto Rosa's plate, and Rosa picked up a fork, reluctantly digging in as Bren filled her wineglass again.

"Well?" Bren asked, wine bottle in hand.

Rosa blew, chewed, swallowed, closed her eyes. "The filling is heaven."

"The crust. What about the crust?" Bren asked.

To her frustration, Rosa took her time answering — scooping up another forkful and blowing on it, then sliding it into her mouth and chewing for what seemed like forever. Just as Bren was about to scream in agony, she swallowed and nodded. "It's good," she said.

"Yes!" Bren pumped her fist in the air. "Like it'll-do good or blows-you-away good?"

"It's pretty damn good," Rosa said, going for a third forkful. "It's Christmas in your mouth. Have some."

Bren picked up her fork and dug a bite out of Rosa's pie.

"What?" Rosa asked as Bren's face fell. "You don't like it?"

Bren nodded, near tears. "It's so good," she said. "It's perfect."

"Why do you look like it's a bad thing?"

Bren closed her eyes and wiped the sweat from her forehead. "I just can't remember what I did differently that time," she said.

Rosa laughed, but Bren wasn't feeling it. This was no laughing matter. Class was tomorrow night, and if she didn't get a recipe down, she was going to humiliate herself in front of her mother, her crazy aunt Cathy, Paula, and God knew who else. She slumped down onto a stool across from Rosa and drank a swig of wine directly from the bottle. She belched and swigged again.

"Oh, come on, it can't be that bad, can it?" Rosa said. "It's good pie. You're a great cook. What's the big deal?"

"What's the big deal?" Bren repeated. She'd asked herself that a million times. What was the big deal exactly? It wasn't like she was a perfectionist in other parts of her life. Why this? "You see, the big deal is this. My kids are gone, Rosa. My husband is downstairs thinking he can play guitar. I have nobody to cook for this Christmas, and I think I should care more than I actually probably do. I haven't had a job in over twenty years. Twenty years, Rosa! Can you imagine?"

"I haven't worked since I married Gilly. That was seven years ago."

Bren snorted. "Seven years? Come back

to me when it's been twenty. And I honestly have no idea if I am even capable of succeeding now. Do you know how that feels, to have no idea what kind of performance you can put in? Give me a diaper to change or a teacher to conference with and I'm golden. Ask me to do just about anything else and it's a crapshoot. I'm like a twenty-year-old just out of college, only I'm missing the confidence of a twenty-year-old because I've lived life and I know how it can knock you down and you never saw it coming."

"Well, that's depressing," Rosa said, her sunny disposition hiding behind a cloud bank for the first time.

"Yes, it is. Very depressing," Bren said. "But at the same time it's kind of exciting, because maybe I can do this. Maybe I can be a huge success and these . . ." She flung her arm around, indicating the house in general. "These people have been keeping me down all these years with their *wash this* and *give me money for that* and *does this smell rotten to you?*"

"Also depressing," Rosa said. She'd pushed the wineglass away from herself, along with the pie, and seemed to be edging off her stool.

Bren swigged more wine. "Exactly! And

maybe that's my real problem. Maybe I'm depressed and I just blame it on other stuff. Menopause, empty nest, no sex, weight gain, whatever. Those things are depressing, too, right?"

"I wonder if they're done playing," Rosa said, glancing toward the stairs that led to the garage.

"Not likely. They've only been at it for an hour. I'm sorry. I'm making you uncomfortable. Have you ever heard of a Chinese redheaded centipede?"

Rosa shook her head, clearly wary of where this new track of conversation was going to lead.

"It's a poisonous centipede that grows nearly a foot long. A foot!"

Rosa's eyes got big. "You haven't seen one around here, have you?"

Bren swigged, starting to feel that loose feeling in her arms that she often got from drinking, and shook her head. "But Chinese redheaded centipedes live in Thailand. You know what else is in Thailand? My daughter. She lives in Thailand. My future grand-children could live in Thailand. They could get bitten by this giant thing and die before I even get to meet them. Now that, my friend, is depressing. So why am I so wor-ried about a cooking class, right? I should be worrying about the funerals of my grand-kids."

"I'm going to go listen to the guys for a while," Rosa said. "Thank you so much for the pie."

She slid off the stool, landing on her tiny high-heeled feet, her back a perfect arch. Bren felt her stomach folds rest on the tops of her thighs. God, had she ever been anywhere near as perfect as Rosa? Probably not, but how depressing to think that if she had, it had all gone downhill in just a few short years.

"Oh, you don't need to go. I'm just vent-ing," Bren said lightly. "Really. I just can't, for the life of me, figure out why my daugh-ter would choose to live among giant centi-pedes and raise potential children there, but who am I to ask why, right? The pie is cooler now. Another piece?"

Rosa's hand went to her belly, even as she continued to edge out of the room. "I'm so stuffed," she said. "I'm sure it will be fine. Surely they have some sort of pest control for those things. I mean, you'd definitely see a foot-long bug coming at you." She gave an uneasy smile and sidestepped some more.

"Good point," Bren said. She took another swallow of wine and smacked the bottle on the counter, rattling a pair of salt and pepper shakers. She pointed at Rosa and winked. "You see? Needless worry. That's all. Come have some more wine. I can open another bottle."

She didn't know why she suddenly felt so desperate to keep Rosa from leaving the room. She'd only minutes ago been thinking of her as the child she had to babysit while Gary and Gilly destroyed the Beatles for two hours. But now she seemed like a friend on the brink of abandoning her. And the last thing Bren wanted was to be abandoned by someone else, surrounded by all this pie. Another reminder of how lost her life had become, at five hundred calories a slice.

"I think I might be driving," Rosa said. She fished in her front pocket and came out with a set of keys dangling from one finger. "I'm sure Gilly's been down there sucking up the beer." She laughed, but it was hollow and uncomfortable. "But thanks for the wine, too."

Fortunately for both Rosa and Bren, as this conversation had certainly reached a point of no return, Rosa had reached the stairs. She practically sprinted down them in her adorable periwinkle heels.

"Okay, well, it was good seeing you," Bren

called, trying to sound cheery, but wondering if she only sounded drunk. Good golly, was it possible to be drunk from half a bottle of wine? She mentally checked for the last time she drank. Had to have been months now. Maybe not since Kelsey's wedding. Hell, maybe not since last Christmas. "Whatever," she mumbled, waving off Rosa. She was a woman child and the two of them were not meant to be close, anyway.

Of course, that felt a lot more comfortable when it was her not wanting anything to do with Rosa rather than Rosa running for her life from scary half-drunk Bren and her centipede rants.

Her shoulder itched as if a centipede were crawling across it. She shrugged, hoping the movement would calm it, but it didn't.

Sighing, she got up, grabbed plates for Gary and Gilbert, and put slices of pie on them. Surely they would be coming up soon to see what had chased Rosa down. The centipede feeling raced across her shoulder again. She shrugged. It got stronger. She shrugged again. It dug in, stung. She couldn't help raking her fingers across it. But scratching did nothing to help.

"Dammit." She dumped the rest of the pie into the trash can, slammed the glass pie plate into the dishwasher, and trudged off to the bathroom. She locked the door, then stood with her back pressed against it for a few moments. She didn't want to take the two or so steps that would have her facing the mirror — that dreaded bit of wall space she'd been avoiding for months now. Facing the mirror meant she might have to look at her shoulder. Which meant she might have to do something about it.

But the itch only intensified as she stood there trying to think of reasons to turn around and leave the bathroom altogether. It was almost burning now, it was so flamingly itchy.

That's just your imagination, Nan had told her. *It's only itching because you know it's there.*

Could be the truth. Could be that her subconscious made the spot on her shoulder itch to remind her it was there and needed attending to. Or it could be — as she'd read on all those self-diagnosing medical websites — that skin cancer itches.

Letting out a breath, she stepped up to the mirror and pulled the neck of her tunic to one side.

There it was. Ugly. Patchy. Now red, from all of the not-scratching she was doing. Kind of raised.

And had it gotten bigger? She thought it

might have, since she last looked. To be fair, that was a while ago and she'd gained a lot of weight, so everything on her had gotten bigger. But cancer grew. It was the one thing that cancer did really well. Okay, one of two things, if you counted "killing people" as a skill of cancer's, which Bren supposed you could. Maybe its best skill.

She poked at it. Ran her fingers over it to see if the color changed or if she felt any pain. Made faces at it. And then quickly covered it again.

Soon. She would make that appointment soon.

Fortunately, the phone rang, jolting her away from the mirror and out of the bathroom, where she could breathe again. Cancer didn't exist in ringing phones. She got to the phone on the fourth ring, and picked it up breathlessly.

"Hello?"

"Mommy, hi!"

Bren checked the clock. It was barely five a.m. in Thailand. Her already-worried system jolted.

"Kelsey, honey, is everything okay? It's so early."

Kelsey laughed, that amazing tinkle that tore at Bren's heartstrings and reminded her of all the reasons why she needed to be

98

baking pies, even if the crust was never, ever right.

"I'm fine, Mommy. Gosh, you sound so paranoid."

"I just wasn't expecting to hear from you today."

"I know! It's a happy surprise, right?" Again with the giggles. Kelsey was such a giggler. Years, decades of giggles throughout the house. And now no giggles. Ever. Who giggled? Bren? No. Gary? Certainly not. Maybe Rosa, but she hardly counted. A giggle-less house, Bren lived in.

"Well, it's always a happy thing to hear from you, of course," Bren said. "Very happy. How has the beach been? Seen any foot-long centipedes?"

"It was beautiful and fun and lovely, of course. We love the beach. What did you say about centipedes?"

"Have you seen any? Been bitten by any?"

"No." A doubtful tone. "Why?"

"No reason," Bren said, feeling an immense (and ridiculous, she was quite aware) sense of relief.

"Mommy, Thailand is perfectly safe. I've told you. I wish you could come down and see for yourself."

"Maybe someday soon," Bren said. What she always said. With the same feeling that she always felt while saying it — the feeling of lying to her own daughter.

"Well, you just let me know. We have lots of room for you and Daddy, and lots of places to show you. How is Daddy, by the way?"

As if on cue, there was a bumbling string of thumps and pounds from downstairs, along with a series of nonsensical guitar notes.

"He's in a band now," Bren said plainly, hoping Kelsey could hear through her tone how ridiculous this was and would agree with her.

"A band? That's so cool!" Kelsey exclaimed instead. Bren sank into a chair, pulling the telephone notepad over. "What's he doing in it?"

"Making noise, mostly," Bren said.

Kelsey laughed. "Oh, Mommy."

"On a guitar," Bren continued. "Right now it's just two of them. A guitar and drums. I don't think either of them are attempting to sing. Thank God. You know your father's voice. He can't carry a tune in a bucket."

"True. But he could probably learn. The mind is everything. What you think, you become." She said this last bit with an air of recitation.

"What is that?" Bren asked. "A song lyric?"

"A Buddhist quote, actually," Kelsey said. "We've learned a lot about Buddhism since we moved here. It's quite beautiful, actually."

Bren wrote down *You are what you think,* wondering why it was that everything in Thailand was so damn *beautiful.* Couldn't just one time she hear how the smell was atrocious or the people rude or the bugs deadly?

"You're becoming a Buddhist now?" Bren asked instead.

"Not necessarily," Kelsey said, and Bren wrote *Learn Buddhism* on the pad. "Anyway, I actually can't stay on the phone very long, Mommy."

Of course, Bren thought. She never could anymore. She was always running off to the beach or getting ready for work or hoping to go see a sunset with Dean. *Beautiful sunsets here, Mommy. So very* beautiful. Yes, yes, they were. Because the sunsets in Missouri were hideous and boring and oh so Midwest.

"I called to tell you some exciting news about Christmas."

Bren perked up, wrote *Christmas* on the pad without even thinking about it, and followed it with several exclamation points. "You're coming home? Oh, Kelsey, that's great news! We still have plenty of time to put together a great Christmas. Tons of time. You won't get to see your grandmother, but you can come to my new class! Did you know I'm teaching a holiday cooking class? I start tomorrow. Maybe I'll save a cookie lesson for when you're here. I know how much you love Christmas cookies. I'll break out the secret ingredients." She wrote *sour cream* on the pad, even though she knew very well what her secret ingredients were and they were most definitely not foreign words she'd need to look up later.

"No, no, sorry, Mommy, I'm not coming home for Christmas. I thought I told you that."

"Oh." Bren tried not to feel her heart sink all the way to her slippers. Tried not to let the disappointment lace her voice too much. Tried not to get tearful. And tried not to feel the blasted itching on her shoulder again. "Yes, you told me. I forgot."

"But I have really good news about Kevin. He called me last night. He's in Tagbilaran."

"Tagbil what?" Bren poised the pencil over the pad, unsure where to even begin on that one.

"Tagbilaran. In the Philippines, Mommy."

"The Philippines? What's he doing there? Are there people in this Tagbeelaron place? Are there . . . things?" *Or just malaria and snakes and foot-long centipedes?* she didn't finish.

"Yes, of course there are people there. And things. What kinds of questions are those? Are you okay, Mommy?"

Bren wrote, *Are you okay?* then scratched a line through it, afraid she would answer honestly. The fact that she was writing it down at all was an answer in itself. "Of course I'm okay. I've just never heard of this place."

"Well, it's actually not that far. Only about fifteen hundred miles."

"Fifteen hundred miles is pretty far."

"Not when you're Kevin. He's traveled all the way to Tagbilaran, what's another fifteen hundred, right? Anyway, so what I was getting at? The really exciting news. Kevin is coming home for Christmas! Home to my house. Can you believe it?"

Bren nearly dropped her pencil. Or snapped it in half. Or snapped it in half and dropped both pieces. He was coming home for Christmas, only home was now on the other side of the earth? Home was where his own mother most decidedly was not?

When the hell did this become okay?

"Mommy? Did you hear me? Hello?"

Bren jumped, scrawled *1,500 miles* on the pad just to ground her back into reality. "Yes, yes, I heard. How . . . wonderful that the two of you will get to spend Christmas together."

"I know, right?" Kelsey practically squealed. Bren wondered if Dean was still trying to sleep and if her daughter's squeals had awakened him. Or if a *beautiful* sunrise had already done that for her? "I'll be honest, I was feeling really sad about not being around my family this holiday season. I was half considering just going for it and buying a plane ticket home. But now I don't have to. Home is coming to me! I'm just so excited. Do you think he looks the same?"

Bren's mind had blanked out on the words *half considering just going for it and buying a plane ticket home.* Damn Kevin and his rambling travels.

"He can't look that different. He's only been gone four months. Maybe some facial hair. Maybe a little skinnier. I don't know how he's been eating."

"Well, I will fatten him up. I'm already planning my menu. I'm going to make satay and fish cakes and coconut rice. Going to go all out."

Bren didn't bother to write those things down. To think she had been worrying about serving brisket for Christmas dinner. Who the hell ate a fish cake on purpose? *Fish* and *cake* were two words that shouldn't even be in the same sentence together, much less on a plate for a Christmas dinner.

"It's going to be so fun, Mommy. Can you imagine? We'll open presents and listen to Bing Crosby and it'll be just like being home. I can't wait."

"You have Bing Crosby to listen to?"

"Well, no, but that's not the point. I can get Bing Crosby to listen to. I'll order it today. The point is the family is going to be together for the holidays. It's so great, isn't it?" Bren said nothing. She was too busy feeling like someone had reached into her chest and ripped her heart right out. Was "the family" so easily represented by just two of them? Was she herself so easily replaced?

There was a time that Kelsey and Kevin couldn't even be in the same room together without fighting. Real knock-down, drag-out sibling hate fests, they were. Lasted for what seemed like forever, Kevin calling Kelsey fat and Kelsey hitting Kevin with a shoe. They pretty much completely avoided

each other in high school, not even bothering to say hello as they passed each other in
the hallways. Kevin was forbidden from
coming within ten feet of Kelsey's bedroom,
especially if she had girlfriends over.

Not that he cared. Kevin was so into
himself, he couldn't be bothered to notice
that Kelsey even had friends, much less
whether they were worth ogling in their
slumber party pajamas.

To think it had bugged Bren to no end to
see her children be so distant from each
other. How she'd nagged and bitched and
whined and punished. How she'd begged
them to forge a relationship. *Someday you'll
need each other,* she'd said on so many occasions. *Someday Daddy and I will be gone
and all you'll have is each other. Someday the
only other person in this whole world who will
know your whole life story will be each other.
Think about it.* Quite the attempt to be both
guilt-inducing and philosophical, Bren
thought, but it didn't work. They didn't care
about each other's life stories.

So why, now that the two were reaching
out to each other during the holidays — the
most important family time, if you asked
Bren — did she hate it?

She knew why. Because she was jealous,
plain and simple.

"Mommy? Are you still there?"

"Yes," Bren said, rattling out of her old memories. "I'm here."

"I said don't you think he'll like that?"

"Sure, sure," Bren said, having no idea what it was that she was committing Kevin to liking, but also not caring much. It was his penance for going *away* away. "It all sounds just" — she glanced at the notepad — "beautiful."

"I know, right?" Kelsey sounded way too squealy and eager for so early in the morning. Bren idly wondered how Dean possibly stood such cheer at the crack of dawn. She wondered how she'd done it for all those years. Well, she'd done it out of pure mother's love. Dean most likely did it because he found it charming and wonderful and was probably every bit as cheery himself first thing in the morning. "I can hardly wait for Christmas to get here now. It'll be so good to see him."

"Did he say anything else about what's going on in his life?" Bren asked.

"Only that he is totally in love with Pavlina. I think he might propose to her, Mommy. Wouldn't it be something if he did it while they were here?"

"He's bringing her?"

"Yes! They go everywhere together now.

107

She's left the university to follow his travels. What a beautiful commitment, don't you think? How could you say *I love you* any better?"

"By at least one of you having a job so you could pay for all those love bills?" Bren ventured, realizing too late how bitter and cynical she sounded.

"Mommy!" Kelsey sounded shocked. "Money is like water. Try to grab it and it flows away."

Bren sketched down a few of the words, losing most of them before her pencil could draw them out. "Is that another Buddhist quote?"

"Yes! How did you know?"

Because it sounds like you're reading from a Woodstock leaflet, Bren wanted to say, but didn't. "Good guess, I suppose."

"They will be fine, Mommy. Have faith. Kevin is smart enough to know when he's broke and needs to come home. But I honestly think they've been finding odd jobs here and there, selling things, whatever. I'll have much more info for you after their visit. And maybe pictures of Pavlina's engagement ring. I hope, I hope!"

Bren drew a rudimentary solitaire ring on the pad and tried to imagine how crushed she would feel to have missed her son's

Christmas Day proposal to a woman she'd never laid eyes on at her own daughter's house. She couldn't even wrap her head around all of the sadness, so she let it go.

"We can only hope," she said, the words feeling false coming out of her mouth, but they must have sounded genuine, because Kelsey continued to rattle on about her plans without so much as a pause.

Gary played a riff that sounded amazingly close to the beginning of "Revolution." Bren fought the urge to scream the opening Lennon shriek. Wouldn't that get Kelsey to stop talking about the beautiful this and the fish cake that and the brilliantly deep Buddhist quotes?

But eventually, Bren could hear shuffling in the background, and the sound of a man clearing his throat.

"I should go, Mommy," Kelsey said. "Should get my day started, even though I'm going to be so distracted now. I have so many plans to make."

"Well, please tell Kevin I said hello if you speak to him again," Bren said.

"Oh, I don't think I will. He said something about spending some time on the peninsula on his way here."

What peninsula? Bren penciled onto the notepad.

"But we will definitely call you when he gets here."

"Okay, sounds like a plan," Bren said, although she didn't add what kind of plan. A cruel plan. A shitty plan. A plan that would likely make her want to choke to death on her cafeteria potatoes and fall face-first right into her Sara Lee pumpkin pie.

With the perfect crust, every time.

"I love you, Mommy! Have a great day!" Kelsey chirped in her ear.

"I love you, too, honey. And I will."

Bren hung up the phone. On cue, she heard a few bangs and twangs and then a warbly voice starting up "Good Day Sunshine."

Rosa's voice.

And it wasn't so bad, actually.

That bitch.

CHAPTER EIGHT

Even after all of the practice runs, Bren could have kicked herself for choosing a pie for opening night.

But the filling was so good, she'd decided to stick with it, even if she ended up with cardboard crust beneath it. She unloaded her tub. Cranberries, pears, cherries, sugar, flour, butter, eggs, oranges, and one perfect unbaked pie that she'd finished only that morning, complete with a crust she was half proud of, half terrified of. She popped it into the oven, hoping that the tiny holly leaves she'd fashioned out of leftover scraps of dough would be beautiful enough for everyone to forgive if the flavor was off. Or, even better, to assume that they were the ones who had gotten it wrong.

That was, if anyone other than her mother and Aunt Cathy even bothered to show up.

The Kitchen Classroom was really coming together. Paula had added faux-brick walls to which she'd attached wine racks and little bundles of garlic and old black-and-white photographs of women in their kitchens. The cooking stations shone, polished stainless steel ovens and black granite countertops reflecting the overhead spotlights. The pantry racks had been well stocked, the vegetables looking every bit as shiny as the appliances. Paula was back in her office and came bustling out when she heard Bren arrive.

"Hello, hello, hello, are you ready?" Paula asked, barreling in full of energy and excitement. "My God, I smell something wonderful already!" She switched on the oven light and peered through the oven window at the pie inside. "Oh, this is good. This is going to be very, very good." She flicked off the light. "I should put out balloons or something. Do you think? Balloons? Streamers? For the front of the store? Maybe I should have bought a Grand Opening sign. You know, to celebrate and get interest. Maybe a lot of people don't really know we exist yet? Though that doughnut shop brings in a lot of business. We've had a lot of walk-bys this week. All eating doughnuts. Delicious doughnuts, I might add. Is it too late to get a Grand Opening sign? What are your thoughts? I love the look of that pie. Gorgeous. Good enough to eat. Ha-ha, get it? To eat? What do you think the turnout will be? Good? I've gotten good responses. Thoughts?"

Bren's head swam a little. She really ought to introduce Paula to Kelsey, and see if they could literally suck all of the oxygen out of a room in one conversation.

"I hope so," Bren answered, tying an apron — red and green for Christmas, of course — around her waist. "I'm nervous."

"Oh." Paula waved her off. "Don't be. This is going to be so successful. I was thinking we could even extend into the new year if you wanted. I'm not worried. But I sure wish I'd bought balloons."

"The new year?" Bren's hand was frozen around her apron tie.

"We can talk about it later; you're right. You just concentrate on wowing the masses." Paula headed back toward her office. "Let me know if you need anything."

"Masses?"

"Oh yes, you've got six students signed up. I didn't tell you? It's practically a full house. Congratulations!"

"Thank you," Bren said through numb lips. Six students? Was it possible that her mother and aunt Cathy had managed to sign up three times? With the two of them, anything was possible.

The door opened, and in walked the two devils, despite her repeated warnings not to arrive too early. "There she is! Are we late?" Joan asked. "What smells so good?"

Bren nearly laughed out loud, the stress taking an unexpected giddy course through her body. "Nope, right on time, Mom. Only forty minutes early."

"The traffic was a disaster," Aunt Cathy said. "Good thing we left when we did. We liked to never get here. So many honkers, too. Why do you suppose everyone was so glued to their horns today, Joan?"

"Well, I have no idea," Joan said, though Bren suspected she could guess. Joan had been a towering five foot one during her young glory days. Now she barely cleared five feet on a good day. And of course she still drove Bren's father's old Lincoln — a hulking giant of a beast with doors so heavy nobody could open one without an *oof,* and a steering wheel that Joan's head didn't technically clear. She was a menace on the road, driving as if there were no other cars around her. Probably because she couldn't see them.

One of these days, Bren would need to have a talk with her mom about hanging up the old car keys. But today wasn't that day.

Today was the day she talked to her mom only about cranberries and cherries and how to get a nice, smooth texture to a pie filling. Which her mother, like all women born in the 1940s, probably already knew when she came out of the womb.

"Can we be helpful, Brenda?" Joan asked, dropping the commute conversation. She was old, but she hadn't lost her wisdom on when to change the subject. Not just yet.

"You can help me distribute these ingredients," Bren said. "I think I should have about six students."

Joan brightened. "Six! My, look at you! Chef Brenda. We'll be seeing you on one of those cooking reality shows before you know it. You'll be rubbing shoulders with that Emeril fellow."

God love moms. "Well, I'm not exactly ready to put on a chef jacket yet, but if we could just put two pears and a bowl of each of the berries at every station, that would be great."

"Did you hear that, Cathy? Six students," Joan said, turning away with a disappointing single pear in her hand. This was going to take forever. Which was probably good, given how early they were.

The hour lead time that Bren had given herself seemed to eat itself up like magic.

She'd only barely gotten all the ingredients passed out and was still trying to figure out the video system that would show an aerial view of what she was doing on a screen behind her when the first two students arrived, their words rising over one another in half Spanish, half English.

"No, you did not park *entre las líneas.* I saw exactly where you parked the *coche.*"

"Gah, you always act like you know it all. *Tan molesto!*"

"*Sí,* that's because I do, especially when it comes to driving. You're terrible."

"Well, if only you knew as much about cooking as you do about driving, maybe *no estaríamos aquí.*"

"Welcome!" Bren said, proffering a basket of warm honey-glazed apple oat muffins, her attempt to create an inviting atmosphere that would make her students feel at home and as if they could trust her. "Muffin?" she asked hopefully.

"No, *gracias,*" one of them said. "We are not hungry."

"Never mind Lulu," the other said. She reached for a muffin, but the other one smacked her hand away. "My sister thinks she always speaks for both of us."

"Teresa," she scolded. "We are here to learn, not to eat."

"Oh," Bren said, trying a breezy laugh. "I'm sure we'll do a fair amount of both."

Lulu smiled. "Teresa needs to do the first before she worries about doing the second. Our business relies on it. *Gracias,* though, for the offer." She motioned with her head for her sister to follow her. Biting her lip, Teresa reluctantly let her hand fall away from the basket and followed Lulu to the back of the room.

The ladies found spaces at two stations near the back, right behind Aunt Cathy, who was listening raptly to the argument, nodding her head as if she had been speaking and understanding Spanish all her life.

Aunt Cathy barely spoke English well, much less any other language. Especially in an argument.

Bren slunk back to her station at the front of the room, trying to look relaxed and inconspicuous, but unable to ignore the fact that soon everyone's eyes would literally be on her. She caught a whiff of fresh doughnut and wished she were next door, pulling one out of the grease right at this very moment, biting into Tod's new prune-berry concoction that he'd been talking about lately.

Oh, but the last thing she needed was another doughnut. She peered down at herself — still trying to be as unassuming as a wallpaper border — and noted that her Mrs. Claus–style apron really looked pretty filled out. In fact, she could be described as *jolly* in it. And everyone knew *jolly* was just another way of saying *fat.*

God, she was a fat cooking teacher. Cliché much?

"I think your sister is right," she heard her aunt Cathy say to one of the ladies at the station behind her, before rattling off a bunch of nonsense that could, at best, be called Spanglish. Bren tried to ignore it, even when she was ninety-nine percent certain she heard the words "hakuna matata" come out of her aunt's mouth.

"Am I late?" a booming voice called. Bren turned to see a large woman in a knee-length flower-print dress beaming in the doorway, a giant purse slung over her shoulder. Everything about her, from the voice to the oversized handbag to the dazzling yellows and reds and fuchsias and emeralds in her dress to the white of her teeth, was bold.

A prim-looking young woman slunk in behind her, squirted past without a word, and slithered to the back of the room, silently taking up residence on a stool and whipping out a notebook. Everything about her was brown — brown hair, brown clothes, brown shoes, brown notebook. She didn't much look like the type to eat muffins — although Bren's muffins did have the advantage of severe brown-ness.

"No, no, you're right on time," Bren said, choosing to concentrate on the woman in the doorway, rushing toward her. "Muffin?"

The woman patted her ample behind and chuckled. "No, thanks. I can probably do with a few less muffins in my life, if you know what I mean," she said.

"I definitely know what you mean," Bren said, feeling herself blush. She wondered if she should pat her own behind to show solidarity, or at least to show that she wasn't talking about this particular woman's butt. She could hear Kelsey's gasp in her mind. *Mother! How rude!* How that child loved to chastise her. It was endearing when she was two, annoying when she was twelve, and now just made Bren doubt herself. As if she needed more reason and opportunity for that.

Rather than take offense, the woman seemed to take this as an invitation for a longer chat. She plopped her bag at the nearest station and placed her hands on her hips. "I told myself, Tammy Lynn, you need a cooking class like you need a hole in the head. I cook too much already, but I can't help myself." She cupped her hand around her mouth conspiratorially and leaned forward. "I suppose it's better than some addictions out there, right?"

"Right," Bren said, glancing uncomfortably at the clock. It had turned seven. Her palms bloomed sweat. She felt so out of control — how could she ever start class while she felt so out of control?

"I have a cousin who snorts stuff. You know? Not cocaine, either. Like . . . stuff."

"Stuff," Bren repeated uncertainly. 7:01.

"His kids' candy and sugar, crushed chalk, whatever he can find. He ain't right. You know, up here." She tapped her temple, and Bren noticed she even wore bold orange fingernail polish.

"No, doesn't seem so," Bren said, wondering how she'd gotten into this conversation at all.

"I keep telling him, Charlie, you're going to rot your brain right out of your head with all that sniffing. But my auntie says he never could keep from shoving things up his nose. She had a pair of tweezers that were just for digging stuff out of there when he was little."

Bren noticed the prim woman with the notebook sit up straighter, a look of disgust crossing her face. She gave her as apologetic a look as she could muster without being overtly rude.

"The man probably has no nasal passages left. I wouldn't be surprised if it was just one big cavern up in there." Tammy Lynn waved her hand around in front of her face. "Just boogers and blood and gummy worms everywhere."

This last sentence came out particularly loud — loud enough to make everyone stop talking. All eyes turned to Tammy Lynn and Bren. Bren felt her forehead flood over. She wanted to tell them that she was not a part of this conversation at all, that it had waylaid her, that she was dull and slow from the doughnut addiction, and that they should all have mercy on her because her own two flesh-and-blood children had betrayed her this holiday season.

In the long moments of silent staring that followed, Bren imagined herself flinging the muffin basket over her shoulder and bolting for the door, possibly moving to a new town. And then she imagined just taking up residence in another one of the class stations, looking expectantly toward the front of the room, and then after a few minutes wondering aloud who the teacher was supposed to be, and if they all shouldn't just give up and go home since she hadn't shown.

But then her aunt Cathy started cackling — long, slow, guttural guffaws that sounded a bit like someone had tossed a handful of rusty nails into an old coffee can — and Bren knew she had to do something to save this train wreck, or she would never get out alive. Once a laugh like that came out of Aunt Cathy, it was hard telling what kind of humiliation would follow.

"I should . . . Good evening, everybody," she said, trying to be Bright and Cheery Bren, which was, admittedly, not a Bren she'd been in a long while now. She thought about Gary, who was probably wrecking "One After 909" right at that moment. It helped. She had something to smile about as long as she wasn't there to witness that.

She hustled to the front of the room, not even registering whether anyone had responded to her. Her hands were shaking as she set the muffin basket on the floor, so she clasped them together on the cutting board in front of her to still them. She remembered that her cutting board was broadcast onto the big screen behind her, and clasped them together tightly to make them stop. And then worried that her white knuckles would show instead. Mistake,

mistake, this was such a mistake.

But she was in it now.

"I'm Bren," she said, hoping her voice wasn't shaking as much as her hands. "Epperson," she said, then cleared her throat. "Uh, Bren Epperson. This is a holiday dinner course." She closed her eyes. This was ridiculous. She had to get over it. "We're, uh . . . we're going to be trying some new recipes, and uh . . . learning some basic techniques. Like, uh . . . piecrust."

An image of Kelsey and Kevin flooded her eyelids. The two of them, sitting down to dinner together — some funky, trendy attempt at dinner, something *beautiful,* no doubt. They placed their napkins in their laps, tucked into their plates of fish and banana leaves, and mocked the droll and backwoods holiday the bumpkin family must be having back in Missouri.

When she opened her eyes, the edges around things were sharper. The sky was crisper, the passersby redder in the face. The scent of the completed pie more intoxicating. Christmas was in the air, and these people, these wide-eyed women staring up at Bren with anticipation, they appreciated it. They cared. She pulled open the oven door, the aroma of butter and berries and cooked flour billowing into her face like a warm kiss.

"Today," Bren said, picking up her pie and holding it up for everyone to see. This was her big moment. Her opening line. Her chance to do this holiday up right. "We make dessert!"

"Oh no, you don't," she heard, the front door banging open one last time, letting in air that was suddenly a lot less magical holiday and a lot more bleak winter day.

Bren turned to find a woman with white hair curled so close to her head that her scalp gleamed under the Kitchen Classroom's fluorescent lights. She had a dog so old he looked nearly mummified tucked under one arm and a cane gripped in the hand of the other.

Bren blinked, taken aback. Trying to make sense of what she was seeing. Was this a student? With a dog? Was that allowed? She wondered if she should go to the back, try to find Paula. Surely there were health department regulations about such thing. "Excuse me?" she said in her sweetest voice. "Can I help you?"

The old woman, whose left eye got squintier and squintier the longer she stood in the doorway — was the dog's left eye squinting to match, or was it Bren's imagination? — took the time to gaze at each woman in the room, in turn. It seemed to take forever.

"I said there will be no dessert," the old woman finally said. "Not tonight. Not ever."

CHAPTER NINE

From the smell of things, she had thought her apartment was on fire. And that the blaze was set by one of those potpourri candles that women were always falling all over themselves about. One of the stores farther down the square, something with a stuffy name that involved a whole lot of cursive writing that Virginia couldn't make out, sold those candles. Virginia and Chuy avoided the sidewalk in front of that shop. The stench stuck in her clothes, and it took at least two washes to get that awful per-fumey smell out.

And at this time of year, the place took the happy stench up a notch.

Cranberries, pears, and . . . was that piecrust she smelled?

Virginia scooped up Chuy and rushed down the stairs, only to find that the town was not ablaze, but it was the sidewalk in front of her very own front door. Ablaze, not with an out-of-control potpourri fire, but with light, spilling through the front window of that ridiculous Kitchen Classroom. How she'd hoped something would happen to close it down before it got up and running.

Worse, the smell was coming from within.

And even worse than that, there were cars lined up in front of it, their cooling engines giving off ticks and hisses and hideous engine vapors that intertwined with the rancid sweetness (though if she had to choose one over the other, she would definitely go for the engine oil).

She didn't even need time to think, although she could still hear her dear old Ernie in her head: *Think it through, Ginny,* he'd always tell her. *You can't just go charging in like a bull in a china shop.*

"The hell I can't, right, Chuy?" she muttered, and then stumped right through the front door into the haze of berry-scented hell itself. The fiery undershorts of Satan couldn't have reeked more.

"Today, we make dessert!" a chubby woman on a riser was saying, holding up a pie as if it were a baby being presented to the gods.

"Oh no, you don't," Virginia said, not caring one whit that the heads of all the dumb broads lined up in the room had whipped around to gawk at her. *Let them gawk,* she thought. She even narrowed one eye to give them something to gawk at.

"Excuse me? Can I help you?" the flustered woman asked, setting her stinky pie down.

"I said there will be no dessert . . . ," Virginia said, and then, not liking the tentative trail in her voice — they could stop gawking at some point, for heaven's sake! — gathered herself up sturdier and added, "Not tonight. Not ever." There. That sounded final.

It was then that the herd began looking at one another with confusion, whispering, which brought Virginia's confidence back up a notch or two. The one on the riser in front actually started sputtering a little.

"I'm sorry," she said, cocking her head to one side and pasting on a smile that was way too tentative for Virginia Mash not to believe she could crush it in an instant. "This is a holiday cooking class. Are you a student?"

"If she is, she'd better not get dog hair in my pie," a kooky-looking elderly lady near the back said.

"Shh, now, Cathy," another lady next to her warned.

Cathy, affronted, placed her palms on her chest. "I've got allergies."

"You do not."

"Yes, I do. I'm allergic to dogs."

"Catherine Marie, I have known you all my life and you have never had one single sniffle around dogs," the lady said, pulling herself up off her stool and leaning in toward Cathy, the elastic waist of her perfectly pressed pale blue slacks peeking out from under her cardigan. "You know I hate it when you start fibbing. You used to have a dog of your own. Don't think I've forgotten about Petey. He had a full coat, too."

"Mom," the one up front said through gritted teeth, "not now."

Virginia Mash watched the scene with astonishment. Here she was, shutting them down, and they were only arguing with one another about dog hair? Chuy growled low in his throat, as if telling her to put a stop to this.

"I'm sorry," the woman said, seeming to gather herself as she came down off the riser and offered her hand to Virginia. "This is our first night, and we just got started, so you're definitely not too late." She made a concerned face. "But I'm not sure about your puppy here. It might be against some kind of code. I can get the owner."

Chuy growled again, and she yanked her hand away, stuffing it instead into the front pocket of her apron.

"I don't need to see the owner," Virginia snapped, moving Chuy away from the offending hand, even though the fat cook had already hidden it. "I need to be able to breathe in my apartment. Between those infernal doughnuts and your pie, it stinks to high heaven. And it's hot. These ovens are making it hot."

The fat cook shook her head, looking confused. "But we haven't even turned the ovens on," she said. "Just this one."

"I feel my throat closing up," the woman named Cathy piped up, scratching at the front of her neck. "I'm going into anaphylactic shock."

"You are not," the other woman said. "Maybe you're just talking too much."

"Oh, that's rich, Joan. That's very, very rich. Go ahead and make light of it. And then when the paramedics have to punch a hypodermic into my heart, we will see how much you're laughing."

Dios mío, a dark-haired woman muttered behind the two old ladies.

The fat cook whipped around. "Aunt Cathy! Not a good time," she whispered.

"And all the cars! How can anyone concentrate with all that traffic going up and down these streets all the time?" Virginia Mash pounded her cane on the floor, making several of the women jump.

"It was okay to park there, wasn't it?" a woman in a flowery dress asked, and general murmurs followed her question.

"Yes, of course it was," the leader said.

"Good, because I would have frozen if I'd had to walk," one of the dark-haired women said. "Since this one can't park to save her life." She jerked her thumb toward the woman next to her.

"No, no, the flyer said 'convenient parking,'" the other dark-haired woman said.

Unbelievable! Unacceptable! They were totally missing the point! "It's not that you *can't* park there," Virginia stormed. "It's that it's miserable for those of us who live here. It's loud, and it stinks."

"It's hard to get used to a new apartment," the fat cook said, reaching out toward her again. What was wrong with this woman that she couldn't keep herself from pawing at people? As if reading her mind, as he so often did, Chuy barked, a high-pitched string of his most terrifying yaps. The fat cook jumped away. Virginia used the moment to her best advantage. She thumped the floor with her cane again.

"Now, listen here," she commanded, and everyone stopped and stared with great wide eyes, even the one with the dog allergy, long red fingernail streaks running down the front of her throat. "I have lived upstairs in that apartment for eleven years. And I'll be damned if I'm going to see it turn into a commercial venture. Eleven long years, all alone. By myself."

She felt her throat close up at the words. *All alone. By myself. Eleven years.* Had it really already been that long? She glanced at Chuy for proof. His eyebrows — yes, he had eyebrows, dense, bushy tufts of fur that gave him the look of an old man — had grayed. His whiskers were no longer straight. He was missing teeth and his bark was hoarse and he walked with the slightest limp. Most days Virginia knew exactly how Chuy felt. She imagined them growing old together and dying together, yet she knew that Chuy would die before her. It wasn't the way it was supposed to be. Losing Chuy would be like losing so much more than just a pet, and the very thought of it filled her with such despair she refused to think about it.

"Maybe I should just see if Paula is still in her office," the fat cook was saying.

"Don't bother," Virginia said. "I've already talked to her. Dumb as a box of rocks. Next she will be hearing from my lawyer."

Virginia didn't have a lawyer. But that didn't stop her from making that very threat more times than she could count in a single week. What was wrong with the world these days, that you had to threaten someone with a lawsuit every time you turned around? Why was it the only way to make people listen? Had the whole world gotten so obsessed with money?

"Oh," the fat cook said. She licked her lips and took a small step backward, her hands fluttering to the front of her apron. "I'm very sorry we've disturbed you."

"Yes," Virginia said. "Disturbed. You did. And if you don't keep the noise down, I'll be calling the police."

Chuy barked again. A petite girl in the back of the room wrote something down in her notebook.

"And I recognize you," Virginia said, lifting her cane to point at the girl. "You're that Rebecca Aaronson person, the one from the newspaper."

The girl sat up straighter, her reporter's face so icy Virginia could practically feel it coming off of her.

"You're a reporter?" the fat cook asked.

"I . . . I . . . Nobody told me about . . ."
She seemed incredibly flustered by the
news, her hands now leaving the front of
her apron and running themselves through
her hair instead.

"Aaronson?" Aunt Cathy said. "You don't
even celebrate Christmas."

"Catherine Marie!" Joan scolded.

"What? Aaronson? Isn't that Jewish?"

"That's just not something you say, Aunt
Cathy," the fat cook said. "Reporter? You're
sure?"

"We actually celebrate both in my family,"
Rebecca Aaronson said coolly from her
stool. "And, yes, I'm a reporter. For the
Tribune. But I'm here to learn to cook.
See?" She turned her notebook around, and
everyone leaned in to study it.

Everyone except Virginia, of course. She
was done talking. Done fighting. Done just
trying to get some peace and quiet. Done
begging for privacy. She was so very tired.
It felt like she'd been trying forever.

Well, you have, Ginny, she heard Ernest
say. *You've been fighting for eleven years.
Might as well be forever. Maybe it's time to
wave the white flag. Stop fighting. Just get
along.* Ernest never knew what he was talking about.

The fat cook had turned to her. "I'm

sorry," she said. "I don't really know them yet. Well, those two are my aunt and my mom. But the others . . . You don't think she's going to write an article about the class, do you?"

Virginia knew what the right thing was to say and do. She knew she was supposed to tilt her head to one side, offer a soft smile, and maybe even rub the fat cook's arm as she told her not to worry about a thing, that her class would be wonderful, these ladies would turn out to be great friends, and any article written would say nothing but positive things.

Instead, she gathered herself into a hard little bundle — her favorite posture — and frowned.

"Keep the noise down or I will call the police!" she said, then, seeing the horror wash over the fat cook's face, felt satisfied. She nodded once, then turned and plunged out into the cold, the wind whipping her bare arms into goose bumps instantly.

Chuy barked three times as she placed him on the sidewalk, then coughed, hiked his leg, and peed on the door.

CHAPTER TEN

Now that Gary had enlisted a bass player, "Let It Be" was somewhat recognizable.

Although Bren still had a hard time thinking of John as a bass player. She knew what he really was — an accountant with a beer belly and a great secret recipe for grilled burgers that he refused to share with anybody, not even his best friend of twenty-some-odd years.

But apparently once one middle-aged man dug out the electronic toys, his friends couldn't help dusting theirs off, too. Because, shockingly, John had a bass guitar, brittle and scratched, from college, that he was just dying to practice his — also brittle and scratched — skills on.

Yet he had somehow managed to improve the sound coming from downstairs, which Bren followed, her heart too heavy from the weird thing that happened at her first class to even begin to concentrate on the appetizers she was practicing for the next class.

After that old woman had left, Bren had a hell of a time getting back on track. Even though the ladies had seemed open to it, once they'd ironed out that Aunt Cathy was a lot of offensive things but anti-Semite was not one of them, and that they could, indeed, park in front of the store, and that dog hair hadn't really drifted into anyone's berries, which didn't matter because — and her mother had mountains of evidence on this that seemed to span back to nearly the turn of the damn century — nobody was actually allergic to dog hair anyway.

"What was that all about?" Tammy Lynn had asked when Bren passed her station on the way back to the riser.

"I honestly have no idea." Bren had noticed she was shaking. Her legs felt weak, like she really just needed to go home.

"Well, it was incredibly rude, whatever it was," Tammy Lynn said. "But don't you worry. We'll get right back on track. Forget about her."

"Right. Yes. Pie."

But Bren couldn't help doubting when she got to the risers. Teresa and Lulu were back to squabbling, Tammy Lynn was looking at her expectantly through long fake lashes, and what on earth was that Aaronson

137

woman writing in that notebook?

Her brain had filtered through every moment in her life that she'd ever felt unloved and unwanted. Ridiculous. Why couldn't her brain work that quickly when she was trying to remember how to get downtown or recall the name of her prescription? She had been back in those moments with lightning speed, knock-kneed and sweating as she realized she was the only one in fourth grade still wearing overalls. Nauseated while standing in front of her American Literature class, about to present a report that was so unlike everyone else's it might as well have been written in a foreign language. Sobbing as Gary, newlywed and fiery, sped off in an angry huff, with promises to never return. Flushing as Kelsey and Kevin giggled over something out-of-touch and stupid she'd said . . . and then worse, when they stopped laughing at her indiscretions because she was just that old now, so old that laughing at her would be mean.

She'd considered backing out — just leaving Paula in the lurch. That wasn't usually her style, but so much of her life had been not her style these days, it was impossible to tell what her style was anymore.

"Well, who cares what that old bag of bones thinks?" Aunt Cathy had called from the back of the room.

"Catherine!" Joan chided.

"What? I didn't cuss. And I want pie. Brenny? Are we here to learn or aren't we?"

In a way, this was one of the reasons Bren would be nothing but glad to have Aunt Cathy in the class, warts, bad manners, and all, because it was that last sentence that had sparked her into movement. Her hands went on autopilot; her mouth made words that her own ears didn't hear. And somehow, when the class ended and the ladies filed out, each was holding a glistening pie. The kitchen smelled like heaven — Christmassy heaven — and Bren had even leaned against the hood of her car for a few moments and enjoyed the glow of the lights from within, the warmth of the pine garland that lined the front window, the sweet spice in the air, the buttery scent of warm pastry. She watched as Paula moved slowly around the empty kitchen, wiping down counters and double-checking stove dials, inspecting the timer on the dishwasher. Her flannel wrapped her up like a blanket, and Bren had cinched her scarf higher up on her neck as a chill swept down the back of her shirt.

This was a magical time of year. *Beautiful,* to quote a certain daughter of hers. She would like to say she hadn't given another thought to the older woman who clearly didn't appreciate Christmassy heaven, but that would have been a lie. She'd driven away, peering up toward the dimly lit apartment windows above the Kitchen Classroom, and wondered what the heck she was going to do if the woman showed up again.

But that was a problem for tomorrow. In the meantime, she had a certain musician to seduce. Or at least to try to entice into recalling that she still lived there with him.

"Let It Be" got a lot more difficult to decipher the closer she got to the basement. Apparently, John's sweet musical stylings were not so much styling as they were plodding, and he seemed to be at least two beats behind everyone else. But from the expression on Gary's face, he knew no difference. He looked so proud, so happy. Bren almost felt guilty about the song breaking up completely when she slipped into the room.

"Hey, there, Bren," Gil said, attempting to twirl a drumstick around his fingers. It flung sideways and clattered to the floor. Gil, God love him, didn't even have the sense to look embarrassed by the mistake. He simply palmed a new drumstick and pounded out what Bren suspected was supposed to be a riff, but succeeded only in sounding like someone falling down a staircase.

"Bren," John said, dipping his head down shyly. John had always been bashful around her. She could never figure out why — they'd raised their kids together, played poker together, eaten watermelon on July fourth together, gotten drunk during Gary's ridiculous moonshine phase together. He was brother close in Bren's book. No shyness necessary.

"Don't stop on my account," Bren said, her voice dripping with lightness and enthusiasm. "I was enjoying it!"

All three men grinned like they'd just won a prize. "You were?" Gary asked.

Bren nodded. "Just like the fab four themselves. You need a singer!"

On the inside, she cringed at the idea of a singer joining the band, but kept her smile plastered on, chalking it up to one of those white lies that are told in all marriages, just like the time Gary swore she was a knockout during her god-awful Hawaiian dress phase.

Gary's face lit up. "We were just talking about that, actually. John's got a friend who sings. And we were thinking of putting together some Christmas rock songs and trying to get some gigs."

Bren's stomach shrank. "Gigs?"

"Sure, you know, office parties, bars, that kind of thing." He twanged a couple of guitar strings, and Gil thumped the bass drum in agreement.

"Are you sure you're ready for that kind of thing?" Bren asked. "I mean, you sound great, but don't bands usually have to practice for a long time before . . . ?" She trailed off, not liking how this was sounding. Doubtful, unsupportive, embarrassed. She was all of those things, but she didn't want them to know that. She'd been operating under the premise that if she supported Gary's various hobbies and interests, eventually he would land on one that was less obnoxious. And he would remember her on his deathbed as a golden angel for having always been by his side. Although she supposed it was slightly morbid to do things just so someone would say nice things about you just before they blinked out of existence. But still. Motivation was motivation.

Instead of answering her question, Gary furiously scrubbed at his guitar strings, the other fellows joining in with their instruments, making Bren's eardrums vibrate, her chest buzz. After a few moments, she recognized what might have been a version of "Rockin' Around the Christmas Tree," if perhaps played by musicians not actually in the same room with one another. Or state. Or country.

But since she recognized it, she smiled and nodded and even bounced her knees a little in what might have been a dance. She was enjoying this, her face said. This was rousing entertainment! This was fun! A garage — er, basement — band was the best idea ever! She even poked her two pointer fingers in the air, getting some hip action in as she bopped the air with them.

The band didn't so much finish the song as peter out into a trickle of clangs and screeches and bangs, but the guys looked around at one another triumphantly.

"Take five!" Gary crowed, and they all disentangled themselves from their instruments. "Whatcha got to eat, Brenny?"

Bren jumped, flustered. "Well, I was working on some appetizers," she said. "But those are for my class."

"Perfect!"

The men rushed up the stairs, Bren hurrying after them, barking instructions. "Now, the crab cups are still warm, and the tomatoes haven't been stuffed just yet. There's a pistachio cream in the refrigerator — let me just finish those up before you — now, Gary, don't get into it just yet."

But she was too late. By the time she pushed her way into the kitchen, Gary already had three spoons and had uncovered the bowl of pistachio cream that she'd spent hours perfecting — crumbling bacon, adding just the right amount of scallions to give the cream a good green color to contrast with the red tomatoes — and John was tossing a handful of roasted pecans into his mouth. A handful. The nuts whose coating recipe she'd labored over all morning. The nuts that made the kitchen smell like the inside of love. The nuts that she'd carefully poured into her grandmother's wedding bowl. Tossed in like a pack of airplane peanuts. One missed his mouth and stuck to his lapel. Bren sighed.

"I see you've found everything," she said. "The cream is supposed to go into the tomatoes."

"I can do ya one better, Brenny," Gil said, and tipped the plate of carefully cored tomatoes — the ones she'd made hamburger out of her fingers to cut just right — into the bowl of pistachio. "Voilà! Cooking made easy."

"Rosa's got herself a handyman in the kitchen, eh?" Gary joked, elbowing Gil. The two of them dipped their spoons into the bowl and came back out with tomatoes and cream piled high.

"Real good stuff here," Gil said. He reached over to one of the three cooling racks that seemed to have taken up permanent residence in Bren's small kitchen now, picked up a crab cup, tossed the whole thing in his mouth, and nodded approvingly while he chewed. "Real good," he repeated, sounding like he was talking through a mouthful of cotton.

"Well, I guess I'm glad it was at least edible," Bren said, hoping she'd remember the recipes so she could make another batch before her next class.

"More than," John said before quickly tipping his head back and stuffing his mouth full of nuts again.

"Oh, here, John," Bren said, resigned. She stepped forward, plucked the pecan from his shirt, and held it up to his mouth. He opened like a baby bird and she popped it inside, then patted his shoulder a few times as his face turned a shade of deep red that brought to mind Santa Claus.

The pathetic bunch. Who couldn't love them?

"Go ahead, take it downstairs," she said. "Enjoy, enjoy."

"You're the best, Brenny," Gil said, pocketing two more crab cups on his way toward the basement. "You should hang on to that one, Gare."

"Yeah, yeah, she's a real peach," Gary

said, and Bren couldn't help feeling a little stung at the lackluster way he said it, as if he was only going on autopilot, or as if he maybe didn't mean it at all. Hardly the demeanor of deathbed adoration.

"And don't you forget it," she said, turning on Charming Bren, even poking John in the gut playfully as he followed Gil. "Practically an angel. Now you get down there and learn that Beatles Christmas song. What was it called?"

"Oh, the one with Yoko whatserface in it," Gil said, his voice getting muffled by his and John's footsteps.

"That's the one," she said. She grabbed Gary's arm as he passed her. "Wait a minute."

He turned back, looking irritated, the way Kevin used to look when she'd make him come inside for a bath when all of his friends were still outside playing. "What is it?"

"Nothing, I was just . . . I was thinking. Maybe we should go out on a date or something."

Another impatient glance toward the basement door. The footsteps had faded, and now there was only the rumble of deep voices coming up from the basement. A soft clang of a cymbal getting nudged. The sound of the basement fridge opening, a beer hissing to life.

"A date? What for?"

Bren put her hands on her hips. "What do you mean, what for? For us. For . . . for closeness."

A quick bass warm-up thrummed from the basement. "But aren't we going out on Christmas? To Lucky's Café? That's a date."

"That's not a date. And it's not a café. It's a cafeteria. It's a surrender. And it's also a month away."

Gary gestured toward the basement door. "I've got the band now, and we have a lot of work to do. You said so yourself."

"Oh, do you ever," Bren said, but managed to keep it under her breath enough that he was too busy inching toward the door to notice. "Gare, come on. I miss you."

"How can you miss me? I'm right here every day. With the kids gone, we see more of each other than we ever did before." His eyes widened. "Oh. That's what this is, isn't it?" Bren breathed a sigh of relief. "You're just missing the kids. You should give them a call. Or Kelsey, anyway. You always feel better after you've talked to her. It's okay. I won't mind the long-distance charges." He kissed her on the forehead.

She couldn't believe her ears. Over their

decades together, she'd heard Gary sic the kids on her more times than she could count. *Where's your mother? Go find Mom. I don't know, you should talk to Mom about that. Ask your mother.* All these years she'd assumed he was getting *them* out of his hair.

But maybe he was getting *her* out of his hair instead. Occupying her with the children.

"This is not about the kids. This is about us."

"What about us?"

"We don't know each other anymore. We don't spend time together. We don't talk. Don't you miss talking? I miss talking."

A few drumbeats wafted up the stairs. "The guys are waiting. Can't we do this later?"

Bren pursed her lips. This was definitely not going the way she'd planned. In fact, it was going absolutely nowhere. She had managed only to feel worse now than she had before they'd ever started talking. She reached back and picked up the crystal bowl that she'd filled with the roasted pecans. It still had John's fist-shaped dent in the center. She thrust the bowl at Gary.

"Fine."

He gave that clueless look that she so loathed. "You mad?"

Of course I am, she snapped inside her mind. *I'm more than mad. I'm the furniture. The ignored. The phone call when one of the kids can squeeze me into their busy schedules. The chef good enough to cook your food and laundress good enough to wash your shorts but not the wife good enough to actually pay attention to. Yes, I'm mad. I'm beyond mad.*

I'm hurt.

"No, it's fine," she said instead, though she hoped — unreasonably, she knew — that he would see in her body language that she was not fine. That she was wounded. That she needed him.

He squinted, the nuts pressed into his chest. "You sure?"

"*The guys* are waiting for you," she said, evading the question in her best passive-aggressive maneuver, sneering the words *the guys* just in case he should miss the bricks-over-the-head clues she was leaving. *Come on, Gare, the guilt is right there in front of you. Do the right thing. Pick it up and grovel. Beg for forgiveness.*

"Okay," he said. "I'll bring up the bowls when we're done." And he was gone, actually trotting down the stairs like a damn teenager racing to a girlfriend.

"No, you won't," she mumbled. She'd

been living with him long enough to know that he would say he would do it and would maybe even intend to do it. But two days from now she would be looking for the crystal bowl for something else and would eventually track it down to wherever Gary'd had it last. Because she was also good enough to be his maid.

She made her way back to the kitchen island and sank onto a stool, placing her head in her hand. What had she thought was going to happen? That she would ask Gary for a date night, and that his face would light up with possibility? That he'd ask her to take his black suit to the cleaners so he could spoil her with that fancy place downtown — the one with the dim lighting and the amuse-bouche and the palate-cleansing sorbet before the main course and the snooty sommelier? That she'd plan her day tomorrow around shopping for a new dress, get her hair cut, and maybe even spring for a manicure? That she'd even decide a pedi wouldn't be too much extravagance for a big date night, a big rekindle, an intimate holiday reconnection heavy with the scent of pine needles and melted butter and cinnamon candles? That she'd even splurge on a negligee, and that Gary would be so thrilled with all of it, he'd forget about

150

his stupid band or dune buggy or archery lessons or whatever the hell else was occupying his mind for one night and would remember he'd once looked forward to the day it would be just the two of them? That he'd dance with her in candlelight, an old Kenny G CD unearthed and spinning in the bedroom stereo? That she would become his new hobby?

Yes, sadly, there was a part of her that had thought those things might happen. Or maybe she'd just longed for it, the same way she longed for Kelsey to change her mind about Thailand or Kevin to settle down and pick a college already or any of the other million things she longed for that didn't come to fruition.

"Hello, hello!" she heard from the front door. Heels clicked on the entryway tile.

"In here," Bren called, jumping up from her stool, as if sitting there would betray her dismal thoughts to the world.

Rosa peeked around the corner and gave a shy wave. "Hey there!"

It was weird. Of course things between them would be weird after the way practice had ended last time. Bren was fairly certain that Rosa thought she was a nutcase at best. Maybe a dangerous lunatic, or the terminally depressed, and who would blame her?

Here she was, walking in on yet another moment of Bren's insecurity and failure.

Dear God, *was* she a nutcase? Was she terminally depressed? Well, not terminally, no. But depressed? She shook her head. She wouldn't think about it.

"Hello," Bren said as cheerfully as possible, hurrying to the fridge. "Wine?"

"No, I couldn't," Rosa said. "I'm here to drag Gil away. We've got plans tonight."

Bren pulled the wine out of the refrigerator anyway, then hoisted up onto her tiptoes to reach the glasses, which Gary had put on the highest possible shelf. She couldn't help noticing how out-of-date and dull her kitchen looked compared to the Kitchen Classroom. She was still pulling things out of a white refrigerator — where was her stainless steel? "Plans? I hope it's not an office Christmas party or anything boring like that." She pulled the cork and tipped an inch of wine into each glass.

"Ugh, no, that's in a couple of weeks, after Thanksgiving. I'm dreading it. Gilly's boss is such a pompous ass. And he thinks he's a real ladies' man. Very proud of his assets, if you know what I mean." Bren nodded, though she wasn't one hundred percent sure what Rosa meant; she was only one hundred percent sure that she didn't want to know.

"No, tonight we are going out, just the two of us. Going to try Le Foyer, the new French place downtown? It's supposed to be amazing. Have you been?"

Bren picked up her wine and slugged it all back in one swallow, trying not to feel insult-to-injury-ish. "Not yet. Gary and I will wait until the crowds die down. Maybe" — *when hell freezes over* — "after the holidays." She pushed Rosa's wineglass toward her and refilled her own.

"That's a good plan," Rosa said. "Gilly's just such a sap. He can't wait that long. Once he gets an idea in his head, there's no stopping him."

"How very romantic," Bren said, wondering if the bitterness she felt on her tongue was seeping through her words. She noticed the telephone pad and pencil on the countertop near her wineglass, and had the sudden urge to write *Le Foyer* on it. Something else to look up. Another way to live vicariously through someone while getting nowhere herself. Her notepad was so exciting!

Maybe the urge was to snatch up the stupid pad and rip it in half like those musclemen did with telephone books, instead.

"So how did the class go?" Rosa asked.

Bren took another drink, forcing herself

153

to sip. "Oh, it had its moments," she said. "We made the pie."

"Wonderful! How did it come out?"

Bren shrugged. The comfort she'd felt leaning against her car that night was gone, and now her desperate attempts to create a holiday recipe that was meaningful seemed like a huge waste of time. "Everyone took one home," she said.

"So, what's the next lesson?"

Bren drained her glass again — my, how she must look like a complete alcoholic to Rosa at this point — and chuckled. And then the chuckle turned to a giggle, the giggle to a laugh, and soon she was crossing her legs for fear that she might laugh a pee right out of herself. She held a hand out, trying to calm herself and to assure Rosa that she was okay, and not the lunatic that was appearing before her. Rosa's eyes looked huge in her bobblehead on top of her tiny little body.

It really was all so ridiculous, when she thought about it. After all, everyone had left with a pie. And a damn good one. Why on earth would she let the onetime griping of a cranky old biddy unnerve her so much?

"I'm sorry," she said, gulping for air. "Appetizers, but I'm afraid the boys have snatched them and run. I guess it's a good sign. They're edible."

"I don't know," Rosa said, turning her lips down. "Gil will eat pretty much anything."

Bren let out another gulp of laughter. "Good point. I suppose those three men aren't the definition of selective. I could have served them any old slop."

"Oh, that's not what I meant! I'm so sorry! That came out so rude!"

Bren, still laughing, wiping tears from her eyes, nodded. "It really did. But maybe they saved you some. Feel free to go on down. Don't forget to search John's shirt for some nuts." And then the laughter renewed itself.

"I won't," Rosa said, her voice jovial, as if she wanted to join in Bren's cheer, but her face showing the same wariness she'd worn when escaping Bren's kitchen before. It wouldn't be long before Rosa wouldn't want to come inside the house at all, a prospect that worried Bren on one level, but thrilled her on another. She didn't care for adorable Rosa and her date nights at Le Foyer, but she liked the idea of Rosa being able to tell her friends about the laughing, depressed alcoholic married to her husband's guitarist even less.

Rosa disappeared downstairs, and soon the music — which might have been a rough extraction of Bob Seger's "Sock It to Me

Santa," if that song were played by drunken apes — petered out. A smile spread across Bren's face as she imagined teeny, adorable Rosa bringing down the hammer and busting up the fun for a stuffy date night. *Take that, Gary. Thought you'd weaseled your way out of it, didn't you?*

Bren poured herself another glass of wine and took a long sip. She stared at the tomatoes left on her windowsill — shockingly red for November. She might as well start cooking again. The ladies would like these appetizers. She could only imagine what Aunt Cathy would relate to the crab cups, and what stories would come out of her mouth.

She had just dumped the tomatoes into a colander when she felt a soft tap on her shoulder. She jumped, turning, to find John there, looking pink-faced as ever. He was holding the crystal bowl out to her.

"Oh, John. You scared me. Just put that on the counter. I'll get it in a minute. You liked them?"

He nodded slowly, his eyelids drooping as if he were half drugged. "They were great. Thank you."

Bren's eyebrows scrunched together as she took him in. "Sure, Johnny, anytime. You like some wine or anything?"

"I shouldn't."

The water ran over Bren's fingers, cold out of the tap, turning them numb. Why was he looking at her so strangely? "You okay?"

She noticed a flicker behind his eyes. Discomfort? Embarrassment? Gas?

"I'm really good," he said. "Those nuts were fantastic, Bren."

He cleared his throat before leveling his gaze at her again. The water continued over her fingers, little sprays kicking up the rotting-food smell of their decade-old garbage disposal. She needed to toss a lemon rind down there. Below, she could hear the others, talking, heading toward the stairs.

"Good," she said, the crease in between her eyebrows deepening. Was he okay? Did he have a nut allergy she didn't know about?

Rosa could clomp up a flight of stairs pretty fast in such high heels, but for a change Bren was glad of it, as the noise seemed to jolt the awkwardness out of the room.

"Let's go, my princess," Gil said, swooping through the door so close to Rosa they almost appeared to be one person. Rosa giggled and slapped at his hands and ran through the kitchen on her tiptoes. Nauseatingly cute. Even Kelsey would have had a hard time finding anything beautiful in an overweight, middle-aged man chasing after his hot young wife in a crowd. Well, if you could call Bren and John a crowd. Which you really couldn't, but John had been making the room feel very crowded.

"See ya tomorrow, Gare!" Gil yelled down the stairwell.

"Yup," she heard Gary call back, just before the clanging of something dropped on the hard basement floor.

"Thanks for the snacks, Brenny," Gil said, leaning over and placing the pistachio cream bowl on the counter.

"Yeah, bye, Bren! Enjoy your class," Rosa said, pulling Gil's hand and leading him out of the kitchen.

"You bet. Enjoy your . . . escargot."

"Ew, snails," Rosa said. "I wouldn't dare."

"I would," Gil said. "If I got to eat them out of your belly button." He nibbled on Rosa's ear. Bren wanted to gag.

"Okay, see you later," she called loudly, turning off the water and shaking the colander with too much force for tomatoes. She couldn't help herself; she wanted to shake the ick off of the conversation.

"Bye. Thanks!" they called in unison, heading toward the front door.

"Yes, thank you," John said. He reached

over and put his hand on hers as she tried to dry it off, the paper towel caught between them.

"You're welcome," she said, aware that it came out of her mouth as a question rather than a statement.

"Thank you . . . for everything," he said.

More of the awkward staring.

"You're welcome . . . for everything," she said, a dim fear seeping into her that perhaps John was having a stroke. At their age, you had to be vigilant for signs.

He grinned — was that a wink or had a flick of water gone into his eye? — bit his bottom lip, and then slid out of the room, leaving Bren standing by the sink holding a dripping colander full of slightly battered cherry tomatoes.

He whistled a familiar tune as he walked. "I Saw Mommy Kissing Santa Claus."

She stood rooted in her spot until long after the front door had shut behind him. Gary was making more noises downstairs. It almost sounded like he was trying to play the drums now. He was actually — God knew how — worse on those than he was on the guitar.

Bren set the colander back in the sink, grabbed her wine-glass, and emptied the bottle into it, filling it so full she had to bend over and slurp some off the top, before picking up the glass and holding it in her pruny and numb hand, John's whistling and wink-grin running over and over through her mind.

"What in the hell was that?" she said aloud, and then dumped her wine into the sink, grabbed a paring knife, and started coring.

CHAPTER ELEVEN

As expected, Aunt Cathy seemed to have a hell of a time pressing the dough into the muffin tin.

"You know what I think?" she exclaimed. "I think you bought yours, that's what I think. You're just trying to make us all look bad. Nobody could get this crab cup nonsense to work. Why does it have to be in a cup anyway? Can't you just put the fish on a cracker like everyone else?"

"I got mine," Joan said. "See?" She held up her muffin tin, which looked like it had been hit with an explosion of flour and eggs and dough. Revolting. Maybe Bren should have rethought the complexity of this dish. Though, to be fair, how complex was flour and egg, really?

But the tomato thing had gone so poorly, especially after Aunt Cathy had loudly compared the pistachio filling to "a Christmas sneeze" and Tammy Lynn had laughed so hard a false eyelash had fallen into her cream cheese. Only Rebecca had been able to get her tomatoes stuffed, and Bren had eventually just moved on.

She should have started with the nuts. Those were toss-and-bake.

"Oh, look at hers," Tammy Lynn said, pointing to Rebecca's muffin tin, which was perhaps even more perfect than Bren's had been. Rebecca reddened and shrank back onto her stool.

"She cheated," Aunt Cathy said. "She brought those from home."

"Aunt Cathy, she did not cheat," Bren said, hurrying to their station. She lowered her voice, leaning into Joan's space. There was flour all down the front of Joan's Christmas sweater, which was blocked red and white rectangles with kittens in various poses of garland entwining appliquéd to the front. Bren really needed to talk to her sister-in-law about buying those awful things for Joan every year — *amlright?* "Mother, can't you do something about her?"

Joan shrugged. "Don't you think if I could I would have by now? She's been this way her whole life. No changing now. You just have to live with it. Like taxes."

"Or a cold," Tammy Lynn added.

"Or genital warts," Aunt Cathy crowed. "Say, she's writing again." She pointed at Rebecca, who had taken a break, perched on the stool with her notebook placed on her knee. "What are you writing in that thing? Nasty newspaper exposé? Or maybe for one of those what-do-you-call-'em?" She turned to Joan for help.

"Tablet magazines."

Aunt Cathy snapped her fingers. "That's right, the tablets. Maybe one of you is secretly sleeping with George Clooney and she's tracking you down. My money's on one of you two." She pointed at the two ladies behind her.

"She's probably writing down the recipe," Lulu said. Teresa nodded in agreement. Lulu leveled her stare at her sister. "Something you should be doing, *hermana.*" Teresa clicked her tongue and looked away, her arms folded across her chest.

"No, she's writing a steamy romance novel," Tammy Lynn said. "Wouldn't that be a kick? She could title it *Heat Me Up.*" She brushed her hands together, a plume of flour fogging the air in front of her.

"She could call it *Caliente Cook,*" Teresa said.

"Oh, nothing hotter than a Latino chef," Lulu added. "*Hijo de puta,* these cups."

Joan held a rolling pin in the air. Why was she using a rolling pin? This required no rolling pin. "Or she could call it *Kiss the Chef.*"

"Or *Nookie in the Cookies,*" Aunt Cathy added, and everyone groaned.

Everyone except Rebecca, that was. She simply wrote more furiously, her fingers gripping the pen so tightly it appeared to have started to bend under the pressure. Her eyes flicked up only once, accusatorily, Bren thought, and then she went back to her intensive scribbling.

What was she writing? Bren wondered. She hardly ever spoke, didn't even crack so much as a grin during the search for the missing eyelash, and she was forever jotting notes into that book. Aunt Cathy was right — it was unnerving.

"You know, why don't we go ahead and get our cups in the oven?" Bren said, heading for her station. "And we'll start glazing our nuts while they cook."

Aunt Cathy snorted. "Now, there's your title right there," she said, snatching Joan's rolling pin and pointing it at Rebecca, who didn't even notice.

"Catherine," Joan said, but she was smiling while she said it. Tammy Lynn let out a huge bark of laughter that made everyone jump.

"Sorry," she said through hiccups of giggles. "Continue."

Bren hopped up onto her stage and pulled the bowl of pecans under the projector. "Okay, we're just going to add a little —"

Just then the door opened, letting in a whoosh of cold night air that made everyone shrink into themselves. Over the past two days, winter had really begun to set in. No more wearing a button-down and a scarf to ward off the chill. No more running out in just a Windbreaker. It was coat time.

A young, impossibly fit girl wearing spandex and neon tennis shoes — the expensive kind that Bren's sister-in-law bought by the armload for her kids — rushed in, alongside a man so round he made Humpty Dumpty look like a personal trainer.

"You ready?" the girl said, pulling a pink headband down over her ears. Her cheeks were red, as if she'd been outside for a while. Come to think of it, Bren hadn't seen any headlights. Had the girl walked here?

"I'm in the middle of a cooking lesson," Tammy Lynn responded. She turned to Bren with an uneasy smile. "This is my daughter, Janelle. And my husband, Elwood. We just call him El."

Bren waved, but the girl only glanced at her impatiently. "Mom," she said through clenched teeth. "We need to go."

Tammy Lynn seemed to flush. "I'm sorry, I've just been a big old jumble of distraction today, haven't I?" she said. "I've just put the crab cups into the oven, Janelle. Can't it wait ten minutes?"

"No," the girl said. "I've got a spin class to get to. This has waited long enough, if you ask me."

"Just let your mother cook her things," El said. He offered Bren a smile, which hoisted his massive cheeks and lit up his entire face. *Santa,* Bren thought. *If he were only white-haired, he could be Santa with cheeks and a belly like that.*

"She has cooked enough things, Dad," the girl said. "And you've eaten enough things. You both have. Why you let her take this class in the first place, with us trying to make some progress, is beyond me."

"Janelle, honey," Tammy Lynn said, although she didn't look up from her hands, which were resting in her bowl of pecans. For the first time, she seemed timorous, maybe even a bit meek. Even her brightly made-up face seemed to pale. "You're embarrassing me."

Bren flicked a glance around the room.

Everyone was trying not to look interested, but she knew they all were. Tammy Lynn was such a lighthearted person, and this felt like a private moment that they couldn't escape from. "There are only eight minutes left on the cups," she said, trying to be helpful, while knowing that she wasn't.

"Come on, we're embarrassing your mother. We'll wait outside, Tammy," the man said. He tugged his daughter's sleeve, but she didn't move.

"I'm sorry if I'm embarrassing you," she said, "but this is important. Much more important than embarrassment. The doctor told both of you if you don't lose the weight, the next heart attack could be the one that kills you. And that you are just as much of a ticking time bomb, Mother, as Dad is. So I'm sorry if I'm embarrassing you, but Murphy and I are getting married in two months, and I would like my children to have grandparents who are alive." She looked from Tammy Lynn to El. "Well?"

Tammy Lynn nodded slowly, still not taking her eyes off her hands. But after a moment, she pulled her hands free and untied her apron, slipping it over her head and folding it up.

She let out a breathy, self-conscious laugh. "Janelle is studying to be a personal trainer.

She's been working so hard. It's a lot of hard work, isn't it, honey?" She stuffed her apron into her cavern of a purse, not bothering to wait for Janelle's answer, which was good, because it amounted to not much more than an impatient *come on* gesture. Tammy Lynn snapped her purse closed and pushed it up onto her shoulder. "Would you be so kind as to make sure my cups don't burn?" she asked Joan.

"Of course," Joan answered, her voice low and uncertain.

"There are low-fat alternatives," Bren blurted, not sure where on earth that came from. She knew it must sound rich to this skinny young thing to have someone Bren's size talking about low-fat anything. She was clearly high-fat everything, and after witnessing this little scene, was feeling a little painy in the chest area, too. Was her left arm going numb? Or was it supposed to be the right? She never could keep symptoms straight. The very thought scared up an itch on her shoulder. She scratched at it absently. "In fact, I was just telling your mom that I have fat-free cream cheese in the walk-in for just such substitutions." Her heart quickened. She was lying, right here in front of everyone. But it quickened in a giddy way, especially once she caught Tammy

Lynn's eyes and saw the gratitude in them. *Just please, please don't let Aunt Cathy start talking,* she thought.

"Right," Tammy Lynn said. "We were going to use low-fat cream cheese. And crabmeat is good for you. Lean protein, just like the doctor said."

"And the rest is just vegetables and seasoning," Bren supplied. "We even discussed using a cauliflower dough option instead of flour."

"And you know I love cauliflower," Tammy Lynn said, rubbing her belly.

"And our other dish is tomatoes," Teresa said.

"Heart healthy," Lulu added.

"Pecan?" Joan said, offering the young girl a bowl. "More protein. Looks like you're going on a run. You could use the energy." She looked so kindly, so innocent, an old lady who would have nothing but one's best interests at heart. The type of lady who would invite trick-or-treaters in for fresh-baked cookies, and would meet the garbage collectors at the curb with lemonade on a hot summer's day.

But the woman could lie like a convict, and at the moment — and not for the first time, either — Bren loved her with every fiber of her being for it.

The girl turned her nose up at the nuts. "I've eaten," she said mildly. "And those are covered with sugar. You do know sugar is the culprit behind our world's current obesity epidemic, right?" She shifted from foot to foot, and then rolled her eyes. "Fine. Just don't dawdle when you get done. I don't want to miss too much of my class. I'll meet you outside. Not you, Dad. I don't trust you to be standing around by the doughnut place. Stay in here, where the food is at least . . . healthy." She said the last word like it was a dirty word, even though she looked to Bren like the type to eat an artichoke leaf and call herself full. You never knew with those girls, though — she could live on a diet of pasta and candy bars, for all Bren knew. She sucked in her gut self-consciously. Or doughnuts and lattes.

"Here, El, you can help me with the crab filling," Tammy Lynn said, waving her husband into her station as Janelle sulked into the night air. Bren could see her neon shoes, but that was about it. She appeared to be stretching, and then ran off down the sidewalk. Jogging to warm up for her workout, she supposed. Definitely the artichoke type.

It took a minute for things to settle back

to normal, as everyone hopped around and rubbed their arms against the cold and Bren tried to re-corral her jumbled thoughts. Something had just happened here, but she couldn't really define what exactly.

Tammy Lynn retied her apron, while El took a wooden spoon to the crab mixture. He stirred so hard his jowls jiggled, and Bren could have sworn he was humming something while he did it. "The Little Drummer Boy"? Yes, that seemed to be it.

Tammy Lynn's eyes flicked up to Bren very briefly, her smile full of gratitude, the color back in her cheeks. They'd lied for her. And it was then that Bren was able to pinpoint what had just happened — they had become a unit, this class. Not just a bunch of strangers failing at crab cups; a bunch of strangers failing at crab cups *together.*

Bren let out a big breath. "Okay. So we'll start with some cayenne. Not much, just enough to give it a little kick. A little heat at the end of the sweet — that's how I like to think of it."

"Oh, like Venezuelan chocolate," Aunt Cathy said. She elbowed Joan in the side. "Like the kind we had in South America, remember?"

"We've never been to South America."

"Yes, we have. Remember, the place where I got that food poisoning from the chicken salad right in the middle of my hot rock massage? Dear Nelly, that was a mess."

"Oh," Joan said. "Yes. That wasn't South America. That was our trip to Louisiana."

"Same thing."

"No, it's not the same thing at all."

Aunt Cathy planted her hands on her hips. "It's south. It's in America. What's the damn difference?" She spun and pointed to Rebecca. "And don't you write that down. I'm a Christian woman. I can't be immortalized saying Satan's talk."

"Satan's talk?" Bren asked. She'd known Aunt Cathy to be a lot of things, but a Christian woman was not one of those. "You curse all the time, Aunt Cathy."

"Not when there's a reporter present."

Bren squeezed her eyes shut and shook her head, and when she opened them again, she saw it was already eight o'clock. On track. She had to keep them on track, or they would never get out of there. Out of the corner of her eye, she saw pink running shoes streak past again.

"Back to the nuts," she said.

"Oh, title of Rebecca's novel," Lulu said, and she and Teresa leaned into each other, snickering.

"What's that she said?" El asked, his arms nearly covered to the elbow with cream cheese. "What novel?"

"Oh, never you mind. You just spoon some of that filling into the cups. Go ahead, Bren. We're listening."

Bren nodded. "So you've got your cayenne, now let's add some sweet spices. You've got cinnamon, nutmeg, allspice, cardamom, whatever, it's up to you."

"Tammy," El said.

"Not now, El. Let the woman talk. I'm spicing it up over here."

"Title of the novel!" Lulu and Teresa yelled together.

"What novel?" El asked.

"El, I'm busy. We've got to hurry before Janelle comes back. You know she'll be mad if we're not done when she gets here. Put the filling in the cups."

"But that's what I was going to say," he said, pointing into the bowl.

"After you've got your spice profile worked out, go ahead and set that aside. We're going to toss the pecans in egg white and vanilla vodka."

"Tammy Lynn, where is the —"

"Shh, now, I'm separating eggs. You know my eggs break when I'm nervous."

"Title!" Lulu and Teresa shouted again.

They had to sit down to catch their breath from all the laughter.

"What on earth are they talking about with the novel?"

"Just stuff the cups already, would you, man?" Aunt Cathy shouted, bringing the room to a standstill.

"Well, that's what I'm trying to tell you," Elwood finally said, his voice going high and loud, beads of sweat popping out on his balding forehead. "There are no cups to fill!"

"What do you mean, no cups?" Tammy Lynn said, finally looking up from her pecan bowl.

And it was in that moment that Bren smelled the smoke. "Oh my God! The cups!" She rushed toward Tammy Lynn's station, forgetting about the platform and stumbling off it, landing hard on her knees. "Get them out! Get them out!" she said, reaching up from her position on the floor. She knew she looked pathetic, and that her knee was definitely going to smart later, but she was too busy noticing, with horror, the haze of smoke that was rising above them as the ladies each pulled out their burned crab cups.

At first there was nothing but silence, punctuated by a few quiet coughs from

Rebecca's station. Everyone seemed to be gazing forlornly at their blackened appetizers.

"Oh, so those are the cups," El said softly.

"Maybe they're salvageable," Joan said, and as Bren pulled herself to standing, she could see her mother bravely chipping at the charred sides of one cup, blackened pieces skittering across the counter.

"Sure, once you put the filling in, you won't even taste it," Aunt Cathy said, in a surprising display of support. But it was a lie.

Bren leaned over Aunt Cathy's disastrous cups and made a face. The stench of burned flour filled her nose. "You could put a partridge in a pear tree in that thing and you would still taste it. I'm so sorry, you guys."

And even though the room echoed with soothing forgiveness — *It's okay* and *It's not your fault* and *We should have been watching them better ourselves* — Bren couldn't help feeling like this was a huge failure that was all her doing. She should have quit when her gut told her to. She shouldn't ever have come into this place to begin with. This was a whole elaborate message from God that binge-eating doughnuts on a Thursday morning is nothing but a bad idea piled on top of bad ideas.

Although she could have really gone for a Hole Shebang caramelized Vidalia–filled Bismarck at that moment.

She tried not to feel the familiar tingling in her nose that meant tears were close by. She wouldn't cry. Not over this, not now, not in front of everyone. Later, she would get out her telephone pad and look up dengue fever, think about eating congealed diner gravy, listen to Yoko Ono warble about war being over, and cry her eyes out. She would cry until her tongue felt fat. She would cry until Gary actually noticed.

But right now she was the teacher. The leader. She was supposed to be in control and in charge. She would act like this was just another bump in the road to exceptional and creative holiday cooking. She would lead these ladies to an excellent holiday meal.

"Right," she said. "This is a good opportunity to see how easily crab cups can be burned. Very quickly, in fact. Now that we've seen what not to do, let's go ahead and dump them out and start over."

Lulu rubbed her eyes with one hand and waved a dish towel in the air with the other. It was doing no good. Teresa looked utterly perplexed by what had happened. Her crab cups looked like the burning was the least of their problems.

"Maybe we should prop the door open," Tammy Lynn said, fanning the air in front of her face as Elwood thunked the muffin pan against the side of the trash can, emptying it, the burned mess clinging valiantly to the sides of the pan.

Teresa shook her head. "It's freezing out there."

"But the smoke is killing my contacts," Lulu said.

"Don't be such a baby," Teresa said. "You get the truck so smoky I feel like I'm in a hookah den."

"Truck?" Aunt Cathy asked.

Lulu waved her hand dismissively. "Taco truck." She turned her attention to Teresa. "And if you could cook, you wouldn't have anything to complain about with the smoke. But obviously this is doing you no good. Look at these *cangrejo* cups. *Patético.*"

"Maybe if we open the door just a crack," Bren said. She went to the door and reached for it, but just as she got there, it flung open, with that same old woman who invaded the last class standing in the dark on the other side. That same scraggly dog tucked under her arm like a grizzled, growling football.

"What in Sam Hill is going on here?" the

old woman asked, thumping her cane on the ground.

"You have got to be kidding me," Bren muttered. No way was this happening, too. As if the night hadn't been disastrous enough on its own.

"I was watching my shows up there, minding my own business, even though you're all so loud I could barely hear the TV over you, and next thing I know, I'm seeing smoke coming up through my floor."

"I'm sorry," Bren said. "We had a mishap."

"This whole class is a mishap. I never got to talk to that boss of yours, but this is your last warning. Either this class goes or the cops come. And move your cars. I can barely get Chuy to the grass without rubbing your car dirt all over my clothes."

She turned as if to go, but Bren hurried to step between her and the door. "Please. Ma'am. I know you're upset, but, really, those are public parking places. There's nothing you can do to keep people from parking there."

"I can take my key to the sides of their cars."

Behind Bren, Tammy Lynn gasped. "You wouldn't."

"Don't think I won't."

"Someone ought to take a key to —,"

Aunt Cathy started, but Bren held out a hand.

"I'm very sorry this has been so upsetting to you. But, really, it was an accident. We'll try to keep from burning things in the future. Maybe you should join us. But you simply can't keep bursting in here on us like this. We have a right to hold this class."

The old lady held her gaze for an uncomfortably long time, during which Bren held her breath. Outside, she was poised and calm — assertive, even. Inside, she was shaking like a leaf.

Finally, the old lady simply turned and disappeared into the night with her dog, letting the door close behind her. Bren didn't know exactly what she had been expecting the woman to do, but she knew she hadn't been expecting that. A feeble fight, maybe. A parting verbal jab. A threat of some kind. Anything but silence.

But Bren could scarcely wrap her mind around what had happened and what to do next when the door was whipped open again. She half expected it to be the woman, coming inside to fling flaming dog poo at her, or maybe to let the pup tinkle on her shoe. But instead, what came in was a blur of pink shoes and black spandex.

"Mom, Dad, we really have to . . . Was

there a fire?"

Bren opened her mouth to answer, but it was at that moment that the smoke detector started buzzing, and only seconds later that the sprinklers kicked on, drenching everyone in a shrieking, flour-gooey frenzy.

This time Bren didn't keep the tears from rolling. Not like anyone would know the difference anyway.

CHAPTER TWELVE

She needed bigger pants. Not exactly the Christmas gift she had been hoping to give herself, but she supposed if she stopped gifting herself midnight bags of potato chips, the pants wouldn't be an issue.

Not that Bren had anything better to do at midnight. Not with Larry, Moe, Curly, and Ringo downstairs until all hours, farting around with hard rock versions of songs that should never hear an electric guitar. Songs like "O Holy Night" and "Christmas Shoes." Terrible, terrible stuff.

And they had added a singer. Or what you might call a singer if you didn't actually know what a singer was. This man — Jeremy — was to singing what blackout-drunk people were to dancing. He couldn't seem to retain the words to even the simplest Christmas song — songs most kindergartners knew by heart — and resorted to filling in imaginary words with a strange *fnnn* sound to them.

Who wouldn't be driven to the soothing arms of grease-saturated vegetables fried to a crisp and coated in sour cream and onion powder?

Besides, buying new pants meant getting out of the house, for which Bren was grateful. Inside the house, she only waited for the phone to ring. For Paula to fire her for water damage. For Paula to fire her for complaints from the upstairs neighbor. For Paula to fire her for being a general, all-around disaster.

The square was the quaint part of Vargo. The traffic was slow and easily managed by stop signs. The stores were cozy and expensive. The coffee was made to order and the garland bells and snowmen and bows shimmered in the breeze. But beyond the square was the city, such as it was. Stoplights and strip malls and coffeehouse drive-thrus. And traffic. All of which was annoying during the summer, mind-numbing during the spring and fall, but which carried with it a sense of excitement and energy during the holidays. Bren didn't mind being out in the holiday hullaballoo. Even if she didn't have much reason to celebrate this year, nor much of anyone to celebrate with.

Given that it was a weekday, and not really that close to Christmas, Bren didn't have to fight for a parking space. She'd recently vowed to start parking farther away from doors, anyway, a feeble yet still defensible attempt at correcting the problem. But the wind was blustery that day, and had a hint of snow scent to it. She hadn't watched the forecast in days, so she had no idea if it was actual snow she was smelling or just the hope of snow — of something, if only one thing, that reminded her of a normal, happy holiday. Even if white Christmases were actually pretty rare.

She was wearing her winter coat — the big quilted one that she'd planned to get rid of three winters ago, but was still wearing. Three years ago she was easily two sizes smaller, and now she felt stuffed into the thing, her arms barely able to bend comfortably and the snaps periodically freeing themselves when she stretched at the waist. She tugged it around herself as she sprinted across the parking lot, one hand on her head to hold her crocheted hat in place. Her hair would be a disaster after this, but she wasn't here for a fashion show. Did anyone ever even think about their hair while they were buying bigger pants?

She nearly mowed over a bell ringer, who

looked entirely too relaxed and cheerful to be out in this wind, and Bren was instantly ashamed. Another vow she'd made — to start carrying cash for the red buckets — remained unfulfilled. Upon closer inspection, the man ringing the bell was eighty if he was a day. Surely he was an icicle inside of his coveralls, yet he was still smiling and God-blessing everyone who walked by. Including Bren, whose response to the embarrassment of having nothing for the kettle was the same as it always had been — to duck into the store quickly and pretend she hadn't noticed him at all.

Of course, ducking into the store quickly meant she nearly bowled into the greeter, who stood far too close to the door, dressed in shiny satiny holiday finery, looking as if she were about to head out to a Christmas pageant, her moussed curls fluttering as one with the wind that suctioned through the vestibule.

"Welcome to Saints Department Store. Our latest flyer," she said, pressing a glossy into Bren's hand. Cheerful. So cheerful. Probably related to the bell ringer. "Lots of great deals."

"Thank you," Bren said, and took the flyer, though her first glance showed sales on candles and ornaments and platters.

Precisely the things she didn't need this year. Knowing that she wouldn't be fighting to the death for a marked-down tablecloth threatened to set her into another fit of depression, and she had enough of that going on with the increase in derriere, thank you very much, so she veered through the juniors department and tucked the flyer down the back of a mannequin's skinny pants.

Served them right. Not even mannequins looked good in skinny pants.

Saints had more than compensated for the cold outside. Within seconds, Bren felt a drip of sweat roll down her back, right into her waistband. Great. She always felt fatter when she was sweaty. Peeling off damp too-tight jeans was second in discomfort only to putting them back on again when she was done trying on clothes.

The Jackson Five sang, at an impossibly high volume, "Santa Claus Is Coming to Town," a rendition Bren always felt was too manic for Christmas. Christmas was for soothing songs. Quiet ones with heavy undertones of reverence that bordered on sadness. Baby-rocking songs. Songs that lent themselves well to easy-listening voices and choirs and church ladies. Not that there wasn't any place for happy holiday music.

Who didn't smile when Bing Crosby sang about Frosty? But it wasn't Frosty you thought of when you thought of Bing, now was it? No, it was that half-agonized David Bowie duet, wasn't it? *Pa-rum-pum-pum-pum,* pass the Kleenex.

Ah, but even Bren recognized that perhaps she was just in a different place this year. A place where jiving to the Christmas beat required way too much energy and far more optimism than she had inside of her.

And she was sick to death of the scent of cinnamon. When did cinnamon become so inextricably entwined with the birth of Jesus, anyway? And why did every department store, retail store, craft store, and auto supply store have to carry a heaping stock of reeking pinecones? Pinecones were supposed to smell like pine. Was she not the only one who realized this? There was no cinnamon pine tree. And from the looks of things, nobody was buying them, anyway. Always, the bins were overflowing with wafting bags of tree offal, and Saints's bins were no different. Bren made a wide arc around them, suddenly aware that all she really wanted was to get the damn jeans and get out of there.

A woman walked by, a coffee in one hand and her cell phone in the other, loudly stressing about a gift that she was, apparently, unable to find anywhere. Bren did not miss those days.

Maybe Kelsey and Kevin had given her a gift after all. Maybe they'd given her the greatest gift — the gift of a stress-free holiday. Really, who could complain that their biggest holiday shopping frustration was finding the right pair of jeans for themselves? Nobody, that was who.

She wound her way through the jewelry department, past the handbags — taking the time to inhale deeply and let the scent of leather cleanse her nasal passages — and into the plus-sized department. She didn't like anything there. She never had understood why so many plus-sized clothes were so loud and unattractive. Big ugly flowers and decades-out-of-style paisley and so damn much elastic, as if overweight women had somehow lost the skill of buttoning a pair of pants. Not a belt to be found anywhere.

Listlessly, she pulled four pairs of jeans off the rack and headed toward the dressing room.

She had tried on only the first pair when her phone rang. Bren almost let it go to voice mail, but the sixteens she'd been trying on hadn't fit, and in a fit of frustration she had stripped them off and plucked the phone out of her purse with every intention of turning it off mid-ring.

Instead, she saw KEVIN light up across the screen, along with a photo of him arm in arm with her on his graduation day, both of them squinting into the sun so hard and smiling so wide it looked painful.

"Kevin?" she answered.

"Ṡwạṡdī mæ̀!"

Bren pulled the phone away from her ear and double-checked. There was her son, graduation cap in place, gazing back at her. Dear God, it was her nightmare, come true. A stranger, somehow in possession of her son's phone, calling for help she couldn't provide because she didn't speak the language of whatever country he had lighted upon this time. And her telephone pad and pencil nowhere in sight!

"Hello? Sir? Is everything okay with Kevin?" she asked in a panic.

She could tell by the laugh that it was, indeed, Kevin. "Sorry, Mom."

"Oh, it is you! You had me worried. I thought some vicious person had stolen your phone and was calling for ransom."

He laughed again. "Still the same with your paranoia, huh?"

"It's not paranoia. Bad things happen

every day. It's reality. You never know. And you were speaking a strange language."

"I was saying, 'Hi, Mom' in Thai. Is Kelsey not speaking the language yet? I would think she would have at least taught you that much. She's been here a lot longer than I have."

This was something Bren had never considered. It was a terrifying concept — her kids having whole languages in common that she couldn't even understand. As if the language of Siblings United Against the Parents wasn't enough. "I don't know," she said. "You do? Speak Thai, I mean?"

"Well, not fluently. Not yet. I haven't really spent enough time here yet to pick it up as well as I'd like. I was hoping to practice on her." He sounded disappointed. "I'd still rather speak French or Arabic."

She pushed her clothes off the corner bench into a rumpled heap on top of the jeans she'd just shucked off, and sat on it, the plastic cold against her underwear-clad bottom. "But you took Spanish in school."

"I didn't really like Spain all that much," he said. "It was too gray. Although Pavy thinks we should go back. She thinks it will be much more romantic if it's just the two of us, without all the others." Bren rolled her eyes. Pavlina. A girl he'd known for how long? A month? She was now Pavy, the romantic and worldly Pavy. *Pavy thinks.* Bah.

And who were all these others? Kevin had embarked on this journey alone. It was what had worried her most about his going. Who would take him to the emergency room if a snake bit him on the knee and he was unable to walk to the nearest medicine hut? Who would flag down help if he flipped an ATV or fell into quicksand or had a heart attack or God only knew what other dangers might befall him? Now that she knew he had a group — Pavy and "the others" — she was almost even more frightened. What if one of these "others" robbed him? What if they were unruly? What if they fought and bullets flew? She had no idea what any of these "others" could be like. Bearded and filthy with foul mouths and smelly clothing. Shifty and intelligent with beady eyes and complicated schemes. Buxom and writhing with movie-star lips and an eye for gold. Bren could think of a hundred more, a hundred worse, things these "others" could be. A thousand, maybe. A million, while sitting right here on Saints's cold bench — that carried the bum germs of more strangers than she even cared to think about — if only she put her mind to it.

No. She refused to put her mind to it.

"So does this mean you're in Thailand?" Bren asked instead, wishing she'd brought the telephone pad with her. Hurriedly, she hunted through her purse for a pen and something to write on. She found an old candy bar wrapper and turned it inside out so the white paper side was spread across her bare leg, a stolen Marriott pen clutched in her hand.

"Ko Sichang," he said.

Cozy Chang, Bren wrote. "What does that mean?"

"It's a place. Not too far from Bangkok. But away from all those tourists. Just me and Pavlina and the monkeys."

"Monkeys? They have monkeys in this Chang place?"

He laughed again. Bren was starting to dislike this laugh. It made her feel small, the same way he'd made her feel toward the end at home. As if he were so much more knowledgeable than she was. He probably was. No, he definitely was. But he didn't have to show it so much. She never showed it when he was a little boy and she was the one teaching him everything. She never tied his shoes and then said, *In your face, stupid!* She'd been glad to share her knowledge with him. For as short a time as that had lasted.

"Yes, there are monkeys and a jungle and the remains of Judhadhut Palace."

Jude had Hut, Bren wrote.

"Mom, I'm telling you, there's a whole world outside of Kansas City that you don't even know. There's just something so very intellectual about the ocean, you know what I mean? Connectedness, the whole universe. When I'm eating cashews right off the trees in Koh Phayam or drinking I-don't-know-what with the *chao ley* in Koh Jum, I feel like I'm flowing through a universal artery. You know what I mean? It's like . . . it's . . . I can't explain it. The only explanation I can give is that you just haven't lived until you've snorkeled in the Andaman Sea. You haven't been enriched until you've made love in the lagoon off of Koh Phra Thong."

Bren's face burned with a blush. She crossed her legs, suddenly feeling too naked to just be sitting around in a public place. When did her son — her sweet-faced little boy — begin "making love"? And, more to the point, when did he begin feeling comfortable talking to his mother about it? Her pen hovered over the candy bar wrapper, trembling slightly. He'd spouted so many words, she couldn't keep up. She thought he might have said something about a thong, but it was too close to the "making love" comment for her to possibly have concentrated enough to get it on paper. And there was no way she was going to have him repeat all of that.

"Are you still there? Mom?"

"Yes, yes, I'm here," she said. "Um, it sounds like you're having a wonderful time. Is Cozy Thong your favorite place? You sound very excited." She winced, her use of the word *excited* in describing his time at the place where he is clearly "making love" a dreadful, and scandalous, choice of words.

"I don't know. I still have to get to Bhutan. I mean, how can you hike the mountains of the happiest place on earth and not feel some sort of connection to humanity, some sort of centering? I think Pavy and I could really take our relationship to a new level there. You know what I mean?"

Bren blinked. "Disneyland?" She wrote down *Disneyland*. And then, next to it, *possible wedding???*

"What?"

"You said the happiest place on earth. Isn't that Disneyland?"

"What? I don't know. No, Mom, pay attention." And there it was again — that condescending tone. "Missourians," he added scornfully. Bren felt stung. "No, Bhutan. It's in the Himalayas. It's supposedly the happiest place on earth. They're all zenned out over there or something, I don't know. I'll find out. After the first of the year, that's where we're heading. I got a job back in Rome — crazy place, would not recommend it — and we managed to save up enough to get us most of the way there."

"Most of the way? What's most of the way?"

"I don't know. Depends on how we decide to go. Pavy and I aren't planners. That's so very American, I think. You know what I mean?"

Bren wished more than anything that he'd stop asking her if she knew what he meant. Of course she didn't know what he meant. She didn't understand why suddenly asking a reasonable question made you a *Missourian,* said with such contempt. And she didn't understand what was wrong with being a planner, or being American, for that matter. She didn't understand when her son became so above it all, he and his "others." He and his lovemaking Pavy with her cozy thong.

"So we're planning to head up to Pak Kret in a few days, make it an extended visit. You know where Pak Kret is, right?"

"Of course I know where it is," Bren snapped. She may not be as worldly as her children, but she at least knew where her daughter lived. She had joked to Kelsey while helping her pack that a place called Pack Rat was perfect for her. Kelsey had not appreciated her humor.

He laughed. "I was just making sure you didn't think it was in Universal Studios or something."

Bren glared, but she had nothing to glare at, so she settled on glaring at herself in the mirror. She could hear noise of the fitting room filling up around her. Voices, happy voices, women thrilled to be out shopping, just as she and Kelsey might have been if this were a normal Christmas. If Kelsey hadn't abandoned her.

There was a soft knock at her door.

"Yes?" Bren asked, sitting up straighter, snatching her too-small jeans off the floor and draping them over her lap modestly, as if the knocker had X-ray vision and could see through the door.

"Excuse me, ma'am? Are you all right? You've been in there for a while."

"Who's that?" Kevin asked. "Are you not at home?"

"Nobody," Bren said.

There was another knock. "Ma'am? Are

you okay? Should I get someone?"

"I should let you go. I thought you were at home."

"No, no, it's fine. I'm fine." Then, realizing she'd said this last bit into the phone, said it again, louder, to the door. "I'm fine."

"I can call when I get to Bhutan."

"Everything's fine; I'm just doing a little shopping, is all." Suddenly Bren was desperate to keep him on the line. He may have been treating her like a down-home servant, but he was still her son, and hearing from him was still rare enough for her to not want to let it go easily. "I can talk and shop at the same time."

"Ma'am, if you're not trying on clothes, I'm afraid I'm going to have to ask you to vacate the fitting room," the voice on the other side of the door said. Why would they not just leave her alone? What was wrong with giving someone a little bit of privacy?

"I'm fine!" Bren called again, going for cheery, but sounding as manic and desperate and confused as she felt.

"I'll just let you go. I'm sure Kelsey and I will call on Christmas Day."

But Christmas Day seemed forever away.

"Wait," Bren practically shouted. "What about Pavlina? You're sounding awfully close. I mean . . . do you have plans with her? *Those* kinds of plans? The big kind? You're not thinking of making things permanent, are you?"

There was a pause on the other end, during which the woman on the other side of the door knocked again, only this knock sounded suspiciously like a pound.

"Ma'am, there is a line out here. I'm afraid if you don't come out, I'll have to call security."

"I'm naked, okay?" Bren shouted, and then blushed with embarrassment again as the silence from Kevin's end grew even longer.

"Listen, Mom. About me and Pavy. It was a crazy time, and I meant to tell you about it. But we couldn't wait. We are just so connected to the universe together. You know what I mean? It was a whim. I barely even told Kelsey."

"Told Kelsey what? What crazy time?"

There was a longer pause, during which the pounding on the other side of the door seemed to get echoey and faraway. In that moment, Bren wouldn't have cared if the woman busted down the whole door. She slid from the bench to the floor, aware that anyone looking under the door could see her nearly bare bum and not caring. She attempted to hug her knees to her chest, but her stomach made that impossible, so she simply bent them, pressing her back into the mirror.

"What crazy time?" she repeated, this time her voice low and cold as it left her lips.

"Mom," Kevin said, and she had a wild moment of wondering where his patronizing laugh was now. Was craving it, really. Hoping he would chuckle and tell her she'd misunderstood everything. "Pavy and I, um . . . well, we kind of got married already. Maybe."

Bren tingled from top to bottom. Suddenly she was cold, too cold, and her vision felt wonky, like she might faint. "Married? And your sister knew?" was all she could whisper.

"Barely," he repeated.

Bren felt the hold slip on her calm. It didn't help that the Saints clerk was still hammering away at the fitting room door, and that Bren possibly might have also been hearing voices of other women — impatient shoppers — out there. "How can someone barely know something? Either she knew or she didn't. And how does someone kind of *maybe* get married, anyway?" she snapped.

"We're not even sure if it's totally legit," he said. "Me being American, her being Czech, neither of us being Italian. I told you it was crazy." He laughed again, but it had lost some of its cockiness. At least he had the decency for that. "It's not a big deal, Mom."

He sounded like a little boy. Like a little boy, guilty of something. Like the time he cracked Gary's windshield with a baseball. Or the time he put a hole in his bedroom wall. Guilty and afraid to admit what he'd done, trying to downplay it by making Bren sound so unreasonable.

It was enough to send her completely over the edge.

"Ma'am, I've called security," the voice said.

Bren struggled to standing, whipped the door open, and snarled, "Call the FBI for all I care. I've got bigger problems than whether or not I'm hogging the dressing room." She slammed the door on the clerk's shocked face, barely even registering the glares of at least a half dozen women clutching armloads of clothes standing just behind her. She pulled the lock and put the phone back to her ear.

"How can you say it's not a big deal, Kevin Joseph? Marriage is a very, very big deal. And you're barely eighteen years old."

"I didn't mean that —"

"And the fact that you don't think it's a

big deal makes it plain that you are too young to be married. Not to say anything of the fact that you think you are only *sort of* and that your sister *barely* knew. Do you even hear yourself talking right now? Do you sound like a married man?"

"Mom, you're freaking out about —"

"No, you don't. You sound like a boy. And I don't care how connected you and Pavy and whoever the others are to each other or to the universe or to a cow in the river."

"What others? Calm dow—"

"And I don't care how romantic it was or wasn't in Spain or if your time in Rome was crazy or if monkeys are giving you god-damned piggyback rides in Cozy Chang. The fact that you could even sort of get married without your mother there is . . ."

Bren trailed off. She didn't even know what word would be the right one to finish with. *Bad* wasn't strong enough. She needed something more like *reprehensible,* only with less of an admonishment-in-court sound to it. *Careless? Irresponsible? Mystifying?*

"Hurtful," she finally said. She gulped, realizing that tears would be coming. Once she was able to wrap her head around this properly, surely they would flow. She was a mother-in-law now. To someone named

Pavy who didn't like shoes. "I'm hurt, Kevin. You've hurt me."

There was a long silence, in which Bren was aware of two things: one, her breath sounded like thunder in the phone, and two, the knocking had ceased. Both of these things alarmed her, but neither more than the thought that Kevin may have hung up on her.

"Hello? Are you still there?" she asked, then added, "Young man," to keep some of her angry edge.

Finally, he spoke. "Mother Teresa said when you love until it hurts, there is no more hurt, only more love," he said.

Bren blinked. "What the hell is that supposed to mean?"

"Listen, Mom, my battery's about to die. I've got to go. We'll call you when we get to Kelsey's, okay? We can talk more then."

But Bren knew the men of her family. *We'll talk more about this later* meant *We will never, ever talk about this.* She sank back down onto the bench.

"Okay," she said. "That's fine."

"And I'll e-mail you and Dad a picture of Pavy," he said, and he had the gall to sound completely happy about it. The word *hurt* might never have been bandied about at all. It had had no effect on him whatsoever.

"Sure, all right," she said.

"Okay, love you, Mom."

"Love you, too, Kevin," she said, though the words were coming out automatically, her thoughts so jumbled she was barely aware of speaking. "And, Kevin?" she asked at the last moment.

"Yeah?"

"She's not sort of pregnant, is she?"

He laughed, the haughtiness right back in place. "Of course she's not."

"Well, at least there's that," Bren said.

She sat for another long moment after they'd hung up, staring at his contact photo. He was such a handsome young man. No wonder Pavy wanted to sink her claws into him. She'd led him astray. Bren knew that as well as she'd known anything. What type of girl would think it's okay to marry a man without his family there? A girl who didn't care a whit about family, that's what type. Already Bren didn't like her. She would look at the photo he sent tonight, but it wouldn't change anything.

Finally, Bren slid her phone back into her purse and picked up her crumpled jeans from the dressing room floor. They were too tight — she could barely breathe in them — but she no longer cared about rectifying that situation.

She left the jeans she'd been trying on discarded in a crumpled wad on the floor, stepping into her shoes and shouldering her purse, and then opening the dressing room door and casually walking out as if nothing had ever happened.

Three ladies stood by, scowling at her with arms crossed angrily and hips cocked to one side.

"Next," Bren said, pasting a smile on her face.

It wasn't until she was in her car, pulling out of the parking lot, that it dawned on her that all of those women had seen her in her underwear.

She stopped the car, leaned her forehead against the steering wheel, and laughed until she cried.

CHAPTER THIRTEEN

It was when the square was quiet that she liked it the best. When she and Chuy could take their walk without having to dodge worker bees and snooty shoppers or choke on exhaust. When Chuy could do his business without the fear of some nosy Nelly wanting to put their intrusive hands all over him. It was like nobody understood that a dog his age had to work slowly up to a good poo, that the slightest distraction could make his business creep right back up inside his intestines and that it might be hours before he could find the nerve to have a go at it again. Or, worse, that the nerve would strike suddenly and at a most inopportune time. The only thing that smelled worse than those dratted doughnuts was a spare bedroom full of dog doody.

At times, Virginia Mash felt guilty about her "relationship" with the shop owners and shoppers around the square. She was hardly an ambassador of goodwill, welcoming one and all to her fine city. But, really, there was so much more city to shop in. The highway led to strip malls, and twenty minutes away, in Kansas City proper, there were shops galore. Twenty more minutes would have them in their beloved suburban malls. They loved their cars so much, why not sit in them on their way to their shopping sprees? Imagine the bliss of juggling cell phone and traffic while headed to a parade of glorious price tags, just waiting to be owned.

But, reason and rationale aside, she did feel guilty at times. She did worry that she would drive away good business by acting bad. She did know that some of the shop owners — that short, dark-haired woman who owned the children's boutique on the southeast corner, for example — had children to support. She knew that some of them — the shoe repair couple directly across the way — were trying to carry on generations-old family businesses. She knew that some of them — Bill, the surly antique restorer on the other side of the Hole Shebang — were living out a lifelong dream, after decades of toiling away at faceless corporate jobs until retirement. She knew these things, and they ate at her, and yet she couldn't help wishing, just a little, on the inside, that their businesses would fail. That they would all pack up shop and leave her be.

But on days like these, when the square was dead — just a few courthouse government drones smoking on the lawn, the random deliveryman rushing in and out of city hall — Virginia Mash kind of loved it. It was cold outside, true. Too cold, really, for walking around. Even the most dedicated to Vargo chose warmth over supporting local commerce. But the cold didn't bother Virginia. She could handle much colder than this. Had done so on many occasions, in fact.

Had done so on the worst occasion.

But she didn't like to think about that.

This day, she'd donned her quilted flannel shirt, the brown and red one that reminded her of Thanksgiving. Hard to believe that just tomorrow, families would be gathering together over their turkeys and stuffing. She had bought Chuy a special can of food, the expensive kind he never usually got. She'd bought herself a frozen turkey dinner. She didn't see any reason to go out of her way for just the one of her.

Ernie, oh, how he'd loved Thanksgiving. It was his favorite holiday, truth be told. It didn't have the hectic overcommercialization of Christmas, he'd always said. It was relaxed and cozy. And there was football. He loved sitting in his robe after dinner watching football, a pie plate balanced on his stomach, a coffee with Baileys steaming on the end table.

She didn't often miss Ernie. Or, more accurately, she only ever missed him as he was when they first met. He was kind to her, kind to everyone. But they'd lived through too much together. It had all begun to fall apart at the end. They'd lost each other. To be specific, he'd lost her, but she couldn't find herself, so how was she to come back to him? She was sorry to see him go — so sorry — and she grieved him deeply. But her heart had already been broken before he went. She didn't have the capacity to grieve him the most.

He'd gone quickly and easily in his sleep. He'd looked peaceful when she woke up the following morning and found him there. She'd wondered who he'd found waiting for him on the other side. She was ashamed of herself for being a little bit jealous that he got to know first.

Chuy had a nearly matching brown and orange flannel dog coat. It was goofy, and too short, not really made for a dachshund, but he was old and his arthritis didn't always love the cold, even if he himself didn't mind it. Plus, he was maybe a little bit cute in clothes.

Virginia wanted to take a long walk today. The kind of walk that stretched out of the square and all the way up toward the business park off State Route 1. If worse came to worst, she would carry Chuy, wrap him up in her shirt. They would keep each other warm that way. But she didn't think it would come to that. She and Chuy had walked that route many, many times before.

She hadn't done it in a long time, though. Maybe since the winter before, even. She couldn't remember making this trek in the heat recently, which meant that they must not have gone over the summer at all. Funny how Thanksgiving seemed to bring out the nostalgia in her, seemed to make her want to relive old memories. Even the terrible ones.

As if she didn't relive the terrible memories enough right in her very own apartment every single day.

Traffic picked up as she got out of the square, past the majestic historic homes, past the smaller homes in various states of disrepair, dogs, also in various states of disrepair, barking at Chuy, their muzzles pushed through the diamonds of chain-link fences. Chuy occasionally stopped, his ears perked, sniffing the air in their direction, but he rarely barked back. When he did, it had a definite raspy, cantankerous *Who do you think you are, talking to me like that?* quality to it that made Virginia oddly proud.

"Okay, boy," she would mutter after letting him have his say. "No need to be rude just because they are," and she'd give his leash a soft tug, prodding him to keep moving. "In one ear and out the other." And on they would continue through the neighborhood and toward the main thoroughfare.

Truth be told, Virginia Mash preferred the neighborhood surrounding the square over any of the subdivisions in Vargo. The subdivisions were filled with carbon copies of the same house occupied by manicured types, always tapping something into their cell phones. They were the rude ones, the ones who took cooking classes and burned things, thinking nothing of how it would make her apartment smell. She'd had to sleep with the fans running that night, but did any of those women care? Had a single one of them stopped in to apologize? Not that she would have answered the door even if they had, but it was the principle of it.

She'd called, of course, and left messages for that owner, that red-haired Paula.

Several messages. So many that Paula no longer so much as paused when Virginia shouted after her on the sidewalk the few occasions she'd seen her locking up the building and heading home for the night. So many that Paula, when she was finally cornered, Virginia and Chuy taking up camp behind her car, which just happened to be emitting exhaust that would float right up into her living room window, had she been able to pry it open, had called Virginia's efforts at communication "harassment," and had threatened to get the police involved.

Virginia could scarcely believe it. *Getting the police involved* was her threat. She didn't love the way it felt coming at her instead of from her. Terrible feeling, actually.

Not that she was scared of the police. She was an old woman living alone with her geriatric dog — the kind of person police treated like their own grandmothers. Not to mention, she'd complained to them about so many things over the years, they were all on a first-name basis anyway.

The enormous oak trees thinned out as Virginia and Chuy passed the last house — a brown gingerbread-style house with peeling paint and one shutter missing — and then they turned onto Missouri Trafficway, the business park laid out before them at the bottom of the hill.

Virginia's heart began to thump harder, and despite her cold fingers, she could feel sweat break out under the flannel. She didn't like to even look at the building, so why on earth did she make herself come here? Why had she moved to an apartment so near it in the first place?

As if he could read her thoughts (and she wouldn't have been surprised to find that he could), Chuy paused and gazed over his shoulder at her. He knew exactly why she'd moved so near it, and so did she.

"Yes, sir, we are going down there. Don't look at me like that," she said.

He seemed to accept this unpleasant fate and continued his slow march. Virginia followed him, trying to log details about their walk to keep herself distracted. The elementary school had gotten a new slide on their playground since she'd last walked past. Looked like half the school was hanging off of it — she couldn't make out the kids, but could hear their squeals and see their silhouettes in the sun — which didn't seem extraordinarily safe to her. The MRI center had gone out of business, as had the little Chinese restaurant next to it. It had been an odd location for a Chinese restaurant, anyway, she'd thought, and they'd put peas in their egg drop soup the one and only time she'd ever ordered it, about seven years ago. Who in their right mind would eat peas in egg drop soup?

There were three houses in a line on the other side of the street. But they were up high, separated from Missouri Trafficway by a tiny outer road that served only those houses. One of them had been painted recently. And the color was terrible. Baby puke brown, if Virginia had to put a name to it.

She looked for other things — a new sign marking the beginning of the walking trail that took pedestrians off into the (unsafe, in her opinion) woods, the grand opening of a veterinary center (looked too expensive), and the price of gas at a local gas station (ridiculous) — but no matter how hard she tried not to notice that she was coming up on the cancer center, she couldn't help feeling it, a tugging in her gut, a dread in her throat, a burning behind her eyes that had nothing to do with the cold or the wind or even the glare of sun high up in the crisp sky.

R. Monte Belle Cancer Treatment Center. It was still there. Still beige brick–faced and still with the tinted front doors, so that the people who slipped in were gobbled up by anonymity immediately thereafter. A new doctor had been added across the bottom of the sign in bold black letters: Jeanette A. Patrick, MD.

"Oh, Chuy, you know what that means," Virginia said. "There's demand."

It broke her heart to even think about it.

"Well, come on, I suppose I should at least let you sniff a little," she said, pulling Chuy onto the lawn surrounding the center. He immediately went for the sign, gave it a couple of whiffs, then turned and hiked his leg on it.

She let him lead for a while, follow his nose, and tinkle to his heart's content. This always led to a meandering, often circling, many times all-out stopping tour of the grass and even sometimes of people's tires. Which she didn't mind. *Piss all over those tires, Chuy; that's my boy. Give 'em a good soaking,* she'd been known to say more than once.

But today she just didn't have it in her, and neither did Chuy. After sniffing the entire perimeter of the sign, he seemed content to simply lie down in the grass, panting softly. Maybe he was finally too old to make this trip. Maybe it was a sign that they both needed to let the R. Monte Belle

Cancer Treatment Center go. God, that was so much more easily said than done.

She decided to let Chuy rest for a while. She hooked her cane over the brick pedestal that the sign had been mounted in and let her backside lean against it. She was covering the words, but she didn't really care. If someone passed the center, they would see it on their way by the other direction. Besides, didn't everyone have one of those PGS contraptions that told them exactly where to go all the time now anyway? Nobody had to think for themselves. Cars were selfish little coffins-to-be, everyone too busy worrying about and listening to and looking at their contraptions they forget that they were essentially turned into mobile weapons in those things.

Deadly. Cars. Cancer. All of it.

She watched the door. A couple went inside, the woman's head wrapped in a pink bandana. A child came out, her bald head exposed to the world. A perfectly healthy-looking man strolled inside. But wasn't that how they all looked initially? On top of the world, as if nothing could possibly be wrong with them? As if they were going to be one of the few who beat it.

"We should do something, Chuy," Virginia said absently as she watched a man carry another child out. The child was far beyond carrying age — maybe as old as eleven — and was draped over him in complete exhaustion. "We could make a difference."

But what difference could they make? If anyone knew that even the kindest gestures couldn't take away the feelings of despair and futility, she knew it. If anyone knew that no matter how sympathetic they were to your cancerous plight, you would still look at them with bitterness, with contempt that they were so unfairly healthy, even if you felt guilty for thinking those things, she knew it. What difference, indeed?

"Let's go," she said, abruptly pushing off the wall and giving Chuy's leash an admittedly too-harsh tug. His tags rattled as he struggled to catch up with the movement. She grabbed her cane and slowly the two of them thumped back up the hill, through the neighborhood, and toward the square. She catalogued nothing on the way back. She noticed nobody. No peeling paint, no missing shutters. Even Chuy didn't bother to sniff at the barking dogs.

That fat blond cook was the first thing she saw when she rounded the northeast corner of the square. It was late afternoon. The sun was going down, and even Virginia had begun to feel a little chilly. But the cook was bundled up so tight she looked like she was heading for a month of dogsledding.

She gave an exasperated sigh, stopped, leaned against her cane, and watched. Dammit. The last thing she needed tonight was an overwhelming food stench riding along a wave of imbecilic laughter. It was Wednesday — not even their regular night. They must have moved it for the holiday. Could they not have just taken Thanksgiving week off?

The cook struggled with a very large aluminum pan of something that she had pulled out of her backseat. Something orange dripped over the side, out from under the foil she'd covered it with. In the midst of her struggle, she happened to spot Virginia. She tensed, looked quickly over each shoulder, as if possibly Virginia had a couple of henchmen waiting in the wings to rub her out, and then continued trying to shut her car door with one leg as if Virginia hadn't been standing there at all.

Chuy let out three sharp barks.

"You're a good judge of character, my friend," Virginia said, and then thumped toward the cook. Her feet were tired. Her right bunion throbbed. But she didn't care.

"You're not planning to have another class tonight, I hope," she said.

The cook jumped, and more orange stuff sloshed out of the pan and down the front of her shirt. "Yes, I am," she said. She sounded like she was going for nonchalant, but the quiver in her voice gave her away. "There's no reason why I wouldn't. I have every right to teach a class, and in fact an obligation to do so. People paid good money for it."

She stepped up onto the curb blindly, seemed relieved that she'd made it, and then proceeded to wrestle with the logistics of getting the front door open. Finally, flustered, she let out a grunt.

"I don't suppose you'll help me out," she said.

"Not if it means I'm going to have to have my apartment fumigated again," Virginia countered, though, to be fair, she'd only considered the fumigation thing, and had decided she wouldn't actually act on it until the class was officially over and the Kitchen Classroom was officially out of business. Which wouldn't be too long from now if she had her way.

"I didn't think you would, but it was worth a shot," the fat cook said. She set the pan on the ground, opened the door, held it with her hip, and then picked up the pan again. "Have a good night."

"You won't get away with this," Virginia Mash yelled at the door, which was closing behind the fat cook. She hated not getting in the last word. She yanked the door open. "For your information, I've hired an attorney."

"Great. Tell that to Paula. I don't own this place, she does." The fat cook had set the pan on a counter and was busy wiping the front of her shirt with a paper towel. Looking for all the world like she didn't really care if Virginia Mash was even in the room with her.

"I will sue you."

The fat cook looked up and smiled, but it was sour underneath. "I just work here," she said. "Would you like to stay? We're making barbecue sauce." She pulled back the foil, and a plume of steam mushroomed to the ceiling. Virginia Mash pinched her nose shut. "For brisket. Family recipe."

"I would sooner starve to death."

"Then you wouldn't have to worry about the smell anymore," the cook said, her voice agreeable but her message nasty.

Virginia Mash was aghast. She was used to a fight. She was used to tears. She was even used to dirty looks and hateful whispers. But she wasn't used to such . . . pleasantness.

"When does the redhead get here?" she asked.

"Oh, I'm sure she's here. Probably in the back or something. Would you like me to fetch her for you?"

Virginia scowled. Not really. After the walk, the cold, and this new attitude, not to mention the kids at the cancer center, she just really didn't have it in her to fight tonight.

"Just be sure you don't burn the place down," she said. "And if you interrupt my TV shows tonight, I will be back."

"Bye now," the cook said, tossing the paper towel in the trash and offering a friendly wave. "We'll save a station for you. Just in case you change your mind."

"Over my dead body," Virginia said, storming back out onto the sidewalk. But halfway up the stairs, the creak of the wooden steps echoing the creak of her bones inside her feet, she realized what she'd said.

Over her dead body.

Given the day she'd had, it seemed like the world's poorest choice of words.

CHAPTER FOURTEEN

Why on earth had Bren let Aunt Cathy bait her?

Really, she knew better. She knew the crazy old bat would try to get her to tackle a project only for the sake of saying she made her tackle it. She was, after all, the aunt who'd dared her to stick her tongue on a light pole during that fourth-grade snow day. She was the one who'd claimed it wasn't possible to play human bowling on the stairs with a helmet, a flattened cardboard box, and three overturned buckets. She was the one who'd bet — actually bet an eight-year-old child! — that she couldn't jump from her second-story window into the swimming pool below.

Bren had been falling for Aunt Cathy's bait since she could say the words *Uh-huh, I'll prove it to you!* She was more than old enough to know better now.

But there was something that just snapped

inside of her when Aunt Cathy looked up skeptically from her plate on Thanksgiving Day and said, "This is just a turkey."

"What do you mean, *just a turkey?*" Bren had said, feeling herself blanch. She had been up since the crack of dawn basting that turkey. Her eyeballs felt packed with sand thanks to that turkey. Her kitchen was a disaster because of that turkey. Granted, she hadn't gone all out the way she would have if the kids had been home, but she had pulled down and dusted her grandma's china, had whipped an entire bag of potatoes for just the four of them, and had gotten the name-brand cheese for the broccoli-rice casserole.

"I'm just saying, you're a cooking professional now. I expect more of you."

"I'm hardly a cooking professional. Besides, this is a traditional Thanksgiving turkey. You can't do more with a Thanksgiving turkey," Bren said defensively, but she could see on the faces of Gary and her mother that they maybe agreed just a little bit. Plus, the turkey was a little on the dry side. "Well, what do you think I should make?" she asked, a question she now realized was entirely, entirely stupid. "Since you want me to wow you."

Aunt Cathy thought about it for a moment, swirling her spoon listlessly through her gravy, drumming the fingers of her other hand on the brown and orange tablecloth. Everyone stared at her. She stopped drumming and tapped a forefinger to her chin, making a production out of her decision making. "A turducken," she finally said.

"What's a turducken?" Gary asked.

"It's a chicken inside a duck inside a turkey," Aunt Cathy said, miming stuffing things into one another with her hands. "Or something like that. I saw it on that food channel."

"I've heard it's delicious," Joan said. "I've never had one. I'll admit I've always been kind of curious, though."

"See?" Aunt Cathy said to Bren. "Nobody's curious about plain old turkey. People want to see you stick a chicken up a duck's ass."

"Catherine, Bren probably doesn't know how to make a turd-whatsis," Gary said. Bren shot him a *Thanks for the vote of confidence* look.

"Turducken," Aunt Cathy, Joan, and Bren all corrected at once.

"Exactly," Gary said. "Bren here probably has no clue how to do that."

Bren stared down at her plate. The turkey looked so . . . beige. Was turkey always so beige? She'd never noticed its beigeness before. Aunt Cathy was right. It was a cop-out. Not even a challenge, really. She could do better. Or at least she'd hoped she could.

"I absolutely know how to make a turducken," she blurted. All eyes looked skeptical, but that only spurred her to keep going. "I've made them."

"When?" Gary asked. "I've never had a chicken in a duck's ass."

"Before we got married," Bren answered without missing a beat.

"You have not made a turducken before," her mother said.

"Mom, you just didn't know about them," Bren said, but she couldn't look her mother in the eye while saying it. "But I've made them. Tons."

"Yeah, she's made tons of them, Joanie," Aunt Cathy said, slapping Bren's mother on the arm. She was enjoying this way too much. "She probably has the best turducken recipe anyone's ever tasted. Right, Brennie?"

The old woman's eyes sparkled with *gotcha.* So Bren smiled sweetly.

"The perfect recipe."

"And I'm sure you'd be willing to share it with your class, since I'm sure all of your students would love to know how to shove a chicken up a delicious duck's ass," Aunt Cathy challenged.

Bren refused to break gaze. "Of course I will." She set her fork down, lifted her arms, victory-style, and declared, "Next week, we make turducken."

But now it was next week and Bren couldn't believe she'd let Aunt Cathy trick her into making a turducken, which, of course, she had never even contemplated making before, much less actually made.

Really, could it be that hard? Any harder than making a regular Thanksgiving turkey, even? Slap a little butter on that beast, some salt and pepper, cram some stuffing into the delicate regions, and bake it. Easy peasy.

Not so much. First was the fiasco of trying to find a damn duck — not so easy peasy in Vargo, where people lived off hamburger and chicken and the occasional pork chop. Then to find just the right size duck that would easily fit inside a turkey, while still allowing room for a chicken? Impossible.

Bren was still trying to wedge them together when a noise sounded behind her. She jumped as John appeared out of nowhere, gazing up at her from under his eyebrows, as if he were up to something.

"Oh, jeez, John, you scared the crap out

of me. Gary's not here yet. He and Gil went to get guitar strings. They should be back in a few minutes. You can go on downstairs if you want."

But he didn't go. He just stood there, staring at her, awkwardly shifting his weight from one foot to the other, that weird horror-movie grin creasing the bottom half of his face again.

She tried to get back to work, but found herself unable to do anything without periodically glancing over her shoulder at him. Maybe she should call Cindy. Make sure there aren't any mental health concerns going on with her husband these days.

"You can go on down," she said again.

"What are you up to here?" he said, and she noticed he'd moved a few inches closer to her. "Looks like you got a mess going on."

"Making a turducken for my class," she said. "Or trying to, anyway. But you're right, all I seem to be making is a mess. I don't know how on earth you're supposed to fit a chicken inside of a duck. They really aren't all that much smaller." She tried wedging the chicken inside the duck again, but her hands slipped, and the chicken only managed to flop onto the floor with a wet splat. At this rate she was going to have to antibacterial-bomb her entire kitchen. "Dammit."

John chuckled softly, then bent to pick up the chicken. "You have to bone it first," he said. His face was extraordinarily red when he straightened. He held up the chicken. "This. You have to bone this."

He moved to the sink and rinsed off the chicken, and then brought it to the cutting board and placed it on its back.

"Can I borrow?" he asked, pointing to the knife that lay on the counter near the other two birds.

"Of course," Bren said. She handed the knife to him. He took it slowly, more of that smiling. Something felt so awkward in the air, yet she couldn't really say what, since all the man was doing was taking the bones out of some poultry for her. Yet she wished Gary would get home already.

"You have to have a soft touch," he said, and Bren felt herself blush. Great, now the blushing was contagious.

He worked deftly, as if he'd boned a lot of chickens in his lifetime.

"I had no idea you were such the chef," she said, moving over to the sink to wash her hands. "Maybe you should be teaching this class instead of me."

"No, no," he said. He drew a delicate slice

in the chicken's skin. "I'm no teacher. I'm only good in intimate situations." His voice cracked. He cleared his throat. "Besides, you're doing great. A natural, from what I hear."

"Where would you hear that?"

His lips quivered as he stared intently at the chicken. "I just know you're good at it."

Bren shut off the water and grabbed a paper towel, which required her to lean across his arm. She really needed a bigger kitchen. "Well, I'm not. I don't know what I'm doing half the time. I've practically burned down the place, and then spent a whole class period on barbecue sauce. And now I'm making a turducken just because my aunt Cathy gets my goat. Look at me. I didn't even realize you have to take the bones out of the damn thing to make it fit in the other damn thing."

She wadded up the paper towel and tossed it in the trash.

John pushed the flayed chicken to one side and picked up the duck. "You shouldn't be so hard on yourself, Bren," he said. "You're wonderful. Best I've ever seen."

"Thanks, John," she said. "I wish I could believe it." She sank onto a stool. "I don't feel so wonderful these days. The kids don't want to come home. Kevin had a crazy night in Rome that I don't know if I should even tell Gary about. My life's just kind of feeling a little out of control right now." As if on cue, her shoulder itched. She scratched at it impatiently.

"If only you could see Bren Epperson through my eyes," he said, working, his back to her. "You would never doubt yourself again if you did."

There was a ruckus as Gary and Gil popped through the front door, a tornado of noise and rustling plastic bags.

"Hey, Johnny's already here!" Gary said, plunking the bags down on the kitchen table.

"I thought you were getting guitar strings," Bren said, eyeing the multiple bags. She got up and peered into one, which held what looked like thirty-seven bags of beef jerky.

"We wanted food. There's never food in this house."

Bren had to work to keep her eyes from bugging. "No food?"

"Duck's done," John said. He set the knife down and turned to face Bren proudly. His smile faltered when he saw her face.

"No food?" she repeated. "Are you kidding me? I'm a cooking teacher, Gary."

"That's why John is doing this for you," he said. He elbowed Gil and snickered. Bren narrowed her eyes at him.

The tips of John's ears reddened, and he turned toward the sink, where he commenced to washing his hands, scrubbing so vigorously, Bren feared he might throw out a joint.

"He's not doing it for me," Bren said, although she knew it was kind of true that he was, in fact, doing it for her. "Well, I didn't ask him to," she amended. "I've never made a turducken, Gary. Have you?"

"I thought you made tons of them before we were married."

"Never mind."

"What in the world is a turducken?" Gil asked.

"It's one of those things where you squish a bunch of poultry together," Gary said.

Gil pondered for a moment. "Sounds like it needs bacon."

Gary gestured toward Gil in a *See? This is what I'm talking about* sort of gesture. "Bacon," he said. "That's the kind of food we need here. Jerky. Beer. Not froufrou poultry and pies with berries and seafood sawdust cups."

He laughed in the kind of way Gary was wont to laugh whenever he was showing off for friends. Bren knew the laugh well — of course she did, after so many years of marriage. But he also knew when his wife was not finding his humor the least bit funny.

The mood in the room turned heavy. Gil skittered down the basement steps without a word, grabbing two of the plastic bags on his way. John ripped off a paper towel, the sound loud as a firecracker, as Bren and Gary stared each other down.

"I'll just . . . you should . . . um," John said, stutter-stepping toward them.

"I just meant that we wanted real food," Gary said, gulping. "Man food."

"I think you meant junk food," Bren said. "Jerky and beer and cheese curls. That's not real food; it's junk food."

"Okay, fine. Junk food, then," he said. "We wanted junk food. Sue us." There was a thump as Gil sat down at his drum set downstairs. Gary glanced over his shoulder. "Don't take it so personally." He turned, grabbed the last three plastic sacks, and headed toward the basement. "Come on, John. We've got to work on 'Jingle Bell Rock' some more," he said from the stairwell.

There was a beat, during which Bren and John both stood stock-still in the middle of the kitchen. Bren knew she should feel embarrassment or humiliation over Gary's friends — her friends — having witnessed that. To her, it was painfully obvious that she and Gary had lost touch with each other, and she wondered if they would ever find each other again. She wondered if John and Gil could see the same thing. If they sided with Gary. If they felt sorry for her at all. She wondered if they even cared, or if they were judging her. God, she didn't want to be judged. Not by guys like these.

She walked over to the kitchen table and sank into a chair. She stared through the archway into the living room, gazing at the fireplace, which was completely bare. Normally, it would be draped with garland and white lights, the kids' old stockings clinging to it. Kelsey's was the typical red felt getup, the white cuff around the top tinged yellow, the "y" rubbed off her name. Kevin's was knitted, from back when her mother and Aunt Cathy used to do that, and had been snagged by one of Kelsey's cats, creating a hole in the toe that let M&M's escape. Bren had vowed for years to do something about that hole, but she'd never gotten around to it. And now it was too late. Now she didn't know if she'd ever hang a stocking for Kevin again. Or Kelsey, for that matter. Did you hang stockings for your married children? This seemed a bit of Christmas etiquette nobody had ever passed on to her.

Ordinarily, a huge tree would be standing next to the fireplace as well. A real one, its needles falling off at an alarming and frustrating rate, clogging Bren's vacuum cleaner, sticking to her bare feet. It, too, would be draped with all-white lights, although she had toyed the past couple of years with the idea of switching over to colorful ones. The LED types that were so bright they didn't look real.

She used to love sitting with the Christmas tree late at night, sipping a cup of tea, flipping through a catalogue or wrapping gifts on the floor.

"There's no tree," Bren said softly.

"I'm sorry?" John asked, looking more uncomfortable than ever.

Bren shifted back into reality. "Oh, sorry, John," she said. "I didn't realize you were still here. They've all gone down."

"I know, but you were saying something about a tree?"

She waved her hand. "I'm being silly," she said, and swallowed when she realized there was a lump in her throat. "I was just realizing that Gary and I didn't bother to put up a tree this year. How awful is that?"

"Not awful," he said. "You're busy with your new job."

Her lips drew into a hard line. "If only

that were it." Music started up downstairs, the first few bars of "Santa Claus Is Coming to Town." "I think that's your cue, Santa."

"Sure is," he said. "Listen. About the turducken. You're going to want to only partially bone the turkey. That way it'll still look like a real turkey once you have it all stuffed together. Otherwise, you're good to go."

Bren had forgotten all about the turducken. How could she have forgotten? The food argument was what had caused this whole thing. She could still smell raw poultry in the air. "Thanks for your help, Johnny," she said. She stood and put her hand on his arm. "You're so kind."

She felt something then. A jolt of what might have been electricity. She pulled her hand away, mystified, when she realized John was gazing at her, his face gone all slack and serious. He licked his lips. "Any—," he started, but the rest of the word seemed to get caught in his throat. He cleared it and tried again. "Anytime."

Bren took a step back, a weird feeling coursing through her — something embarrassing and wrong. She turned toward the poultry, her face pointed to the floor, and started slicing into the turkey, unsure what she was doing or where she was cutting.

Surely her mind was playing tricks on her. She'd known John for decades. She was friends with his wife. He was best friends with Gary. Anything she felt transfer between the two of them was a mistake. A bad, bad mistake.

By the time she looked up again, and gathered enough courage to glance over her shoulder, he was gone.

A few minutes later, she heard his amplified voice singing backup, something about Christmas in the jailhouse. He sounded extra energized.

CHAPTER FIFTEEN

"So you still haven't told him about it," Nan said, tapping Bren's shoulder with her comb. The touch made it begin itching anew.

"I still haven't gone to the doctor," Bren answered. "The specialist."

"You know, it could be psoriasis or something. Bend your head down."

Bren did as instructed and felt Nan comb out another swatch of hair, tuck a piece of foil under it, paint it, and fold the foil over. "That's why I haven't gone. Why waste money on a copay when it's most likely nothing?"

"Not true." Nan combed up another swatch of hair. "I've known you a long time, Bren Epperson, and you are so lying right now. You're scared of it, and that's why you haven't gone."

Bren pretended to consider this as a new thought, but she knew Nan was right. Ever since she'd found the eraser-sized brown spot high up on her shoulder, she'd been terrified. In fact, she was relatively certain that the damn thing didn't actually itch. It only prickled when she was thinking about it, or thinking about other things that made her nervous and scared. Then it bristled like a son of a bitch. And, of course, since she was already worried or nervous or scared in the moments that it began nagging her . . . well, it wasn't a terribly long leap to her death by melanoma.

"It's probably nothing. You use sunscreen, don't you?"

"Not always."

Nan stopped, leaned over so she was looking into Bren's face. "You don't?"

"Who does?"

"Everyone does."

"Well, I try. But it's impossible to always be prepared." Plus, she thought, there were all those careless days in college, the ones where she and the girls would go to the dock with nothing but their underpants to keep the sun off their skin.

"I'm sure you're fine regardless," Nan said. "But you really should start wearing sunscreen."

"Oh, trust me, I will," Bren said. She'd more than once thought if she renewed her vows to healthy skin care, maybe the spot would go away. But that didn't appear to be how life, and the universe, worked.

"So how's the class going?"

Bren sighed and absently rubbed the scratchy spot on her shoulder. From one sore subject straight to another. Why did she even come to Nan, anyway? Nan was nosy. Maybe she should start seeing a stylist somewhere else, someone who didn't know her. Someone who liked silence. She could lie — make herself out to be someone way more fabulous and less pathetic than she was.

"It's going, I suppose," she said. "Going right into the toilet."

"Aren't you just full of Christmas cheer these days?"

"Nothing to be cheerful about," Bren answered. Nan turned her, so now she was looking at an old lady getting curled two chairs down. The old lady had a serene smile on her face, her eyes half closed. "It has its really good things, you know? The students are fun. Most of them. Not my aunt. She's a pain in the butt. But the other students are fun. And they like to cook. And they don't seem to complain too much when I mess up."

"You mess up?"

"A lot. Oops, sorry." She'd realized she'd been nodding, and Nan was chasing her hair with the bleach brush.

"So it sounds great. What's the problem?"

Bren sighed. "This woman upstairs. She lives alone with her dog, and she's so sour and nasty. It's like she lives to complain about us. We can't get through a whole class without her crashing it, threatening to call the police, to have us shut down. It really dampens the whole mood."

"Wow. That is some kind of crabby. Look down again."

"Yeah," Bren said as she lowered her chin again, thinking about the last class. The old lady had come in with eyes a-blazing and had clomped right up to Tammy Lynn's station. Before Tammy Lynn could do anything to shield herself, that dog had sneezed all over her turducken . . . or her turducken-like bird wad. All hell had broken loose then, with Aunt Cathy swearing her throat was closing up, Joan trying to wipe invisible dog snot off everyone's birds, Tammy Lynn squawking with her palms up at her shoulders, Lulu and Teresa launching into *preach it, sister* mode, wagging their manicured nails at the old woman, the dog yapping its ever-loving head off, the old woman going on and on about code violations, and Rebecca calmly writing in her notebook. "She is definitely some kind of crabby, that is for sure."

"Maybe she's just lonely," Nan suggested. "Maybe griping at your class is her only form of entertainment."

"I don't know," Bren said. "She sure has a way of trying to make friends, if loneliness is her problem. And I don't think it is. Not entirely. I think there's more to it."

"Like what?"

But that was what Bren had been asking herself lately. More like worrying herself over, actually. Because it had occurred to her that maybe the old woman didn't have anyone else in her life. And maybe someday that would be Bren. Kelsey in Thailand, Kevin and wild-night Pavlina God knew where, Gary on some sort of motorcycle tour of Australia or studying kung fu on a mountaintop, or maybe just out in the garage not speaking to her for the umpteenth year in a row. And there she would be — grumpy old Bren, tottering around on a cane with her natty old cat wedged under her arm like a football. *I'll sue you. And I'll sue you. And I'll sue you and you and you, too,* she imagined herself saying. What a bleak image of the future.

"I don't know what exactly is behind it.

But something not good," she said.

That night they worked on sweet potatoes. Three ways, as if there were even one way to make sweet potatoes taste good, in Bren's opinion. She hated the things. Never made them.

Which made her decision to teach an entire class on cooking them correctly seem really, really stupid.

And the old woman had wasted no time complaining. Had practically been lying in wait for it, bursting in and waving what she claimed was a cease-and-desist letter above her head. Could have been a grocery list, for all Bren knew, but it didn't matter. She'd been shaken by the interruption once again. Gary was right about one thing — she wasn't a good enough cook to teach others how to make sweet potatoes one way, much less three. And that was when she wasn't rattled.

The first way — mashed and loaded — came out gloppy and stringy. The second way — baked, with butter, brown sugar, apples, and walnuts — should have been a no-brainer, except Bren forgot to bring the bakers' potatoes themselves. And she couldn't even remember what third way she'd had planned.

"You okay?" Tammy Lynn had asked, as she passed Bren's station on her way to the pantry to put away the unused brown sugar. Bren was sitting on her platform, her head in her hands, wondering how she would break it to Paula that she was quitting, and how much Gary was going to gloat when she did.

Tammy Lynn eased down onto the riser next to her with a grunt, her cosmic-patterned culottes hitching up over her knees. She'd painted her nails deep plum to match.

"Well, now you have to tell me, since it will take two men and a truck to get me up off this floor," she said.

Bren let out a listless chuckle. "I suppose she's getting to me."

"I suppose she's getting to all of us. Lulu said next time she comes in, she's going to call the police herself, for her disturbing the peace. Teresa's talked to the owner about it, and the owner is at her wits' end. Costs her money every time that old kook has her attorney send a nasty gram. And Cathy's threatening to —"

Bren held out her hand. "Please don't tell me what my aunt is threatening to do. I'm stressed enough already. She's been dying to firebomb somebody since the mid-sixties."

"Oh, honey, don't be stressed," Tammy Lynn said, reaching over to pat Bren's knee. "We're all having a blast, even if things get burned and don't come out right and a dog sneezes into our food. None of us here are chefs. Well, except maybe Lulu. I haven't quite figured that out yet. We're all just trying something new."

"You know what would be new?" a voice said, and Bren looked up just in time to see Aunt Cathy lowering herself to the floor beside Tammy Lynn. "Whiskey."

"Whiskey isn't new," Joan said, eyeing the ground as if she wanted to join the others but didn't quite trust making a trip that far down.

"Mom, don't. We'll stand up," Bren said, but Joan was already lowering herself, and had made it to the floor without incident. She looked very pleased with herself for having done so. She laboriously kicked off her house shoes and wiggled her stockinged toes.

"Whiskey is old as the hills," Joan repeated. "And so is drinking it while you're cooking. I'm onto you, Catherine. I know exactly what you're thinking, and the answer is no."

"But drinking it while we're cooking *here* would be new," Aunt Cathy said. Her glasses had slipped down to the end of her nose, and she looked schoolmarmish, gazing at her sister over them. If a schoolmarm wore floor-length denim skirts with peace-sign appliqués, that is.

"We could do a shot every time that woman and her dog showed up," Lulu said. She and Teresa had joined them, their matching Christmas sweaters dazzling Bren's eyes with their reds and greens and golds.

"We'd all be *borracha* before we put a single thing in the oven," Teresa said.

Lulu giggled. "Which would be a good thing when it comes to you, Teresa."

Teresa flung her palms up. "I'm learning; what more do you want, *perra*? I think some whiskey might improve your attitude."

"And who would drive us all home?" Bren asked. "Thanks, ladies, but no, thanks. I'm just . . . I think she's won. You know?"

"Who?" Tammy Lynn asked. "You don't mean that hateful woman?"

Bren nodded. "Yeah. I can't concentrate — not that it's all her fault — and I can't seem to make a single thing. You all saw the turduckens."

Aunt Cathy snickered. "I won ten bucks

off that fiasco."

"I'm so happy for you, Aunt Cathy. But I bought five hundred dollars' worth of dead bird, and did anyone go home with something edible?"

The ladies all exchanged glances. Just when Bren was about to drive her point home, a voice piped up from the back of the room.

"I did."

They all straightened and peered over the stations, looking like a pack of meerkats poking their heads up out of a hole to watch for intruders.

Rebecca stood from her stool, flipping her notebook closed, and pushing it into the back pocket of her corduroys.

"Mine came out just fine," she said, taking a few steps toward them.

"Who is that? I can't see," Aunt Cathy said.

"Well, who do you think it is?" Joan answered. "It's that girl in the back of the room." She whispered very loudly and slowly, "The reeepooorterrr." Bren rolled her eyes. How her mother and Aunt Cathy got around on a normal day, she would never know. She would just thank God that they somehow made it into their beds safe and sound each night.

"It was a little bland, but that was because I was too afraid to salt it because of the sausage in the stuffing. I thought it would get too salty, but you were right, I should have been more liberal with it."

"Did it look like roadkill, though?" Lulu asked. "Mine looked exactly like a raccoon we hit with the taco truck last week." Teresa nodded in agreement.

Aunt Cathy's bracelets jingled as she pantomimed the shape of her turducken. "Mine looked like a headless baby. I thought about freezing it for a Halloween decoration next year."

"That's disturbing," Tammy Lynn said.

"I left mine on the top of my car," Joan said. Everyone got quiet. "I forgot I put it up there while I was trying to help Catherine put the seat belt around hers."

"You seat-belted your turducken?" Bren asked.

Cathy shrugged. "I told you, it looked like a baby."

"So what happened?" Tammy Lynn asked. "To the one on the roof?"

"Oh, it fell off about the time we turned onto the highway," Joan said. "Bounced right off the hood of the car next to us. Landed in the gutter. There was too much traffic for us to stop, so I figure someone would pick it up with the dead raccoon."

There was a moment of pregnant silence, during which Bren could hear the tinny sound of "The Little Drummer Boy" — again! — over the speakers. And then all of them burst into laughter.

"Imagine," Tammy Lynn said, holding her stomach with one hand and wiping her eyes with the other, "you're driving along and all of a sudden this naked turkey just sproings across the hood of your car."

Even Joan chuckled, after at first looking a little annoyed. "I suppose it's a shock enough when a live bird flies into your car. But a plucked one . . ."

"A plucked one with stuffing hanging out its behind," Cathy said, and there was more laughter.

"So Rebecca's the only one who cooked hers?" Bren asked, after the laughter had died down.

"Oh, I cooked mine," Tammy Lynn said, "but Janelle wouldn't let us eat it. The sausage. And the butter. She took it to work." Her face got serious. "Come to think of it, we haven't heard from her since."

"Dear God, you better check to make sure she's still alive," Joan said, and there was more laughter.

Bren couldn't help it. She felt better.

There was something about this group of women that could do that for her without even trying. Without even knowing about Kelsey and Kevin and Gary's basement band. Without knowing about how beautiful Thailand was and how wild those nights in Rome could be. Without knowing that she had no Christmas tree in her home, no stockings or garland, not even a single drop of eggnog.

"Seriously, though, I think Tammy Lynn is right. We should try something new," Teresa finally said.

"Like what?" Bren asked. "My batting average with 'new' isn't the best."

"We could all bring in our favorite dishes and share them," Joan said. "I could bring creamed corn. Catherine could bring that root beer cake she makes."

"Oh! And tamales!" Lulu cried. Teresa nodded vigorously. "We always make tamales for Christmas Eve anyway."

"I've got a great cranberry salad recipe," Tammy Lynn said. "I could bring that. And maybe Elwood could come with and make some of his famous Italian cornmeal cookies."

They'd all begun standing up again, excited about their new plan.

"This just sounds like a potluck to me,"

Bren said, standing with them, but also more than a little relieved to be off the hook for trying to find something new and exciting to teach them for the next class.

"We'll all bring recipes and give fifteen-minute demonstrations," Teresa said.

"It will be like team teaching," Lulu added.

Tammy Lynn clapped excitedly. "I love it. It's settled, then. Next Tuesday is potluck night. I'll tell El."

"Let's stop by the store for root beer," Cathy said to Joan, and they all began to move toward the door.

"Wait a minute," Bren kept saying, but she couldn't get anyone's attention. "But that's not . . . I'd have to ask Paula. . . . That's going to be a lot of smells in one place . . ." Nobody listened. Instead, they packed up their belongings, shut down their stations, and left in a cluster of excitedly chatting friends.

"But that doesn't do anything to solve the problem," Bren called, just as the door was shutting on the last of them. She sighed. Well, at least she was off the hook about cooking. She'd just wait for Paula to get back and see what she thought about a team-taught potluck night.

She went to cleaning out her station,

completely forgetting about Rebecca until she heard the snap of high heels on the floor, coming toward her.

"They're right about one thing," Rebecca said. "We do need to do something new. But a potluck isn't the answer."

Bren paused, then wet a sponge and began wiping down her station. "I'm afraid I don't know what is. I've tried everything. I've tried being nice and inviting her to join us. I've tried being firm. I've tried acting like I don't care. Nothing works."

"Have you noticed anything peculiar about the woman? The one with the dog?"

Bren chuckled. "I've noticed a lot of things. None of them good."

"A coat," Rebecca said, and when Bren gave her a quizzical look, went on. "She doesn't wear a coat. Ever. It's what, forty degrees outside? It's supposed to snow tomorrow. And she's outside walking that dog in a flannel shirt. Sometimes in short sleeves only."

Bren blinked. She hadn't noticed it before, but Rebecca was right. In all of her confrontations with the woman, she had never been wearing even so much as a light jacket.

"You think she doesn't have one?" Bren asked.

Rebecca nodded. "It's totally possible.

We've done a lot of stories about the elderly who are in need during the wintertime but don't ever reach out for help. It's more common than you realize. She's living alone in that apartment. Who knows what it's like up there? Maybe she's really poor, and what's coming out as grumpy is actually a cry for help?"

Bren felt a surge of sympathy for the old woman, imagining her apartment filled with ratty old things from decades long past — fat decades of wealth. She envisioned her wrapped in an old quilt, too destitute to afford much heat, eating soup out of a dented can, sometimes sharing her dog's food because that's all that was there. That could be her someday. Could be anyone, really. You just never knew.

"Anyway. I don't really know what the answer is. She seems pretty determined to shut the place down." Rebecca cracked a tiny smile — the first one that Bren had seen out of her. "Would be a shame if she succeeded." She went back to her station and began getting her things together. Bren saw her make a short notation in the notebook and stuff it into her bag.

She couldn't help herself. "Speaking of all the stories you've done, you aren't really writing a scathing review of the class, are you?" she asked. She pointed at Rebecca's purse, where the notebook had been stashed. "Because I'm not a real cook. If you listened to my husband, Gary, I have no business teaching a cooking class at all. I just like butter." She chuckled at her own lame joke, which, even to her, sounded strange and disjointed. "You're not also try-ing to get us shut down . . . ?"

Rebecca shook her head, pressing her smile into a tight-lipped frown. She looked like she wanted to bolt, but seemed to think better of it, and took several lurching steps toward Bren, pulling her notebook back out of her bag.

"My mother has Alzheimer's," she said. "Early onset. She's only fifty-five. Some days she doesn't even know who I am. She can't remember a thing of the past, and what she does tell us, we never know if it's real or imagined."

"I'm so sorry," Bren said. "I didn't mean to . . ."

Rebecca waved her off. "No, it's okay. A lot of people look at me strange, because I am a reporter and I'm always writing in this thing. But the truth is, it's just a diary. It's habit to carry one of these around, anyway, because of my job, but I'm off the clock here. And I want to remember everything in my life — all the good things, at least — in case there's a day that I can't remember any of it. And in case I have kids someday, they'll know what my life was like. They'll know what is a real memory and what is imagined. It sounds silly when I say it out loud. But I'm writing a book to myself, just in case I should ever need to read it." She rummaged through her purse, then pulled out the notebook and plopped it in front of Bren. "Go ahead, you can take a look."

"I don't need to do that," Bren said. "I'm so sorry I doubted you."

Rebecca opened it to a random page and read. " 'I've learned a lot about patience in the kitchen through this class. And maybe these are lessons that transcend the kitchen into real life. You have to work slowly and carefully or you could make a mistake. Yet somehow mistakes don't seem like mistakes when you're sharing them. The ladies in the class seem to thrive off of their burned crab cups. It's like they're sharing a trauma. It's humanizing everyone. Mine came out perfect, and in a way I was hoping they'd burned, too, so I could belong.' "

"Oh," Bren said softly. "I didn't . . . I don't . . . You do belong. . . ."

"It's fine," Rebecca said on a smile. She closed the book. "The fewer friends I have, the better off I am. I can't imagine how it must feel to my mom to have lost so many friends. Or maybe she doesn't know. I hope she doesn't. I've kind of been avoiding that subject. Or all subjects with her." She took a deep breath, let it out. "Anyway, so that's what I'm doing back there. It will hopefully never be read by anyone. Or maybe it will. But either way it's important to me to get it all down. Even though it seriously annoys your aunt."

Bren rolled her eyes. "Everything seriously annoys Aunt Cathy. Don't take it personally. And whatever you do, don't let her talk you into things. Like turduckens."

They both laughed.

"It's okay, really," Rebecca said. "I kind of think it's fun to annoy her. Makes the project even more worthwhile somehow. She's colorful."

"*Colorful* is a good word for it," Bren said.

"So anyway, why don't I bring matzo ball soup to the potluck? We could add a little dreidel spinning to our holiday cooking class, too, eh?"

"Sounds like a great plan."

But after Rebecca had said good night and thrown on her coat and taken her things with her, leaving Bren to clean up, the self-doubt chased her down again.

She put away the food and wiped the counters, and then turned off the lights, all except the strand of Christmas lights that ringed the front window. She sat on her stool in the dark and listened to "The Little Drummer Boy" — seriously, did they ever play anything else? — feeling fully and securely like a total failure. Now the class was taking over. That was really what the potluck was code for, wasn't it? Saving the instructor.

Even though she knew damn well she could cook an amazing holiday dinner, for some reason she just couldn't translate it into the Kitchen Classroom. Or maybe she'd just been fooling herself all this time.

She felt restless. Like she needed to go home and translate all the words on her telephone notepad and look up more, so she could sound worldly and unaffected when her kids called again. Or maybe she needed to go out and buy gifts — tons and tons of gifts, gifts for family and friends and complete strangers — and take them home and wrap them in the expensive heavy-duty paper. Or she needed to buy a tree to decorate and put the gifts under. And a second cat to snooze on the hearth in its romantic glow. A kitten, even.

Or maybe run around the block or eat a

chicken dinner or detail her car or appliqué a sweater.

Just something. Something that would remind her that she was still here. That Christmas was only one out of 365 chances for success each year, that Thailand was just another country, that wild nights in Rome could happen to her, too, and, by God, that she could belt out "Last Christmas" in a basement just as well as the next guy. Something to prove, even just to herself, that she was alive and participating. That her life mattered and made a difference in this world.

And that was when she saw it. The door tucked between the Kitchen Classroom and the Hole Shebang swung open with an industrious squeak, and the old woman stepped out. She set the dog on the ground and trailed after him. She coughed twice and turned to brace herself against a gust of wind.

Rebecca was correct about one thing — they were forecasting a snowstorm. Bren could feel the snow on the air all day. The atmosphere felt wet and heavy and so cold, breathing in made your nostrils feel stiff.

And yet the woman was out there with no coat.

Bren sat forward on her stool, hiding in

the shadows of the kitchen, wondering if she should do something. Rush outside and wrap the woman in her own coat, perhaps. Invite her inside for a cup of hot cocoa or offer to make her some soup.

The woman coughed again, leaning hard against her cane. The cough sounded painful; even the little dog looked over his shoulder at her while he stooped to do his business. It was more than Bren could take.

She went to the front door and opened it, hanging outside, her body immediately tensing against the cold.

"Excuse me," she called into the night air. The woman didn't respond. "Hello?"

The woman finally turned. A scowl immediately imprinted itself on her face. "What?"

"I was wondering if you'd like to come inside for some coffee? Or if I can bring you a wrap of some kind?"

The scowl deepened. "Why would I drink coffee at this time of night?"

Bren gestured to the sky, and another gust of wind ripped through her, pushing the bangs off her forehead. "To warm up," she said. "Snowstorm is coming."

"I can watch the news myself, thank you very much," the old woman said. "I know exactly what's coming."

Bren faltered. "I just thought . . . since you're not wearing a coat . . ." She didn't know how to finish the sentence.

"Who are you, the fashion police? What if I like being cold?"

"Nobody likes being cold," Bren said, but her words were lost on the wind. She pulled herself back inside the shop and let the door close it out. Her nose tingled with warmth. Despite the sweet potato disasters that had occurred there, it still smelled sweet and comforting in the classroom. She looked on as the old woman turned back to watching the dog squat, coughs racking her body every few minutes. And then, sneakily, the hand that was holding the dog's leash crept up the woman's back and very sturdily gave Bren the bird.

Bren gasped, and then laughed. That was one spiteful old woman. And stubborn.

But Bren could be stubborn, too.

No, Rebecca was right — a potluck was not the change this cooking class needed. Not at all. Bren found a piece of paper and a pen, crusted with cracker crumbs at the bottom of her purse, and bent over her counter, writing out a plan.

She would e-mail everyone before the potluck. She would get everyone on board.

And then she would see who was flipping the bird to whom.

CHAPTER SIXTEEN

"Happy holidays, Bren," Tod exclaimed as she walked into the Hole Shebang the next Tuesday on her way home from her very important errand running.

"They certainly are, aren't they? What very merry concoctions do you have awaiting me today?"

Tod raised his eyebrows. "My, you're in a jolly mood. Things going well next door?"

"Not even a little bit," she said, but he was right — she couldn't pry the smile off her face with a crowbar. Her plan had been set into motion beautifully. To her surprise, and excitement, all of the students seemed to be on board. Tonight was the potluck. They were going to learn how to make tamales and root beer cake, and as a bonus they were going to do something nice for someone who honestly didn't really deserve it. Bren felt like Oprah Winfrey. "But it's all good. 'Tis the season for giving." She practically giggle-squealed the last and had to talk herself down, reminding herself that maybe — just maybe — she was the weeest bit too excited.

"Indeed," he said. "Well, we have here a mint jelly cruller. And this is a sweet potato fritter. Delicious. Better than apple by a landslide. Flying off the shelves. Oh, and if you want to really eat outside the doughnut box, you can try my breakfast special." He pointed at a lumpy monstrosity on the shelf behind him. "It's got scrambled eggs, sausage gravy, and hash browns inside a glazed exterior." It sounded horrific, and Bren had begun to think that there just might be something seriously wrong with a man who could create something like that.

"I'll just take a chocolate long john," she said. "Two, actually. I'll take one home to Gary for a change." It was a lie and she knew it. Gary didn't like doughnuts. She would eat it in the car on the way home and then would need to spend an hour laid out flat in the recliner while her stomach tried to make sense of what she'd just done to it. She knew this from experience.

But she didn't care, because today was going to be a good day, no matter what Gary liked, or what it did to her stomach.

After Tod had given her the doughnuts

and she'd left the shop, she went directly over to the Kitchen Classroom, where Paula was standing at the head station, paperwork spread out before her.

"Oh, hey," Paula said when Bren came in. "I was just going over our new schedule. How do you feel about a class in January? Maybe Healthy Eating for the New Year?" She eyed Bren's doughnut bag — Bren tried not to see judgment in her look — as she said this, but her smile never wavered.

"Oh, I don't know if I'm the person for that one," Bren said. "Maybe a Break Your Resolution in Record Time cooking class would be more my speed. Or How to Cheat on Your New Year's Diet in the Privacy of Your Car. We'd be eating marshmallow Peeps before Valentine's Day even rolled around."

Paula tapped her pen on her chin, her necklace bouncing softly against her turtleneck with the movement. "You know, you may be onto something there," she said. "People are oppositional these days. I can see them getting excited over an anti-resolution movement. We'll give it some more thought."

Bren wrinkled her nose. "Actually, I don't know if that's such a good idea. I'm not the best teacher."

Paula's eyebrows creased and she shuffled back through her papers. "That's not the feedback I've been getting. The students love you, across the board. I've even got a couple on a wait list. You think you could handle as many as ten next time?" Bren felt a wave of happiness wash over her heart. *The students love you, across the board.* Wasn't that what her goal had been from the beginning? Just to have some friends? Someone to hang her holidays on?

"I think I can't handle the ones I've got," Bren said, and then put her hand over her mouth, surprised that she had said this aloud. She lowered it and pulled the stool that Tammy Lynn normally sat on over to the station. "What about the woman upstairs? She's not getting any easier to deal with."

A frown melted Paula's gleeful look. "Don't worry about her," she said. "I've already talked with my lawyer. She can't do anything to us. She's the landlord's problem. So we just keep doing what we're doing."

"Yes, but she will just keep doing what she's doing, too," Bren said. "It's very distracting." She chewed her lip. "And humiliating."

Paula smiled. "We'll figure something out.

So I can count you in for a January class, then?"

"Uh . . . ," Bren hedged, but in the end, the conversation went right where she knew it would. She was locked into teaching another class when she couldn't even finish the one she was working on now.

But at least maybe her plan might resolve the other little problem — the one upstairs.

Since she wasn't actually cooking tonight, Bren had a couple of hours to kill before she had to leave for class. Even her talk with Paula and thinking about Virginia Mash hadn't killed her mood. She felt free and alive and eager to put her plan into motion.

But first. Gary.

He'd left her a message. The band couldn't meet tonight — something about Rosa dragging Gil to see *The Nutcracker* — so he would be home all night. She took that as a sign. An opportunity. He would be home . . . all night. The old Gary would have been saying that with wiggling eyebrows and groping hands. Maybe new midlife Gary would take that as an opportunity to remember how fun it was to make love to something other than his cheese puffs and guitar strap.

This could be their chance to rekindle

things. To get back to each other. To work it out, just like the Beatles sang. Snow on the Roof had been trying to sing it themselves.

Bren started by putting a roast in the oven, ignoring the years of grime that coated the oven window. Roasts could be sexy, right? After twenty-seven years of marriage, food was definitely sexy, along with conversation and the occasional actual eye contact. Roast, potatoes, carrots, all of it smelling perfect. Not like the perfect disasters she'd grown accustomed to in the classroom.

She lit candles. Not so many that he would begin to complain about his sinuses getting overloaded by "all those conflicting smells, and why do we pay money for that, anyway, it's not like we live in a hut filled with oxen" and start doing that thing where he squeezes one nostril shut and blows through the other to try to clear it. She'd seen it more than enough times to know it was decidedly unsexy. She blew out three of the candles she'd lit.

She remembered a movie she and Gary had once seen a long time ago. One where the wife waited, all wrapped up in a Saran Wrap dress, for her husband to get home. The husband had practically blown a gasket when he'd arrived, afraid that someone might have seen her, completely missing the point of her seduction. *I'd have had you unwrapped before I put my briefcase down,* Gary had told her after watching that scene. *I'd have had to rip into you like a birthday cake,* he'd said.

That was a long time ago, but maybe he still felt that way.

She knew exactly where to wait for him. The one place he would be most geared up to go. Her competition: that damned basement band set. At first, she thought she'd skip all pretense and go completely naked — after this many years of marriage, time and frugality worked against cute ideas like Saran Wrap — but the drum seat was way too cold against her bare butt.

She tried lingerie, going for the frothy red getup she'd bought for their twentieth wedding anniversary (and then had hidden and promptly forgotten that she had it at all until the night was over). But she was a good thirty pounds lighter back then. And lingerie showed way too many bad doughnut decisions, especially once she sat down.

She finally settled on one of Gary's old tried-but-true favorites. She got one of his dress shirts out of the closet and put it on. It was tighter than she'd have liked it to be, but once she unbuttoned it to the navel it didn't matter anymore. She let one of his ties hang loose between her bare breasts, and finished the look with a pair of black heels — the ones she'd gotten for her brother's wedding many moons, and years of younger feet, ago. She limped/walked down to the basement and waited.

It was only about twenty minutes before she heard his car pull up outside, and moments later a car door slamming. She rearranged herself, draped sexily across the snare drum, a little bit of nipple showing, the heel of her left shoe hooked sexily around the chair leg. She held two drumsticks loosely in one hand, hoping that she looked suggestive.

"Down here!" she called as soon as she heard the front door shut. "Come on down; I've got something to show you!"

She pressed her palm into her mouth to stave off giggles as she followed the sound of his footsteps through the entryway, the kitchen, and slowly down the basement steps.

"Feel like banging something?" she purred, giving her chest an extra little pop forward.

Only it wasn't Gary standing in the doorway — a fact that took Bren, and her exposed nipple, far too long to register.

"John!" she screeched, lurching backward.

"Oh!" he yelled, turning and covering his eyes with one hand.

The backward motion tipped the stool she was sitting on, and next thing Bren knew, she was crashing to the hard basement floor, flashing God knew what to Gary's best friend, who was not supposed to be there, by the way — the goddamned practice was canceled; hadn't he gotten the memo? Her foot kicked out, her heel slicing a hole clean through the bass drum, and her flailing arm knocked over a cymbal with an earsplitting crash.

"Get out, get out, get out!" she yelled, rolling around on the floor, trying to get herself righted and save as much of the drum set as she could from getting ruined. Gil was going to kill her. And would probably want a new seat when he found out what had been on it.

It took her a long moment to get herself sorted, and by the time she did, yanking the lapels of Gary's shirt together as she struggled to sit upright, John was gone, the sound of hurried footsteps and the front door slamming the only thing left in his wake.

If she hadn't been so mortified, and if her butt hadn't hurt so much from hitting the floor, she might have laughed.

As it stood, she could only sit on the floor miserably, taking in the damage she'd just caused, knowing that Gary was going to be livid to see the broken drum and bent cymbal, and at best what she could look forward to when he got home was fighting rather than lovemaking. Yet she couldn't help but wonder, above all else . . . What in the world had John been doing there in the first place?

CHAPTER SEVENTEEN

Gary hadn't been quite as outright furious as she'd been afraid he'd be. *What on earth were you thinking?* had come out of his mouth a record seventeen times, and twice he'd accused her of beating up Gil's drum set in a fit of jealous rage, but after that he'd seemed to mostly let it go.

He'd also turned right around and gotten into his car, mumbling something about owing Gilbert a new bass drum as he backed out of the driveway.

Not exactly the homecoming she'd been planning. Stupid John. Stupid John, who'd now seen her lady bits. Oh God, how would she ever face him again?

But all the fuss and mayhem had indeed killed those two extra hours she'd had, and soon Bren found herself standing in the Kitchen Classroom, giddily waiting for her students to arrive with their contributions to tonight's special class.

Tammy Lynn walked in first. "Gloves!" she sang, waving a pair of bright pink and green striped gloves over her head. They matched her outfit, which was far more spring in a color palette than winter. "And cookies on the way." She gestured outside, where Elwood was wrestling with a Tupperware container and the car door.

She dropped the gloves on Bren's station. "Oh, Bren, I think this is the best idea. To think, reaching out to combat ugliness with kindness. We should be on a viral video on the Internet, don't you think? How do you go viral? We should try it."

"I don't know about that," Bren said. "I'm not much of an Internet video type of person." Though she would be, if it meant she got to actually see her kids instead of just talk to them over the phone. But Kelsey was always claiming that Dean hadn't yet set up whatever something or other was necessary to make that happen, and old wild-night Kevin didn't even own a computer. Even though, in Bren's estimation, a computer could really make him feel at one and connected to the entire universe, without his having to make love on some strange beach she couldn't pronounce.

"Well, I think it's just fabulous. Maybe she'll have a change of heart and feel differently about us after she gets all warm and cozy," Tammy Lynn said.

"I wouldn't count on it," Aunt Cathy said, coming through the door with a cake pan and a plastic bag. She tossed the bag at Bren, missing her station by miles. It skidded across the floor and came to rest at the wall. "There's your scarf. Stayed up all night knitting it, and now my arthritis is acting up."

"You don't have arthritis, Catherine," Joan said, toddling behind her sister. "And you bought that scarf at the Walmart."

"How would you know?"

"I was with you, Miss Cranky." Joan bent to pick up the bag Cathy had dropped — which took a great deal of effort and grunting — and handed it, and another one, to Bren. "We got two, just in case she's the kind who likes to double up. And boots, just like you asked. And never mind your aunt there. She's just crabby because she missed *Wheel of Fortune* while we were at the store. You know how she is about Pat Sajak."

"I try not to think about it," Bren said.

"And all for that ungrateful cow, too," Aunt Cathy added. "Bet she won't even appreciate it. Ten bucks says we don't even get a thank-you card."

"Well, now, that's not why we're doing

this, Aunt Cathy," Bren said, pulling the scarves out of their bags and setting them on her station.

Lulu and Teresa came in, bringing with them what seemed like an entire kitchen, and a blanket.

"I could have gotten the ingredients for you," Bren said, rushing to hold the door.

"No, you wouldn't have gotten the right ones," Teresa said.

"How would you know what are the right ingredients to anything, Teresa?" Lulu scolded. "Two trays of taco meat in the trash in one day. What am I going to do? You're going to put the truck out of business." She shook her head. "What Teresa means is that we were already out buying *el edredón* for our friend upstairs." She pulled out a beautiful quilt.

Teresa ran her hand over the blanket, ignoring Lulu's complaints. "I have one just like it. It will keep her very warm." She shot a look at Lulu. "And you can't just guess at tamale ingredients. You might accidentally put too much cayenne into the meat."

Bren took the blanket to the front of the room with the other things. Rebecca had slipped in, unnoticed, while her back was turned, and had deposited a clutch of stocking caps on her station as well. They were all varying shades of brown.

"So how are we going to do this?" Tammy Lynn asked. She winked and nudged toward Bren's side with her elbow. "You know, make the drop?"

Aunt Cathy pumped one fist in the air. "We'll just go up there, knock on the door, and say, 'Here, maybe this will calm your crabby butt down.' "

Joan gasped. "Catherine! We will do no such thing."

"We can't very well just hand it to her and say nothing," Tammy Lynn said.

"That would seem very weird," Lulu agreed.

Bren carefully placed each new item in the giant gift bag she'd bought. At the bottom was the new coat she'd picked up earlier that day — fluffy, turquoise, knee-length, warm. Expensive.

Bren had thought about the delivery many times, actually. And she'd considered so many possibilities for how it could go. They could drop it and doorbell ditch, just like kids, although the thought of her mother and Aunt Cathy racing down a flight of stairs seemed laughable, if not altogether terrifying. They could wait for her to come in to complain and present it to her then. Bren had even considered burning some popcorn real quick to get her downstairs. But she wasn't sure if that was the best time to give someone a gift — right in the middle of their yelling at you. She'd even imagined them knocking on her door and singing a sweet Christmas carol — probably "The Little Drummer Boy," because, well, obviously — before presenting her with the gift. But there was nothing about that old woman that suggested she would appreciate such a gesture on any level.

"Anonymous," Rebecca said, and everyone turned to stare at her.

"Did she just say something, or is my hearing aid on the blink again?" Aunt Cathy stage-whispered to Joan. Joan shushed her.

Rebecca gave her only the slightest glance and then continued. "It needs to be anonymous. She's a proud person — we can tell that much already. If we try to just give it to her, she'll refuse it. Leave it as an anonymous gift. Bren, you should take it."

There were murmurs affirming what Rebecca had just said, and Bren nodded. This also had been a scenario she had toyed with. Leaving the bag after they were done for the night, and just letting it sit there until the woman found it the next day.

"Okay, done," she said. "Now. Who's hungry for tamales, cookies, and cake?"

CHAPTER EIGHTEEN

Those dumb cooking bimbos had been in high spirits last night, that was for sure. They'd kept her up until nine o'clock with their giggling and their thumping around and their car engines. Even Chuy had rested only half as well as usual. He'd gotten up and shifted positions at least three times.

It didn't help that she had this damn cold. She hated colds. The fact that she was still getting them made no sense whatsoever. She couldn't remember the last time she'd had personal contact with anyone. She never even let anyone touch her cane.

She'd probably picked it up just by stepping inside that godforsaken class. There were what, six of them in there? All with their germs flying right out of their flapping gums and hanging in the air, just waiting for an unsuspecting victim. The very idea of eating anything cooked in that petri dish made her want to puke.

She would be fine. She knew that much. The world was too cruel for this cough to be anything more serious than a cold, what with how long she'd been waiting to meet her Maker, and whomever else happened to be hanging out with Him. She had some guesses who. It was a real party up there. A corker. Something these cooking bimbos knew nothing about. So she would be fine, but in the meantime, she felt certain she was going to cough up her toenails, and standing outside in the slush the wet snow had left behind seemed like courting disaster. She'd taken Chuy out only once, in the morning, and after coughing for a solid twenty minutes after, had given in to letting him go on paper inside the apartment. Made for a stinky day, but she was so congested she didn't care anyway.

And because she wasn't leaving the apartment, she'd had to just let those cooking bimbos party away. She'd watched them as they trickled out, each of them carrying pans and yelling at one another to have a good weekend. One — the really loud one with the really loud husband — had a strand of red garland wrapped around her head like a sorority girl. She'd overheard that one getting yelled at once by someone who seemed to be her very fit daughter. Virginia had pretended she hadn't heard a thing, but she'd been witness to all of it. It was embarrassing, and she thought she could even see the glimmer of a tear in the woman's eye. She felt sorry for her in that moment. Wanted to shake the daughter, tell her to appreciate her mother while she was still around. *Life is too short to fight,* she wanted to say, but then she remembered that she didn't really believe that fully. Life was about fighting, and she intended to be the winner. If you didn't fight, you ended up alone.

Worse. If you didn't fight, you left other people alone.

She never did see the head bimbo — the fat cook — leave. She must have snuck out when Virginia wasn't looking.

Despite having been kept up until all hours of the night from that fuss (she made a mental note to include that phrase — *that fuss* — in her next letter to Buckley Finster, attorney-at-law), somehow she'd managed to get enough rest to feel better this morning.

Which was good, because Chuy was a sophisticated man who didn't appreciate having to do his business on the sports section any more than he absolutely had to. He was practically jumping in circles at the front door.

"Okay, okay," she said. "Hold your fur, would ya?"

She dressed in a pair of red sweatpants and a green flannel shirt — her one begrudging nod to the upcoming holiday — and stuffed her feet into gym socks and her old brown loafers, the ones Ernie would have called her *sensibly hideous shoes.*

It was cold out there. She could tell just by looking at the sky. The snow was turning to slush, yes, but overnight it would freeze again and again and never really go anywhere, except to form smooth, treacherous patches of ice. She would have to be careful. The last thing she needed was to fall and break something. Who would take care of old Chuy if she was laid up in traction?

She had a promise to live up to. A promise to give old Chuy her undying care, and she intended to keep it.

"Let's go," she said, pulling Chuy's leash from its hook by the front door. He squirmed with excitement. Or rather writhed in what was a close arthritic approximation of excitement. "Calm down, now. You're no spring chicken. You're getting too old for all those acrobatics."

She was so busy talking to Chuy, she almost fell ass over teakettle on top of a giant bag that was sitting at her front door.

"What in the world?" she asked.

Chuy barked at the bag, then lifted his leg and peed on the wall next to it. He'd reached his waiting limit. Ah well, at least he was sort of outside.

She bent to peer into the bag. All she could see was color. Bright color in patches and stripes and swatches. And cloth. Lots of cloth.

She looked left and right, and, of course, there was nobody to be seen. The stairs led only to her apartment. Whoever had left this here, had left it for her.

"Change of plans, Chuy," she said. She tossed her cane back into the apartment and used her free hand to drag the bag inside, too. Slowly, methodically, she pulled out its contents — a hat, two scarves, a pair of gloves, a coat, a blanket, boots.

She stood by her couch, eyeing the things she'd just laid on it, her arms folded across her chest. Chuy barked once more, then seemed worn-out and lay down on the blanket, his thoughts of a walk chased away by thoughts of getting in a quick snooze.

Someone had given her these things as if she were some sort of charity case. As if she were in need.

Well, she was in need, all right, but what

she needed they couldn't very well give her, now, could they? And a coat, of all things. Gloves. Scarves. Did it ever occur to anyone that maybe some people had vowed off such things for a reason? Maybe they'd worn their last coat because that was what they wanted. Because that was what was right.

"Well, I can't take them," she said to Chuy, though he was sound asleep. "But I know damn well what I can do with them."

She rebagged everything — upending Chuy from his spot on the blanket, causing him to give her quite the accusatory glare — and placed the bag by the front door.

Chapter Nineteen

Bren had hoped that her high from the potluck class would have stuck with her long enough to get her through the next day. But it didn't. She drove to her mother's house, absently scratching her shoulder while she drove.

Joan's eyes lit up when Bren walked into the kitchen. "Well, what a surprise! I wasn't expecting you."

"I wasn't expecting me, either," Bren said, sitting across from her at the table.

"Let me call Catherine. I'll get a pot on."

Bren reached across the table. "No, there's no time for that. I've already had my coffee anyway. I was hoping you'd want to come with me today."

Her mother's hands clamped tight around her coffee mug. She was already dressed for the day, bright and early, as she always was, humming the birds awake. "Where are we going?"

Bren wanted to tell her. She really did. Just like she wanted to tell Gary, and maybe even Kelsey (but not wild-time-in-Rome Kevin, because, really, would he even care?). She maybe even wanted to tell Rosa, despite the rhinestones and yoga pants. But so far the only person she could tell had been Nan, and only because Nan had noticed her scratching, had noticed the spot on her shoulder, and had insisted that she wouldn't cut another strand of hair until Bren fessed up. And she'd told her doctor, of course, although all he'd done was promptly lateral her off to the R. Monte Belle Cancer Treatment Center. A cancer center. Where people with cancer went. *Just for testing,* he'd said, but how did someone not get freaked out about having to have anything done — even if it was *just a little testing* — in a cancer center?

She'd put off making the appointment. And then rescheduled it. Twice. And then the news about Kelsey not coming home and Kevin's little bombshell, and the class, and it had become easy to forget that *just a little testing* was necessary in her life. But the itch. It was always there. Always reminding her.

She couldn't put it off anymore. What if she died before she could work up the courage to go in?

But telling all of this to her mother proved impossible. Joan was so fragile, so frail, her face so open and kind and loving. It always had been. She'd been a great mother. Always there for Bren, with open arms, open heart. Bren literally could not think of one time in her entire life that her mother was too busy to attend to her. Truth be told, she was a way better mother than Bren herself was.

Knowing Bren had this problem would upset her. Knowing it had gone on so long without Bren's telling her would hurt her. Knowing what it could possibly mean would frighten her.

But Bren needed her mommy.

"Christmas shopping," she lied, opting to buy herself some more time before spilling. "You up for it? I also have to run a quick errand I hope you'll go with me to, if that's okay."

"Oh, sure, sure," her mother said, jumping into action, pulling her sweater closed over her shoulders and taking her mug to the sink. "I need to get a canister of popcorn for the mailman. I forget him every single year. How can I forget him every year? He never forgets me. Not for one day."

"He's sort of paid to remember you, Mom."

"A paycheck is not a thank-you."

"Well, it kind of is."

"A thank-you is a canister of popcorn."

Bren knew her mother. When her mind was made up, there was no changing it.

"Then to the mall it is."

So they braved the mall the week before Christmas, something Bren wouldn't do on a normal year. She'd had to drop her mother off at the door and park all the way out in the Chili's parking lot, halfway on a curb, and pray that nobody towed her. Of course, if someone towed her, she would miss her appointment. Silver lining.

There was a choral group singing "Gloria" in the middle of the food court, their voices drowning out the sounds of the cash registers and blenders and cappuccino machines and the food court workers hawking free samples as people way too stressed out about their checkbooks and their lists blew past them without so much as a glance.

Bren checked her watch roughly every ten seconds as they bought tins of popcorn for each of their mail carriers, a Precious Moments doctor statuette for Joan's endocrinologist, candles for the chiropractor and the podiatrist, and boxes of sausages for every nurse Joan had ever come into contact with. Even Bren got suckered into picking up a box of chocolates for her dentist, whom she wouldn't even see until the end of February. Not to mention, what dentist appreciated a box full of sugar for a gift?

Even after all that shopping, and the requisite standing awkwardly in front of the choral group, smiling appreciatively, there were still two hours until her appointment. She couldn't take it.

"You hungry, Mom?"

Her mother checked her watch. "It's only eleven."

"Lunchtime. I'm starving. Come on. You in the mood for pizza or baked potatoes?"

"Neither. It's still morning."

"Chinese food it is."

Bren led her mother to Asian Matters, a trendy fast-food Chinese restaurant that specialized in sweet-and-sour everything. Bren ordered pork and chicken, a bowl of lo mein, and two egg rolls. And a coffee for Joan.

"How can you eat lunch so early?" her mother asked, sitting in the same posture she was in at the house — hands wrapped protectively around her coffee cup, shoulders hunched, placid look of tranquility on her face.

"Well, I haven't killed my gut with twenty gallons of coffee," Bren answered, biting into an egg roll, which squirted a stream of grease into her mouth. Guilt, guilt, guilt. When she dropped dead of a heart attack, and Gary was left to find her, she would have nothing to blame but her love of sweet cabbagey grease.

"Is there something bothering you, Bren? You seem on edge lately. Not your usual sunny self. Is it the kids?"

Bren took a bite of lo mein and chewed. "It's everything, Mom," she said. "It's the kids, it's Gary, it's the class, it's this." She stared down at her tray of food. If she looked around the food court, she could see that nobody else was eating like she was. This was embarrassing, what she was doing to herself.

"What's going on?" her mother asked, placing her hand on top of Bren's. "Something's wrong with Kelsey?"

Bren sighed. "Not Kelsey. She's fine." Beautifully *fine, in fact,* she thought. "But Kevin may be married."

Joan sat back, her eyes wide, blinking, her mouth hanging slightly open. "What do you mean, 'may be'?"

"He doesn't even know for sure. Something about a wild night in Rome. How wild can it get when the Pope is right there? I mean, a wild night in Rome is accidentally drinking too much wine and maybe jumping into a fountain, right? It's not accidentally marrying someone your parents have never spoken to."

"You don't know the girl? Who is it?"

Pavy. And the others. "Her name is Pavlina. He met her somewhere in the Czech Republic. Or maybe it was Russia. Or . . ." She wadded up her napkin and tossed it into her remaining lo mein, suddenly too disgusted to eat. "Or the Congo, for all I know. I have no earthly idea where he even met the girl. Where did I go wrong?"

"Oh, honey," Joan said. "You didn't go wrong. You raised independent kids who aren't afraid to go out and live lives and make mistakes. That's what you're supposed to do, right? That's being a successful parent."

Bren shook her head. "But why do they have to be so independent from so far away?"

"They'll come back."

"How do you know?"

Joan smiled, a nostalgic smile. "Because I have a couple of independent kids myself. Remember your brother going away to college on the East Coast? It felt so far away, and I was sure he'd get attached and stay there forever. He met Kelly there, and I thought, *This is it. I've lost him.* But here they are, right back home, twenty minutes away." *AmIright?* Bren thought. "And you sowed your oats, too. But you came back. And now I'm so proud of you. You raised these amazing kids, you're a successful teacher, you've got Gary."

Bren grimaced. "I wish I could agree with you on a couple of those things." She reached under the napkin and picked at a noodle, snapping a piece off and putting it in her mouth.

"There are problems with Gary?"

Bren shrugged, petulant. "We'll be fine, I'm sure. But right now he seems a million miles away. Like he could be having a wild night in Rome and I wouldn't even know about it. I'm pretty sure he'd rather be having a wild night in Rome than ever be with me."

"Be patient. Being empty nesters takes time to get used to."

"You and Daddy didn't seem to have any trouble adjusting."

Joan's smile deepened. "That's because that's what we wanted you to think. All I have to say is thank goodness Catherine moved in right across the street, and thank goodness she always had plenty of gin on hand."

Bren chuckled, then pulled her half-eaten egg roll out from under the napkin and ate it, feeling better about her vice, knowing that her mother had vices, too.

"Brenda? What else?" Joan was looking concerned now. Her mother could always tell when she wasn't being entirely honest. And she could always tell when something was wrong. Not just with her, but with her brother as well. It seemed the woman was forever bursting into a room a half a second before they broke something valuable and was already rushing toward them before they managed to get hurt. Bren thought of it as her mother's superpower.

"Okay," Bren said. "I actually have some-place else I want you to go with me today. It's a doctor appointment. At the cancer center."

Joan blanched but didn't say a word, which for some reason scared and upset Bren even more. She took a bite of sweet-and-sour chicken, feeling tears prickle the corners of her eyes while she chewed.

"How bad is it?" Joan finally said.

"It's this," she said around the food, and pulled the collar of her sweater to the side. Joan squinted at her shoulder, then got up, moved around the table, leaned in, and squinted harder.

"Why, it's just a mole," Joan said.

"But it itches. And now it's sore from all the scratching."

"So stop scratching it."

Bren let go of her collar. "It's not that simple, Mom. Women my age can't just get new moles."

Joan made her way back to her seat. "Why the hell not?"

"Because." Bren rolled her eyes, picked up her fork, removed the napkin, and went back to town on the Chinese food. "Because women my age get cancer, not moles."

"It's not even a big mole."

"That doesn't make any difference!"

"Sure it does. What did your doctor have to say about it?"

"He said to get my ass to the cancer center. You don't think I would just decide to take myself there, do you?" Actually, she kind of had. What her doctor said wasn't so much *Get your ass to the cancer center.* It was more along the lines of *It looks like a mole, but if you're that concerned about it, you can have it followed up on by a specialist.*

Which, in Bren's mind, was basically the same as *Get your ass to the cancer center.* Okay, in Bren's mind it was *Get your ass to the cancer center before you die, die, diiieee.*

But Joan didn't need to know any of that.

There was a pause, and then, to Bren's surprise, her mother began to giggle. She held her coffee cup in front of her mouth, presumably to hide how funny she thought Bren's immediate demise was, closed her eyes, and laughed.

"I'm glad you think it's so funny," Bren said, scooping the last few grains of rice off her plate. "You've been hanging around Aunt Cathy too long." And when her mother kept laughing, added, "Who does this? Who laughs about having to take her daughter to an oncologist?"

"I'm sorry, I'm sorry," Joan said. She took a sip of her coffee and pulled her sweater up over her shoulders again. "I'm not laughing at you. I'm just . . . well, you had me worried."

"That's a fine way of showing it," Bren pouted. She got up and tossed her trash into the bin behind their table.

"Oh, don't be so pouty, Brenda," Joan said. "I'm sorry. Of course I'll go with you. And I promise not to laugh. Let's go."

Bren wanted to be a nervous wreck in the waiting room. She wanted to be chewing her fingernails to nubs and growing pit

291

stains on her shirt and pacing a hole into the carpet. But her mother had robbed her of all of that with her laughter. Now she felt relaxed and as if there was most likely nothing to worry about. Damn that woman.

The lobby was hot — overcompensating for yet another incoming winter storm that Aunt Cathy's favorite weatherman was predicting. This one was supposed to dump as much as three inches on them. Oh, how Bren of yesteryear would have been excited about this. If the weather kept up this way, it would be a white Christmas. Heaven. Was there anything more peaceful than a snowy Christmas Eve? Any better proof that God did exist, and He was good?

The lobby Christmas tree was small and nondescript, decorated with angels, each one bearing a name. Bren hated to think what that meant, although she was pretty sure she knew exactly what it meant. She tried not to look at the other patients awaiting their turns. So many of them children, playing despite the obviously serious path their lives had now taken. Instead, she watched the small TV mounted high up on the wall in the corner by the reception's desk — Martha Stewart making something out of pinecones. She couldn't follow along, because the sound had been turned all the way down to make way for the Christmas music droning over the loudspeaker. "The Little Drummer Boy." Of course.

The nurse who rescued Bren from the waiting room was full of small talk — *Are you traveling for the holidays? Do you make a big dinner? What do you think about this weather?* — and barely peeked at Bren's shoulder before whisking out of the exam room, as if she had never been in there at all. Bren tried to read her expression but could tell nothing about the direness of her situation from the nurse's face. Maybe that meant it was really bad.

Joan sat in a chair in the corner of the exam room, thumbing through an ancient *People* magazine, while Bren sat on the table, wondering why no one had given her a gown. Surely once the doctor saw that she had this . . . *lesion* on her skin, he would want to see everything. To look for how far it had spread.

But, no. It turned out he didn't. He asked her a few questions, dug a magnifying glass out of his coat pocket, leaned over her shoulder, poked her skin a few times, then kicked his little rolling stool back a few feet, and said, "Looks like a mole."

Joan snickered, but when Bren shot her a look, she was bent over the *People* magazine again, looking very interested in an article about Ben Affleck. Bren knew for a fact that Joan had no idea who Ben Affleck even was; she was just trying to keep her eyes down. Smart lady.

"That's it?" Bren asked, knowing she should feel relieved, but instead feeling slightly irritated. This was how people ended up on those prime-time news shows. *I went to doctor after doctor, and nobody took me seriously. And now look, my nose is gone. Fell off right in the middle of the grocery store. Right in front of the Pop-Tarts.* "Shouldn't you, like, test it or something? It didn't exist before. And it itches."

He touched her shoulder again with his rubber-gloved fingers. "You have a little bit of dry skin here. That's probably what's causing the itching. You have a patch on the bottom of your chin as well. Has it been itching?"

She hadn't really noticed it — she'd been so concentrating on the itchy cancer cells eating her shoulder — but now that she thought about it, yes.

"I'll prescribe you some cream for the dry skin. And we can remove the mole if you wish. We can even biopsy it, I suppose. Or you can leave it be and keep an eye on it. If it changes, gets bigger, gets painful, irregularly shaped, that kind of thing, come on back. But I've seen a million moles, and I'm telling you this is no mole to be worried about."

"Are you sure you don't want to look at it again? Maybe a little closer this time?"

He gave her one of those *I would humor you, but no* head tilts. He scribbled onto a prescription pad and then ripped off the top page and handed it to her. "You can schedule a removal date at the front desk."

She held the paper in her hand, staring at the door for a long moment after he left.

"Not a word," she said to her mother, who snickered again.

"Oh, come on, don't be so sore about it, Brenda. It's good news. Don't you feel so much better?"

She thought about all these months of worrying and hiding, scratching and contemplating what the world would be like after her death. All the stress, all the fear. And the man hadn't even done much more than give it a cursory glance through a magnifying glass. It just didn't seem right. It was too quick. If she'd had test results to wait for — maybe for a few days or even a few weeks — the relief would be bigger.

"I guess. Let's go," she said.

She didn't even bother to make a removal

appointment.

"I can't believe he was so rude. Did he seem rude to you? He seemed rude. A quack. I should probably make an appointment for a second opinion," Bren was saying as she and Joan walked across the parking lot. "From someone less rude. Someone who knows you can't just tell something is cancer by looking at it; you have to —"

Had the dog not barked, she might not have even noticed it. But just as she was getting ready to open her car door, she heard a familiar yap, ringing out across the parking lot. She knew that bark well. She'd heard it in her nightmares. Nightmares where Aunt Cathy starts gagging on imagined allergies and someone gets a wad of fur lodged in their turducken skin.

"No way," she said aloud, and hurried into the car. She slid down in the front seat, but not so far down that she couldn't keep an eye on the old woman and her dachshund, who were just entering the parking lot from the sidewalk. "What the hell?"

"Just leave me behind, why don't you," Joan was saying, taking her sweet time lowering herself into the passenger seat.

Bren waved frantically for her mom to sit down. "Get in here. Don't you see her?"

"See who? My goodness, you are strange

today. I think you need a vacation. Maybe instead of a second opinion on that mole, you need to make an appointment with a psychiatrist."

"Her," Bren said, pointing through the window.

They both stared as Virginia Mash made her way across the parking lot, leaning heavily on her cane, Chuy barking up a storm as he lagged slightly behind her. In one hand, Virginia Mash carried the gift bag Bren had left on her doorstep.

"Good Lord, is that the woman from the cooking class?"

"Yes," Bren said, realizing she was whispering, but not knowing exactly why. It wasn't like Virginia Mash could hear her even if she was speaking full voice. "She must have walked all this way."

"And without a coat. She should be freezing. It has to be twenty degrees outside. Didn't we give her a coat?"

"Yes," Bren said again, seething. Really, did the old woman hate them so much that she couldn't even accept a gift from them? Was she so ugly, inside and out, that a gesture of kindness would be rebuked? "I ought to ask her to give it back, the ungrateful old jerk."

But no more were the words out of her

mouth than she saw Virginia Mash stop as a child came out of the building. The old woman bent and talked to the child and the child's mother for a long time, and it didn't look like she was ranting or yelling or being rude in any way. After a bit, she reached into her bag and pulled out the stocking cap that Rebecca had donated. The child pulled off her bandana to reveal a gleaming scalp beneath. Smiling, she allowed Virginia Mash to pull the cap over her head. They ended with a hug, and the child and her mother went to their car, happy looks on their faces.

"Did you see that?" Bren whispered.

"I did. I don't believe what I saw, but I saw it," her mother answered.

They sat there for a while longer — just long enough to see Virginia drape her new quilt over a man leaving the building in a wheelchair.

Bren could barely believe it. The woman wasn't wearing her coat, but it wasn't a spiteful thing. It was a pay-it-forward thing. And she looked like she was enjoying it.

What Bren couldn't figure out was why.

CHAPTER TWENTY

Gary looked like he would rather be just about anywhere else. The DMV? A prostate exam? Holding Bren's purse outside the ladies' fitting room at Macy's? All of the above.

But Bren didn't care. He'd promised for better or for worse, and if worse for him was a table for two at Olive Garden, so be it.

"Stop pulling on that thing," she said, splitting a breadstick in half. She laid both halves on her plate and scooped up a huge portion of salad, making sure she took both black olives. Gary didn't like olives. Didn't even like them to be touching his plate. It was one of the unspoken understandings of their marriage that Bren would always eat the olives. Sacrifice.

He yanked on his tie once again, making a face. "I don't see why I had to wear it. People are in jeans here."

"*People* may be, but we're not. It's supposed to be a nice date, Gary. Can't we just have one nice date? Gil went to *The Nutcracker,* for Pete's sake. Ballet. Besides, you wear a tie to work every day. What's the big deal? Here." She scooped salad onto his plate.

He shook out his napkin angrily. "The big deal *is* that I wear one to work every day. At night I like to come home and relax, not come home and relive the workday."

Bren bit into one of the breadstick halves, trying maintain her light attitude. "Well, hopefully having dinner with me isn't that much work," she said sweetly. She considered kicking off her pumps under the table and running a bare foot up his leg. Of course, she mostly wanted to kick them off because they hurt her feet. At least Gary was accustomed to wearing his getup. She was cramming sneaker feet into sex heels. It wasn't a pretty picture. She tried changing the subject. Maybe life at the telecom farm, where Gary'd been working since Kelsey was in elementary school, would be a safer bet. Until recently, he'd seemed to be an endless font of corporate triumphs and complaints. Lately, though, mum had been the word. "How is work going, anyway? You hardly ever talk about it anymore." Translation: *you hardly ever talk to me at all anymore.*

Gary set his fork on his plate of untouched salad. "That's because I don't want to talk about work. These are my twilight years, Bren. I want to have a little fun."

"I couldn't agree more," she said, the sweetness in her voice getting an edge. "I want to have fun, too. Breadstick?" She turned the basket toward him. He angrily snatched a breadstick out of the paper.

"And getting all dressed up to eat pasta on a Wednesday night is fun?" He mumbled this to himself, almost as if he were cracking a joke that only he would think was funny.

"Well, for me it is," she said. "I don't see what's so damn fun about murdering Christmas songs in your basement all night long. How about that?" As she'd predicted, he flinched, stunned. She raised her eyebrows in a challenge. *Want to be sour? We can both play at that game.*

"We're coming together just fine," he said.

"I suppose," Bren countered, biting into her breadstick again. "If you call making 'Jingle Bells' unrecognizable and forcing stray animals into hiding *just fine.*"

Gary's eyebrows drew together and he bent forward over the table. "Well, it's better than killing strays with the scraps from your failed food experiments."

Bren's mouth hung open. She really had no response for that. He may be deluded enough to think his band was good, but she couldn't even pretend for a moment that her classes were going well. Not that he knew the first thing about her classes. He'd never even bothered to ask.

"It's about more than cooking," she said.

"Yes," he agreed. "It's about trying not to kill your students or burn the place down, I would guess."

"Gary Stephen!" Bren practically shouted. The couple at the next table glanced over at them. Bren sat up straighter and smiled, fussing with the sleeves of her dress as if nothing had happened. When they finally looked away, she narrowed her eyes at her husband again. "I have been cooking for you for decades, and you have never once complained. I have raised two children off of my cooking, and never has there been a problem. Now, just because you want your so-called twilight years — which you can't really claim until you're at least retired, by the way — to be all about reliving your youth, you think anything refined is some-how bad. But I'm refined, Gary. Or at least I want to be. And if you want to be with me, well, then I guess you want to be refined, too."

"At the moment, I want to be with my band. They understand what it's like to be me. Which you clearly don't. If you did, you wouldn't be making me wear this." He stuck his fingers behind the knot of his tie, loosened it, and pulled it over his head, flinging it so it landed in the salad bowl of the table next to them. The same staring couple stared again.

"Oh my God, I'm so sorry," Bren said.

"These breadsticks really make your hands slippery," Gary added jovially, wiggling his fingers at them. They fished the tie out of their bowl and held it across the aisle until Bren sheepishly took it.

"I'm so sorry," she said again.

The waiter arrived with their entrees, which created a stir of plate wrangling, since they had hardly touched their salads. He grated some cheese onto Bren's plate and then left them to silently pick at their dinners.

After a while, Bren couldn't take it anymore. "Kevin got married," she said. She saw Gary stop chewing momentarily and glance up at her, surprise registering.

"What?"

She nodded. "And Kelsey knew about it. They kept us in the dark. But it happened in Rome. Maybe. And I'm not sure when."

He seemed to consider this, his eyes taking on a faraway look. Finally, Bren could see him flick the surprise away. So easy. "I see."

"That's it? You see?"

He nodded. "He's married. I see."

"Well, what are you going to do?" Bren asked. "You're the boy's father."

He took another bite of lasagna and chewed it maddeningly slowly, then picked up his napkin and dabbed at his lips. "What *can* I do about it? He's not a boy anymore. He's halfway around the world. Am I supposed to storm to Thailand and ground him?" His shoulders had crept up around his ears. "What are you going to do? You're the boy's mother."

"Aren't you even curious who she is? Or what happened? Or when?"

He shrugged. "I'm assuming she's someone I don't know. And what does the rest even matter with him there and us here?"

"It matters, Gary, because your eighteen-year-old son is now a husband to someone who may not even speak English. What if she wants to live in Europe? What if they have kids that we never meet? Or . . . or what if she breaks his heart? Gives him a disease? Robs him blind and leaves him for dead in Asia? Don't you care about those things, Gary?"

"Of course I care about them. But you said it yourself. He's eighteen. He's eight thousand miles away. I'll try to talk some sense into him when he calls next, but otherwise, my hands are just as tied as yours."

Bren stared at her husband, everything about him suddenly becoming unfamiliar. The way he chewed. The calluses on his fingers. His thick fingernails and the gray hairs in his eyebrows. When did his lips become that color? When did he start parting his hair on that side? What happened to the man she married, the one she'd thought she knew from top to bottom and inside out?

"How can you say that? Any number of things can happen between now and the next time he calls. He's your son, Gary. Your family. Have you forgotten about us entirely?"

"Of course not. You're being dramatic now."

There were a lot of things Bren hated, and being called dramatic was one of them. Gary knew this. He knew that words like *dramatic* and *irrational* and *hysterical* would trip her switch.

"Fine," she said. She wiped her mouth with her napkin, even though she really hadn't eaten anything. "I'm dramatic. But I'm also lonely, Gary, and that's definitely your problem."

"Then do something about it."

"I'm trying to," she cried, gesturing at the table. "What do you think this is about?" She could feel tears coming on again. "I almost died of cancer, and you didn't even know."

This got his attention. He froze, his fork poised over his plate. "What?"

"Well, it was technically just a mole, but I had to take my mother with me to the appointment, because you weren't there for me."

"A mole?" His temple pulsated as he ingested this news, working bits of food in his jaw. "Like, a melanoma?"

"No, it was just a regular mole, but that's not the point."

"You scared me to death. Dammit, Bren, that was low."

She knew it was. She already regretted it, but a part of her was a little happy, too, to know that the thought of losing her was still scary to him. "I'm sorry," she said, casting her eyes down toward the tablecloth. "But I wouldn't have said it if I didn't feel like I needed to say or do something major to get your attention."

"Well, you got my attention, all right." The waiter wandered near the table and Gary gestured him over. "A couple of boxes and the check, please?" The waiter scurried off and Gary turned to Bren. "I'm done."

"Wait. *Done* done? With us?"

The waiter set the check and a couple of mints in front of Gary. "Thank you. Done with this dinner. There you go, being dramatic again."

Swiftly, the quickest Bren had seen him do anything for quite some time, Gary paid the check and boxed their leftovers. He did so wordlessly, then picked up his tie and stormed away from the table, not even waiting to see if Bren was following him.

The drive home was silent, a talk radio show babbling in the background. Bren cried softly as she stared out the window. It had been strange between the two of them for some time. That much she knew. But this was more than strange. This was more than strained. This was worrisome.

"Gary?" she asked when he pulled into the driveway.

He turned to her. She could see the anger still on his face.

"Are we going to make it?"

He stared at her for a long time. "Yes, of course we are. You're being really unreasonable these days. I think it's best if we just don't try to talk tonight. I'm going to call the guys," he said.

He started to get out of the car, but she stopped him, placing her hand over the keys. "Leave them," she said. "I'm going to get dessert."

If she was overdressed for Olive Garden, she was definitely overdressed for Ice Dreamery, a mom-and-pop ice-cream shop tucked on a side street two blocks off the square. A team of elementary school–aged basketball players was tearing up three booths in the back, the noise deafening. Bren sat at a nearby table, smiling wistfully at them, missing the days of shushing her own kids in public. Man, in the moment it seemed like those days would never end, like she would never get a break. But now, what she would give to have those days back. They weren't so bad, these kids. They were just being kids. Excited. Energetic.

She'd ordered the Three Heifer Dream, the biggest sundae on the menu. Three oversized scoops of ice cream, loaded with hot fudge, peanut butter sauce, caramel, chocolate chips, pecans, whipped cream, and a heavenly four maraschino cherries. If you were confident enough — or had given up on yourself enough — to step up and order a dessert with the word *heifer* right in it, the payoff was entirely worth it. Bren could make that sundae last half an hour, the bottom a soupy mixture of wonderful by the time she reached it. She sometimes walked away feeling as if she might need to lie down for a while, but it was a blissful misery.

Tonight she needed that bliss. She already had the misery. She wondered if she and Gary had maybe finally gone too far. If it was more than a cafeteria dinner for the holidays and more than dune buggies and lonely cheese toast dinners. She wondered if maybe they'd been broken for a long time now, and she'd just always been so focused on the kids that she hadn't noticed it.

Don't forget to have a life of your own, Bren, her mother had told her often when the kids were young. *You need a job or a hobby or something, because these kids will be grown up before you know it, and if you've devoted your life only to them, you won't even know where to start.* Bren supposed her mother spoke from experience, but she'd always just assumed Gary would fill in those empty spaces once the kids were grown.

She must have been wrong.

Gary didn't seem interested in filling anything.

The basketball team got up and whooped and hollered their way out. The three booths they left behind looked as if they'd been hit by a bomb. Ice cream, napkin shreds, empty cups, straw wrappers everywhere. A hapless teenager in an Ice Dreamery uniform came out with a rag, shoulders drooping, muttering, "You have got to be kidding me," over and over again. Bren had half a mind to help the poor kid clean up.

Alone, without even the rowdy crowd noise to distract her, Bren checked her watch. It was nearly nine o'clock. Flurries had begun falling outside. Someone in the back turned up the music — "The Little Drummer Boy."

Ice Dreamery would be closing soon, and she would have to go. They probably couldn't wait for her to finish up so they could start shutting things down. After all, what kind of crazy nut goes out for ice cream in the snow a week before Christmas? *Just me,* Bren thought.

The door opened. *Okay, just me and one other crazy, desperate nut.*

The other woman — large, bundled up as if she were heading for a month in the

Arctic, ordered a Three Heifer Dream. Bren thought she recognized the voice. But it wasn't until the clerk handed the woman her ice cream and she turned to leave that Bren put a brightly colored face to the name.

"Tammy Lynn?" The woman stopped, turned. Bren waved. "Hi." She held up her nearly empty plastic tub. "Like minds, I guess."

Tammy Lynn bounded toward her. "Oh, Elwood thinks I'm crazy going out for ice cream like this. Crazy for ice cream, he means." She threw her head back and laughed. The motion knocked her coat hood right off her head, revealing a mess of unruly, staticky brown curls. She dug into her sundae. "Look at you, all dressed up. Big night?"

Bren shrugged, turned her eyes toward her lap. "Was supposed to be, but things didn't exactly work out as planned. You?"

Tammy Lynn took another bite of sundae. She had a dot of whipped cream above her upper lip. "I'm sort of hiding. You remember Janelle, my daughter?" Bren nodded. "She's just bound and determined that we are to lose weight. Isn't going to rest until we take off a cool buck between us — that's what she says. She means a hundred pounds. A hundred, can you believe it? We can't lose all that. We'll starve."

"That's a lot," Bren agreed. "I can't imagine."

"Thing is, she's right. As much as I hate to admit it. I'm sick of every ache and pain I have explained away by my doctor as being because of my weight. Even though she's probably right about most of it. And I'm sick of aches and pains. But, oh, Bren, I hate dieting. And I love ice cream; what can I say?"

Bren looked down into the bottom of her pail. All that was left was a brownish liquid, the dregs of melted deliciousness. The rest of it sat disagreeably in her stomach. She hiccupped. "I totally understand."

"Anyway, Janelle actually had plans tonight for a change that didn't involve harassing us about cholesterol or going for a quick run. So I came here. Did you know that when you run in this weather, your nostril hairs freeze and feel all crunchy up in there?" She wrinkled her nose. "I hate it."

Bren couldn't help laughing. There was something about Tammy Lynn that was so forthright and honest. Something good in her.

"You want to hear something shocking?" Bren asked.

"I love shocking," Tammy Lynn said around a mouthful of ice cream. "Lay it on me."

So Bren told her about seeing the old woman and her dog at the cancer center. She told her about the woman still not wearing a coat, and giving away the cap and the quilt to patients of the center. Tammy Lynn's eyes grew rounder and rounder as she listened.

"How strange. How can someone be so hateful one minute and do something so kind the next? You don't suppose it was a passive-aggressive thing, like she was giving it away because someone gave it to her out of kindness?"

Bren leaned over and tossed her cup into the trash. The teen employee had finished up the three booths and was now going through the dining room with a broom, every so often giving Bren and Tammy Lynn pointed *get out* looks. "I suppose that's possible, but why?"

"Wouldn't it be something if we left gifts on her doorstep every day?" Tammy Lynn said, laughing. "Then we'd find out if she was doing it just to spite us, wouldn't we?" She had reached the end of her sundae and tipped it up to drink the remains from the bottom. "My grandma always said you could kill ugly with kindness."

"Mine, too," Bren said, but she was already lost deep in thought. She'd seen the way the woman had looked when she'd given that child the stocking cap. It wasn't spite. It was satisfaction. It was maybe even pride. Happiness?

"We'd probably kill her if we left stuff there every day." Tammy Lynn sighed, peering into her cup. "I wish they made a Four Heifer Dream. If you're gonna cheat, might as well go big, right?" Bren didn't answer; she was still staring off in space. "Hello? Earth to Bren. Is something wrong?"

Bren blinked, came to life. "You know, what if you're right?"

"I love being right. But about what?"

"About the old woman. What if we left her gifts every day? What if we killed her with kindness? I mean, not literally kill her. But even if she is giving them away through anger, they're still going to a good place, right?"

Tammy Lynn shook her head like she didn't quite understand where this was going. "I guess."

"We have, what, seven days until Christmas?"

"Don't remind me. I'm not done shopping."

Bren snapped her fingers. "One hundred gifts." She turned excitedly toward Tammy Lynn, grabbing her hands. "One hundred Christmas gifts. It's brilliant. We can hand-make things. Candles, scarves, stationery, cookies, whatever. Little things. There are seven days, and seven of us. That's" — she calculated in her head — "like, two gifts per person per day. You think you can get Elwood and Janelle on board?"

Tammy Lynn thought about it, frowning and leaning her head to one side. "Probably. Although if Janelle gets involved, the old woman will be getting chia seeds and homemade quinoa protein balls. That, literally, smell like our old hamster cage. And don't taste much better."

"Perfect!" Bren shouted. The teen employee leaned on his broom and eyed her curiously. "I'll let everyone know. We'll start tomorrow. Forget cooking class. We are now a gift-making class. Well, not class. More of a group. A club. You know what I mean."

"Okay," Tammy Lynn said, clutching Bren's hands in hers now. Bren recognized that they probably looked ridiculous, the two of them, holding hands and squealing as the snowstorm picked up speed outside.

But when they finally left, the Ice Dreamery sign blinking out behind them, she had a plan firmly in place.

She stood on the walk in front of her van and tilted her head up, watching the flakes rain down from an inky black sky. She stuck out her tongue to catch a few.

Kill ugly with kindness.

There wasn't much she felt in control of these days. But this was something she could do.

CHAPTER TWENTY-ONE

"I can't believe we're doing this, but I'll admit it's kind of nice," Lulu said when she came into the Kitchen Classroom the next day. She stomped on the doormat to shake the snow off. It was a white, white world out there, the weather predictions panning out for a change, and Bren had been worried that maybe none of them would be able to get to class.

"Don't let her fool you," Teresa said coming in after her. "She's counting this toward her church goals this year. It's only nice because she feels like she can skip Mass to work on her gifts. Plus the truck gets no business in this snow."

"Not true," Lulu argued, but a smile spread across her face. "Okay, maybe a little."

"Sisterly love," Aunt Cathy deadpanned. "Leave it to a sister to never let you get away with anything."

Lulu and Teresa looked at each other, confused.

"We're not sisters," Lulu said. Teresa shook her head.

"But you look like twins," Aunt Cathy said.

"We get that a lot. We're just best friends who like to share beauty secrets," Teresa said.

"And we're coworkers," Lulu added.

"At a taco truck, right?" Joan asked. She was busy dropping spoonfuls of monster cookie dough onto a cookie sheet.

"Hot Tamales Taco Truck. We actually own it," Teresa said.

Bren stopped cold. "Wait. You own it?"

Both ladies nodded. "Yeah, why?"

"I thought you just worked there," she said. "But you're . . . actual chefs."

Lulu held up one hand. "I wouldn't go that far. I'm a cook. Teresa is a disaster."

Teresa nodded again. "It's true. It's an embarrassment to my mother that I'm so bad. That's why we took this class. So I could get better. It's working, I think. I've learned a lot about what not to do." Teresa gestured around the classroom.

Bren wanted to die of embarrassment. She laughed out loud. "This class must have seemed like a hot mess to you."

"Oh, no, no," Lulu said. "It's good for me to see that these things don't just happen to us. Once Teresa set the truck on fire. And my apron."

"I thought those tamales tasted professional," Aunt Cathy said. "I just figured you two cheated and bought them from someone and tried to pass them off as your own."

Teresa grinned. "We were testing out a new menu item. We were thrilled that you guys liked them. And the best part is I made the filling myself. With no help. See? Getting better."

"So what is our first batch of gifts going to be?" Tammy Lynn asked. She'd come alone, but, as predicted, Janelle had sent along a bag full of protein bars.

"I made soaps," Aunt Cathy said, proudly holding up a red, white, and blue blob.

Bren squinted. "Is that the Republican elephant?"

"You bet your American ass it is!"

"Where on earth did you get the molds for that?" Tammy Lynn asked, picking up a soap.

"Had 'em for years. Finally found a use for 'em."

"I've got candied nuts," Joan said, shaking a can. "And I bought a can of coffee. Can never have too much coffee, I would guess."

"Great," Bren said. "I made dog biscuits."

"Should have made those in the shape of Democrat donkeys," Aunt Cathy said.

"We brought Hot Tamales gift certificates. But we thought we'd make sopapillas while we're here."

"Rebecca?" Bren asked.

Rebecca held up a book, bound in beautiful map-themed paper and a bright red ribbon. Bren noticed that she'd tied a matching ribbon in her hair — a tiny pop of color in a sea of brown. "It's a journal," she said. "In case she wants to write down the memory of getting all these gifts."

"Okay," Bren said. "I thought we could all make cookies while we're here today, too. A whole variety. I brought tubs to put them in. If I'm counting correctly, then we have fifteen gifts today. A great start!"

They all shifted into busy mode, heading for different parts of the kitchen — the pantry, the cooler, their stations. Bren piled the premade gifts next to the Christmas tree that Paula had put up.

"What will we say if she comes in to complain today?" Joan asked as they set to work.

"We tell her to buzz off and we give this stuff to someone who deserves it," Aunt Cathy said. "And then we lob a little Molotov cocktail into her apartment for good measure."

"Catherine!"

"She won't come in today," Bren said.

"If you really believe that, you must be crazier than I already think you are," Cathy said, dumping a cup of flour into a bowl and squinting at the recipe card Bren had laid out for her.

"No, no, she's got the right idea," Tammy Lynn said, wielding a bottle of vanilla. "Good karma and all that. We're putting positive energy out into the world, so today she won't come."

Everyone paused and gaped at Tammy Lynn, then snickered and went back to work, not a one of them believing a word she'd just said.

But she'd been right.

They'd worked long into the night.

And Virginia Mash hadn't come down once.

CHAPTER TWENTY-TWO

Poor old Chuy was sick. And not just gobbled-something-he-shouldn't-have-out-of-the-trash sick, either. Not sore-from-his-walk sick. He was *sick* sick. The kind of sick where he didn't leave his bed at all for two days, not even to eat a bite or take a single lick of water. Virginia had resorted to sucking water up into an old eyedropper and squirting it in through the side of his mouth. He didn't even fight her when she did it.

She knew this day would come eventually. Sooner rather than later, in fact. Chuy was old. He'd outlived what a dachshund reasonably should live. He'd outlived three of those damn cats.

He'd outlived Jamie. His owner.

Damn him.

They'd both outlived her.

Truth be told, Virginia was not a dog person. Not an animal person, actually. Not in the least. She'd always felt like she had her hands full enough with Jamie. She'd been forty when Jamie was born, so while life was colorful and busy and vibrant, it was also exhausting. She was a working mom. She had no time for pets.

But, oh, how Jamie had always wanted one. And so she'd bought one the very minute she got her own place. Senior year of college, she'd brought home this adorable little mound of brown fur. Had him zipped up against her inside her coat. She'd stood on the porch, shit-eating grin on her face, and pulled down the zipper, and out popped a head.

"Oh, Jamie, you can't take care of a dog. You've got too much on your plate as it is. You're in college; why do you want to tie yourself down?" Virginia had raged, but Jamie hadn't heard a word of it. She'd been too busy pressing her nose to Chuy's nose, scratching behind his ears, holding him like a child while he slept.

"Who couldn't love a face like that? What could I possibly be doing that could be more important than loving this little guy?"

And so she had. Jamie had loved Chuy like he was the sun and the moon and the stars all wrapped up into one long, ornery, short-legged body. She walked him faithfully and held birthday parties for him and

323

only left his side when she had to.

Boys came and went. And eventually men, too. But Chuy was the constant.

Virginia heartily believed that it was Chuy who kept Jamie alive for as long as she was. She believed that Jamie was prepared to leave her parents and her friends. It was the little dog she couldn't bear to go without.

After . . . well, just *after,* it was nearly impossible for Virginia to even so much as look at the dog. She wanted nothing to do with him. She wanted no reminders. Carrying on without Jamie was hard enough without a constant living, breathing reminder of who she was and what she loved lapping up dog chow in the kitchen. But Jamie had made Virginia promise, and so she'd promised. It would have broken her daughter's heart to know that Chuy suffered without her. It would have shattered her if Virginia had given him away.

Oh, but the dog did suffer without her. Wouldn't leave the dining room, where they'd set her up in the end. He'd sit at the foot of the bed, looking, waiting. And then they'd had the bed removed, and he'd sit where the bed used to be. He'd lie in there at night and whine. He'd curl up on her old blanket, which Virginia had left in a corner on the dining room floor, unable to bear the thought of moving it, washing it, putting it away.

Even as he got over the loss of Jamie, the dining room remained Chuy's room.

And then when Ernie died, and it was just the two of them, the memories seemed to be everywhere, echoing around them all the time, choking them. She imagined Ernie being greeted by Jamie in heaven. She imagined him holding her in his arms again — only she wasn't sick; her body wasn't ravaged by the cancer. She wasn't having seizures four, five, nine times a day. She was beautiful and bright and laughing, leading a whole pack of Chuys while Virginia and the actual Chuy were stuck in that old house, growing more and more bitter with each passing day that they weren't with her.

Virginia had packed Chuy up and moved to a dismal little apartment above an unrented space on the square. The windows were painted shut and the place was clogged with traffic and visitors, so many happy mothers and daughters, so many playful families. It was more than either of them could take.

Virginia loved Chuy because he loved and missed Jamie just as much as she did.

And now he was sick, and it was the kind of sick she recognized. The unfixable kind.

"Oh, Chu, come on, now, how about a little bacon?" she'd asked, trying to hand-feed him some leftovers from her breakfast. He perked up long enough to lift his head and give it a sniff, but then he only licked the air a couple of times, sickly, and dropped his head back down onto his bed. She lowered herself so she was sitting on the floor next to him, and then tipped over, laying her head on his bed. She could feel his breath on her neck; she was staring him right in the eyes. "Don't do this to me, Chuy," she said. "If you go, I'll be the only one left who loved her."

Downstairs, the idiotic ladies were having a hell of a party, it sounded like. Lots of thumping and bumping and giggling. Like a bunch of overgrown teenagers. It was disgusting, really, the way people refused to grow up. She could smell cookies baking. Her stomach growled. She'd been so worried about Chuy, she hadn't left his side, even to go grocery shopping. She was down to her last few cans of soup, and hadn't eaten a thing all day.

There was a loud clang, like something had gotten dropped. Virginia Mash nearly jumped out of her skin. Damn those morons; didn't they understand what disturbing the peace was? Didn't they understand that an old dog sometimes just needed his rest, not all this noise and bustle?

"Don't worry, Chu, I'll go down there and make them shut up so you can sleep."

But Chuy only barely opened an eye in response to his name. He let out a feeble cough — more of a wheeze than a cough — licked his muzzle again, and went back to sleep.

Virginia Mash lay her head down next to his again. "Okay, okay, I'll stay," she said. "But only because you get so cranky when you're hungry and I'm not here to feed you. You really should work on that, Chu. Nobody likes a crab." She snuggled in closer, listening as there was more bustling noise, some laughter, some shushing. She closed her eyes to try to ignore them better. "You know, crab sounds really good right about now, Chuy, doesn't it? Jamie loved crab. When she was a little girl, she used to eat a piece and then squeeze lemon directly into her mouth, like a shot chaser. Was the funniest thing." She opened her eyes and stared at the ceiling. "I used to make a big old pot of crab and shrimp boil on New Year's Eve for that girl. I think it was her favorite meal of the whole year. I'd just throw everything into one pot. Crab legs, shrimp, sausage, corn, potatoes. We ate it all with our fingers and wiped our hands on dish towels. Those were fun times, Chuy. I bet you can even remember one or two if you try real hard." She turned again to face him, though his eyes were still closed. "I'll tell you what, old dog. You get better, and I'll make us a shrimp boil all our own this New Year's Eve. It'll be our special dinner. We'll share it."

She reached over and scratched him behind his ears. Once again, his eyes fluttered open. She thought she even saw his tail try to wag a little. So she kept doing it, even though her elbow creaked and the arthritis in her hands screamed with each movement.

They lay there for a long time. So long, in fact, Virginia was half afraid she wouldn't be able to get up again. So long the noises below stopped and she heard the familiar *whump* of the front door of the Kitchen Classroom closing again and again.

At one point, she thought she heard the shushing of soft footsteps coming up her stairs. She perked up, waiting for a knock on the door, but it never came.

Eventually, Chuy began snoring — deep and guttural — and Virginia sat up, watching him sleep.

"I'll bet you're excited to see our Jamie," she said. She pulled herself to standing, which required less work, but more grunting, than she'd anticipated. "Me too, old pal. Me too."

CHAPTER TWENTY-THREE

Bren's Friday had been busy. She'd made loaves of rye bread, baskets of pumpkin muffins, had looked up and made an Amish bread starter that they could all work off of, had made two Christmas ornaments out of dough, and was busy working on garden soap. She'd also stopped by the bookstore and had bought an armload — everything from thrillers to classics, and even one Bible, although she was fairly certain the woman upstairs was not much of a church-goer. It was the whole *love thy neighbor* vibe she wasn't getting.

She'd been in touch with everyone. Together, they had managed to make forty-eight gifts, and they all agreed to meet at the classroom to drop off what they had so far. Tonight's haul up the stairs would probably take two treks. Bren was practically giddy at the thought.

More snow had dropped overnight, but

then the sun had come out, so the world seemed impossibly bright and glittery, the snow like a dusting of diamonds. Instead of watching the news, Bren dragged her kitchen chair — the one that wobbled when you moved around in it — to the window and watched as neighborhood kids played, building snowmen, hurtling down hills on sleds, their feet leaving little trails of joy behind them everywhere they went.

"The guys are coming over," Gary said, popping his head into the kitchen at one point. He was officially on Christmas vacation, not that it made any difference in Bren's life. As she watched him scratch his belly, wearing only a T-shirt and sweatpants with tired elastic, she tried not to remember the way they used to talk about spending Christmas in the mountains, at a ski resort, a roaring fire warming their feet and glasses of wine warming their bellies and *It's a Wonderful Life* warming their hearts. They'd once had plans.

"Uh-huh," she said. She picked up her toast and bit into it. It was dry and tasteless. Needed something.

"You think you might be willing to make us some snacks?" he asked. He'd opened the refrigerator and was bent inside of it, so was spared the incredulous look that she couldn't keep from her face.

"You're kidding, right?"

He straightened. "What?"

"You expect me to cook for you now." She slapped the toast down on her plate. Crumbs flew, but she didn't care.

"You don't have to cook. Just if you could whip up a little something."

She stood, took her plate to the sink. "I have a class tonight," she said icily.

He reached out and tried to touch her shoulder; she ducked away from it. "On a Friday? Oh, come on, Brennie, don't be like that. We had a bad night. It was just a fight. We've got our big dinner coming up."

She rinsed her plate and put it in the dishwasher, and then turned to face him. "Don't wait up."

She had been so furious when she left her house, she'd had to stop for a coffee on the way to the square. Okay, technically, the coffeehouse was not so much on the way to the square as it was all the way across town in the opposite direction, but she really, really needed that time to think.

Was he being genuine? She honestly just couldn't tell anymore. A sad statement after so many years together.

By the time she got to the Kitchen Classroom, everyone was already there. There were loads of gifts by the tiny tree — enough to instantly brighten Bren's sour mood — but she could tell as soon as she walked in that something was wrong.

"Hey, what's . . . ?" She stopped when she saw Paula standing at her station in the front of the room, her arms crossed, her mouth turned down. Very serious pose. "What's going on?"

Bren set her things with the other gifts under the tree and walked up to the front of the classroom, taking time to look at everyone, trying to determine what was happening by the look on her mother's face, or Aunt Cathy's. But she was only able to ascertain that Something Bad had happened.

"We're *terminado*," Lulu said. She made a slicing motion across her neck with her finger.

"What?" Bren's hands automatically clasped at her own throat.

"She's shut us down," Aunt Cathy said. "The old cow." She tipped her head up and shouted at the ceiling, "I want my elephant soaps back!"

Bren slowly unwound her scarf and took off her coat. "I don't understand. She shut us down?"

Paula gave a look and held up a sheet of paper. "She got a restraining order against you. Us. All of us. Something about dumping trash on her property. I don't know. It seems sketchy. I don't know if she can actually get a restraining order against a business right beneath her feet. But she's also been making reports about us disturbing the peace, and I'm being threatened with fines if we don't take care of the problem." Paula spread her hands apart. "I'm out of money."

"But she's the problem," Lulu said. "All we're doing is cooking."

Paula held up another handful of papers. "I honestly don't know how legit it all is, but she's exhausted what little I had for legal help. I can't fight her. I'm just going to have to . . ." She shrugged helplessly. "Quit."

"Quit? But we haven't been dumping. We've been leaving gifts."

"Killing ugly with kindness," Tammy Lynn interjected. The ball on her Santa hat flopped around when she moved.

"Yes. That," Bren said. "We're not leaving dog doo on her doorstep. It's cookies. And stocking caps."

"It's out of my hands. I'm so sorry," Paula said.

Bren thought that she should maybe be

relieved. She had, after all, never been certain about her ability to actually teach this class. And she had proven herself to be failing miserably. How many times had she wanted to — even tried to — quit? But instead of relief, she felt hopelessness and failure. How could this be? She needed this class. She needed Tammy Lynn and Lulu and Teresa and even quiet Rebecca. She needed to make gifts for the old woman upstairs. She needed to see this project through, even if she didn't quite know why.

Or maybe she did know why. Maybe she knew that she needed this project because it was all she had left. Maybe she knew that good and well, but didn't want to face it.

"We should talk to her," Aunt Cathy said. "I'll go."

"No," Joan said, blocking Cathy in with her stool. "That's the last thing we should do. You of all people."

Aunt Cathy gasped, affronted. "You're saying I can't be polite?"

Tammy Lynn patted her hand. "Don't take it the wrong way, dear, but yes."

"Yeah," Paula said. "Don't antagonize her. Really, we shouldn't even be here. I just wanted to let you all know. I'll refund everyone the rest of your money, and I'll let you know if I get this worked out in time for a

New Year's class like we talked about. But I wouldn't count on it. I'm so sorry, Bren."

"It's okay," Bren felt herself saying, but it wasn't. It wasn't okay at all. Nothing was working out for her anymore, and she was sick and tired of pretending that everything was okay.

Slowly, they put on their coats and picked up their purses and filed toward the door.

"We brought a lot of things," Teresa said as they neared the Christmas tree.

"We should leave it on her doorstep to spite her," Aunt Cathy said. "Just one more time."

"Not if it's going to get us arrested," Joan said.

"I wouldn't mind it," Tammy Lynn said on a shrug, "if I knew I'd gotten her goat one last time. I could use a few days off of my diet." She laughed, but it fell flat as they all stared forlornly at the gifts.

"Not me," Aunt Cathy said, breaking the silence. "If I'm going to jail, I'm gonna firebomb her."

"Cathy!" Rebecca gasped.

"Oh, don't worry about her, honey," Joan said. "She's been threatening to firebomb people at least three times a week since the Nixon era."

"How do you know I've never gone

through with it, huh?"

"Oh, come on," Joan said. She picked up her gifts and headed out the door.

Aunt Cathy bent and picked hers up, too. "Well, if I can't burn her apartment down, I'm sure not going to give her these socks. They're good socks."

There were mumbles of agreement, and while Bren grew more and more despondent as it became clear that they were all giving up on the project, she couldn't help but pick up her gifts as well. She stood by the door, saying good-bye to each of them as they left. Finally, it was just her — and Paula boxing up some things in the background.

"Paula?"

"Hmm?"

Bren shifted her weight. "I'm really sorry. If I were a better cook, maybe this wouldn't have happened."

"We'll get it figured out," Paula said. "And it seems to me whatever you were doing in this class, it was working just fine. The real kicker is I had two more people call today, wanting to sign up for our New Recipes for the New Year cooking class. You'd have had a full house."

Bren tried to imagine what the classroom would look like, all filled up. She wondered how badly she could screw things up with even more people, more pressure. Not to mention new recipes that she'd never tried before.

Funny thing was, she actually could imagine it.

And she liked it.

CHAPTER TWENTY-FOUR

December 21 had always been Bren's busiest day of the holiday season. It started back when the kids were little, and the twenty-first was their last full day of school before holiday break. The day always sprang up on Bren, as if she didn't know it was coming, and she found herself horrified and energized by the length of her to-do list. Over the years, the habit stuck, and even though she had no real reason for it, other than perhaps to take her mind off of her many troubles, Bren found herself cleaning the house top to bottom on December 21.

She started with the kitchen, making it tidy and lemony fresh, and then changed the sheets on all the beds — even the two guest beds — and vacuumed and dusted and reorganized the hall closet. And still it wasn't even lunchtime yet.

Gary was in the house somewhere, though Bren had no real idea where. She honestly didn't care. She was still angry with him for that night at Olive Garden, and the last thing she wanted to do was admit to him that she'd lost her job at the Kitchen Classroom, so avoidance seemed like the best policy at the moment.

She supposed he was knocking around downstairs in the basement, so she lingered upstairs in their bedroom, eyeing the attic hatch and thinking that the only way she could get farther away from him without actually leaving the house would be if she were to go up there.

But the attic was dusty and probably full of spiders, and the only things up there were her father's navy trunk and the Christmas decorations, anyway.

She'd been gnawing on her fingernail, but she suddenly stopped. The Christmas decorations. She stayed still for a few moments, thinking, and then sprang from the bed.

"Well, why the hell not?" she said aloud before hooking her finger through the pull string and lowering the attic door.

After all, just because her too-worldly-for-the-world kids couldn't be bothered, why should she go without her lovely tree? Just because Gary's twilight years had no room for tradition or cheer or gifts didn't mean her life had no room for those things.

Christmas may have moved on without her, but that didn't mean she had to move on without Christmas.

She climbed up the wooden ladder, wiping cobwebs, or what felt like cobwebs, off her face and out of her mouth as she went. Normally she would make Gary go up and do this, and now she remembered why. It was dirty and cold, and she was guessing it was going to be a real feat of acrobatics to get the boxes down the ladder rungs. But that was okay. She didn't need him. She could do it on her own.

It was dark in the attic, and she had to fumble for a few moments to find the pull cord for the one bare lightbulb that hung from the ceiling. She pulled it, and the attic was bathed in stark light, creating shadows that were perhaps scarier than the shadows that were there in the dark. Bren went straight to the six boxes that held the decorations and groaned. This was going to be a damn lot of work.

Somehow she managed to wrestle all six boxes out of the attic and downstairs to the living room without breaking any bones or knocking any holes in the walls. She was sweating by the time she was ready to go through them, but it was a good sweat. Like a workout. The most exercise she'd had in a while, and she kind of liked it. For the first time in a long time, she wasn't hungry.

Just as she opened the first box, there were a few clicks of wood hitting wood and then some tentative drumbeats rumbling up through the floor from the basement. Bren sighed. She bent in front of the entertainment center and sorted through their old CDs, her fingers leaving prints in the dust on top of them. Goodness, how long had it been? She flipped through until she found what she was looking for. She held it up and wiped the dust off the cover. Bing Crosby. Her favorite.

She started the music, cranking up the volume to drown out Gil's drumbeats, and then turned to the first box. Before he got to "White Christmas," she had unearthed and assembled their ancient first Christmas tree, which was so short she could put the angel on top without so much as standing on her toes. It wasn't a real tree, but it would do. Actually, it would more than do. It was cute. And festive.

Oh, those had been the days. She and Gary in that old apartment with the clanging pipes and the furnace that never really worked all that well. How they'd been so excited to buy this little tree. It was their first moment of legitimacy, their first item of permanency. How she longed to go back to that first Christmas. He'd bought her a simple gold bracelet. She'd bought him a toolbox. They'd bought each other a bottle of expensive champagne and cooked steaks on their filthy stove and watched movies while balancing their plates on their laps. Why had they been so eager to grow out of that? Why had she worked so hard to get them . . . here?

She shook off the thought and continued wrapping the tree in blue garland. She picked through the ornaments, choosing only the ones that meant the most to her — the triangle reindeer head Kevin had made out of popsicle sticks in preschool, the clay snowman Kelsey had painted green when she was three — and hanging them lovingly on the tree.

When she was done with the tree, she moved on to the hearth, placing her wooden Santa Clauses just so, lost in memories and in thought and feeling so happy that she'd decided to decorate. Soon "It's Beginning to Look a Lot Like Christmas" queued up and she began humming, then moving her hips, then flat-out dancing around the room, straightening the gown of the angel with her fingers. Her dance partner.

The song ended, she placed the angel on

top of the tree and curtsied to her. And in that dead airspace between "It's Beginning to Look a Lot Like Christmas" and "Christmas in Killarney," she heard it. Applause. Only it was real and in the room with her and the sound of only one person clapping.

She whipped around, her hands automatically going to her heart. John stood in the doorway between the kitchen and living room, leaning against the doorframe, smiling at Bren. He stopped clapping and crossed his arms over his chest.

"Oh, goodness, I didn't know you were here," Bren said, rushing over to turn down the music. She was struck by the thought that she'd said that to him a few times recently. Why did it seem like he was always creeping up on her? "I'm so embarrassed." She swiped her hair out of her eyes as she stood.

"Don't be embarrassed. I liked it." More of that disturbing smiling. Bren's stomach twisted as she realized what she supposed she'd already known for a while now — that this was no ordinary visit, no ordinary smile, and that John was not here to see Gary or to play in the band.

"Gary's downstairs," she said nervously. "You can go on down."

Instead, he pushed away from the doorframe and sauntered toward her, his head ducked so that he was looking out at her from under hooded eyes. "It looks great in here," he said.

"Oh, that." She glanced toward the decorations and then waved them away breezily. "It's not what I'd usually do, but it's kind of nice."

"I think you're kind of nice," John said, and took another step toward her.

Bren backed up a step. Her throat was suddenly very dry. "Wh-what?" She tried to smile.

"Come on, Bren, we've been doing this for weeks. Maybe longer. You know Cindy and I are split up."

"You are?" she barked. She'd at one time been good friends with Cindy, but they'd fallen out of touch. Cindy was a gigglier, tinier version of Bren herself. "I had no idea. Does Gary know?"

He squinted. "For months now. Of course he knows."

"He didn't say a word." *About anything,* she thought bitterly. Of course he wouldn't think it relevant information to tell her that two of their oldest pals had split. Why would she care? "I'm so sorry," she practically whispered. "I hope it was amicable."

He rubbed her arm with an index finger.

She felt it like an electric jolt to her skin, but she was too shocked; this was all happening way too fast for her to move. "And I know you and Gary are having a hard time."

She swallowed. "We're . . . Has Gary said something?"

But John seemed to ignore her question. "I've felt it, and so have you. All that stuff about the nuts?"

"Nuts?" Bren was really lost in this conversation. Nothing he was saying was making sense. Did he really say he and Cindy were no more? "I'm sure you and Cindy will work this out."

"And then the boning," he continued. He ran a finger up her other arm. She finally found the power to move both arms behind her back.

"Boning?"

"The birds," he said. "And that day with the drums. Tell me that was an accident."

"It was. I mean, what do you mean an accident? That was for Gary. And I had to make a turducken. You came in and boned . . . them. Oh God."

John had wrapped himself around her so swiftly, she didn't even have time to move her arms back. She was trapped under the most uncomfortable hug she'd ever felt.

"I've wanted you for so long, Bren Epperson," he breathed into her neck. "I know you want me, too."

"No, I . . . John, I think you're misinterpreting. . . . Gary is right downstairs."

He continued to hold her for a moment, and Bren would be lying to herself if she didn't admit that it was at least kind of nice to feel a man's arms wrapped around her once again. It had been so long, and he smelled so good — like spices and soap. And he was warm.

But this was wrong.

Unexpected and nice.

But wrong.

She wriggled under his grasp until she was able to put her hands on his chest. She pushed him away. "I'm sorry," she said. "I need to do something upstairs."

And without looking back, she raced up to her bedroom and locked the door behind her, feeling flushed and excited and mortified and confused all at once.

Downstairs, very faintly, "Mele Kalikimaka" started up on the stereo.

CHAPTER TWENTY-FIVE

Chuy had improved just the tiniest bit. She could at least get him to eat now, little bits at a time, and she'd finally taken him for a short walk around half the square. Even though it was bitterly cold, he'd started panting before they'd even reached the flower shop, and she'd picked him up and wrapped him in her flannel, carrying him back, clucking at him while she stroked his face. She'd walked slowly, so he could see the lights on the buildings. He'd never said so — well, of course not; he was a dog — but she always suspected he enjoyed Christmas lights. Especially the yellow ones, because they lit up the night with a goldish glow that just felt peaceful. Old Chu liked peaceful.

Speaking of peaceful. It was not lost on her that the Kitchen Classroom was empty, lights out, sign on the door flipped to CLOSED when she walked by. Not even that obnoxious redhead inside to yell at. She and Chuy had stood outside that window, too, and gazed at the shadowy reflections of themselves on the glass, framed by the dormant equipment inside. It was so dead in there. So . . . boring.

But the wind had driven them home, and Chuy hadn't once done any business while they'd been outside. Instead, he was going on the newspaper in the guest bedroom, or sometimes just wherever he sat. Which was messy and unpleasant but, given that he wasn't feeling well, temporarily forgivable.

She probably should have taken him to the vet long before now. She knew that. She felt a little guilty for not having done so. But he wasn't suffering — or at least he didn't appear to be. He seemed happy, but tired, so tired. If she'd had any hint that he was in pain she would have had him put down. Or at least she'd liked to have thought she would. She'd like to have that strength for Jamie.

For Jamie.

Everything she ever did with Chuy was for Jamie, and that included squeezing out every last minute that she could with him. If there was even a chance that he'd have another good day, another half trip around the square with her, then by God she would give that to him.

Probably people would think she was cruel for it. People had found her cruel for many, many things in her lifetime. And maybe for good reason.

She understood that she wasn't the easiest person to like. She knew that she was persnickety. Outspoken. Demanding. Opinionated. She hadn't always been like that, of course. Life made her that way. If people wanted to blame something for the way she made them feel, they would just have to turn their little faces upward, clasp their little hands together, and thank God. Or the universe. Or whatever it was that drove her life down this path.

She was once just as pie-eyed and hopeful as the rest of them. It was a disgusting way of living. Unrealistic. She never thought she'd have reason to be any other way, but she'd been wrong. It was a terrible lesson to learn in this life. An unforgettable one, too.

Those women downstairs probably thought she was cruel. And over the past two days she had been wondering if maybe she'd been a bit too harsh with them. She'd talked to Chuy about it at great length, stroking his back as he lay next to her limply on the couch.

"You think I should have let them be,

don't you, Chu?" she'd asked. He'd rolled his eyes at her and then gone back to sleep. This was on one of his better days — a day when he could limp to the food bowl mostly on his own. "Well, I know what you're thinking — that I was jealous of their fun. But it wasn't about that. It was that they were so loud with their fun. All that talking and yelling and clanging pots and pans and giggling like teenagers. Really, they needed a wake-up call, someone to tell them to act their age. Now, don't you sigh at me, Chuy. You're a soft heart, but you can't be soft-hearted with people like that. They don't know when to stop. They push and push and will just keep pushing until you push back. Leaving all those things on my door-step. What do you suppose that was about, anyway?" She leaned over to check Chuy's reaction, but he was snoring again. His ear twitched. "I'll tell you what it was about. It was about making me feel guilty. And it didn't work."

But the truth was it did kind of work. She couldn't quite figure out their game — that much was true — but the gifts were nice. And it had felt really good to pass the first ones on to those kids at the cancer center. She'd only wished Chuy hadn't gotten sick so she could take more down there. Brighten more bleak days. If that was possible. There wasn't much of anything bright about having cancer.

But there was also something too personal about the gifts. She didn't have friends because she didn't want any. She didn't have family — well, of course she had family, those dimwit nieces and nephews of hers, who served only to remind her of what she didn't have and never would — because she didn't want any. She had no one but Chuy, and that was on purpose. She didn't need a bevy of moronic housewives trying to wend their way into her life. She didn't need people to care about. She had enough cares with Chuy.

Which was why she couldn't explain what it was that made her repeatedly open her front door, looking to see if the idiotic cooks had left more gifts there. Of course they hadn't — she'd made sure they couldn't — but still she looked just the same. Opening her door, even stepping out to peer down the stairs to make sure they hadn't just decided to leave the things on the sidewalk, and then closing the door slowly with a soft, defeated click. She'd expected more fight out of those women. They'd let her down by giving up so easily.

She hated it when people gave up.

Jamie had given up. She had. She didn't fight near as hard as Virginia wanted her to. She'd said she was fighting, but it didn't seem like enough of a fight from Virginia's perspective. She remembered standing by Jamie's bed on that last day, looking down at her veiny eyelids, her sharp cheekbones, a younger, oblivious Chuy tucked under her arm, and thinking, *Dammit, why didn't you fight harder? You had some still left in you; I could feel it. A mother can feel it.*

And then when Ernie went with no fight whatsoever, Virginia had only looked on with bitter jealousy.

"Maybe that's my problem, Chuy," she said, trying to interest him in a spoonful of peanut butter. He shifted, lifted his head, and gave the spoon a few tentative licks. "That's a good boy." She ran her fingers over the top of his bony head. "Maybe I should give up a little easier, you know?"

Indeed, her life would be easier. Or at least filled with less fighting. Imagine if she didn't have to continually set people straight on what they were doing and how it was affecting her. Imagine if she could just toddle through life with a dippy grin like most of the general population did. Her IQ would suffer, certainly, but at least she wouldn't have to worry so much about so many things. She would just sit in her stuffy little apartment. Leaky faucet drip, drip, dripping all night long? No problem. Stench of burned flour poofing up through her floorboards on clouds of smoke? No big deal. Loud, rumbling car engines waking her up in the morning, keeping her up at night? She was getting too much sleep anyway! *No worries, friend* as her catchphrase? Of course!

Bah. She could never be that person. She hated to even be in the same room with that person.

"But can you believe it, Chuy? I used to be that person." She turned the spoon so the lump of peanut butter he'd pushed to the edge wouldn't fall off. "I used to tell Jamie all the time to suck it up, live and let live, turn the other cheek. And look where that got her. Look where it got both of us. No, wait, sorry, Chuy, all three of us, you're right."

No, Virginia was not at a loss every day to notice exactly where all those morals, all that nobility, all that living and letting live got her. She was surrounded by it, literally, every day of her life. Shabby walls, wood floors with the varnish worn off, peeling paint everywhere except around the windows, where it was thicker than cinder blocks. Appliances that worked only when they wanted to, noise, noise, noise — always the noise of people having happy days, people spending their money, spending their time, as if they had unlimited quantities of both. Did those people not know that there was suffering around them all day every day? Did they not understand what their laughter did to the lonely?

Chuy understood. She could see it in his eyes, which had become so red around the rims they looked almost bloody. He understood what it was to be left behind. And he also understood what it meant to do the leaving.

"It's okay, old man," she said. "I'm used to it."

But as she turned on the TV to take her thoughts away, and wiped the insides of her glasses, which seemed to have gotten smoggy all of a sudden, and thought about getting up to check on the doorstep one last time before bed, she couldn't help wondering if she *was,* in fact, used to it.

She began to wonder if she ever would be.

CHAPTER TWENTY-SIX

Bren couldn't blame the ladies for not wanting to finish the gift project. They were angry. So was she. Who wanted to deal with such unpleasantness just three days before Christmas? It was supposed to be a time of joy!

She'd never gotten to share her figgy pudding recipe. That was the thing that kept going through her mind as she sat in her kitchen, ignoring the gurgle of the dishwasher. It was probably the sound of the old thing getting ready to go out, and when she was trying to watch TV, the noise annoyed her, but at the moment if she let herself hear it, the noise would serve only to upset her more. She never got to bring them some damn figgy pudding.

Who in the world still ate figgy pudding, anyway? As far as she knew, nobody. But it was the tradition of it, the undeniable Christmas-ness of it. It was in songs, for goodness' sake. *Bring us some figgy pudding.* She'd found a figgy pudding recipe; she'd bought the dates and figs and had even picked out which ramekins she would use. They were supposed to eat them warm right there in the classroom on the twenty-third — what was scheduled to be their last class before the holiday. Their farewell until January.

She'd been such a flop as a cooking instructor, it seemed like a figgy pudding was the least she could do for them. They'd done so much for her.

And now that was a flop, too.

And she had all these godforsaken dates and figs in her kitchen.

"You're home early," Gary had said two evenings before, standing at the counter, dumping half the spice cabinet into an overflowing bowl of popcorn.

"Oh, don't get me started about that," she'd said, unwrapping her scarf and draping it over a kitchen chair. "You know that old woman who lives above the kitchen?"

He was actually clueless enough about her life to look upward and appear confused, as if she literally meant a woman living above the kitchen in their home.

"At the Kitchen Classroom, Gary. Where I'm home early from?"

"Oh," he said. "Old woman, huh. Friend of yours, I guess."

She rolled her eyes. "No. Come on, I've told you about her a hundred times. She's a nasty old thing who lives upstairs. And she's always complaining. Everything we do is wrong and disturbing her and, well, I've just never met anyone so miserable in all my life."

He'd picked up the bowl and was cradling it to his chest, looking impatient. This was a look she'd gotten to know quite intimately — his *get on with it, because I'm not listening anyway* look. "Yeah," he said.

"Well, she's been threatening to shut us down since day one. Threatening to put Paula out of business, and —"

"Uh-huh." Eyes roving toward the basement door.

Bren pulled off her coat and draped it over the chair with the scarf. "Well, I never thought she'd come through on any of her claims, but today I go into the kitchen and —"

There was a clang of cymbals downstairs and a "Check, check" into a microphone. Her head jerked toward the door.

"Practice again tonight?"

Finally, he looked interested. Invested. His eyes lit up. "We've got a lot to do. Gil thinks

358

he might have gotten us a gig in the Holiday Inn lobby on the twenty-third. If the rest of your story can wait . . ."

"Not really."

"We won't be too late tonight, I promise. We can talk then." Already, he was halfway to the door.

"No. Gary, I'm really upset. I need to talk now."

He sighed, edged toward the door but inclined his head toward her. "Okay. What?"

Bren hesitated — he just looked so put off by having to pay attention to her — but decided she would take what she could get. She walked over to the table and sat down. "Well, it's just that this woman . . . She's made us so miserable this whole time, so we decided to leave her gifts. Blankets and gloves and homemade things. Little from-the-heart things, you know? It takes work and money, but we were willing to do it, because, you see . . . well, I thought I saw her give some of them away to kids with cancer, and . . . well, that part's a long story." She rested her head in her hands. The class really was more than willing. They were excited about it. Excited about sharing with her, making a difference. "But then today when we got there and Paula had been shut down, I just . . ." She looked over her shoulder to where Gary had been, but he'd moved.

He now stood at the basement door, turned completely away from Bren as he leaned to look down the stairs.

"What the hell?" Bren demanded, and he jerked toward her, his face a guilty oval.

"What? I was listening."

"No, you weren't." She pounded the flat of her hand on the table. "Jesus, Gary, is it so hard to pay attention to me for even a few minutes?"

"No," he said, having the gall to look angered by the accusation. "But if we can just talk about this later . . ." He gestured downstairs with the popcorn bowl. "This is really important to me, Bren."

She let out a gust of air, suddenly so tired it just didn't matter anymore. She brushed him away with a backward sweep of her hand. He turned and bounded down the stairs like a teenager. It wasn't fair — his empty-nest-crisis hobby was working out just fine for him. She slid forward and folded her arms, laying her head down on them for rest. "But what about what's really important to me?" she asked the table.

And now, today, Sunday, Gary was gone. Out with the guys, buying sheet music or a microphone stand or a buffalo in a tutu —

Bren hadn't really been paying attention. Not only had they not finished their talk later; Gary hadn't even come upstairs until well after midnight, and Bren had been sound asleep, earplugs firmly in place, for hours.

She didn't even bother to speak to him when he left. Simply ate her toast and watched her news and read her magazine, just as she'd done so many times before the Kitchen Classroom had opened. Life. It had a way of just going round and round in circles, didn't it?

Bren spent most of the day listlessly wandering the house, everything looking dull and lifeless to her. Back in the day, December 22 had been exciting. So much energy the house felt like it was buzzing. She and the kids would be making sugar cookies — as they got older, someone would always try to sneak a penis onto a gingerbread man or snowman just to see if she would notice — decorating them with colored icing and sprinkles and even those silver candy balls that were so hard they damn near broke your teeth.

They would be playing Christmas music — John Denver singing about the wide-open range and the Peanuts gang full of happiness and cheer — and humming along as they made huge messes of pies and pinecones and garland and those little Italian cookies that Bren could never seem to get exactly right, their joy bouncing off the wood paneling (and, later, the wallpaper, and, later again, the green paint) of the kitchen walls.

Normally she would take them to her mom's. Her dad would still be there — smoking clove cigarettes and rubbing his belly through a thin T-shirt, laughing at a sitcom or watching a football game or sometimes doing both at once, remote finger madly flipping back and forth, back and forth.

Her mom would be in the kitchen with Aunt Cathy, arguing over whether to put oysters in the stuffing or giblets in the gravy or who would make the better presidential candidate for the next term or whose hair had the best platinum rinse or whether the Beatles were a good band that changed the face of music forever or a bunch of noise made popular by a bunch of screaming teenagers. Or God knew what else. It didn't matter what else. It was the holidays, and Joan and Cathy's arguments were as much part of the reverie as anything.

Sitting at her kitchen table, a crossword nearly filled out, but stuck on an eleven-letter word for *victorious* also beginning with *V*, it seemed to Bren that the Christmas she remembered so dearly happened so long ago. Almost like something that had happened in a dream, but not in real life. People had died since then. Left this planet.

People like her father and her uncle George, but also like the kids she'd seen the old woman — that Virginia Mash, or whatever her name was — giving hats and blankets to. People like mothers and sisters and young ones who had so much life left in them.

It seemed so pointless, celebrating this one day out of the year, didn't it?

She placed her pen on the magazine and closed it, even though she'd figured out the word — *vanquishing* — and emptied the dregs of her hot chocolate in one bitter swallow, certain that she knew what she really needed right now. She needed to go back in time.

She needed to see her mother. That was what she needed.

The first thing Bren heard when she walked through her mother's front door was Aunt Cathy's voice. She sighed. She loved her aunt, but sometimes she took so much energy to absorb. And sometimes, even when you were damn near fifty yourself, you just needed Mommy Time.

". . . told that customer service representative, first off, your name is no more Michael than mine is . . . ," Aunt Cathy was saying. She stopped when Bren walked into the room. "Well, look who the cat coughed up," she said. Her usual joke. Or at least Bren thought it was a joke. Knowing Aunt Cathy, she may very well have thought that was how the saying went.

"Well, hello, Brenda. I wasn't expecting you," her mother said, sitting in her usual spot, coffee mug on the table in front of her, hands wrapped around it for warmth. "Did you shut the front door? It's so cold out there — the storm door isn't good enough."

"Gets dark as a well digger's ass in here with all the doors shut," Aunt Cathy chimed in.

"I think the saying is *cold as a well digger's ass,*" Bren said.

"How do you know how cold a well digger's ass is?" Aunt Cathy said. "Seems like it would be pretty warm to me."

"Well, how do you know how dark one is?" Joan asked. "Seems like we're all making guesses here."

"Touché," Aunt Cathy said.

"Or *tushy,*" Bren supplied. "Given the subject at hand." They all giggled. It felt good to laugh, but it also made Bren miss the ladies at the Kitchen Classroom all the more. She got herself a cup of coffee, even though her gut was already sloshing from the hot chocolate.

"So what brings you by, Brenda?" Joan asked.

Bren shrugged, sipped her coffee, added a healthy dollop of creamer, sipped it again. "I was just missing Christmas, I guess. Where's your tree, Mom?" She brushed dust off a Santa figurine her mother had placed in the center of the table.

"Ah, just too much of a hassle this year. Not going to have one."

"That's what I was afraid you'd say." Bren slid into the chair across from her mother.

Joan eyed her daughter. "Something wrong? Another mole?"

"You can come help me put my tree the rest of the way up, if it's that important to you," Aunt Cathy said. "Thing's a heavy pain in the ass. I don't know why I bother."

Bren pointed at Aunt Cathy. "That. That's what's wrong. You have no tree, I almost had no tree, Aunt Cathy hates her tree. Doesn't that bother you?"

Joan and Cathy exchanged confused

365

glances. "No," Joan said. "Should it?"

"Yes!" Bren exclaimed. "Yes, it should! I mean, what keeps us from becoming just like that old woman?"

"What old woman? Is she talking about us?" Aunt Cathy said. "I'm not old. You are, but I'm way behind you."

"No, not you. Virginia Mash." Bren realized that she was getting a little loud. "The woman upstairs?" Like Gary, both her mother and Aunt Cathy looked upward. "Above the Kitchen Classroom," she said, exasperated. "She's so miserable. Alone. Mean as a snake. And what would you bet she doesn't have a Christmas tree in her apartment, either?"

"Well, I don't know, I think it's a far cry from us to her, don't you think?" Joan said. "Just because your arthritis — or a mole — is bothering you and you don't want to mess with a tree for one year doesn't mean you're going to act like that woman."

"But don't you miss it, Mom?" Bren cried. She stood up, paced to the sink and back, suddenly flooded with energy.

"It's just a tree, Brenda."

"Not the tree, all of it. The kids and the cookies and the wrapping paper and the fire in the fireplace."

Her mother looked into her coffee cup.

"Well, sure, sometimes I miss those things. But there are still good things. Catherine and I watch movies, and we have a grand time. Don't we, Catherine?"

"I want to watch the Chevy Chase one tonight. The one where the squirrel gets stuck on his back. You can watch with us tonight, Bren, if you're that bored. It's a funny scene, that one." Joan nodded in agreement.

"I don't want to watch *Christmas Vacation*," Bren said. She dumped her mostly full coffee cup into the sink. "I want to still be making my own Christmas vacation."

"Well, why can't you?" Joan asked.

"Because it's different now. The kids are gone and Gary's busy and you're going to Vegas, and nothing is the same. And I miss it." She paced back over to the table and sat again. "Mom, don't you miss Daddy?"

Joan's face went slack. "Of course I do," she said. "Why would you even ask such thing?"

"Because he's gone and I miss him. He was the first one to leave our Christmas, and now there's no more tree and no football and no kids or cookies or clove cigarettes."

"Oh, I hated those damn cigarettes," Aunt Cathy said, wrinkling her nose. "Smelled terrible as a well digger's ass." And while she still had the saying wrong, Bren didn't correct her, because it seemed like a fair comparison. "I'm glad they're gone."

"That's not the point," Bren exclaimed. "Oh, just . . . forget it. Forget I said anything."

Joan reached across the table and patted Bren's hand. "What's really going on, Brenda? Something tells me this isn't about clove cigarettes."

Bren slid over into the chair next to her mother and laid her head on Joan's shoulder. "Oh, Mom. It's everything. It's the kids and that class and the old woman upstairs. And it's Gary. I think he's fallen out of love with me. He doesn't want anything to do with me. All he can think about is his band."

"Oh, honey, I'm sure he still loves you. Men just go through these kinds of changes differently. He probably misses the kids just as much as you do."

"I don't know," Bren said. "You can't tell by talking to him."

"That's because that's not how men deal with these sorts of things. You have to relate to him on his level."

"Jealousy," Aunt Cathy said. "Make him jealous. Go get you a little something on the side."

"No. Catherine!" Joan scolded. She turned back to Bren. "You let him have his space. And then when he gets it all worked out, he'll come back to you and it will be like nothing ever happened."

"And in the meantime, you dip his toothbrush in the toilet every single day," Aunt Cathy said.

"No, you do not!" Joan said, acting shocked, but even she couldn't keep a straight face. Bren giggled into her mom's shoulder, feeling like a teenager again, and loving the image of Gary brushing his teeth with toilet water every morning. It wasn't mature, but then again, he was wanting to relive those old glory days, now, wasn't he? He wasn't exactly interested in mature.

In the end, Bren went over to Aunt Cathy's to help with the tree. She was right — it was a pain in the ass — but they put on *Christmas Vacation* and Joan popped some popcorn, and by the end of it, Bren wasn't so sure she missed Gary at all anymore.

Chapter Twenty-Seven

It turned out that Gil did get a gig for the band. It wasn't a party at the airport Holiday Inn so much as it was the lobby of the Holiday Hotel, a dumpy by-the-hour place on the fringe of the city, out where the skater kids smoked dope and broke their ankles in the loading docks of warehouses and on the steps of the abandoned Amtrak depot.

Snow on the Roof was to play exactly ten Christmas songs. No Hanukkah, no requests. They just weren't good enough. But their encore was an almost-recognizable rendition of "Happy Xmas (War Is Over)," so they were feeling pretty stoked.

When Bren had gotten home from Aunt Cathy's, they were already playing. She sheepishly crept into the house, trying not to think about John being down there — still unsure about what exactly had gone down between them the night before in the living room, and even more unsure about the vague excitement it made her feel on the inside to know that, if she hadn't misread everything, there was at least someone out there who found her interesting enough to want to be with. She was maybe just the tiniest bit unnerved that she didn't feel guilty about that thought, either. Maybe Aunt Cathy was right — if Gary wanted to keep her, he needed to let her know that.

No sooner had she had the thought than the basement door opened, the music swelling. Bren turned from the kitchen counter, where she was bent over watching the news.

John stood in the doorway, looking as shy and hangdog as ever, only with that newfound creepy grin of his.

"Oh," she said, patting her hair. Why was she patting her hair? Hair patting was for swoony girls. She wasn't a swoony girl. Hadn't been a swoony girl in ages. Aunt Cathy was getting to her. "Taking a break?"

"Just me," he said. He held up a Six Flags tumbler. "Need a refill."

She held out her hand. "What is it?"

"Just water. But don't tell the guys. They think it's something more. Truth is, all the beer and junk food have been wrecking my stomach. I'm not twenty anymore, you know."

Bren smiled. Finally. One of them admitted that this was a young man's game they were all pretending at. "Yes, I do know. I'm not twenty anymore, either." She took the tumbler and filled it with ice and water, her back to him. "Somebody needs to tell Gary that he's not twenty anymore, either. I don't see how he's doing it, staying up so late every single night. I'm sound asleep before he even comes up to bed."

She screwed the cap back on the tumbler, but when she turned to hand it to him, she realized he had closed the distance between the two of them. He was close enough to reach out and touch her now, a thought that made her breath hitch with hesitation.

"He's a fool, then," he said, stepping close. He took the tumbler from her hand and placed it on the kitchen counter without breaking eye contact.

"I'm sorry?" Bren asked, her heart pounding in her throat, her eyes nearly crossing trying to focus on him while he was so close. She gulped.

"If he's not coming to bed with you," he repeated. She could feel the heat coming off him. "He's a fool."

"Oh, I don't know about tha—"

But she couldn't finish because suddenly his mouth was on hers, his arms wrapped around her waist, pulling her in insistently. She made a muffled noise of protest, and even put her hands on his chest with every intention of pushing him away.

The problem was . . . she kind of didn't want to. The kiss felt nice. Soft. Warm. Close. She hadn't felt softness or warmth or closeness in so long.

John must have sensed her pushing her hesitation away, because he suddenly kissed deeper, the sensation touching Bren in places that hadn't been awakened in forever. She sucked in air through her nose in surprise, still telling herself in the back of her mind that she shouldn't be enjoying this, should be slapping his face or calling for Gary or screaming like a proper damsel in distress.

But would Gary even care? She was no longer so sure. There was a part of her — a very depressed part — that thought Gary might welcome someone else taking the heat off him for a change. *Whew,* she could imagine Gary saying. *Let her yammer your ear off for an hour about some cranky old woman in her cooking class.*

Finally, John broke the kiss, but he still didn't pull away. In fact, if anything, he ground his hips into hers harder, his hands spreading to take ownership of the small of her back. Still, the music blatted on downstairs, almost as an unidentifiable soundtrack to their indiscretion.

Bren removed her hands from his chest, and pulled back as much as she could without actually breaking his grasp, partly stilled by shock, and partly unwilling to leave the moment of feeling wanted.

"John," she said.

"I know," he said. "I shouldn't. Not here. But I could feel it, and I knew I'd never convince you unless I did something big. So here's something big." He leaned in and kissed her again, this time lighter and less insistent, though his fingers stroked their way up her back and into her hair as he did so.

She let out a moan — she couldn't help it — and then tucked her lips in on themselves, her eyes going big in surprise. When was the last time she'd made that noise?

This time she did push him away. "John," she said again.

"You're right," he said. "This is a bad place. We can meet somewhere later. Anywhere. You pick."

"Meet?" she said stupidly. "Pick?" It was only then that she began to edge backward.

"Just probably not the Holiday Hotel," he said. "For obvious reasons."

"Hotel?" Bren realized she sounded redundant, if not a little obtuse, but she was so in shock she couldn't seem to muster her own thoughts. Was this really happening? Was she talking hotel with a man she'd just kissed, who wasn't Gary? Three days before Christmas? "John, I'm not . . . I'm not . . ." was all she could manage.

He pulled her in tighter. "It's okay, Bren. I understand. I know you're not the kind of woman to just jump in bed with everybody. We have something special. I've felt it and so have you. For years." He leaned his forehead against hers. It was rimmed with sweat. Or maybe hers was — she really couldn't tell, and the fact that she couldn't tell made it all the worse. Her sweat had actually comingled with another man's sweat. This, somehow, felt like even more of a betrayal than the kiss itself.

"But I haven't," she said. Maybe the tiniest lie. She had noticed something off about him, and yet she'd continued to ignore it. Deny it. Even after he'd caught her in the living room that day, even when he'd told her that he and Cindy had broken up, and all that stuff about the nuts and the boning, she'd still tried to deny that it had ever happened. Maybe she was hoping that he'd lose interest, get his senses back.

Or maybe she had enjoyed the attention too much.

She cleared her voice, made it stronger. "I haven't felt anything. I'm devoted to Gary."

He stepped back, incredulity sweeping over his face. With maybe a dash of disappointment. "Why? He treats you like crap, Bren. He doesn't pay any attention to you. He barely even knows you're here."

Even though he hadn't said anything she didn't already know, it still stung to hear it aloud. "With all due respect, John, that's our business."

"And so you'll just ignore what we have, then? You'll just ignore this?" He darted in again, swept an arm around her back, and kissed her with even more passion. Her toes tingled with it, and once again, to her surprise, she did not pull back. That moan may have even made a reappearance. She could have been imagining it, but she possibly might have even leaned into him a bit. Dammit, what was her body thinking? He just . . . felt so warm. So good. And maybe he was right — maybe she needed to give up on Gary. Maybe Gary had given up on her long ago and she was a fool for staying loyal to a man who, even in other people's opinions, treated her like crap.

The phone rang, startling both of them.

They separated with a wet pop, Bren stumbling back two steps. For a moment they simply stared at each other, chests heaving.

Distance. Distance was a good thing. Because from this distance she could see only the man who'd been her husband's best friend for decades. She could see only that he was hurting and struggling and reaching out.

The phone rang again, this time caller ID announcing that it was Kelsey.

Dear God, Kelsey. And surely Kevin and the new wild-night-in-Rome-maybe-bride was with her. Her children, the ones who'd trusted her for their entire lives to make the right decisions. To keep their home stable, even if they didn't want to live in it anymore. And, for the love of God, to not cheat on their father.

Calling right in the middle of her doing just that.

Wait. Was she doing just that? Was it cheating if she was simply guilty of not pulling away? She imagined Gary might think so.

Worse, Kelsey and Kevin might think so.

Bren was suddenly filled with such shame she was nearly unable to move from her spot. The phone rang again. John wiped his mouth, but he was still leering.

Bren shook her head. "I'm sorry," she

377

said, imagining the disappointed faces of her children on the other end of that phone line.

Why didn't you answer, Mom?

Oh, no reason, I was just making out with Uncle John.

God, she wanted to die.

"I'm sorry," she repeated. "But you're wrong. I don't feel anything."

"That's not true," John said, and he may have even been right — it was too confusing for Bren to tell at that very moment — but then he shrugged and reached for his tumbler. Bren had forgotten all about the tumbler, as if they'd been at this for hours rather than just a few moments. Surprisingly, the band was still mutilating the same song they'd been tearing apart when John had appeared at the top of the stairs. "But okay. If you change your mind — no, make that *when* you change your mind — you know where to find me."

Unfortunately, she did. But she would try very, very hard to pretend that she didn't. She would convince herself.

The phone rang a fourth time. It would go to voice mail if it rang a fifth. As John tromped back down the stairs, Bren leapt for it.

"Mommy? I was just about to hang up."

Bren closed her eyes, tried to steady her racing heart. "Hi, sweetie. How are you?"

There was a puff of air on the other end — a sigh. "Oh, fine, I suppose."

Bren's ears perked. Just fine? I suppose? Not beautiful? What happened to beautiful, beautiful Thailand and all its beautiful customs and beautiful Dean and beautiful, beautiful, oh-so-beautiful food? "What's wrong?"

"Nothing." But this was definitely Kelsey's pouty voice. A very irrational part of Bren (and she recognized that those parts were aplenty inside her these days) worried that somehow Kelsey knew — just knew — what had been happening at the moment she called in the very kitchen where she'd eaten her first jar of strained sweet potatoes.

"Doesn't sound like nothing," Bren said.

"It's just . . ." Another puff of air. "It's just that . . . I mean, don't get me wrong, Thailand is wonderful. It's beautiful and the culture is so amazing and everything. It's just so very far away. And it doesn't feel like Christmas here."

"Has Kevin not ever shown up?"

"Yeah, he has." More listlessness. "And Pavlina. And she's nice, I think. She doesn't really speak English that much. But Kevin doesn't know anything about her, not really, and he says he's not even sure if they're actually married." She lowered her voice. "And don't tell him I said this, but I think he's kind of hoping that they're not. I caught him talking to two girls at the market the other day, and later that night we had a few Singhas and he started going on about annulment practices and asking all kinds of questions about whether a marriage was legal if you did it outside the US with no license or anything like that."

Bren scrambled for the telephone pad. Wrote down *Singha.*

"I think he's really embarrassed that he did it, Mommy, but he won't just come out and say it. Instead he's spending all his time at the beach and leaving Pavlina here with me. And we can't really talk, so we just sit around and watch Thai TV together. And I don't understand a word of that."

Bren was taken aback. Maybe this was why Kevin hadn't included her in his wedding and marriage. Maybe he really had been telling the truth about it being a wild night in Rome. From the sound of things, one he regretted. "Well, he's a big boy," she said. "Nothing we can do for him. He's got to figure this out for himself. And not get her pregnant, whatever he does."

"I don't see how he can. She goes to bed

and he's in the kitchen drinking with me." She sighed again. "Not very Christmassy."

"Well, you can't let your brother dictate how your holiday goes," Bren said, though she would be lying if she said she wasn't just a little bit happy to hear that everything wasn't going so beautifully at the moment.

"But Dean is working all the time. Like, round the clock. And since it's not the same here, he doesn't really feel the need to take time off for the holidays. So he's just leaving me with this really awkward situation. And I'm tired of fish. And I want you. I want brisket and corn casserole and pumpkin pie and brownies and homemade bread. I want to come home."

Bren nearly dropped her pencil, John all but wiped clean from her mind. Her daughter missed her. She wanted to come home. She wanted to have Christmas after all. Just as Bren did. "You can always come home," she said, not even sure if her lips were moving in her stunned happiness.

"Not in time for Christmas," Kelsey said. "But I was sort of hoping right after New Year's? I talked to Kevin about it last night. I think we can both swing it. I have enough money for mine and Kevin's tickets. He doesn't really have the money for Pavlina's ticket, but he says that's all up in the air right now, anyway, so . . . Can we come home for the new year?"

Bren smiled so hard her temples hurt. "Are you kidding me? Yes! Yes, of course! Oh, how exciting! Your father will be thrilled. We'll have Christmas dinner in January. I can send you some money. You need money?"

Truth be told, Bren would have sent her anything she asked for at that moment. Money? Boat? New car? Private jet to fly home in? Sure, consider it done!

They became a flurry of plan making. Excited chatter about who they would see and what they would do. Kelsey wanted to sit in on Bren's cooking class, which gave Bren a pang of regret that there was now no cooking class to sit in on. She wanted to listen to Gary's band play — Bren started to wonder how awkward that would be, given what had just transpired with John, but pushed the thought out of her head. She wanted to shop and buy lunches and visit Grandma Joan and Great-Aunt Cathy and spend a lot of time just sitting in the kitchen catching up on things.

By the time Bren hung up, she'd only written the word *Singha* on her telephone pad. She crossed it out, making an educated guess that Singha was beer.

In its place, she wrote *January Visit =
Beautiful.*

And then she went upstairs to wait for
band practice to be done so she could tell
Gary the great news.

CHAPTER TWENTY-EIGHT

It was nearly two a.m. before Gary came to bed. The music had finally stopped around midnight, but there had apparently been quite the after-party in her kitchen. She could hear voices and laughter and the sound of bottles clinking.

She'd also heard the front door open and close just a few moments after midnight. She'd gotten up and pulled back the curtains. It had begun to sleet — hard ice pellets stinging the windows — and bent over against the wind, heading toward his car, was John. Not staying for the party.

He'd looked up at the window just before getting into his car, as if he knew he was being watched — and Bren had quickly let the curtain drop, stepping to the side so he couldn't see her, feeling naked in her nightgown. Granted, her "nightgown" was just an old T-shirt of Gary's paired with some beat-up running shorts that she'd only ever used for laundry day — never for actual running — but she still felt as if letting him see her in her nightwear was a little too intimate for her.

She'd already let things go too far. It was flattering, having someone want you, but she wasn't interested. If she had lost sight of that for a few seconds in the kitchen that evening, her conversation with Kelsey had reminded her. She'd built this life. It was what she wanted. It was worth fighting for.

Being wanted for a hotel room tryst was nothing like being wanted for a lifetime, even through the good and the bad. She needed to remember that.

Over the next two hours, she watched TV, battled drooping eyelids, and listened for the front door to open and close again. It eventually did, just as she was beginning to fear that she'd lose the eyelid battle once and for all. But with the sound of a silent kitchen, she was energized again, champing at the bit to tell Gary the good news about the kids.

Gary tumbled into the bedroom, reeking of bourbon, and flopped onto the bed, facedown, still in all of his clothes. He belched into his pillow.

"Have fun?" Bren asked, trying to sound sweet and interested, not like a pestering wife. Maybe if she just eased up on him, he would come around.

He turned his head so one eye was showing. "What are you still doing up?"

"I was waiting for you."

He blinked and then closed the one eye of his that was showing. Then turned his face back down to the pillow. "I can't tonight, Bren. I don't feel good."

She gazed at him, unimpressed. Even if she had been staying awake with hopes of seducing him — which she most definitely was not — the fact that he didn't feel good seemed to be of his own doing. A realization that was both outrageous and depressing. Turned down by a drunk guy. She tried to tamp down the irritation. "I'm not staying up for that. I have some good news for you. Are you listening to me?"

He grunted.

"Gary. Are you listening?" She shoved him in the side, making him rock like a beached whale and settle back into place.

"What? I said yes." Growled into the pillow.

"Well, you're not looking at me."

"I don't listen with my eyes." He huffed, rolled to his back, and stared at her. "There. Happy?"

The excitement Bren had been storing up

inside of her shriveled to nothing, instantly replaced with annoyance. Could he not let her have one good feeling? Any attention at all? "Not with that attitude, no."

"What is it, Brenda?" he asked, using her full name, when he knew good and well that her mother was the only one who'd been given that free pass in this world. "What is so goddamned important that you just have to have my full attention at two o'clock in the morning? What, is it more installments in the Old Lady Above the Kitchen saga? Because I'm not going to lie. I really don't care."

She gathered herself up and stepped out of bed, feeling for her slippers with her feet. She knew he was drunk. Even inattentive, rude, midlife-crisis Gary wouldn't have talked to her like that sober. But she was done making excuses for inattentive, rude, midlife-crisis Gary. She was done being patient and she was done forgiving and she was done going about her own business and she was so done begging for his attention.

She found her slippers and stuffed her feet into them. "You know what? No. I had some good news — great news, actually — but I'm not going to tell you now. You can forget it. I'm going to sleep in Kelsey's room, and when you've slept it off we can talk."

He pulled himself up to sitting. Rather than be humbled by her anger, he seemed to be affronted by it. "I'm getting damn tired of these games. I'm just trying to live my life, to have some fun, to get through my last ten years or so of working like a rat in a maze. The last thing I need is to come home to a nagging wife and have her waiting up for me just to act like I've done something wrong. What have I done wrong, Bren? Huh?" He wavered a little, like a plant stuck to an ocean floor, belched, and flopped back down. He rested one arm over his eyes. "Huh? What have I done that's so wrong?"

She didn't care that he wasn't looking at her now. She was so filled with rage she almost couldn't stand up straight. A part of her wanted to come to his side of the bed and pummel him with her fists until she knocked some sense into him. She put her hands on her hips, shivering with fury and cold. The ice pellets continued to knock on the window. She wanted to fling herself outside, let them sting her skin, cool her down. She wanted to do something drastic to make him notice her.

"You haven't done anything wrong, Gary," she said. "In fact, you haven't done anything at all. You haven't talked to me, or complimented me, or made love to me, or even noticed me, in months. I can't pay you enough to listen when I have a problem, and now you don't even care when I have something good to share."

"I do, too, care," he said, but he didn't bother to take his arm off his eyes to prove it.

"Oh, sure, you care so much. About your band. About your silly hotel lobby gig tomorrow."

That, he lifted his arm for. "Hey, it's a good gig for a band that's just starting out."

"You'll be playing for the guy at the reception desk. And yet somehow that's more important to you than me."

"Boo-hoo," he mumbled. "Poor Brenny isn't getting all the attention in the world. Can you say *spoiled brat*?"

She sucked in great gulps of air through her nostrils. "Oh yeah? Can you say *affair*?"

This got his attention. He lowered his arm and sat up. "I haven't had any affair. Now you're just being crazy."

"Not you, you jackass." She knew she'd better leave before she said something she couldn't take back later. But still her mouth pressed on, despite her brain.

His eyes narrowed. "Are you trying to say you're having an affair?" He snickered.

"Please. With who?"

"I'm not," she said. "But I could. With John." She saw his face fall slack, and finally she felt the satisfaction of having hurt him. She nodded and pressed on. "He kissed me, did you know that?" She pointed out the bedroom door. "Right there in your own kitchen. He wants to have sex with me, Gary. He wants to go to a hotel and screw my brains out. What do you think of that?"

"John?" he repeated, his voice soft and disbelieving.

If Bren hadn't been hurt, she might have seen what this new knowledge was doing to him — might have seen it right on his reddening face. But he'd drawn first blood and she was too far in now to go back, so she pressed on. "So you better start paying attention to me, Gary Epperson. Because if you don't want to, there is at least one other man out there who will gladly do so."

Before he could respond at all, she turned on her heel and left the room, marching right down to Kelsey's old bedroom — which was now half guest room, half storage room — and slamming the door. She locked it for good measure.

The clock on the nightstand said it was after two thirty, but she was wide-awake now, fuming, mumbling to herself, not at all tired anymore. Where just thirty minutes ago she'd been battling the sandman, now she felt as if she'd never sleep again.

She stood, arms crossed, lights out, and watched the sleet for a little while. It had already been such a wet winter — one of the things Kelsey'd said she missed most about being away from home during the holidays. Normally, the bad weather would serve only to make Bren feel cozier. But now it just seemed cold and wet and unforgiving.

She turned away from the window, hoping maybe if she lay down on the bed she would suddenly become tired. But as she moved, she kicked a plastic bag. She looked down. It was filled with a cross-stitch pattern of a dachshund, some embroidery thread, and a plain white pillowcase — things she'd bought with the intent of including them in the one-hundred-gifts project.

Yet another of her failures staring at her in the face.

She kicked the bag harder, then lay down on the bed and cried.

CHAPTER TWENTY-NINE

By the time Bren woke up, it was light outside. Brilliant light, dazzling light. The kind of light that was torture to eyes that had stayed open half the night shedding tears. She shifted so she was looking out the window. Despite the persistent sound of it, the sleet hadn't really amounted to much of anything. It lay like a grainy topcoat on the snow that had not yet melted from the last storm. Birds hopped around in it, foraging for whatever they could find in the melted patches, and then flitting up into the chestnut tree to take inventory and try again. She felt sorry for them. Almost as if she could relate to them.

She felt delicate and fragile, starving, cold. The world seemed so huge and unrelenting to her at that moment. So barren, as if it could turn its back on her at whim. She felt as if she were circling the same patch of yard, over and over again, just like those birds, and that she was turning up nothing. Nada. Zip. Zilch. Just brokenheartedness and a big old question mark where her life path should be.

"Just give up, little birds," she whispered. "Fly somewhere better than here." But the thought of their heeding her advice was too depressing, so she shifted again, onto her stomach, letting her arm trail over the side of the bed.

Her hand grazed the same plastic bag that she'd looked at the night before, but it was as if that had never happened, or as if it had happened so long ago she had no real recollection of it. Now she fiddled it open with her fingers and pulled out the dachshund pattern. Cute.

That was the one thing she'd been afraid to say during their turmoil with that old woman, that Virginia Mash — her dog was kind of cute. Something about small dogs touched Bren, the way they looked like puppies and old men all at the same time. That woman's dog seemed to be just as crotchety as his owner, but on him it was adorable. He had little gray eyebrows. And wrinkles around his lips. Bren had wondered how old he was — he'd already seemed to be defying the cosmic rules of a dog's life span.

She could tell the old woman worshipped

that dog. That was what had made her so excited about this cross-stitch. She thought the woman would be just the kind who could appreciate a good pet homage.

Who was she kidding? She had been excited about the whole project, not just the cross-stitch. She'd really wanted to show the old woman that kindness ruled. A bit of a social experiment, maybe, but one that would be worth it in the end if she could just heal the heart of the woman who so hated her. It was about heart, right? It wasn't about real hate. What was there to really hate about Bren Epperson?

She didn't want to know Gary's answer to that question right at the moment.

Oh God, Gary. She'd told him about the kiss. In a way she felt like maybe she'd been the drunk one last night, saying things she now regretted with such depth it felt like mourning. She would have to assure Gary that she'd taken care of it. That she'd shut it down and had no intention of meeting John in any hotel. She would even make it sound like it had never been even remotely appealing to her. She would omit the moans. Those had been involuntary; she couldn't be held responsible for them.

But the best way to not think about Gary right at this moment was to think about the cross-stitch. Maybe she would just while away some time with the embroidery thread. Let Gary sleep it off and plug himself full of coffee. Then she would unlock the door and face him.

She sat up in bed, leaned over until she could reach the bag, and pulled it up into her lap. She had all the essentials right there — thread, pillowcase, pattern, sewing box with needles on the top shelf of Kelsey's closet, left over from her Girl Scout days of sewing badges onto sashes.

In two hours, she had a snout, an eye, and most of a neck finished. She needed to pee and to shower. And probably to face Gary.

But when she went downstairs, Gary was nowhere to be found. Not even in the basement, where the band instruments stood like corpses in the dark. Odd that he wouldn't be going over his music or practicing a guitar solo or doing something to prepare for the big gig tonight. Maybe he was out buying the celebratory bourbon.

Bren showered and dressed, feeling much more human now. When she got out, Gary still hadn't come home, so she went upstairs and got the cross-stitch, then brought it downstairs to the living room, where she parked on the couch with a little daytime television. She had a blue dog collar to get

started on — she didn't want her dachshund to be naked.

An hour into the show, her hands had
finally begun to cramp a little. She'd been
at it for hours now, and had most of a dog
to show for it. She heard a car pull into the
driveway, the sun reflecting off it and dancing across the living room walls. Gary. Finally.

But the garage never opened, Gary never
came in. Instead, there was the sound of
shoes scuffing up the sidewalk and the
stomp of someone trying to knock snow off
of them on the front porch. At last, the
doorbell rang.

"I hope I haven't caught you at a bad
time," Tammy Lynn said when Bren opened
the door. "I asked Paula how to get ahold
of you. Don't be mad at her. I can be very
persistent when I want to be. Just ask a
chocolate cake." She chuckled, but Bren
noticed there was no force behind it.

"No, no, come on in. It's so lovely to see
you," Bren said. Out of habit, Bren silently
inventoried what embarrassments might be
lying around the house — clutter, empty
bourbon bottles, dirty panties hanging on
the laundry room door. But that was the
thing about being an empty nester. Most
messes were easily cleaned up. Not much of

anything went lying around for days. Had she not had the fight with Gary last night, she might have never known any revelry had happened in the kitchen at all. "I was just working on a cross-stitch." She flapped the pillowcase around.

Tammy Lynn stomped on the porch again and then came inside, huffing and puffing the way everyone does when they leave the cold. She unwound herself from her coat and scarf.

"Look at you. You've lost weight," Bren said.

Tammy Lynn waved her off. "Oh, goodness, far from it. But it's nice of you to say. Janelle has us working double time. I'm just dying for a McRib, though." She followed Bren into the living room. Bren picked up the remote and turned off the TV, which was in mid–Whoopi Goldberg rant. "Elwood is really struggling with it. Can you believe he actually suggested we just move away and not tell Janelle where we're going?" She leaned in and wrinkled her nose. "And I think he was serious."

"But it's noticeable," Bren said, with only a twinge of jealousy. Tammy Lynn was the kind of person you wanted to see succeed — the kind of person you saw yourself in if you looked hard enough, no matter who you were. "You must feel great."

She nodded. "And I do. When I'm not jogging. Nothing feels great then. Which is why I'm here."

They sat on the couch. Bren laid the cross-stitch on the coffee table.

"We jogged by the old classroom yesterday. Was so sad to see that sign on the door — Closed Until Further Notice. I feel so bad for Paula. But that old woman was out there, carrying her dog under her arm, just like always. Only she didn't look so mean. She just looked kind of sad. And she saw me. I know she did, because she did a double take. But instead of yelling at me about the restraining order, she just turned around and kept walking. No coat, no scarf, no nothing. I was running and I had on a coat and scarf, and I wasn't even sweating. It was that cold."

Bren made the appropriate *tsk*ing noises and shook her head. The nerve of some people. Or the state of this society. Or whatever it was she was supposed to be getting out of this.

"Anyway," Tammy Lynn said. She reached over and picked up the pillowcase, ran her forefinger over the thread. "I just got to thinking. Maybe we gave up too easily."

"What do you mean?" Bren asked. "Paula

had to shut the place down. She didn't have the money to fight anymore."

"No, I don't mean that," Tammy Lynn said. "Don't get me wrong — I miss the class so much — but I mean we gave up on the gift project too easily."

"There was a restraining order."

"But she doesn't know it was us leaving the gifts. She can't prove anything anyway. Besides, I think she kind of wanted them. I think she liked it."

"She gave them away," Bren said. "If she liked it, she sure had a heck of a way of showing it."

Tammy Lynn held up one finger. "That's just it. I think she liked having them to give away. There's something behind that, don't you think? A woman doesn't just wander around the city in no coat and then give one away to a sick kid."

Bren hadn't thought of it before, but Tammy Lynn had a point. She herself had been perplexed when she'd spotted the old woman giving away the gifts, all but freezing herself with no jacket. At the time Bren had chalked it up to the woman being strange and difficult and not worth trying to understand. But maybe she'd been wrong. Maybe there was more to the story.

"So you're suggesting . . ."

Tammy Lynn was nodding so hard her big hair — which looked even bigger with her subtle weight loss — was bouncing around on her head like a bounce house. "That we finish the project. Why not? We all had plans. We can get together. We can do it here. Look — you've already started." She picked up the cross-stitch and held it up for Bren.

Bren smiled, studying the adorable dachshund that had taken shape on the pillowcase. Tammy Lynn was right. What did they really have to lose?

"Okay, why not?"

Within an hour, everyone had arrived. Lulu and Teresa bottled spices and Aunt Cathy painted an ornament, Joan put in two huge pans of brownies, and Rebecca wrapped a pretty fountain pen in red and gold paper. Bren put the finishing touches on her cross-stitch, and Tammy Lynn assembled a recipe book with typewritten notecards.

By the end of the day, Gary still had not come home, but Bren didn't worry about it. She knew he'd come back to get his instruments, at the very least. She could talk to him then. She could try to save things.

And, besides, the Kitchen Classroom ladies were up to a total count of eighty-eight gifts. They stashed them under the Christmas tree. Boxes, small and large, wrapped and unwrapped, tied with ribbon and twine and sprigged with fake holly and plastic mistletoe. Bags in silvers and golds and with gay poinsettias and sparkling snowscapes painted on them, tissue paper springing from their tops in every color of the rainbow. Baskets and jars, filled with goodies, filled with cheer, filled with sweets and mixes and comforting things. Filled with the love and care of a stranger's hand. Together they were an overflowing, over-whelming hill of holiday cheer. A stacked and tumbling statement of goodwill.

Bren's heart swelled when she looked at them.

This.

This was what Christmas was all about.

CHAPTER THIRTY

It was time. She'd known it for far longer than she wanted to admit. To acknowledge that it had been time for a while now would be to acknowledge that she hadn't done what was best for the dog, but only — selfishly, she knew — what was best for her.

But Chuy hadn't been able to use his hind legs for two days now. They'd dragged behind him the few times he'd had the energy to try to move from his spot on the couch. He'd scooted along, never making a fuss, bless his furry little heart, but with eyes rolling around pathetically as if he were asking, *Why can't it just be over already?*

Virginia Mash understood that question. She understood it very well. She'd understood it for a very long time.

Finally, she'd called a cab. "Take your time," she'd said when they told her they'd get someone out to her as soon as they could. If she could blame it on a slow cab, maybe it wouldn't be her fault that it had taken so long to get him to the vet.

But it was time, and she knew it. He knew it, too. He seemed to accept it.

Damn that dog, he still wagged his tail when she talked to him. Even if it was just a pathetic nudge — maybe a centimeter of movement — it was there just the same. And he knew that she understood what it meant. It was a thank-you. An offer of lifelong friendship. It was meant to console her over what she was going to have to do. It was an apology. Anyone in their right mind would probably think she was crazy for reading so many things into a barely wagged tail.

Those people didn't know Chuy.

But she knew Chuy and she knew her daughter and she knew it was time.

When the cab came, she was watching through the painted-shut front window. She was already dressed in her lounge pants and flannel, boots tied. She watched, though, as the cabdriver got out of the car, looked around, perplexed, and then ducked back inside and laid on the horn.

She picked up Chuy, dog bed and all, and, leaving her cane by the door so she could hold him with two arms, made her way down the stairs.

"It's about time," she snapped when she got in the car. It smelled like onions and incense. "I don't have all day to wait around for you to decide you want to come by."

The man only gazed at her through the rearview mirror. "Where to?" he asked.

Cabdrivers were unflappable.

The words wanted to stick to the sides of her throat. They wanted to cling inside, hooking into her soft flesh. "Noah's Ark Animal Clinic. On Third."

He didn't respond. Only nodded and put the car into gear. She grabbed the door handle with one hand as they started moving, if only to keep herself from jumping out, changing her mind.

Surely she could get another week with him. Maybe two. So he couldn't walk. She could walk for him.

But she knew that was a ridiculous thought. She knew it was time.

They rode in silence, Chuy staring up at her the whole way. His expression was peaceful. Calm. Even happy. He seemed to sense what was about to happen. He seemed to welcome it. She absently rubbed her knuckle down the length of his head as they traveled the city.

Maybe he was accepting what was happening, but what about her? She supposed she would ultimately accept it, too. Seemed that was what life was mostly about — accepting the really shitty things that couldn't be changed. But it was the time between acceptance and relief that was the hard part.

Noah's Ark was a hole in the wall. A place beaten down and beaten out by those fancy doggy-day-care-type places, where young couples with way too much money sent their precious little furballs for overpriced activities that, Virginia Mash believed, were not meant to be engaged in by animals. She would never understand this busy generation, so scheduled and to-do'ed, even their dogs had lesson plans to live their days by. She imagined these people had calendars specifically for their "fur babies," as they loved to call them. She imagined these people needed lives.

She loved Chuy, but she would be struck dead before she would step foot into one of those places.

Besides, she loved Dr. Kahn. He was gentle, even for such a big man with such big, clumsy-looking hands, and Chuy liked him. Wagged when he came into the room, even when he was there for shots. Even when he was there for the last shot of his life.

"Virginia," Dr. Kahn said when he came

into the room. "I was just thinking about Chuy the other day, wondering how he was getting along." He flipped through a chart. Another thing Virginia loved about Dr. Kahn — no computer charts like those fancy places. He still used good old pencil on paper.

"He's not getting along," Virginia said, holding her chin up high to show him that she was not going to be emotional about this. The same pose she'd taken at Jamie's graveside so many years ago. And the same one she'd struck at her husband's graveside, too. The picture of stoicism. She had this under control. Control was power; you had to try to wrestle it out of every situation you found yourself in.

"I'm sorry to hear that. Let me take a look. Come here, Chu, old boy."

But Chuy didn't come to him, and when Virginia laid him down on the metal exam table, he didn't even lift his head. His breathing had become quick and labored, and while he wagged faintly at the sound of his name, his eyes didn't seem to be taking in much of anything. Still, Dr. Kahn checked him over, lifting his tail and pulling back his lips and squinting into his ears.

Finally, he gave Chuy a rub along the neck and let out a big sigh.

"I know what you're going to say. That's why I brought him here. Let's just get it over with," Virginia said. She tried for her sharp, snapping voice, but it broke at the end and she had to cut the word *with* short to take a breath.

Dr. Kahn nodded. "I'm so sorry, Virginia. I know what he means to you. You were good to take him in."

"I had no other choice," Virginia said. She found she had to look at the canine aging chart poster over his left shoulder while she talked. She took a deep breath, trying to stretch out the stomach muscles that had gone taut and sore. "But, yes, he's been a good dog. Nothing lives forever."

He continued to stroke Chuy's head, his huge hands working so gently that Chuy barely even moved with the motion. Chuy closed his eyes. A drop of clear liquid fell from one nostril.

"I'll give you a minute," Dr. Kahn said, and he left.

Alone with Chuy, she could hear his breath, quick, ragged, labored. It seemed to rattle around the room in accusatory percussion: *you should have brought me here sooner!* But at the same time, he looked content.

She stepped forward and ran her hand

down the length of his back. She didn't want to be one of those schmaltzy types, someone who gave her dying dog a lengthy monologue of love and devotion before wobbling out of the office a sniveling, sopping mess. Besides, there was so much to say to Chuy, it was impossible to say it all. She knew because she'd spent the past several days trying.

The apartment's going to be empty without you, she wanted to say. *My walks are going to be lonely. Say hi to Ernie for me. Say hi to Jamie. Especially to Jamie. Tell them I'm sorry I wasn't there for them more. You were a good old dog, Chuy. A great friend.*

But instead, all she said was "Good-bye, old pal." She continued petting him until Dr. Kahn came back.

"You can stay if you like," he said. "Or you're welcome to go. Some people like to remember them as they were living. Some like to be here with them until the very end. Either way is up to you."

Once again, Virginia held her chin up. "I have a cab waiting for me," she said. "I should go."

When she got to the door, she ventured a look over her shoulder. Chuy opened his eyes and wagged his tail, big thumping wags. She wasn't sure if he was wagging at

408

her or if he was seeing someone on the other side. And she didn't know which she was hoping it would be.

CHAPTER THIRTY-ONE

Bren hadn't spoken to Gary since the big fight the night before. He'd stayed gone all day, and even into the evening. He finally came in just as the ladies were leaving, the living room full of gifts for Virginia Mash.

"Where've you been?" Bren asked when he came through the door.

"Nowhere, really," he said. He was still pouting. He passed her and went into the kitchen, heading immediately for the refrigerator and a beer.

Bren followed him hesitantly, leaning up against the doorframe between the two rooms. "Listen, Gary. We should talk. About last night. I wasn't thinking when I said some things."

He twisted the cap off the beer and took two long swigs. "It's done," he said, after a belch.

"No, I want to clear the air. I shouldn't have insinuated that I would —"

"It's okay," he said. "Let's just drop it."

Bren knew Gary, and she knew when *drop it* meant she could keep pushing and when *drop it* meant drop it. He meant drop it. But she was tired of dropping it.

"No," she said. "I've been begging you to talk to me for months, and now you're going to do it."

He gazed at her with tired, hungover eyes. "What do you want me to say, Bren? You kissed another man."

She wagged her finger. "No, he kissed me."

"There's a difference?"

"Of course there is," she cried.

"He said you led him on. He said you'd been flirting with him. He talked about you being naked on the day you broke Gil's drum, and that he was here. Funny how you never mentioned that little detail to me." He took another swig of beer. "You gotta admit, Brenda, it sounds a little fishy."

Her face flamed. She wished the memory of that day could just be wiped away forever. "Sure it seems fishy when you put it that way. But you have to give me the benefit of the doubt, Gary. We've been married twenty-seven years, and I've never been devoted to anyone but you. You, on the other hand, have been solely devoted to

411

your little projects."

He stood. "I'm sorry — I wasn't aware that my full-grown wife needed a baby-sitter." He walked toward the living room. Bren hated when he turned his back on her during an argument. He knew this. She took a deep breath to keep her calm.

"I don't need a babysitter, but a partner would be nice," she said, following him.

"So you went for my best friend? Classy, Bren. Real classy." He flopped onto the couch and picked up the remote, but Bren positioned herself in front of the TV so he couldn't use it.

"I didn't go for him! He went for me!" She was yelling now, her calm a thing of the past. "He thought we were having troubles, Gary. He thought I was available. Because of the way you were acting toward me. Think about that for a minute. He thought he could have me."

Gary's jaw set, but he didn't respond. She recognized that look on him — it was the look that he knew, on some level, she was right. She took advantage of the momentum.

"I've been begging you for attention. I took you to Olive Garden, for Christ's sake. But all you can give me is insults about my cooking and promises to talk later. I want a partner, not a fraternity roommate." He set his beer on the table, but still didn't speak. "I got naked on the drums for *you,* Gary. For you. It went horribly wrong, and I'm so embarrassed, and trust me, if I could take anything back, it would be that. But I swear I didn't kiss John. I love you. And that may make me the world's biggest idiot right now, but I can't help but think there's still hope for us. And maybe when you're done being mad at me, you'll have hope for us, too."

He took another drink. "I'm not mad at you," he finally said. Surly, unconvincing.

"You look mad. You sound mad."

"Can't I even say what my own feelings are without you questioning them?" he snapped.

She stood in awkward silence for a beat, waiting for him to say something more or for the right thing to pop into her mind or anything to break this weird bubble between them. He said he wasn't angry, but he didn't look like someone who wasn't angry. It was a part of marriage Bren didn't think she would ever get used to. The part where you were supposed to read each other's minds and just know how to make things better. She really began to fear what this new development meant for them. Maybe they were done. She tried to imagine what that would mean for her. Would she get the house? Would she have to go back to work, learn how to do things like clean out gutters and wash the lawn mower blades?

"Can I just . . . have a minute?" he finally said.

Bren nodded, her heart falling even lower, if that was possible. Here she had just told him how much she needed him, how much she missed him. Had laid herself bare at his feet. And all he wanted was more of the same — for her to go away. She turned and headed back toward the kitchen. She had no more fight left in her.

"Oh, I forgot. The good news," she said when she got to the doorway.

He looked confused for a moment, and then seemed to recollect what she was talking about. "Oh, yeah. What was it?"

"The kids. They're coming home."

"For Christmas?" He didn't look excited. More wary, and perhaps a bit unnerved.

"No, in a couple of weeks."

"I see," he said.

She sighed. "Aren't you happy they're coming home at least? We're going to have a proper Christmas celebration in January. And we can get to the bottom of this whole Kevin marriage issue while they're here. Oh,

Gary, be happy! Our kids are coming home."

"I'm happy," he said. "I'd like to see them. But they aren't staying long, are they?"

She slumped against the doorframe. "I don't know; we didn't talk about it. But I'm guessing if they're coming all the way from Thailand it's not going to be a weekend trip. I'll do their old rooms up for them. It'll be like old times."

"Yeah," he said, a downturn to his mouth.

"What is it?" Bren asked, cross again. She hadn't been expecting him to jump up and down for joy — that just wasn't Gary's style, especially after a big argument like they'd just had — but a little excitement might be nice. A smile, at the very least.

He took a breath, like he might say something, but let it out, and took another. Seemed to hesitate. Finally, he set his beer on the table. "It's just . . . I've waited a long time for this."

"For what?" But she had a sinking feeling she knew for what. For his dune buggies and his golf game and his band. For his freedom. As she'd feared and been unable to articulate until just this moment, Gary was in love with not having to have a family around to drag him down. Gary was in love with being untethered again for the first

415

time in his adult life. The kids were just a reminder that he had things to do, and while he could blow off Bren, he couldn't blow them off.

"For this," he said, gesturing around the room.

Bren glanced confusedly at the curtains, the end tables. "What do you mean? You've had this for almost thirty years."

His forehead creased with irritation. "No, not the house. Us. Alone. Here. Our lives."

"But we've been . . . unhappy," she said. "We've been fighting."

"Well, okay, I don't mean that. I mean having the house and our lives *to ourselves.* I've screwed it up lately, I get that. And I'm selfish. I get that, too. But I still want it. I want to have our dinner at Lucky's on Christmas Eve and I want to be able to eat popcorn and drink beer whenever I feel like it and I want to build models of ships inside bottles."

"Models of ships?" Bren repeated, thoroughly confused now.

"Or make sausage or have sex with my wife on the living room floor, or . . . whatever." He sagged back into his chair and picked up his beer again. "I got excited. I had so many things I'd been waiting to try until they moved out. And you seemed occupied with your shows and your magazines and your cooking class. I didn't think it was a big deal. I didn't realize you were taking it personally."

"Of course I was taking it personally. I was lonely as hell. I told you as much."

"I know," he said. "I just never thought it could drive you to another man's arms." Finally, when he looked at her, she could see the old Gary inside. The tender Gary. The one who'd said *I do* all those years ago. He'd been buried for so long, she wasn't sure she'd recognize him if he ever came back. But there he was.

She knelt in front of him. "It couldn't. It didn't. John was wrong. I never wanted him."

He closed his eyes, and when he opened them again, they looked watery. "For a minute there, I thought I might lose you."

The sky was turning hazy gray outside, nightfall pressing in on them already, bathing the kitchen in grainy twilight. The countertop looked dark and unused in this light. The house seemed heavy and closed in.

But on the inside Bren felt like she could fly to touch the sun. She'd only been waiting for this. This. She reached out and put her hand on his. He flipped his over, and they held hands like that for the longest time.

"Are you thinking about making dinner tonight, or should we go get something? I can pick up some burgers," he said.

Bren blinked. "It's the twenty-third. You have a gig."

He shook his head, drained the last of his beer. "Not anymore. That got canceled. The guys will come by after Christmas to get their stuff."

"But you worked so hard for that gig."

"Sure did. It was fun, too."

"Sorry they canceled on you, Gare."

"I canceled on them." He shrugged. "Things are different now. Easy come, easy go."

She walked over to him, put her hand on his shoulder and rubbed in circles, the way he always liked it. "How about I make something?"

Thirty minutes later Bren floated into Savings Shopper, nothing on her mind but carrots and potatoes and those little pearl onions — ingredients for Gary's favorite chicken potpie.

For so long now it had seemed like he didn't care. Like she had nothing to hang on to with him anymore. Like he just wanted his own life and his own things and his own activities and none of those involved Bren. But maybe, she now realized, he was just comfortable knowing that she would still be there when the other stuff ran out.

And now she was making a potpie for him. Maybe they'd watch a movie. Maybe they'd make love. She didn't know, and didn't care, as long as she was with him.

She turned down the soup aisle, searching for cream of chicken — her potpie cheat — when her thoughts abruptly turned to the old woman who lived above the Kitchen Classroom. Would she feel this way when she found more gifts on her stair this evening? They had been retrieved from under the tree and stacked roof-high in the back of Bren's minivan. All of them. Some wrapped, some in bags, some in homemade cheesecloth pouches, some just wrapped in cellophane and tucked into a big basket Bren had unearthed from her craft experiment days. Bren had stopped by the apartment on her way to the grocery store and hefted them up the stairs, stacking them neatly off to one side of the doorway. It had taken three trips, and the whole time Bren's heart had pounded with nerves that the old woman would open the door and catch her there. How silly to be nervous that someone might catch you leaving them gifts.

But from the looks of things, the old woman wasn't home. The lights were off and there was no sound coming from the other side of the door. Bren drove around the square a couple of times looking for her to be out there loyally following her dog on his leash. She'd even taken a little side trip past the cancer center. But no Virginia Mash.

So wherever she was, she would come home to the gift of giving. Whether the old snot wanted it or not.

And maybe, just maybe, when she saw the gifts, and experienced the fact that the ladies still wanted to treat her with kindness even after what she'd done to them, she would feel the way Bren was feeling now. Hopeful, happy, too cheerful to even bother to stop at the Hole Shebang for a pastrami-glazed chocolate cake doughnut.

She checked her cart — all that was left to get was the chicken. She turned toward the meat department and almost slammed into the cart of a man standing behind her.

"Oh!" she cried. She did a double take, her lips tingling of their own accord. She touched them. "John?"

"Hey, Bren," he said. He ducked his head, doing his level best to really let her see only the crown of his stocking cap, but she bent her knees to look up in his face. His lip was split and he had a hell of a bruise sprouting on his left eye.

"Oh my gosh, what happened to you?" She reached out as if to touch his face, but thought better of touching him in any way and pulled her hand back.

"I should think you would already know," he said, offering a small, painful-looking smile. He leaned toward her and whispered, "Why did you tell him?"

It took her a minute to catch on. "Tell who what? Oh no."

He was nodding, looking thoroughly unimpressed. "Oh yes."

"Gary did this?"

"I figured he would have told you. Stormed into my house, pulled me out of my recliner — spilling my beer, by the way — and punched me twice. He defended your honor. What a guy." All of this came out very deadpan.

"No, I'm so sorry, I had no idea."

"So why did you tell him, then? You'd already shut me down. That wasn't enough?" He tossed a can of soup into his cart, so hard it rattled the beer bottles together. Of which he had many, Bren couldn't help noticing. "If I'd known that kissing you was going to get my ass kicked, I would've stayed away. I would've kissed Rosa instead." This, he said loudly. A woman by the canned ravioli looked up.

Bren burned with embarrassment. Although she was maybe the teeniest bit proud that she had been John's first choice over adorable Rosa. She looked around, trying to appear as if this were just a hilarious joke between her and a good friend, but the ravioli woman didn't look like she was buying it. "I did not tell him so he would come after you. I felt guilty about what happened between us, if you must know."

John grinned again, wincing as his lip split anew. "Which means you wanted it. I knew it. And I told Gary as much." His voice went falsetto. "Oh, please, bone my bird!" He went back to his normal voice. "Come on, what did you expect me to think? You got naked in front of me."

"That was for Gary! I did not want it. I never did anything to get it." She realized too late that her voice had also escalated, and now not only was the ravioli woman watching them, but so was an old man who had just turned his electric scooter down their aisle.

There was a frozen turkey in the old man's basket. *If you're planning on having that*

Christmas Day, dude, she thought, *you are going to be out of luck. Or licking turkey Popsicles.* She giggled, despite herself. Turkeysicles. Tammy Lynn would have appreciated that one, for sure. She could only imagine the jokes they would all riff off of that one. She giggled some more.

John cocked his head to one side. "I'm glad you find it all so hilarious. I could file charges against him, you know."

She shook her head, held up one hand, tried to tell him that no, it wasn't about his beat-up face, but she couldn't catch her breath. And, besides, it kind of was about his beat-up face, maybe just a little bit. It all seemed so absurd now — the band, the kiss, the wild night in Rome.

"I guess I never realized how much like Cindy you are. You two were a great pair," John said.

Bren, still laughing, nodded. "Yes . . . we were." She straightened up, gulped in a few breaths, stilled herself as best she could. "Excuse me. My husband deserves a chicken potpie. Looks like he worked hard today."

She turned and sauntered down the aisle, hesitating at the ravioli display only long enough to pull a can of Beefaroni off the shelf. She handed it to the lady standing there.

"Here, I've found this pairs well with eavesdropping."

She went straight to the meat counter, where she bought the expensive fresh chicken. Gary cared. In his own selfish, weird little way, he cared.

CHAPTER THIRTY-TWO

There were twelve gifts left to make. But it was also Christmas Eve, and Bren knew she couldn't ask the ladies to come over for more crafting. They had their own families, their own traditions to attend to.

Gary had agreed to upgrading their dinner plans to Christie's Steakhouse, where at least their Christmas Eve dinner would be served on china plates with cloth napkins. Bren still missed cooking, but she understood what he was trying to do. He was trying to create a new tradition for the two of them.

"They could only get us in at four thirty," he announced, coming into the living room, holding his suit on a hanger. "We were lucky to get reservations at all, this late."

"We can do four thirty," Bren said, snapping off the TV and checking the clock. "I love four thirty. Lots of time for digesting before bed. Four thirty is our new tradition."

She raced upstairs and poured herself into an old dress that she hadn't worn since her cousin Maxie's third wedding. She'd been an easy sixty pounds lighter back then — and Maxie had been one husband shy of landing on the current husband number — and she couldn't lift her arms above her head without the sleeves pinching her armpit fat into oblivion. But it wasn't like she and Gary were going to be doing any dancing, and it was an A-line, which meant she had plenty of stomach room to fill with steak and potatoes and buttery, buttery cauliflower. As long as her boobs didn't split the side seams and turn her into the dinner show.

Christie's Steakhouse was a bustle of energy and ambience. The lighting was low, but the mood was high. Bren could literally feel a melted butter mist in the air. Decadence and revelry and smart-looking couples in shimmery clothes, families in their church best, little boys squeezed into plaid vests and little girls itchy in white tights and patent leather shoes. Wine at every table. Dessert at every table. Smiles at every table, and people leaned back against their chair backs and clutching their bellies in regretful satisfaction.

It felt like being part of a special club. Maybe it was. A club of people who didn't do things exactly traditionally. Maybe it was a club of people who didn't slave over a stove and dredge out recipes handed down from their grannies and didn't have legions of children racing around, feverish with excitement for Santa's arrival.

But it was a club of people who were together. *Merry Christmas,* Bren wanted to tell all of them as she passed their tables. *Happy New Year. God bless us, everyone! Enjoy! Enjoy!*

"This was such a great idea," she said, sipping the most velvety wine she'd ever tasted. Like ribbons slipping into her mouth. Bright red holiday ribbons. She sipped again, feeling her limbs go warm and relaxed. "A great idea."

"I thought so," Gary said. "Although we can't really get fried okra here like we would have at Lucky's Cafeteria."

"I'll make you some fried okra next week," she said. "This is Christmas Eve. Look! A guy just proposed at that table over there. Oh, gosh, Gary, why didn't we do this sooner?"

He buttered a piece of bread and bit into

it, resting his elbow on the table. "Because we always had those kids hanging around," he said.

Bren rested her chin in her palm. "You really have been looking forward to your empty nest, haven't you?"

"Absolutely. Think about it. We have money now, Bren. Actual money."

"It has been a long time since we had that, hasn't it?" she said wistfully. "In that case, I'm going to want another bottle of this." She turned the bottle to read the label, but it was all in French. "Whatever this is."

"Drink up, my lady; Santa has a little something in his bag for you later." He waggled his eyebrows up and down.

Bren giggled again. It was a naughty thought, but in a way she wished John had kissed her long ago. It had awakened something in Gary.

"Do you miss the band?" she asked. "I mean, I know it's only been a day, but do you miss playing? Are you disappointed about the gig?"

He studied his bread, took another bite. "Not really. I was kind of nervous about the gig anyway. Truth is, we weren't very good."

Bren arched her eyebrows, tried to look surprised.

"It was exciting to think that maybe we

could get that good, but I honestly have been thinking about kayaks."

Bren sputtered around her wine. "Kayaks?"

He nodded vigorously, dropping his bread onto his bread plate. "Have you seen the guys who do that? They're ripped. I'd have chest muscles on top of chest muscles."

"But it's December."

"Yeah?"

"In Missouri."

"Yeah?"

"A little cold for kayaking. Unless there's some sort of ice-kayaking that I don't know about."

"Well, I would wait until the water is warmer, of course. And I thought we could even go out to maybe Colorado next summer, do some river kayaking."

Bren tried to imagine herself on a kayak. She couldn't do it. "And until then? There're a lot of months between now and summer."

"Until then . . ." He thought about it. "I have you, I guess." He held up his wineglass and they clinked.

So Bren knew that come summer, she would become a kayak widow, just as she had been a golf widow and a dune buggy widow and a band widow, but for now she had him, and she would worry about those months when they came.

"So what about you?" he asked, rooting in the bread basket for another piece. "Do you miss the cooking class?"

She smiled. "Why, Gary. I didn't realize you even knew I was doing that."

"Of course I knew. I was just too busy to talk about it. So do you miss it?"

Of course she missed it. She ached for it. Wondered what Tammy Lynn and Lulu and Teresa and Rebecca were doing at that moment. Wished every day that she were planning her New Year course.

But also . . . strangely . . . she missed Virginia Mash. That miserable old cuss. Bren had really thought that maybe she'd been coming around. Just a little. She'd truly believed that she could have helped that along with her project. Despite all of the evidence she had to the contrary, she couldn't help wondering if just a little more effort might have accomplished their goal.

If only we'd gotten to one hundred gifts, Bren thought, and then, *How irrational is that? To think that eighty-eight wouldn't do it, but one hundred would? How silly do I sound right now?*

Not to mention, it was all done now anyway. Christmas was tomorrow, and she couldn't make twelve gifts herself. The only thing she could make twelve of was . . .

She sat up straighter, holding her wineglass midway to her mouth. "Gary. What do you think about stopping at the store on the way home?"

He chuckled. "You're not going to get enough food here?"

"Oh yes, this was wonderful. It's just that . . . I'd like to make a twelve-course meal."

This time his eyebrows shot up nearly into his hairline as he gaped at her. "You're serious?" She nodded. "But why?" He didn't let her respond. He wadded his napkin and tossed it on the table. "I don't get it. I have done everything I can to make this evening a relaxed and special night for you. I even gave up sweatpants and cafeteria bread pudding. And you know how much I love my cafeteria bread pudding, Bren."

"But that's not what this is about," she said, setting her wine down. She was too excited to be offended by his response, or even worried by the aggravation in his voice. "I want to make a meal for Virginia Mash."

He gave his head a shake. "Who in Sam Hill is that?"

"The cranky old lady who lives above the kitchen," Bren said. "It's perfect, Gary. We wanted to make one hundred gifts. We made eighty-eight. If I make her a twelve-course Christmas meal, we will have hit our goal."

"And why would you want to do that?"

Bren couldn't explain it. She couldn't articulate it any more than Bob Cratchit could explain why he wanted to toast old Scrooge on Christmas Day in that classic Dickens tale.

"It's Christmas, Gary," she said, echoing Mr. Cratchit. "She has no one."

"And is it any wonder?" he asked.

No, it wasn't. But Bren had begun to wonder if it was a chicken-and-egg issue with Virginia Mash. Was she alone because she was mean and ugly, or was she mean and ugly because she was alone?

Gary must have sensed what she was thinking. He sighed, his eyes drifting to the old-fashioned Christmas tree in the corner, lit up with twinkling white lights and adorned with a twisting red and gold velvet ribbon. "I suppose there's no stopping you."

She shook her head slowly.

His plate arrived, and he picked up a fork in one hand and a knife in the other. "I suppose it's also what I love about you," he said.

Bren could barely eat her dinner; she was too busy planning her recipes.

■ ■ ■ ■

Brisket with barbecue sauce. Corn casserole. Macaroni and cheese, steaming and creamy. Green bean casserole, with the crunchy little onions on top. Homemade rolls smeared with melted butter. Loaded mashed potatoes, both sweet and regular. Cauliflower, beautiful, whole, smothered with cheese. Pumpkin, pecan, and custard pies — one of each. She even put together a batch of bread pudding, just for Gary.

Bren came to bed, sweating, covered with flour and sugar, smelling like food. Her hair was limp and her legs sore, and yet the brisket was still in the oven, slow cooking until morning. She tiptoed through the darkened room and went straight into the bathroom, where she shed her funky clothes and dove into the hottest and most fulfilling shower she'd had in months.

Everything was wrapped and boxed and put together. She would take it to the apartment first thing in the morning. She would drop it, knock, and run. She could hardly wait.

She had just rinsed the shampoo out of her hair when a shape appeared on the other side of the shower door, startling her. She jumped, her hand slapping over her heart. The door opened, and Gary's face appeared.

"You scared the hell out of me," she said, flapping a hand at him. Little pustules of suds flew from her fingertips and landed on his chest.

His naked chest.

Which was on top of a whole lot of naked Gary.

"Is there room for one more?" he asked, squinting against the shower spray.

"Are you serious?" Bren couldn't remember the last time she and Gary had showered together. The truth was, with her newfound addiction to doughnuts, she wasn't entirely sure there was room for one more. "I'm filthy."

He opened the door farther. Bren couldn't help letting her eyes slide down the length of him. He was still fairly fit for a man his age. Much more fit than she was. Maybe his inane hobbies had served to keep him young after all. "I don't care," he said.

She took a step away from the door, pressed her back against the cold shower wall, trying not to feel self-conscious about her own body, trying to shield herself with her arms while still looking natural. "There's room," she said.

He first disappeared away from the shower door, and next thing Bren knew the bathroom was bathed in darkness. When he came back, he was upon her, hands first, and then lips, his skin soft and warm and bristling with goose bumps.

Bren let him kiss her. And, yes, she moaned.

Chapter Thirty-Three

The first Christmas after Jamie died was not the worst.

It was actually the first Christmas after she was diagnosed that was the worst.

Everything they did — every tradition they upheld, every morsel of food they ate, every family member they visited — was done under a cloud of doom. Not grief — grief would come later. Grief would be a relief. Grief would happen when it was supposed to and grief would ultimately get them through the loss.

The doom was far worse than the grief.

"It won't be your last," Virginia continually told her daughter, whenever she was brooding. "You're young. You have so much fight in you."

But, of course, she hadn't had as much fight as Virginia thought, and maybe Virginia and Ernie even knew that way back then. Maybe they'd sensed it, that she wouldn't fight it, or at least not enough to beat it. That the first Christmas after the diagnosis would, indeed, be the last.

Jamie had died on December 23, exactly eleven years before old Chuy gave up the ghost himself. Almost another Christmas to put in the old memory book, but no. Just short of it.

They were prepared. Well, prepared and not prepared. A mother could never be fully prepared for burying her child. Even if that child had been wasting away slowly, sadly, for months. They knew it was coming none-theless.

So why, Virginia Mash had asked herself a billion times, had she gone shopping? Of all things, shopping. Why had she driven herself to the mall to buy a lousy coat for her daughter for Christmas on that day of all days?

She'd gotten the call just as she was leaving the mall.

"Gin?" It was her husband.

"Yeah?"

"Where are you?" His voice sounded thin and faraway, and she instantly knew, in her gut, why he was calling, even if she continued to deny it, to make him spell it out.

"I'm at the mall. I got Jamie an adorable coat. You know how she's always so cold these days."

"Gin . . ."

"What is it? Is she having a pain issue again? I'll be there in about twenty minutes." The truth was, Jamie hadn't had a pain issue in days. Virginia had known that no pain, in this case, wasn't a good thing. No pain simply meant the home nurse was keeping the morphine flowing round the clock now.

"Honey."

"Just give her the pain pillow. It helps." She felt a tear roll down her cheek, even if she didn't quite know yet why.

"She's gone, Virginia," he'd said softly.

She'd been at a stop sign when he said this, but now she couldn't move. Couldn't pry her foot from the brake pedal no matter how hard she tried. The message left her brain but never quite reached her foot. It was intercepted by those words — *She's gone, Virginia.* A car honked behind her and she glanced into the rearview mirror, but still she didn't move.

"Honey? Did you hear me?" There were tears in his voice, too, and now that she registered the fact, she realized there had been since she'd answered the phone. "Gin? Are you okay?"

The car honked again, but this time she

didn't bother to look. It careened around her, the man behind the wheel taking the time to flip her the bird before peeling away from the stop sign. How odd, she thought, that he'd just flipped off a mother who'd just been told her child was dead.

Dead.

Oh God, dead.

"Gin? I need you to talk to me. Where are you? I can come get you."

But he couldn't. Ernie couldn't get to her then. Nobody could. She'd been busy disappearing down such a long, dark tunnel, he'd never reach her again.

"I'm here," she said, though the words didn't feel like real words. "I bought her a new coat for Christmas." It was a helpless plea to the universe, but to Ernie it must have sounded ridiculous.

"I know," he said, his voice growing thicker.

"I'm at the fucking mall!" she shouted suddenly into the phone. "I'm at the mall, buying her a coat!"

"I know," he said again. He paused, hitched, then sniffed, a huge windy sound into the phone. "Come on home now, okay? You can see her before they . . ."

He trailed off, but she knew what he wasn't saying. She knew it in pictures and images in her head — awful ones. *You can see her before they take her away.* Before they took her away and wheeled her to the morgue and put her on a cold slab. Before they put her in a box or cremated her or whatever it was they would decide to do with her. And it seemed ridiculous, utterly ridiculous, to her that they had never decided in months of watching their daughter die what they would do with her after. It had seemed like maybe she couldn't die, not if they hadn't figured out how to handle her remains.

"Okay," she said mildly into the phone. "Okay." She hung up but still sat at the stop sign, not bothering to move, not bothering to acknowledge other cars that streamed around her, all of their drivers wearing looks of annoyance.

Eventually, when it seemed like Ernie would wonder what had happened to her, she pulled away and calmly pointed her car toward the highway that would take her up north, the coat she'd chosen — patchwork with little gold sequins and buttons sewn here and there; oh, how Jamie would have loved it! — shivering in the trunk.

It would stay in the trunk until spring, when Ernie cleaned out the car. He'd come inside, holding the plastic bag curiously.

"What's this?" he'd asked, standing in the doorway of the bedroom, where Virginia had spent most of her days, sitting in the rocking chair, staring out the window, like some stereotypical grieving mother. She'd barely glanced over her shoulder — she had a feeling she knew what it was without even looking.

"A coat," she said. "It's nothing."

Recognition lined his face then, and he went somber. He'd pretty much been walking on eggshells around her since the day of the phone call, but there were certain subjects, he knew, that just couldn't be safely broached. "What should I do with it?" he asked.

"Give it away," she said, so quickly her words were almost riding over his.

"Okay."

He'd started to leave the room, but she'd jumped up. "In fact . . . ," she said, moving so quickly toward the closet door, she lost a slipper. She walked on without it. "Give them all away." She yanked open the closet door and dove far into the left corner, where she kept all of her coats, whipped them off their hangers, and tossed them at her husband.

He blinked as they hit him in the chest, one by one. "What are you doing?"

"Getting rid of things," she said. She moved into the hallway, opened the coat closet, and pulled out the two coats stored there. "Take them. Get them out of my sight."

He dropped those two, they were coming at him so quickly. "Virginia," he was saying, "Gin. Honey. Now, you're going to need those."

"No." She swirled around to glare at him, directing every ounce of her anger over having lost her daughter at him. She knew it was unfair, unkind, but she couldn't help herself. "She needed a coat, and somehow she managed without one. Now it's my turn."

"Oh, come on, now, Gin, you're being unreasonable."

But just like that, seeing him standing there with an armload of clothing, two jackets pooled at his feet, her anger was gone. All she could think of was sitting down. No, *lying* down. Stretching out and resting her eyes. Her eyes were so tired. "Get them out of my sight," she said.

She'd gone back to her room then, kicked off the remaining slipper, and sunk into bed. It'd felt like years before she'd come out again.

She hadn't worn a coat, visited a mall, or

even driven a car since.

Virginia Mash didn't expect to feel the same kind of loss over a dog. And when she'd left Noah's Ark and climbed back into the cab, ordered him to take her home, she'd felt strong. The circle of life and all.

But she hadn't been able to stop thinking about the day with the coats. She hadn't been able to get up from her chair by the window, gazing out at nothing, her mind, her internal eyes gazing back eleven years.

Chuy had been her constant companion in that rocking chair. He'd been right by her side in that bed. It had been as if he were mourning right along with her.

But now she was mourning alone, and she was mourning both of them. And maybe she was even mourning Ernie, who'd probably been dealt an even shittier hand than she had, because when he lost his daughter, he lost Virginia, too. Surely he'd been lonely.

She missed hearing Chuy's little toenails tapping on the wood floor as he got up in the morning and began prowling to see how the apartment had fared during the night. She missed when he stood on his hind legs to see out the front window and yapped away at the strangers on the street — although he hadn't done that in a long, long while.

And, though if she said it out loud, she would sound stupid, she missed that he was the only other person left in this world who knew and loved Jamie like she did.

Virginia Mash thought these things as she bagged up Chuy's things — his leash, his squeaky toys, his little plaid coat — finding him in more places throughout the apartment than she'd have ever thought she would. She threw away the unusable things and put the rest in a grocery shopping bag, though she wondered idly what she would do with it once she had it all together. Take it to Noah's Ark, perhaps. Donate it to the animal shelter or some such.

A gift.

The word drew her eyes to the front door. Next to it was still piled the mother lode she'd found when she got home from Noah's Ark yesterday. She'd stood at the bottom of the stairs for a while, blinking away the tears that she finally felt comfortable shedding, trying to figure out what exactly she was looking at.

"I threatened them," she said aloud, her voice more full of wonder than anger. "Surely they aren't this stupid."

But as she slowly made her way to the top of the stairs, her boots squeaking off the slush with each step, she could see that

444

clearly they were that stupid. Gay bows and shiny paper and ribbons and Santas, and an enormous basket that looked as if Christmas had vomited in it.

She'd stood on the top stair and gazed at it. But why? Why would they be that stupid?

Her back creaked as she lugged the things inside her apartment, cursing and grumbling the whole while, and left them there, inside, by the front door. She would have to call the police, she supposed. She would have to tell them to take these things away and go arrest those fools.

But she hadn't. Instead, she'd gone to bed and cried herself to sleep, and then had awakened to thoughts of Jamie and those damned coats while she bagged up Chuy's belongings, all the effort at so-called Christmas cheer still sitting, unenjoyed, by the front door.

Hell of a thing, the way life works, she thought.

She went to the kitchen cupboard, where she kept the old yellow pages, and pulled them out. She searched for a few minutes, her finger running down the page, her mouth working over the words, and then picked up her phone and dialed. It rang and rang, and finally a machine picked up.

"Thank you for calling the R. Monte Belle

Cancer Treatment Center. We will be closed on December twenty-fourth and twenty-fifth for the holiday. If you'd like to leave a message for scheduling, press one. . . ."

Virginia Mash hung up, then stared at the unopened gifts by the front door again. What was she supposed to do with all of that? Of course the cancer center would be closed today. Every place would be. And she was just one person. She didn't need all of this junk. She didn't want it. What gall those imbeciles had in assuming she would want it. Not everyone was all about *things* during the holidays. Not everyone was all about the holidays at all. Some people preferred their comfortable solitude while everyone else was out — *I'm at the mall* — picking up their precious things — *I bought Jamie a coat for Christmas.*

Some people were too busy dying to enjoy Christmas.

She would just throw it all out; that was what she'd do. Well, maybe not all of it. Maybe she would keep the cross-stitched pillowcase that was rolled up, tied with a red ribbon, and left to poke out of the basket. Even rolled up, the design clearly looked like old Chuy back when he was a pup, even though he never wore a blue collar. That gift was kind of special. That one she couldn't part with.

She went back into the kitchen and dug through a drawer, finding a trash bag. She pulled it out and shook it open. This would show them what uninvited friendliness would get you.

But halfway toward the door, she stopped, the trash bag dangling from her fingers.

Not everyplace would be closed today. Not at all.

She went back to the yellow pages and searched until she found the number for the taxi company again.

"Yes, hello. I need a cab. I'll be going to Vargo County Hospital. Not an emergency, no. And could you have the driver come upstairs and help me with some bags?"

CHAPTER THIRTY-FOUR

For the first time in more than twenty years, Bren woke entangled in Gary's arms. Her hair was a disaster from falling asleep on it wet, and she was wearing only a T-shirt and panties. Gary, on the other hand, hadn't bothered with pajamas at all. Bren practically blushed when her leg stretched down the length of him, expecting to find his boxers and instead finding only flesh.

"Merry Christmas," he said sleepily. He kissed her forehead. "My little ho-ho-ho."

Bren chuckled and smacked at his chest. "Not funny. I wasn't that naughty last night."

But she had been that naughty — and naughtier! — and she wavered between feeling embarrassed and feeling energized by it. She ultimately decided to go with energized, especially given all of the events of recent months. She didn't know what the future would hold for her and Gary, but she knew that waking up like this with him on Christmas Day was a good start.

"Breakfast?" she asked. "I can whip up some monkey bread. I know it's your favorite."

He stretched, groaning. "That sounds perfect," he said on a yawn. But he had hooked his arm around her neck and was pulling her toward him again. "But first . . ."

Bren showered and dressed while the bread was cooking. The house smelled like cinnamon and brown sugar and butter and coffee. She could hear Gary downstairs in the basement, putting things back the way they'd been before the band. Readying it for who knew what hobby awaited him next. Kayaks. Beer making. Last night he'd talked about learning to oil paint.

At least oil painting was a mostly silent activity.

She put a few pieces of bacon on while he worked.

"Gare?" she called downstairs. "Breakfast!"

He came up, carrying a guitar in each hand. He set them on the floor next to the basement door.

"Just cleaning up," he announced. "I'm going to leave these things in the den, if that's okay with you. I thought maybe we could go see a movie this afternoon? Grab some dinner?"

She forked the bacon out of the skillet and onto a plate. "Okay," she said. "I'm going to deliver these gifts before lunch. That way if she's hungry, she's got something."

"You're a much better person than I am, Bren Epperson," he said.

But not really, she knew. She wasn't doing it to be a good person. She was doing it because she'd promised herself that she would. She was doing it because she needed something, and she couldn't explain why, but this felt like the right something. Maybe it was as simple as she needed to cook for someone, and Virginia Mash was someone.

She was doing it more for herself than she was for Virginia Mash. And she wished she could feel guilty about it, but she couldn't.

The wind was brutal as Bren headed toward the square. The cold was refreezing everything that had melted, leaving slick patches on the roads that caught her by surprise. Bad weather meant dangerous roads, and Christmas was the one day a year that people would get out on them anyway, no matter what.

But the roads were pretty empty, actually.

Everyone was home celebrating with their families. The stores were closed; the restaurants shuttered. And while lights strung across homes and storefronts would glow soft and warm and meaningful when night fell, in the sun and relentless wind, the decorations in store windows and wrapped on light poles just looked garish and tired.

Some of the grocery stores had already been stocking Valentine's Day candy for a couple of weeks now. Booting out one holiday to make room for the next.

Everything on the square was closed. Not a single car was parked in the slanted slots that faced the storefronts. It was a ghost town. Probably just the way the old woman liked it best, she thought.

If she were thinking about that at all, she might have turned around and taken the food home. Fed it to Gary, or maybe taken it to the fire station to see if the firefighters would like a good, home-cooked meal on Christmas Day. She would have let the old woman have her blessed silence at last.

But she couldn't make herself do it.

There was a light on in Virginia Mash's apartment — she could see that much through the window — and if she'd only looked up at the window for a moment longer, she might have seen the old woman, roused by the sound of a car, curiously peek out at her.

Bren had packed all twelve gifts into two boxes. They fit snugly enough that she could stack the boxes, one on top of the other, and carry both up at the same time, although the effort did make her arms shake and her breath come in huffs and puffs.

But it was worth it to get out of this wind.

Unfortunately, carrying such a big load meant she couldn't walk as quietly as she would have liked to, her footfalls echoing loudly to her ears as they landed on each rubber-matted wooden step. God, why couldn't the woman have chosen an apartment with carpet on the stairway?

When she got to the top, she arranged the boxes side by side, and stood with her hands on her hips for a moment, appraising things and catching her breath, before she made her move. It was probably cold enough even in the hallway to leave food outside for quite some time before any of it went bad, but she didn't want to take any chances.

She took a deep breath, rearranged her stance, so that she was pointed down the stairs, her right foot already down one stair, legs bent at the ready to run, fist upraised and only inches from the door.

One, two, three, she thought to herself,

452

and then knocked on the door.

But her knuckles made contact with the wood only once before the door was flung open, catching Bren so unprepared, she didn't even get a chance to run down a single step. She stood there awkwardly in her run pose, her fist still upraised, as the old woman glared at her.

"I ought to call the authorities," Virginia Mash shouted, thumping her cane on the floor, once, hard.

"I'm sorry," Bren said. "I didn't mean to disturb you." She'd finally gotten the presence of mind to move. She stepped down a couple of steps.

"But you did."

Bren gestured toward the food. "I just thought maybe you'd like a nice Christmas lunch."

"So you butted in and left one, just like you've left all the other junk here, and that's illegal. I got a restraining order, as you know. And I ought to call it in."

Bren slumped. "But why?" The old woman looked at her, mouth working but nothing coming out. "Why did you get a restraining order?"

"You were disturbing me."

"We were cooking. That's all," Bren said. "You could have joined us."

Virginia Mash took a step out the door. "I can already cook. I don't need you teaching me how to do it. And I don't need you cooking for me, either, especially given how much you burn food down there."

Touché, Bren thought. "You cost me a job," Bren said. "You cost Paula a dream. And a lot of money."

"This is harassment," Virginia Mash said, using her cane to push one of the boxes precariously close to the edge of the top step.

Bren lunged for it, pushed it back. "This is lunch."

"This is illegal," the old woman said, pushing the box harder and farther this time.

But Bren's hand was still on it and she shoved it back, harder still. "No, you mean old thing. This is friendship." The old woman stepped back a step, her face looking like it had been slapped. "You may not know it when you see it, but that's because you're so bitter. People probably push you away, but that's because you push first. You're lucky we tried another way of pushing, and you're too stubborn to see it. Now just take the damn food and be nice about it!"

Bren shoved the box so hard it bumped

454

into the other, and a tub of gravy jumped out and rolled across the floor, stopping to butt against Virginia Mash's shoe.

Bren steeled herself for the torrent of hate that would come at her, the woman possibly even adding "assault" to her "harassment" charges. She briefly thought about Gary, having to bail her out on Christmas Day, how he would probably say he told her so, that sometimes trying to do the right thing just didn't pay off.

Instead, the old woman batted at the tub with her cane, righting it. "Does it have giblets in it?"

Bren hesitated, unsure where this was going, then made a face. "I hate giblet gravy," she said.

The old woman nodded. "Then I suppose you'll eat it with me." She turned and thumped into the depths of her apartment without a word more. Bren stood, dumbfounded, on the second stair down. She wasn't sure if she should feel victorious or terrified, but at the moment, she was a little bit of both. "You're letting the cold in. You want to pay my electricity bill, too, I suppose?" she heard from inside the apartment. She scrambled and picked up the gravy, restacked the boxes, and carried them inside.

After she shut the front door, she put the boxes down again and dug her phone out of her pocket. To Gary, she texted, *Let's make it an evening movie?*

And to Tammy Lynn, two words. *It worked!*

CHAPTER THIRTY-FIVE

It wasn't until the smell of the fat cook's perfume filled her entire apartment that she realized she'd never had a guest in here before. Not ever.

Of course she hadn't. She'd moved in for exactly that purpose, after all. Left their house, all of their things and memories, packed up Chuy, and came here to hide. She wanted to be alone. She just hadn't realized that when she'd made that decision, she was making the decision to be alone for such a long time.

The fat cook brought in the boxes and dropped them — too hard; it would probably leave a mark — on the kitchen table. She began to unpack them before even taking her coat off.

"Have you had lunch?" the fat cook asked her.

The truth was, she wasn't very sure when was the last time she'd had a proper lunch.

She definitely couldn't remember when was the last time she'd stocked up on food at the grocery store. She just wasn't hungry anymore. Was this what it felt like to finally give up?

But something happened when the fat cook uncovered a foil pan to reveal a browned brisket inside. Her stomach rumbled so hard she was sure the fat cook could hear it all the way across the room.

The fat cook. Thinking of her this way made Virginia Mash feel washed over with shame. Shame irritated her.

"What's your name again?" she asked. "If I'm going to be poisoned, I want to know who to tell the cops to go after."

The fat cook stopped, a piece of hair fallen over her left eye. At first she looked indignant, perhaps even annoyed, but then that annoyance brewed over into something else. The fat cook threw her head back and laughed out loud. "Poisoned?"

Virginia Mash's face remained straight. "I don't know you."

The fat cook laughed some more, shaking her head gleefully as she pulled out a plastic bag filled with rolls. "Bren," she finally said. "My name is Bren Epperson."

Bren Epperson walked over to Virginia's stove and began pushing buttons, her fingers jabbing blindly. She was going to break something. Virginia lurched out of her chair, feeling for her cane. "Stop, stop, stop. You have no idea how to use an oven, do you? No wonder you were always crucifying the food down there." She thumped to the stove. "What do you want it at? Three-fifty?"

Bren nodded. "And if you have a few saucepans . . ."

"Right under there," Virginia Mash said crossly. "And hand me one. I'll show you how to fix the texture on that gravy."

Bren bent and brought out an armload of pots and pans that were dusty from lack of use. Virginia directed her to the cookie sheets and the bowls and the utensils. They moved around each other in the tiny apartment kitchen, a culinary orchestra played on yellowed linoleum and avocado-colored appliances. Virginia leaned her cane against the countertop and barked out instructions, and Bren followed them, whisking and handing off and beating and blending and tasting. They didn't talk about anything else. They didn't need to; Bren Epperson, the fat cook, was a remarkably good student.

In the end, Virginia even taught Bren how to make a flourless chocolate cake — Jamie's favorite Christmas recipe. Virginia hadn't made it since her daughter died. But she still had it committed to memory. They ate lunch while they waited for it to bake.

"You're right; you're a good cook," Bren said, spooning in a mouthful of potatoes. "This gravy is so much better now."

Virginia grunted, but inside she was busy being wowed by Bren's own talents. The brisket was melt-in-your-mouth tender. The sauce that went over it was tangy and spicy and belonged in a bottle on store shelves.

"Where did you learn to cook?" Bren asked.

"My mother," Virginia Mash said. She refused to look up from her plate. "She's been gone a long time now, of course," she added.

"I'm sorry," Bren said. They ate in silence for a while, during which time Virginia was aware of Bren's neck craning to look around the apartment. "Where is the dog?" she finally asked.

It felt like a punch to the heart. She didn't want to have to say it out loud. She never wanted to say these things out loud. Whom had she even told about Jamie, once she'd moved here? With whom had she shared Ernie's death? Nobody.

Bren had stopped eating, though, and had put down her fork. "Oh. I'm so sorry," she said. "I didn't know."

Virginia Mash grunted again, but the grunt was softer this time, as Bren's hand snaked over and landed on top of hers. "He was a dog," Virginia finally whispered, pulling her hand away. "Dogs die."

"Yeah," Bren said, after another pause. She picked up her fork and started eating again. "You want to hear something ridiculous?" Virginia Mash didn't answer. "My son, Kevin, may have gotten married, but he doesn't even know for sure."

Virginia looked up. Bren was using her tongue to clean food out of her teeth.

"Yep. And my daughter is making boats out of bread for Christmas because Thailand is so beautiful. And two weeks ago I ate an entire dozen of the Hole Shebang's glazed with basil. And my husband's best friend kissed me right in my own kitchen, and it was kind of nice because my husband was too busy being sixteen again to notice me at all. And I freaked out over a mole."

Virginia didn't know what to say to that confession. It seemed the fat coo— *Bren's* life was just as crazed as she might have guessed.

Bren tucked back into her food, stabbing at a green bean with her fork. "Anyway," she said to her plate, "I needed a friend, so I took the job at the Kitchen Classroom,

461

even though I'm not that great of a cook. And it worked. And I saw you at the cancer center giving away the things we gave you."

This time Virginia nearly dropped her fork, and when she looked up, Bren was staring at her with wide eyes, a buttered roll perched between two fingers.

"Why were you there?"

I'm at the mall.

I bought Jamie a coat for Christmas.

Dogs die.

Suddenly Virginia felt very, very tired. Exhausted, and even though it was below freezing outside, the fact that her damned window was painted shut seemed like the biggest injustice of all of them. Chuy had been a great companion, but what made him great was the memory of human connection that came with him. What made him great was that she didn't have to try to let anyone in, as long as she had him.

She didn't want this anymore. She didn't want to be alone. She didn't want to be tired. And, most of all, she didn't know who she was going to walk with, now that Chuy was gone.

The timer went off and Bren got up to snatch the cake out of the oven. She set it on the counter to cool off, then came back and dove into her potatoes again.

Virginia Mash also stuck her fork into her potatoes, but her heart was pounding too hard for her to actually bring the food to her mouth. Still, she kept her eyes planted firmly onto her plate. She had to do this.

"My daughter's name was Jamie . . . ," she began.

CHAPTER THIRTY-SIX

Nobody was more surprised to get the call than Bren was. It came midafternoon on the twenty-eighth, just as she and Gary were leaving the art supply store. It was snowing again. Meteorologists were calling this a record-breaking year already. Gary was calling it a perfect excuse to hole up in front of the fire and paint. He wanted Bren to pose for him. Nude. A thought that made her chuckle, while also tossing her heart right into her throat.

"Only if I can have some sort of blanket to wrap around my middle," she'd said. "And if you Photoshop out the fat rolls."

"Photoshop?" he'd said. "I'm not going to take your picture. I'm going to paint you live. Which means a lot of hours of staring at your naked body."

That definitely didn't help Bren feel any more comfortable at all.

But still, he was looking for a way to

include her in his hobby, and she appreciated the gesture. Even if she didn't want to be quite as involved as all that.

"Okay, but you have ten days to get it done. Then the kids will be here, and I'm thinking they don't want to see anything like that."

Kelsey and Kevin had called on Christmas Day. Bren and Gary both listened in — Bren on the kitchen phone and Gary on the bedroom line. The kids were both drunk, but in high spirits. Dean had gone to bed and Pavlina had gone back home. Turned out Mrs. Wild Night in Rome was about as wild about Christmas in Thailand as Kelsey was. And not at all wild about Kevin anymore, especially now that she found out that her American free spirit was indeed tied down to a family back in the States. And not a rich one on TV.

"Don't worry, guys," Kevin had said. "The marriage wasn't ever legal. We never got a *dichiarazione giurata,* and we found out that the guy who did the ceremony wasn't the mayor's deputy after all, but just some drunk guy. Kind of figures, since we ran into him outside of San Calisto." He chuckled ruefully into the phone. "We paid him eighty euros, though. Wish I had the money back."

As for Kelsey, she sobbed over how beautiful it was to talk to her parents, how beautiful her brother was, how beautiful Christmas was, how beautiful the new year would be, all gathered together the way they were supposed to be.

"Mommy, Daddy, I've talked to Dean. After we get back from Missouri, he's going to start looking for something new in the States. Can you imagine? Maybe we could be as close as California or even Chicago."

A year ago, California and even Chicago would have seemed a million miles away to Bren. Too far. But now it seemed like a virtual skip down the road. She almost felt giddy over it.

She joyously rehashed every detail of the call to Gary — the split, the fake marriage, the job hunting — as they wandered the aisles of the art supply store, even though he'd heard every word of it himself. Gary at least pretended to listen as he dropped things into a shopping basket that Bren had hanging over her arm. It seemed like an awful lot of supplies for someone who didn't know the first thing about painting.

The cashier rang them up and sent them on their way, and it was only seconds after they left the store that Bren's phone rang.

"Hello?"

"Bren? It's Paula."

"Oh, hey, so good to hear from you. How was your Christmas?"

"It was good, a little quiet. Yours?"

Gary fussed with the trunk and Bren got into the car, taking her finger out of her opposite ear, which she'd been plugging so she could hear the call better. "My kids are coming home in a few days. That's really all that matters."

"You also paid a visit to our friend, didn't you? Virginia Mash?"

Bren winced. She'd wondered what would happen after their lunch. They hadn't exchanged phone numbers or made promises to get together again or shared a meaningful hug. They'd talked, they'd eaten cake, and Bren had done the dishes and then left. She was only half certain that the matter between her and Virginia Mash had been settled. Now she supposed half was optimistic.

"I did. I made her lunch on Christmas Day."

"I knew it," Paula said. "I just knew it."

"I'm really sorry, Paula. Did I get you into some kind of trouble?"

She heard the clink of dishes in the background. "Just the opposite," Paula said. "Happy New Year, Bren: you've got your job back. Virginia Mash left me a letter in my mail slot. No more restraining order, no more complaints, no more fines. It's like she's done a total turnaround."

Gary got into the car and looked at Bren curiously. She gave him a thumbs-up and a big grin, and leaned her head back against the seat, all smiles.

"Happy New Year it is!" she said.

CHAPTER THIRTY-SEVEN

Aunt Cathy and Joan were the first to arrive. As always. Aunt Cathy was wearing a pair of silver pants and a silver shirt. Sweat dripped from her temples and down the sides of her face.

"What on earth are you wearing?" Bren asked, laying out the ingredients for the *chiacchiere* she planned to make that evening.

Aunt Cathy looked herself up and down. "It's my GoFit thermal sweat suit. Got a resolution this year. Need to drop a few pounds. Dear Lord, what are we making?"

"They're fried pasta dough balls covered with honey and powdered sugar," Bren said. "Good luck for the new year."

"*Good luck fitting your doughy ass into your jeans after eating that* is more like it," Aunt Cathy said. "Is there a diet version? I'm already a dough ball, thank you very much. And speaking of dough balls, here comes the big-haired one."

"Catherine!" Joan scolded. "That's not nice, and you know it."

"I'm giving up political correctness for my second resolution," Aunt Cathy replied.

Bren hustled to the door, holding out a basket of muffins for Tammy Lynn. "Welcome," she said brightly, proffering the muffins. "Happy New Year!"

Tammy Lynn took two steps inside the door and wrapped Bren in a big hug, nearly toppling muffins out of the basket. "Happy New Year to you!" She palmed a muffin.

"You look so good," Bren said.

"That's because I have good news," Tammy Lynn said. "Janelle got a job. Starts Monday. In Lawrence. An hour in the car, and definitely too far to run. She will no longer have a clue what I put into my mouth and when. I'll take two." She reached into the basket and pulled out another muffin. "Hope you made plenty. El is taking the class with me. He's outside parking the car. And, boy, does he love muffins."

Not long after Tammy Lynn found her place at her old station, Lulu and Teresa arrived, this time bringing along a third woman, a tiny spitfire named Renata, whose hands had the telltale chapped redness of someone who cooked for a living.

"This one," Lulu said, thumbing over her

470

shoulder at Renata, "is even worse in the truck than Teresa."

Teresa slapped at Lulu's shoulder from behind. "*Cállate,* now. I have gotten better." She brightened as she hugged Bren. "Worked a whole lunch shift myself."

"Nobody came. Too cold outside," Lulu said, rolling her eyes.

Behind them came Rebecca, who gave Bren a cursory hug, then took her place in the back of the room, wiggled her way up onto her stool, and pulled out a brand-new notebook. She'd ditched the brown for a demure pink palette. It brought out the blue in her eyes.

Bren stood at the door and regarded her class, thrilled that they had all returned. Maybe she hadn't been so horrible after all.

She was just about to take her muffins back up front and start class when the door burst open again. A bundle of muscles wrapped in the tightest yoga pants she'd ever seen sauntered in. Surely any woman who looked like that had to be here by mistake.

"Is this the resolutions cooking class?" the woman asked.

"Yes, welcome!" Bren said, fumbling for her basket. She clumsily lurched toward the woman, looking a little too eager. "Muffin?"

The woman peered into the basket, seeming to study the treats for a long while. She wrinkled her nose as she looked back up at Bren. "Bran?"

"Blueberry cream cheese strudel," Bren said proudly. Or what she was trying to pass off as proudly. She feared she had only achieved mildly self-conscious. And loud.

The woman seemed to really think it over before finally shrugging and taking a muffin.

"I'm Bren, by the way," Bren said.

"Steff." She took a tiny, birdlike bite of the muffin and rolled it around in her mouth before crinkling her nose. "I'm not accustomed to real sugar," she said. "I usually sweeten with applesauce."

"Oh," said Bren. "I used sugar."

Steff nodded slowly. "Did you know that half a cup of cranberries is only twenty-five calories? And they have blood-pressure-lowering properties. Maybe next time?"

Bren felt herself blush. "Maybe," she said, her voice barely above a whisper. "We're making fried dough balls tonight," she added apologetically. "With sugar."

"No worries," Steff said. "I'll work it off later. I own a gym. Maybe you've heard of it? Fit and Lean? It's on the other side of the square, but it's kind of tucked away.

We're a small operation."

Bren had seen it, actually. Once, during the spring festival, she'd had to park in front of it and walk to the Hole Shebang. She'd made sure she'd devoured her entire dough-nut before going back to her car, but had dropped a splotch of chocolate down the front of her shirt. She'd wanted to die of shame walking in front of the windows of a gym that way.

"Would you mind if next time I bring my own sweetener?" Steff asked.

"Of course not," Bren said. "But I'm not sure if things will cook the same. I've never used . . ."

But she trailed off as the door opened again.

"Excuse me," she said, hurrying over with the basket. But she stubbed her toe against the cabinet and lurched forward, and the last three muffins popped out of the basket and rolled across the floor. One bumped against the foot of the young woman com-ing in. She stooped to pick it up. "So sorry," Bren said. "Muffin?" She laughed awk-wardly, taking the muffin from the woman. "Just kidding. I'm sorry."

"It's okay," the young woman said. She took the muffin from Bren, blew on it, and took a bite. "Just a little dirt. Dirt is our friend. Full of minerals. Full of life."

"I'm Bren."

The girl smiled at her serenely. "Sonja, with a *J*." She bit into the muffin. "But you can call me Bluebonnet."

"Like the butter?" Bren asked, casting a worried glance toward Steff, who would probably never approve of butter.

The girl laughed, a tinkling sound. "No, no, like the flower. Flowers are full of color. Full of life."

"Oh," Bren said. She was much more comfortable calling this girl Sonja than Bluebonnet, but she wasn't sure whether she was supposed to do what was comfortable for her or comfortable for the girl.

Finally, everyone was settled, and Bren was ready to get her new-year good-luck *chiacchiere* lesson going.

"What's that smell?" Aunt Cathy said, tipping her nose up in the air.

Bren's mother lifted her chin, sniffing. "I smell it, too."

"Smells like *cigarrillos,*" Lulu said.

Renata mumbled something to Teresa, and Teresa said something back to her. "Burned hair," Renata said, her mouth turned down.

It was the word *burned* that got Bren moving. "Oh, Christ, not already," she whined.

474

She raced to the stove, where her oil had been heating up. She'd forgotten that she'd dropped a few *chiacchieres* into it to test the temperature.

They now floated on top of the oil, smoking and reeking like three petrified turds.

Bren fished them out. Dammit, now her oil was going to taste off.

But her thoughts were quickly abandoned as she heard the thumps above her head. They all looked up, silently tracing the noises as they made their way across the room, and then turned to the telltale thump-creaks of someone coming down a flight of old stairs.

"Oh, shit," Joan said.

"Joan!" Aunt Cathy chastised, but her grin showed that she was thrilled to finally get to be the one doing the reprimanding.

"Surely not," Tammy Lynn said. "I thought she'd declared a truce."

"That was before I burned something," Bren said dejectedly. "I'm so sorry, you guys. I'll go get Paula."

But before she could leave her pedestal, the door flung open, and there stood Virginia Mash, her face etched deep with frown lines, her cane thrown out to the side to prop open the door.

"You burned something again," she said.

"I can barely breathe up there."

Bren nervously glanced around the room, unsure what to do. Did she try to disarm the situation? She and Virginia Mash had had a nice lunch together, but it wasn't like they were best friends now. Bren understood the woman a little better after hearing her story, but understanding and excusing were two different things. Tammy Lynn and the others would surely expect Bren to stand up for herself, after all they'd done and been through. And heaven only knew what the new people were thinking.

Eyeballs, the room was full of nothing but terrified, expectant eyeballs.

Virginia Mash thumped to Bren's station. She peered at the work surface, which had *chiacchieres* in various stages of doneness, including the three *chia*-turds that Bren had just fished out of the oil. "Well, your oil's too hot," she said.

Bren hesitated. "Okay."

"Pour it out and start over. And I'll show you how to make a chocolate sauce to go with these that will blow your socks off."

"What's going on? Is this a prank? Am I in a movie?" Bren heard Aunt Cathy whisper. She heard her mom shush as a response.

"I'll have to see if there's chocolate in the

476

pantry," Bren said uneasily.

"If not, there's some in my pantry upstairs. You can run up and get it. Now move over."

So Bren moved and Virginia Mash struggled up the single step onto the pedestal, hung her cane over the oven door handle, and rolled up her sleeves.

"Don't just stand there; swap that oil," she barked. Bren took off with the hot pan. "And the rest of you can go ahead and pour your oil into your pan while we wait."

By the time Bren came back with a clean pan, Virginia Mash was elbow-deep in *chiacchiere* dough, and everyone was happily chatting and cooking. Even Rebecca, who stopped every few minutes to jot something in her notebook.

"I found some chocolate," Bren said, setting a bag of semisweet chocolate chips on the counter. "What should I do next?"

CHAPTER THIRTY-EIGHT

They had turducken for Christmas in January.

Kevin had grown a beard. And not one of those scrubby-looking, patchy things boys grow; a man's full beard. His eyes twinkled above it, his face tanned and healthy-looking. He was lean — he'd either missed some meals or gotten a ton of exercise, or both. His jeans hung on his hips, filthy and frayed, until Bren made him swap them out for a pair of his father's sweatpants so she could wash them. She had half a mind to burn them. What if these were his Cozy Thong lovemaking jeans? She considered using salad tongs to transport them to the washing machine just to be safe.

Kelsey, on the other hand, had grown plump. Her hair was listless and scraggly, and she looked tired around the eyes. She clung to her mother so hard and for so long, Bren wondered if she might suffocate them both. When she pulled away, there were tears streaking down her face. "Oh, Mommy, I've missed you so much. You look so beautiful," she'd cried. Bren had wiped her tears with the flats of her hands and led her into the kitchen for a cold drink. She heard Gary in the living room, small-talking with Dean. She could hear Kevin groan as he sank onto the couch, and then the flip of channels on the TV. He was right at home.

Joan and Aunt Cathy came for dinner, even though Aunt Cathy was still dieting, and Joan's stomach was so ravaged by constant coffee consumption she rarely ate more than a few scraps of food. But Bren didn't care. She was having her Thanksgiving and Christmas, all rolled up into one beautiful holiday.

She'd left up the tree. She'd even tucked a few gifts for the kids beneath it. She'd played Christmas songs and had Gary light a fire in the fireplace, and they'd all gazed appreciatively at Gary's first painting — a winterscape — which was absolutely atrocious, but he was so proud.

And they'd eaten their turkey and chicken and duck, their mashed potatoes and gravy, their green beans and sausage stuffing, their apple and marshmallow salad and custard pie and white chocolate chip cookies, sharing stories about their lives over the past year. Bren had passed around her telephone notepad and the kids had translated all of the words for her. They'd even gotten a good laugh over her misspellings and doodles.

"Cozy Chang, Mom? Really?"

"Oh, hush. It was hard to hear over those cell phones. And your father's band music." Air quotes around *music*.

"Hey now, Snow on the Roof was a good band. We were just getting started."

"That's what I was afraid of!"

"Oh my God. Singhas, Kevin. She wrote down about the Singhas."

Laughter. "Don't even say the word *Singha* around me again for a while. I'm still nauseous. That was a wild night."

"You seemed to have a lot of those, son."

Embarrassed blushing. "What can I say, Dad? Rome was a blur. It's all good now. Pavy is happy, I'm happy, and we're both happier apart."

"And you'll meet again in Spain? Weren't you telling me Pavy thought it was romantic there? Here, who wanted the potatoes?"

"Who knows where we'll meet again? Or if we'll meet again. It's no big deal."

"Maybe you'll meet at the beach, Kev. Spelled b-e-e-c-h-e, right, Mom?" More

laughter, more passing around of the notepad.

Bren didn't mind. She wasn't embarrassed. That time of her life seemed so long
ago. And it had seemed so permanent then,
yet here it was — a piece of the past.

Finally, the last of the meal had been
eaten, and everyone sat miserably in their
chairs, their pants unbuttoned, their eyes
closing. The doorbell rang and Bren sprang
out of her chair.

"Oh, good! Dessert is here!"

She ignored the groans and protests at her
back as she made her way to the front door.

Bing Crosby was just starting up "The
Little Drummer Boy" — naturally — when
she opened it. There, on the other side, was
Virginia Mash, holding up a covered dish.
The taxicab's taillights shone red on her
gray hair.

"I don't know what took you so long. It's
not a mansion, you know. I'm an old
woman. I don't have all the time in the
world. I might meet my Maker in the time
it takes you to answer your damn door.
Here."

She held up the dish and Bren took it.
Bren held out a hand to help Virginia Mash
up the short step into the house, but Virginia
smacked it away, refusing help the same way

she'd refused to let Gary come pick her up.

"Let me at least take your coat," Bren said, but Virginia had already taken it off and hung it over a hook in the entryway.

"Let's just get this over with," she said.

"You're going to love them," Bren said. "I promise you."

She proudly led Virginia to the kitchen, where Gary was just pulling up another chair. Bren put the dish on the counter and busied herself uncovering it, listening to them all welcome Virginia Mash to their Christmas.

The truth was, she'd made a wonderful dinner. And she could have made a fantastic dessert. In fact, she could have made this dessert. Virginia had shown her how. But instead she'd chosen to make something else. Something that she couldn't quite label. Something that wasn't quite friendship, or maybe it was, and wasn't quite pity, but could have been. Something that ran the line between stubborn and stupid, patience and perseverance. Something that was getting easier every day. And more worthwhile.

She held up the dish. "Chocolate flourless cake, anyone?"

And then set about dishing up the slices.

■ ■ ■ ■

Conversation Guide: The Hundred Gifts

JENNIFER SCOTT

■ ■ ■ ■

This Conversation Guide is intended to enrich the individual reading experience, as well as encourage us to explore these topics together — because books, and life, are meant for sharing.

A CONVERSATION WITH
JENNIFER SCOTT

Q. In the first chapter of The Hundred Gifts, *the protagonist, Bren Epperson, is persuaded to teach a cooking class when she's told, "This isn't a job. It's a friendship." And in your acknowledgments, you thank Roberta for convincing you that you weren't joining a workout; you were joining a friendship. Can you tell us a little bit about why and how friendship can help us enter new arenas and overcome challenges?*

A. I'm pretty introverted, so it's not in my nature to join big groups or seek out a lot of friendships. I tend to stick to my tried-and-true few. It took Roberta many months of asking before I agreed to join her workout group, but she kept after me until I gave in. Little did I know I would be joining something that would, over time, result in many friendships — a tight-knit group of ladies who encourage and support one another while also laughing and struggling together. I wanted Bren to have something similar — a group of ladies from many different backgrounds, with many different personalities, and watch them pull together to have fun and help out one another, but also to help out someone else who needed it. Bren needed that to bolster her courage, which was sorely lacking. I think friendships — especially unexpected ones between people who are not exactly alike — can give you bravery you might not have had already, or maybe sometimes empathy that you may not have had already, or silliness, or gumption, or imagination, or endurance. It's true that there's strength in numbers, and sometimes that strength is inner strength. You just need that someone out there who believes in you so that you can find it.

Q. Bren makes quite a lot of dishes for her cooking class: pies, appetizers, barbecue, turducken. Do you, like Bren, enjoy cooking? Do you have a favorite dish you like to cook for your family? What kind of research did you need to do to write these scenes?

A. I am head chef in the Brown house, and over the past twenty-plus years, I have cooked more meals than I could possibly count. I've had a lot of practice, and consider myself to be a pretty good cook. But I excel at stick-to-your-ribs meals like chicken and dumplings or meat loaf or pasta. I'm nowhere near as "chefy" as Bren, and I wouldn't have the first clue how to make a turducken. But I am totally a closet foodie and would for sure eat one!

Bren's holiday meal, though, is definitely a nod to our own family tradition. My mom has a brisket recipe to die for, and we have the foods Bren mentions — brisket, barbecue meatballs, corn casserole, chips and dips, and even Kraft Macaroni & Cheese — on our Christmas Day menu. It's been that way for nearly as long as I can remember, and we would have it no other way. While other people are looking forward to their turkey and stuffing, we are eagerly awaiting our tailgate party!

Q. There's a lovely range of characters in this story — from Bren, to the crotchety Virginia Mash, to the women in the cooking class, to Bren's hysterical aunt Cathy. Many authors, when talking about their characters, will say they're amalgams of people they've known and their own personalities. Do you think that's true? Were certain characters in the book inspired by people you know? Do any spring entirely from your imagination?

A. I would like to say most of them spring entirely from my imagination, because it would be great to have such a colorful imagination, but the truth is they are probably all amalgams of people I've known and can't even really pinpoint. Bren is the only exception in that she's a pretty good representation of me. We're the same age, and we've struggled with the same mid-forties problems — struggling to say good-bye to grown children leaving the nest, years of bad food choices and their ensuing weight consequences, a lot of self-doubt, and some amount of restlessness in what to do now that we're older. We even shared a "suspicious spot" on our shoulders during the writing of this (just a mole). Bren's voice came easily to me.

By the same token, Aunt Cathy is sort of the anti-Bren. She doesn't take life so seriously, has more confidence than is good for her, and is not at all measured in how she approaches the world. I don't know any Aunt Cathys, but I sure would like to!

Q. What do you hope readers take away from this book? A year after they've read it, what do you want them to remember from it?

A. Always, first and foremost, enjoyment. I love books that are filled with characters who feel like fun friends whom I miss when I'm not with them. So I hope to create characters that my readers enjoy spending time with. But also, as with everything I write, I hope my readers take away a message of connection from this book. It's not always easy to reach out, and it's not always easy to be understanding — especially with someone who is trying their level best to not be understandable! We can never truly know what motivates someone to act the way they do; all we can do is try to have empathy. I will always believe that true connection is the hardest and most important lesson we are to learn in this life, and if I inspire just one person to reach out to another, I will feel good about what I've done.

Q. *You have now written two books,* The Hundred Gifts *and* The Sister Season, *set during the holidays. Do the holidays have a particular draw for you? Does the setting somehow heighten challenges the characters face?*

A. Christmas is definitely my favorite holiday, and I love the entire holiday season. I even love the manic shopping sprees and the loud commercials and "The Little

Drummer Boy" (even if Bren doesn't particularly enjoy any of those things). But there is some amount of pressure there, too, to make everything perfect and magical and wonderful and to engineer it so that your friends and family, and even you yourself, never have any bad feelings throughout the entire season. And we see the media representation of the holidays, and it makes it look as if everyone else is pulling off this perfection. But the truth is nobody's pulling it off, because it's not possible, and the holidays bring out bad feelings — regretful memories, feelings of not being good enough, not being rich enough, not being happy enough — in so many of us. I think it's a season that lends itself well to the exploration of challenges, especially of the family variety.

Q: You write middle grade, young adult and adult fiction. The versatility is so impressive! Can you talk a little bit about some of your other projects and what's coming next?

I have just released my second middle grade novel, *How Lunchbox Jones Saved Me from Robots, Traitors, and Missy the Cruel,* and am now working on the first in a new middle grade series. All of my middle grade books are more lighthearted and silly, while also dealing with unlikely connections!

I am getting ready to release *Shade Me,* the first book in my new YA suspense series, and am currently working on book two in that series. It's an exciting new adventure for me, about a girl with synesthesia who finds herself immersed in an assault investigation she doesn't want to be part of.

QUESTIONS FOR DISCUSSION

1. When *The Hundred Gifts* begins, the protagonist, Bren Epperson, is an empty nester, eating her emotions as she ponders the quiet holiday season she's about to endure without her children. Who is she by the end of the book and what has contributed to her changes? Think specifically about the roles Bren plays in her life, including those of wife, daughter, mother, teacher, and friend. What contributes most to her changes through the book?

2. In chapter two, we meet Virginia Mash, a solitary older woman living above the Kitchen Classroom. What is Virginia's role in the beginning of the book and how does that change by the end? As you did with Bren, consider Virginia's roles as a wife, mother, and friend.

3. Bren and her husband, Gary, view and

deal with the absence of their children in very different ways. Do you think this is typical in a marriage? Were you surprised by Gary's admission that he was looking forward to having time for other pursuits — and time for Bren and him alone? Have you seen this in your own marriage or in those of your friends and family? How do they work to come back together?

4. In the beginning of the novel, Virginia Mash has few attachments in her life, but she does have a dog, Chuy. Talk about the role of pets in Virginia's life and in your own. What does Chuy represent to Virginia? What voids does he fill? What does he bring to her? And are there ways in which he hinders her?

5. Food becomes a source of conflict in this novel as a group of women gather together for cooking classes. But it might be most noticeable for Bren and Tammy Lynn. Discuss the different ways these two women approach food. What are they like at the beginning of the book? At the end? How do Tammy Lynn's daughter, Janelle, and the new class member, Steff, play into this conflict? Is there a character you most identify with regarding her attitude toward food? Why?

6. As the cooking class begins, a variety of characters come together, including Bren's aunt Cathy and her mother, and Tammy Lynn, Teresa, Lulu, and Rebecca. Did you have a favorite character? Who was it and why was he or she your favorite?

7. As the title suggests, giving gifts is a central theme in this book. The women are dedicated to making homemade gifts for Virginia Mash. Do you think homemade gifts are more meaningful than store-bought gifts? Would you, as Bren's nephews do, prefer a gift certificate or cash? What is the line between being pragmatic and being heartfelt in the art of gift giving?

8. Bren's final gift to Virginia Mash is a twelve-course meal she delivers on Christmas Day. However, when she tries to deliver it, Virginia Mash tells her, "This is harassment." Bren counters, "This is lunch." Virginia Mash then responds, "This is illegal," to which Bren exclaims, "No, you mean old thing, this is friendship." How is it friendship? When a potential recipient rebukes an offer, how does one know when to back off and when to keep pushing? How assertive should one be in pursuing friendship?

9. Many people would say *The Hundred Gifts* has a happy ending — and they might be tempted to criticize the story for that feature. Yet the happy ending is a valued element in many types of books, from Jane Austen novels to contemporary romances. What do you think of happy endings in novels? Are they unrealistic and simplistic? Do they inspire hope and give us strength to face new challenges? Are they some mixture of the two? Do you prefer stories with happy endings?

10. Is there someone in your own life who might benefit from one hundred gifts? Or perhaps just one? Who is that person and what would that significant gift be?

ABOUT THE AUTHOR

Jennifer Scott is an award-winning author who made her debut in women's fiction with *The Sister Season*. She also writes critically acclaimed young adult fiction under the name Jennifer Brown. Her debut YA novel, *Hate List,* was selected as an ALA Best Book for Young Adults, a *VOYA* Perfect Ten, and a *School Library Journal* Book of the Year. Jennifer lives in Liberty, Missouri, with her husband and three children.

The employees of Thorndike Press hope you have enjoyed this Large Print book. All our Thorndike, Wheeler, and Kennebec Large Print titles are designed for easy reading, and all our books are made to last. Other Thorndike Press Large Print books are available at your library, through selected bookstores, or directly from us.

For information about titles, please call:
  (800) 223-1244

or visit our Web site at:
  http://gale.cengage.com/thorndike

To share your comments, please write:
  Publisher
  Thorndike Press
  10 Water St., Suite 310
  Waterville, ME 04901